SURRENDERING TO A KISS

"Lianne . . ." He lifted his hand to cup her cheek.

"No . . ." Lianne murmured in protest. She knew she should move away and break the contact, but she couldn't. She was helpless to deny herself what she needed most . . . a moment of affection . . . a moment with someone who cared about her . . .

In the delicate shadows of the night, Adam found Lianne even more lovely. His gaze dropped to the curve of her mouth.

"Ah, Lianne, you're so beautiful." He sought her lips with his own, capturing them in a kiss.

Lianne's first reaction was to draw back. This was the arrogant Adam Trent . . . the man who'd taken her home and who'd treated her in such a condescending way. The man she hated. But even as she fought inwardly to deny what was happening, his lips broke down the last fragments of her resistance and she gave up her struggle to refuse his kiss . . .

BOBBI SMITH

PIRATE'S PROMISE

ZEBRA BOOKS
Kensington Publishing Corp.
www.kensingtonbooks.com

ZEBRA BOOKS are published by

Kensington Publishing Corp.
850 Third Avenue
New York, NY 10022

All Kensington titles, imprints, and distributed lines are available at special quantity discounts for bulk purchases for sales
promotion, premiums, fund-raising, educational, or institu-
tional use.

Special book excerpts or customized printings can also be created to fit specific needs. For details, write or phone the office
of the Kensington Special Sales Manager: Attn. Special Sales
Department. Kensington Publishing Corp., 850 Third Avenue,
New York, NY 10022. Phone: 1-800-221-2647.

Zebra and the Z logo Reg. U.S. Pat. & TM Off.

ISBN-13: 978-1-4201-0039-6
ISBN-10: 1-4201-0039-4

First Printing: September 1988

10 9 8 7 6 5 4 3 2

Printed in the United States of America

This book is dedicated to the real Lianne—Leann Shoaf. I hope the real Adam finds you soon!

Thanks, too, to Cindy Swanson and to SS who keeps telling me that romance and love are NOT logical!

A special note of thanks for their help to Dr. Alberto Soto, M.D., and Cathy Perrine, C.R.N.A. (and to Betty Kolb for her loving, unfailing support through the years).

Prologue

Gulf of Mexico—1849

"Captain Shark!" Lewis Grimes, a mate on the fleet ship *Banshee,* pounded on the door to his captain's cabin unmindful of the earliness of the hour.

The man known only as Shark to his crew awoke with a fierce growl. Angered at being wakened, he cursed Grimes loudly as he roused himself from the comfort of his bunk. In an impatient fury, he pulled on his clothes then threw wide the door to his quarters.

"What the hell is it?" Shark snarled. His overlong dark hair was wild about his face, and his black eyes were afire with the power of his wrath. He was a big man of hulking proportions, and he towered threateningly over the hapless seaman who'd dared to disturb him.

Shark was known as the "Scourge of the Sea" and with good reason, the cowering Grimes thought as he stared up at him. It was rumored that when Shark raided he never left a victim alive, and at this moment he found that easy to believe. As far as he was concerned, his captain looked much like Satan incarnate, and Grimes knew he had a disposition to match. He had seen him lose his temper with some crew members earlier in the voyage, and he had no desire to anger him further. He swallowed nervously several times and fi-

7

nally managed to croak out an answer.

"It's a ship, sir! Mr. Johnson spotted one off the port bow!"

"A ship?" Shark scowled even more blackly at the news as a sudden sense of urgency possessed him. With the illegal cargo he was carrying, the last thing he needed was a run-in with authorities. His irritation at being awoken forgotten, he rushed from his cabin.

When Shark pushed past him and disappeared down the companionway, Grimes collapsed weakly against the wall. Relief flooded through him at having been spared a taste of his captain's viciousness. Pulling himself together, he drew a shaky breath and quickly hurried after him.

Shark emerged on deck and was immediately joined by his first mate, Will Johnson. Will was a dark-haired mountain of a man whose stern control and harshly-meted-out disciplines were second only to his captain's.

"What d'ya got, Will?" he demanded brusquely.

Will pointed out to sea over the port bow where the billowing white sails of another vessel were visible on the horizon. "Looks to be headed this way."

Shark roughly snatched the spyglass Will had been carrying and focused on the ship in the distance. He was tense as he studied the other boat, and only after long minutes of consideration did he relax again. It was not the law, but a slow, lumbering merchantman. His own contraband cargo was safe.

"Hold steady on course, Will. I think it's time we had a little fun on this voyage," Shark ordered, not about to let such prime pickings get away. His expression, once so grim, lightened.

Will had thought that his captain would want to avoid the other ship, and he was puzzled by the order. "You don't mean to—"

"Are you questioning me?" Shark's tone was as cold

8

and deadly as the obsidian gaze he turned upon his first mate and longtime comrade.

Though Will stared at him in disbelief, the implied threat in his words effectively silenced his objections. He knew it would be a lethal mistake to cross him. "No, Captain," he finally replied with just the right amount of deference.

"Good." Shark's smile was feral as he glanced back toward the unsuspecting, oncoming frigate. It had been quite some time since they'd had the opportunity to raid a ship, and the thought of it sent excitement charging through him.

"I was only concerned about our cargo," Will offered in the way of an excuse, his thoughts centered on the hundreds of blacks chained together in the dark confines of the *Banshee*'s hold. Surely, the slaves they were smuggling into Louisiana were worth far more than any treasure they could steal from this merchant vessel.

"No need." Shark dismissed his concern. "We're going to strike so quickly and so unexpectedly that there'll be no danger to us, only profit."

He nodded, silently deferring to his captain's wishes, and then moved off to give new instructions to the helmsman.

Aboard the Crescent Line's main merchantman, the *Windwood,* Captain Adam Trent strode the quarterdeck with his fiancée, Elise Clayton, enjoying the bright freshness of the new day. A tall man, with lean, chiseled features and dark hair and eyes, Adam had an air about him of a man used to command.

This morning, however, Adam had willingly turned his duties over to his first mate, Beau Hamilton. Since they'd departed Houston several days before, he'd been far too busy to spend much time with Elise, so today he wanted to rectify that. They lingered at the rail now, his arm about her waist in as intimate an embrace as he could manage there in the open before the crew.

Adam gazed down at his fiancée, his brown eyes warm upon her. She was petite, gloriously blond, svelte of figure and sweet-tempered, and he felt certain that Elise was the woman for him. They had met at a ball in Houston a little over a month ago, and it had been love at first sight for the both of them.

Adam had had no plans to marry when he'd sailed into that Texas town. He'd always enjoyed his freedom and had lived the life of a bachelor to the hilt. He had quite a reputation as a ladies' man, and he'd earned it. Strangely enough, though, he'd found himself proposing to Elise soon after they'd met.

Now they were making the return voyage to his home in Charleston accompanied by Elise's maiden Aunt Odile as chaperone. Elise would meet his sister, Becky, there, and then they would be married. Adam was surprised to discover that he was actually looking forward to settling down with Elise. He was in love for the first time in his life, and he liked it.

"I have something here for you . . ." Adam told Elise as he reached into his pocket to draw out a small black jewelry box.

"You do?" She stared at the box as he held it out to her and then up at Adam, her blue eyes sparkling with excitement. "What is it, Adam?" she asked with all the open delight of a guileless child.

"Open it and see," he teased, giving nothing away. "I hope you like it. I had it made just for you . . . for us . . ."

Elise eagerly opened the box and found two golden, crescent-shaped medallions on fine gold chains within.

"Oh, Adam, they're beautiful." She raised glowing eyes to his as she reverently lifted one of the medallions from the box.

"I had one made for each of us," he told her earnestly. "If I hadn't come to Houston on Crescent business, we would never have met."

Elise held one necklace out to him. "Put mine on for me, please . . ."

When he took the chain, she presented her back to him, lifting the heavy mane of her golden hair so he could fasten it behind her neck for her. The warmth of his fingers at the nape of her neck sent a tingle of excitement through her as he secured the necklace.

"Thank you, Adam. I love it, and I promise you that I'll wear it always," she vowed as she turned back to him.

Elise longed to throw her arms about his neck and kiss him, but held herself in restraint. Now was not the time. Later, when they were alone, she would thank him most properly.

Motioning for him to turn around, she took his matching chain from the box. "Now, I'll do yours for you . . ."

Adam waited patiently as she fastened the clasp at the back of his neck. When he faced her again, she lifted the medallion and slipped it inside his shirt.

"I want you to keep it close to your heart, for that's where I always want to be," she told him, her face aglow with the joy of their love.

Their gazes met and locked. Desire smoldered deep within them, but they knew they would have to wait. Their entire future lay ahead of them, and, at that moment, it appeared very bright indeed. Taking Elise's hand in his own, Adam lifted it gently to his lips and pressed a tender kiss upon it. Elise's eyes never left his as she shivered with delight. They turned back to the rail then, Adam once again drawing her to his side.

Adam turned his attention out to sea to try to distract

himself from his growing passion. It was then that he spotted the unidentified clipper, heading full-sail directly toward them. A sudden feeling of gut-wrenching dread filled him. Gone were all thoughts of love and their future happiness. There was something very sinister about the speed with which the other vessel was traveling toward them, and the multitude of heavy cannon he could see protruding from both sides of the deck, glinting harshly in the brilliant sunlight. Adam went still, tensing at the danger that was near and closing fast.

"Elise . . ." Adam kept his tone level and quiet. Never taking his eyes from the menacing, approaching ship, he ordered in a voice that brooked no argument, "I want you to go below with your Aunt Odile, and I want you to stay there until I come for you."

Chapter One

The moment Elise was out of sight, Adam shouted to Beau, who was at the helm. The sound of Adam's call brought Beau's head up instantly. He recognized the urgency in his tone and wondered at it. Turning the wheel over to Rob, the usual helmsman, he hurried across the deck to where Adam stood.

Tall, lean, and dashingly debonair, Beau Hamilton was the blond counterpart of his longtime friend, Adam. They had been as close as brothers since childhood and neither ever expected that to change. They believed they could accomplish anything they set their minds to, and so far they had not been proven wrong.

Adam and Beau loved the sea, and they had sailed together since they'd gotten their first boats in their youth. When Adam's parents died and he inherited the family's firm, Crescent Shipping, he took Beau on as a partner. The rest was history. With a lot of hard work and ingenuity, they had parlayed the small shipping firm into a major, very profitable competitor. For men who were only now in their late twenties, they were doing very well, and their future prospects looked even better.

"What is it?" Beau asked as he came to stand at Adam's side.

"Look." Adam pointed out the oncoming clipper. "What do you make of it?"

A sense of unease gripped Beau Hamilton. It was obvious that the other ship was making no effort to steer

13

clear of the slower, more heavily laden *Windwood*. In fact, it seemed to be heading straight toward them. He lifted his glass to study the sleek vessel.

"Strange . . ." He paused to glance at Adam. "She bears no outward markings. It's like she's keeping her identity a secret."

"They're not keeping their guns a secret," Adam came back tersely, the feeling of impending trouble refusing to abate. "I don't like this, Beau. I don't like this at all. She's not flying any flags . . ." He broke off as the ship began to turn sharply. "Good God!" Adam watched in horror as the looming craft turned broadside and brought its guns to bear on the unsuspecting *Windwood*.

"They're really going to do it!" Beau could not believe what was happening. "They're going to attack!"

"Arm yourselves with whatever you can find, men!" Adam shouted without further hesitation. "Beau! See to our guns! I'll take the helm."

Even as he said it, Adam and Beau both realized the futility of his order. The two small cannons they carried were of limited range and would be no match for the pirate vessel's more lethal weapons.

It was then that Adam thought of Elise and her aunt, below and unprotected. He rushed to the helm.

"Robby! Go below to my cabin and stay with Miss Clayton and her aunt. I have weapons in my trunk. Hopefully, we'll take care of things up here so you won't have to use them, but, should the situation arise, don't hesitate."

"Yes, sir . . ." Robby responded nervously as he cast a quick glance back at the threatening ship.

"I don't want anything to happen to them, Robby," Adam told him sternly.

"I understand, sir." He disappeared down the companionway determined to do his captain's bidding.

As Adam personally took over at the helm, his dark,

troubled gaze focused on the attacking ship. A chill of doom shook him at the sight of the cannons pointing directly at the *Windwood*. Grimly gripping the wheel, he rapidly called out to his men, exhorting them to prepare.

Steering hard astarboard, he struggled valiantly to bring his ship about, out of harm's way. As he felt the ship begin to respond, the fleeter clipper let loose with a lethal first volley. The accurate, deadly fire strafed the riggings and the deck and snapped the *Windwood*'s mainmast like a twig. The huge beam splintered as it fell. It crashed to the deck killing and maiming many of the crew, trapping them beneath its weight.

Surrounded by sudden death and destruction, Adam fought desperately to maintain control of his ship, but the loss of the mainmast rendered the *Windwood* virtually helpless. She was, for all purpose, dead in the water.

A cold dread filled Adam as the pirates maneuvered even closer. He could see the crew of the other craft swarming about on deck, readying themselves to board their hapless prey.

Adam caught sight of Beau and several of his men still struggling with the cannons amidst the wreckage. One gun had been damaged by the falling timber, but the other looked to be sound. Abandoning his place at the helm, he charged through the carnage to help. Though his injured and dying men called out to him, Adam knew there was no time to stop and comfort them. They would all end up dead if he didn't help Beau get a round off.

Every second brought the pirates closer, and it was that very nearness that gave Adam and Beau hope that their small gun might actually do some damage. With Adam's added strength, they finally managed to position the cannon and, as quickly as they could, they loaded it. They got off a shot, but it was destined to be their last. The round caused some damage as it ripped across the deck of the attacking ship, but the glory of the moment was lost as the raiders snared the *Windwood* with their grappling hooks.

Shark had expected their own accurate cannon fire to crush any resistance aboard the merchantman, and he was surprised and angered by the return fire. A few of his crew were killed by the unexpected return volley, and Shark was outraged by the other captain's daring. Their refusal to surrender filled him with murderous rage, and he incited his men to bloodlust, assuring them of a generous share of whatever loot was taken. Shark led his crew aboard the wrecked trading ship, scrambling over the *Windwood's* side with deadly intent.

Adam was determined to protect his vessel. Yet, as he watched the invaders come, he realized it would be a hand to hand fight to the death. As the screaming horde charged aboard, there was no time to think, only time to act. He and Beau exchanged a quick look of silent understanding and then rushed to take up the weapons of their fallen comrades.

"Let's go, men!" Adam urged his men to action. Armed with pistols and sabers, the defenders attacked the superior force, desperately trying to drive the pirates from their ship.

Even as Shark was angered by this continued, futile opposition, he felt reluctant admiration for the outnumbered and outgunned force. He had expected the crew to throw down their weapons and beg for mercy in the face of their invasion, but they showed no signs of giving up. Shouting encouragement to his own men, he led them forward in a brutal attack.

The sound of gunshots echoed across the gulf, and blade met blade in a deadly clash. Though they were determined not to surrender, the *Windwood's* insufficiently armed defenders were no match for the well-armed, bloodthirsty plunderers. Adam and Beau fought side by side, but their efforts were largely futile as Shark's men drove relentlessly on, mowing down all resistance. In a final savage surge, they pressed the last tattered remnants of the crew ahead of them until they had cornered them near the bow.

Beau went down, wounded by one of the vicious saber-wielding pirates. Adam, witnessing his friend's distress, fired at the man responsible, killing him instantly. He continued to urge his men to fight, pressing his own attack with reckless abandon. He had no concern for his own safety. All he could think of was Beau lying on the deck appearing mortally wounded and Elise below virtually unprotected. Adam knew he could not give up.

When Shark heard Adam issuing commands he recognized him as the captain. Knowing that the embattled crew would surely give up if they saw their leader fall, he snatched a pistol from one of his crew and took steady aim. His shot was true and the bullet struck Adam in the head. The surviving crew of the *Windwood* stared in horror at the sight of their captain sprawled lifelessly on the deck.

"Fools! Give it up before you're all slaughtered!" Shark called out as his superior force surrounded them. "Save your own skins! Lay down your arms!"

Certain now that there could be no victory or escape, the demoralized men threw aside their weapons and fearfully huddled together.

"A wise choice," Shark sneered. "Guard them, and if anybody moves . . . kill 'em!"

"Aye, Captain Shark!"

"The rest of you get below. I want anything and everything of value brought up on deck. Any man caught trying to keep something from me will pay a price greater than these . . ." Shark gestured to the dead strewn about the scene of the fighting.

17

As his men rushed anxiously below to loot and pillage, Shark and Will moved off, away from the *Windwood*'s crew. They stood alone together surveying the destruction they'd wreaked.

Beau had only just regained consciousness when he heard the two men approaching. He went completely still. Though violent pain wracked him, he knew that even the slightest movement on his part would give him away. He almost groaned aloud when the men stopped near him and began to talk, gloating over their triumph. He was helpless to act. He had no weapon, and, even if he had had one, he didn't have the strength to use it. The knowledge filled Beau with impotent rage.

"So you approve now, do you?" Shark's tone was smug as he spoke with Will. "I've never known you to be so lily-livered before."

"It was a great risk . . ."

"I'm a risk-taker, Will. You, of all my men, should know that," he mocked him. "What is life without risks? Without excitement? Without challenge?"

"There would have been quite a bit of excitement if our ship had been damaged. You know your partner wouldn't have been happy if anything had happened to the blacks."

Shark shrugged indifferently in response. "We're ahead of schedule. If anything had happened, there would have been plenty of time to make repairs before we're due in New Orleans. Besides, Will, what she doesn't know . . ."

The agony of Beau's wound grew too overpowering for him as they continued to talk. With the last of their words echoing through his mind, he slipped into unconsciousness again, no longer able to resist its offer of blissful escape.

The sound of shots being fired belowdecks alerted Shark that there might be something of even greater value on board than he'd suspected, and he and Will hurried off to investigate.

Only minutes after the shots were heard, the terrified screams of the women resounded from the depths of the ship. The men of the *Windwood* heard the shots and cries and reacted instinctively, lunging forward to go to the ladies' aid.

"Get back!" Shark's men shouted as they leveled their guns threateningly at them.

But the *Windwood's* crews' emotions drove them onward. At their continued challenge, the guards fired without hesitation. Three men were killed instantly. The cold brutality of the act effectively cowered the other men and they fell back, outraged over their inability to save the women from the pirates' savagery.

It was some time later when the crew of the *Banshee* transported the last of the valuables to their own ship.

"This is the last of it, Captain!" one of his men shouted.

"Good! You men have worked quickly and have earned your reward!"

A raucous cheer went up, for they were drunk on the power of their murderous victory.

"Will, lock the rest of their crew in the hold," Shark directed malevolently, "then torch the boat as soon as you're through."

"What about the women?"

The smuggler's glance was utterly ruthless. "Forget them. Let's just get done and get out of here."

Will was surprised by this order, but did not question it. He hurried to do his bidding. With the help of the other mates, he quickly herded the men of the *Windwood* belowdecks.

The blaze successfully started, Will led his crewmates

back to safety aboard their own boat. Within minutes, the raiders had set full sail and were rapidly distancing themselves from what they thought was a funeral pyre.

The acrid smoke from the feeding fire seared its way into Adam's lungs, forcing him back to consciousness. Convulsing in his need for air, Adam began to choke violently. He struggled to awareness, pushing himself upright and bracing himself weakly on one arm as the ship seemed to spin around him. He was dizzy and disoriented for a moment. Blood from his head wound stung his eyes, and he wiped it away with his sleeve. The pain in his head was excruciating, but he fought against it as his memory of the battle returned.

Adam could hear the screams and shouts of his men, trapped as they were belowdecks. He staggered to his feet intent only on releasing them before they were roasted alive. Gasping for breath, he reeled unsteadily through the carnage toward the hatch. When his strength would have failed him, his resolve drove him ever onward. It seemed to Adam to take an eternity to reach the cover, but he finally made it.

"Men!" Adam croaked, his voice hoarse from the smoke.

"It's the captain! We thought you were dead, sir!" Came the resounding cry of the exultant men.

"Hang on . . . I'll try to get this open . . ." He worked feverishly at opening the hatch unmindful of the blood still seeping from his injury. With a final valiant effort, he managed to throw the cover wide.

In ecstatic jubilation, the crew scrambled from the hold. They banded together in earnest to fight the fire and try to salvage what was left of the ship. Only Harnett, the *Windwood*'s physician, did not take up the fight. Instead, he paused to aid his captain, who was swaying unsteadily on his feet.

"We thought all was lost, Captain. Thank God you're

still alive," Harnett told him. "Sit down. Let me see what I can do for your head . . ." He would have examined the wound, but Adam brushed him aside.

"No! There's no time," he argued selflessly, ignoring the throbbing in his head. "I have to find Elise and Beau . . ."

"Mr. Hamilton's got to be dead, sir. The way he was cut . . ." Hartnett hung his head in despair as he mourned Beau.

Adam broke away from him to rush to where Beau lay on the deck. From what the doctor had said, he'd honestly expected that it would be too late, but as he dropped to his knees beside Beau, he was stunned to find that his friend still breathed. Though Beau's pulse was weak, it was steady. Adam called out to the doctor as he began to apply pressure to the bloody saber wound.

"Beau, damn it!" Adam spoke his name insistently. "Don't die on me! Fight!"

Adam's voice came to him from what seemed like a great distance as consciousness slowly returned. Harrowing, agonizing pain burned through Beau's chest, and he groaned as he opened his eyes to see Adam and Harnett at his side.

"Beau! Thank God!" Adam's hand tightened on Beau's arm in a desperately emotional grip.

"What happened?"

"They torched the ship before they left," he told him, "I've got to go below and find Elise!" He was a driven man as he lurched toward the companionway.

Forgetting his own agony for a moment, Beau called out, "Adam! Don't go down there!" But it was too late to stop him. With a vile curse, Beau turned to Harnett who was trying to bind his wound. "Forget about it!" he ordered. "I've got to go with Adam. Help me get up."

A jagged jolt of red, agonizing pain blazed through his side as the doctor helped him stand, but he refused to give in to it. Beau only gritted his teeth against it and directed Harnett to help him below. He was forced to move so slowly that by the time they reached Adam's cabin, it was too late.

Adam was standing motionlessly beside his bunk. His quarters were in total disarray as if some great struggle had gone on there. Robby's body lay near the door, Adam's pistols still clutched in his hands even in death. There was a body on the floor near the windowseat that Adam had somehow already managed to cover with a blood-splattered sheet. But it was the woman lying on the bed that drew Beau's attention and rendered him momentarily speechless. It was Elise. Naked and curled in a defenseless fetal position, she lay completely still upon the blood-stained bed.

"Adam, Elise . . . is she . . . ?"

Adam turned on Beau like a madman, his expression fierce. "It would have been better if they *had* killed her . . ."

Then, mindless of his own pain, Adam drew a quilt over her and took her slight form into his arms. He sat on the bunk and cradled her to him, wanting to comfort her, wanting to ease the hell she'd suffered. But there was no answering response in her. Elise's eyes were dazed, her expression completely blank. Tormented by the thought that he'd been unable to protect her, Adam remained there, holding her in his arms and speaking to her in low tones as Beau and Harnett backed from the room.

Chapter Two

Four months later on the Gulf . . .

The captain of the clipper *Merryweather* stood at the helm as he watched the unidentified clipper that was swiftly angling toward them. Fine-lined and sharp-hulled, the sleek, fully-rigged craft was outfitted for speed, and he knew that whoever was in charge of her was a master.

"I don't know what they want, but stay steady on course, helmsman."

"Yes, sir, Captain Wright," the sailor replied.

Ghosting through the smooth sea, the approaching ship gave the seasoned commander pause. Never in all his years at sea had he seen a craft move with such quickness and precision. Always an admirer of a fine-looking ship, Wright thought the boat quite innovative for the precise set of its sail and its obvious speed, but he grew a bit apprehensive as to the reason for its intersecting course. It was then, as the ship drew closer and then veered to a parallel path, that Wright saw the guns.

"Blast it! We haven't a chance to outrun her! Bring her to heel, now!" Wright bellowed.

The terrified crew of the *Merryweather* exploded into action. Scrambling as quickly as they could, they climbed aloft to take in sail. They were not fighting men, and they understood their captain's decision to surrender without a challenge. It was the only sensible thing to do. The *Merryweather* carried no guns to speak of, and, as fleet as the other ship was, there would be no outrunning them. The merchandise they carried could be replaced, but human lives could not.

Almost as soon as Wright had issued the order to take in sail, though, the coming craft fired a threatening volley over their port bow. The captain cursed under his breath, fearful that he'd made the wrong decision in giving in so easily. What if he'd put the fate of his ship and crew into the hands of some bloodthirsty killers who wouldn't be satisfied with just taking their wealth?

Wright momentarily considered trying to flee. But one last look at their closing assailant reaffirmed what he'd realized instinctively at the start. Escape would be impossible, and, as far as protecting themselves went, armaments on his ship were next to nonexistent.

"Easy, men. There'll be no fighting. We'll give them what they want," he ordered judiciously.

The captain hoped it was a good sign that the challenger had chosen to fire only a warning volley when it could have easily put them on the bottom. Keeping his men under tight control, he made sure they did not resist as the raiding ship moved in and they were boarded.

The men from the attacking clipper swarmed aboard the *Merryweather* fully armed and prepared for a fight. A group of them separated to surround and guard the ship's crew and officers.

Tensions began to mount as the captain of the invaders came aboard. Everyone fell into a stunned, frightened silence as he strode purposefully across the deck. Tall and leanly-built, the master of the attacking ship was dressed all in black and wore a concealing, ominous-looking mask. Behind the disguise, his dark eyes shone with a conquering fire, and, as he moved forward to speak to his men, he smiled ferally.

"What is it you want?" demanded Captain Wright.

The mysterious leader wheeled about to face him. Wright could feel a cold deadliness emanating from his unknown adversary even with the mask hiding his features. The pirate didn't respond to his question as his dark eyes bored icily into his own, and, after a moment, he turned back to direct his men.

"Search the ship," he commanded.

The men who were not guarding the *Merryweather*'s crew hurried off to do as he'd ordered. They boldly scoured the surrendered vessel. The men searched, but to Wright's confusion, they did not plunder. When they reported back to their captain and told him that they'd found nothing, he only nodded.

The masked raider's presence was fearsome as he turned to Wright. Wright stiffened as he awaited his pronouncement. He didn't know what he was expecting from this ferocious, threatening figure, but it was not what came next.

"My apologies for the inconvenience, Captain," the captain told him in an almost cordial tone that was at odds with the feeling of danger and tension that exuded from him.

"What? he was stunned. "Who the hell are you!"

"My name is Spectre. Remember it," the raider answered harshly.

"Spectre . . ." Wright repeated. The tension eased from him a bit as he sensed that his ship and men were in no danger.

"I'm searching for the pirate named Shark whose ship looks much like yours," he offered as an explanation for the search. "Have you seen or heard of him?"

"I've heard of him," Captain Wright said. "He's a

bloodthirsty bastard. Rumor has it that when he raids, he never leaves anyone alive . . ."

"What you've heard is true, but mark my words, his raiding days are numbered. I intend to put an end to his murderous ways."

"Why not go to the authorities?"

"Shark is mine," the man known as Spectre declared, and smiled chillingly.

Wright could sense the hatred Spectre had for Shark. A shiver of apprehension ran down his spine as he wondered what the killer pirate had done to Spectre to create such an unrelenting need for revenge.

"Spread the word. I want it known that I'm after him," Spectre directed. "I want Shark to know what it feels like to be the hunted instead of the hunter."

Before Captain Wright could respond, the raider was gone.

The men of the *Merryweather* made no moves as they watched the raiders return to their own vessel. As the other ship sailed away and they were free to resume their original course unscathed, their talk was of the dreaded Shark and this strange man known as Spectre. The crew speculated on his reasons for keeping his identity unknown and for tracking the pirate. They knew when the confrontation did occur, it would be bloodly and deadly.

Spectre stayed on deck until they were well away from the *Merryweather* and then, after instructing the helmsman to continue plying the main trade routes into New Orleans from the south, he went below. As he slammed into his cabin, he tore off the mask and threw it negligently to one side. His shoulders slumped in frustration as he recognized the futility of his efforts. He had been searching for months now and had turned up nothing.

Spectre went to his desk and sat down, raking a hand through the dark thickness of his hair in a weary gesture. He got out his charts and maps of the Louisiana coastline near the delta and began to pore over them for what seemed like the thousandth time. When the knock came at the door, he didn't even bother to look up.

"Come in."

His cabin door swung open and Beau Hamilton entered the room.

"What is it, Beau?" he asked tersely, his temper stretched to the limit by the disappointment of the raid.

"I want to know what you're going to do now, Adam," he told him as he came to sit in the chair before his desk.

Adam's dark eyes glowed with an inner fervor. "We'll keep searching, Beau. We're going to keep it up until we find the bastard, and then I'm going to kill him."

"But, Adam, you've been combing the Gulf for months now with no success!"

"Don't you think I know that!" Adam came to his feet in an uproar. "Don't you think I know that this is like looking for a needle in a haystack!"

Beau nodded in silent response as he watched his friend pace about the room. Beau realized that Adam was a changed man since Shark's raid, and he reflected on all that had occurred. They'd been rescued at sea shortly after the attack and returned home to Adam's plantation home in Charleston. Adam's sister, Becky, had taken charge and nursed his own and Adam's wounds personally, and she had quietly seen to Elise's desperate needs.

Though Adam's physical wounds had healed rather quickly, deep within the heart of him the emotional wounds he carried were raw and agonizing. He blamed himself for what had happened to Elise. When the

27

numerous doctors and specialists whom Becky had engaged to treat Elise announced that there was no hope for recovery, that she had withdrawn from life and showed no signs of ever improving, Adam had been devastated.

It was then that Adam had decided to track the murderous pirate down and kill him. His heart had hardened, and he became obsessed with the thought of making the killer pay for his deeds. With only the few clues Beau had overheard while pretending to be dead on deck to guide him—that the pirate's name was Shark, that he'd been smuggling slaves, and that he had a female partner in New Orleans—Adam had begun to plan.

Beau had been weeks longer recovering, and Adam had spent that time preparing to go back to sea. He'd ordered his fastest ship, the *Sea Shadow*, re-outfitted with enough guns to blow the pirate right out of the water. As soon as Beau had been able to sail again, Adam had entrusted Elise to Becky's care and then had gone back to the sea . . . back to find and kill the brutal savage who'd destroyed his world.

Viciously determined, he had begun combing the Gulf for Shark. Not wanting his real identity known, he'd adopted the disguise of a masked avenger named Spectre. He was a ghost from Shark's past, and he meant to haunt him until he could claim his complete revenge.

Adam had concentrated his efforts in the trade routes near New Orleans, challenging and stopping every clipper that resembled the pirate's. He'd released all innocent vessels without looting or damage, but always made sure that those aboard knew of Spectre and of his quest to find Shark.

"There's got to be a better way," Adam declared, no longer fully confident that his plan to catch Shark at sea would work now that the months of useless searching had left him desperate. It was time to come up with a new strategy.

"Right," Beau agreed, "but what is it? The man's as slippery as an eel!"

"Look, we know he's smuggling slaves into New Orleans, and that's what we've been centering our search on, hoping to catch him coming in to port. But maybe there's an angle here that we haven't considered yet." Adam turned to face his friend, wanting Beau's opinion on the new plan he'd devised.

"Such as?" Beau was immediately attentive. He was more than willing to do whatever it took to pay Shark back for the pain he'd caused.

"What would you think if I told you I was going to pay a lengthy visit to New Orleans?" Adam asked, his eyes narrowing as he considered it.

"You're going into New Orleans? As Spectre?"

"No, as the rich Adam Trent, Charleston plantation owner, on a slave-buying trip," he explained. "We have family friends there—the Whitneys—and I'm sure I'll be welcome to stay with them. They should be able to introduce me to society so I can make the contacts I need."

Beau caught his drift instantly and felt a spark of excitement. "You're going to try it from the other angle . . ."

"That's right. You can assume Spectre's identity and keep on searching the trade routes, while I'll start trying to locate this female partner of his."

"It just might work, Adam."

Adam met his friend's gaze across the cabin. "It's got to, Beau. I'm not going to rest until Shark's paid for the attack with his life."

* * *

It was dark and noisy in the riverfront dive in New Orleans. Huddled nervously across the table from the infamous Captain Shark, Miller, a weaselly, skinny little man, relayed all that he'd heard.

"He goes by the name of Spectre," he informed him, "and he told us all that he was lookin' for you."

"Why would he tell you?" Shark sneered.

"I dunno. All I know is what I heard, and what I heard is that he's lookin' for Shark and he ain't gonna stop 'til he finds you," the sailor finished off with relish.

"What's he look like?"

"That's the worst part," Miller said with a shudder, his fear obvious.

"What are you talking about?" Shark snapped, grabbing him by his shirt front and almost hauling him across the tabletop.

"I mean he wears this disguise . . ."

"Disguise? What kind of disguise?"

"Well, he dresses all in black, but he wears this mask. It covers most of his face, see, and all you can see of him is his mouth."

Shark was suddenly tense as a haunting premonition jolted through him at the thought of this Spectre hunting him down . . . masked, secretive, and determined never to give up. He tried to imagine who among his enemies would come after him this way, but came up with no one.

"You say he's got a fast ship?" he queried, shoving the messenger back down in his chair.

"The fastest!"

"No ship's quicker than the *Banshee*," Shark scoffed.

"This one'll give you a race," Miller replied, afraid to tell Shark that he really believed Spectre would be able to run him down with ease. "Why do you suppose he's wearin' that mask?"

"I don't know. But I'm sure I'll find out," he replied,

acting as though it were of little concern for him, but in truth, the icy fear that had come with his premonition was still with him.

Quickly, forcefully, he shrugged the threat of danger away. Spectre was obviously a coward, Shark told himself, that was why he was hiding behind the mask. When their paths finally crossed, he'd take great personal pleasure in running him through. No one had ever bested Shark before, and no one ever would.

Chapter Three

Six weeks later, north of New Orleans . . .

From the end of the curving drive, the Ducharme plantation home, Belle Arbor, appeared immaculate. Framed by moss-draped oaks, the massive, yet gracefully designed white house bespoke of great wealth. Six huge Corinthian pillars supported the pitched roof, and the balcony that graced the front of the structure was trimmed in ornate wrought iron. The twin garçonnieres that flanked the center section were smaller, identical copies of it, adding to the mansion's overall appearance of grandeur.

Yet as one approached the pillared home, it became apparent that all was not well there. Paint that seemed perfect from a distance was fading and peeling. The hot, humid Louisiana weather and a lack of care had taken its toll. The wide expanse of green lawn and the flowering shrubs that surrounded the house were no longer perfectly manicured. Instead, the bushes were growing wild, and the grass was just barely under control. If outward impressions were anything to judge by, it was clear that life at Belle Arbor was no longer troublefree.

Lianne Ducharme sat at the desk in the cool seclusion of the study, her elbows on the desktop, her head resting in utter weariness in her hands. It was not readily evident from her posture that she was a lovely young woman. This afternoon, with her lustrous red-gold hair twisted back in a tight, practical bun, wearing her plainest, most practical daygown, Lianne appeared far older than her twenty years. There was no light of joy in the emerald depths of her gaze, and no smile brightened the loveliness of her features. She was exhausted and it showed.

Lianne pushed away from the desk and moved slowly to stand by the floor-to-ceiling casement window. The view from the study window of Belle Arbor's beautiful reflecting pond usually cheered her, but today she felt only frustrated and empty as she stared out across its mirrored depths. Time was running out. She knew she was cornered.

After her older brother Mark's death in a duel a year ago, Lianne had felt certain that she could hold the plantation together. It was their heritage, their family's roots, and she wanted to save it for herself and for her younger brother, Alex. She'd managed well for a while, but now she was beginning to have doubts that she could do it. Somehow, no matter how hard she worked or how many hours she labored, there just didn't seem to be enough money. This troubled her, for things had been wonderful when Mark had been alive. Their cotton and sugar cane had flourished, prices on the market had been stable, and money had never been a problem.

Lianne frowned as she considered all that had happened. Their crops had continued to be good, prices hadn't fallen. Yet, she was still finding herself in dire financial straits. Even Antoine Ducharme, their uncle who'd been appointed their guardian when Mark had died, was encouraging her to sell Belle Arbor. Lianne had adamantly refused to consider that terrible possibility, for she was determined somehow, someway to keep her home. It was all she had left of her past . . . all that remained of the happiness and love she'd once known.

Lianne's mouth twisted in disgust at the thought of

her fraternal uncle. Being a woman, she'd had no recourse when he had been named their guardian. He was, after all, their only living blood kin. Even so, his appointment had left her feeling decidedly uncomfortable, for in no way did he resemble their beloved, long-deceased father, Richard. Her father had been tall, lean, darkly handsome and filled with loving warmth. Antoine, on the other hand, was short and fat, and though he gave the impression of caring deeply for her and Alex, Lianne sensed a certain coldness in him. He'd immediately refused to come live at Belle Arbor with them, claiming that his business interests forced him to stay in New Orleans, and Lianne sensed that Antoine was relieved when she and Alex had chosen to remain on the plantation rather than stay with him.

Lianne grimaced as she thought of his visit to Belle Arbor the week before. He had been very aware of their failing financial situation. Instead of offering to help them, he had tried to convince her in his irritating, arrogant male way that running the plantation was no job for a woman. He'd emphasized rather bluntly that she was in danger of becoming an old maid and that it was time she started seriously thinking about marrying . . . for her sake and for Alex's.

Lianne sighed. During the past few months, several men had attempted to court her, but she harbored no deep romantic feelings for any of them. She'd always wanted her own marriage to be a love match, just as her parents' had been. She had always imagined herself falling madly in love with a wonderful, exciting man who would sweep her off her feet and into ecstatic marital bliss. Now she was beginning to wonder if it would ever happen.

Her heart was heavy and her mood depressed as she realized the truth. There would be no handsome prince to rescue her from her fate. She was the one who had to take responsibility for herself and Alex. There was no one else. It was up to her to keep Belle Arbor afloat.

Mark entered her thoughts then, and at the memory of her strong, tall, older brother, tears stung her eyes. If only he were here, she was sure things would be different. He would know what to do . . . he would know how to help her . . .

Suddenly, Lianne was frightened about her future, and with that fear came a desperate fury over the injustices of the past. If only Mark hadn't fallen in love with Suzanne Labadie! Everyone had known how wicked that gorgeous blond really was. She used men as it pleased her and then dropped them without a thought. Lianne had tried to warn her brother about Suzanne, but he'd been too enamored at the time. He had declared himself in love with her and believed that she loved him too. He had even planned to propose to her . . .

The deep, abiding hatred Lianne felt for Suzanne welled up inside her as she remembered the duel Mark had fought over her honor and his senseless death. The other woman had barely shed a tear over it all and had returned to the social scene on the arm of a new beau one short week later.

"Damn her!" Lianne suddenly exclaimed, no longer able to hold it all inside. "Damn Suzanne Labadie to hell!"

Her fists clinched in useless rage as she realized the helplessness of her situation. She had tried so hard to be strong, but now she was cornered by circumstances and she could see no way out.

"Miss Lianne?"

The soft call at the study door took her by surprise and she hurriedly struggled to bring her runaway emotions back in check.

"Yes, Sarah, come on in." Lianne was struggling to

35

control her raging temper as the servant entered the room.

Sarah had been with the Ducharme family for all sixty years of her life. Short, happily rotund, and always filled with a sense of life's joy, Sarah was not only Lianne's mammy, but also her dearest friend. She had raised Lianne, and she loved her as if she were her own.

"I thought you might like something to drink," Sarah offered as she crossed the room.

"Thank you—" Lianne managed in a tight voice.

As Sarah drew nearer she saw the distress reflected in her eyes, and a frown creased her brow. "What is it, honey? What's troubling you?" she asked as she placed the tray on the desktop.

"Nothing . . ." Lianne tried to deny it, and then, desperately needing someone to talk to, to confide in, she answered "Everything . . ."

"Tell me, darlin'. What's wrong?" Sarah went to her, and, when Lianne didn't protest, she took her in her arms, giving her the support and reassurance she needed.

"I don't understand it, Sarah. Nothing's working out right. If Mark was still alive, none of this would be happening . . ."

"Easy, little one," she crooned, remembering how she had comforted Lianne in the same way when she was a little girl facing the death of her parents. It had been a much simpler matter to dry her tears and help her confront her fears then, for the future had not seemed nearly so threatening while Mark was alive. Now, though, Sarah knew that Lianne had no one to turn to, no one to rely on but herself. Sarah had already decided that Antoine Ducharme was no good. She couldn't say exactly why she didn't trust their uncle and guardian, it was just a feeling she had about the man, and Sarah always trusted her feelings. "It's not as bad as you think.

36

You know you can do anything you decide to do!"

Lianne sighed deeply in her distress. "God knows I'm trying, but sometimes it all seems so useless . . ."

"You saying that working to save your home is useless?" she demanded.

"No . . . no, of course not. I guess I'm just tired. . . ."

"And grieving," Sarah added. "You know you've never mourned Mark the way you should have. You were too busy being strong for Alex to ever stop and realize what had really happened."

Lianne knew she was right, but it didn't make what she was feeling now any easier to deal with or any less painful.

"I'll tell you one thing, Sarah," Lianne swore with a vengeance as she drew away from her, her back stiffening as her sense of pride returned. "I don't know how I'm going to do it right now, but some day, some way, I'm going to pay Suzanne Labadie back!"

"If ever a woman deserved payin' back, it's that one," Sarah agreed bitterly.

"And you know what?" Lianne said avidly.

"What?"

"I'm going to enjoy every minute of it!" Lianne's green eyes glittered like shards of brilliant glass. "Every minute!"

The tense, emotional moment was shattered as young Alex came charging into the study. "Lianne!" Unaware of the undercurrents in the room he raced to his sister's side without hesitation. His face was flushed with excitement as he held up the jar he'd been clutching for her inspection. "Look what I just caught!"

Somehow Lianne managed to put aside all the hatred she felt for Suzanne as she gazed down lovingly at her little brother. At eight, he was a sturdy boy whose dark good looks held the promise of great manly appeal. With the deepest of affection, she ruffled his already tousled sable hair and gave him a quick warm hug as she studied the butterfly he'd managed to trap.

"It's beautiful, Alex."

"I know, and I'm going to keep it forever," he told her breathlessly, his chocolate brown eyes aglow at the though of such a wonderful pet.

"You know, butterflies don't live very long when they're held captive," Lianne explained, frowning slightly.

"They don't?" He was troubled by this news, for he treasured the creature and wished it no harm.

"No, honey." She softened her tone. "But I imagine if you let it go sometime today, it'll be all right."

"That's what I'll do," Alex agreed. "I'll just keep it for a little while."

As Lianne watched him leave the room, she couldn't help but compare herself to the butterfly. If she followed her uncle's suggestion and married just anyone, she'd be trapped in a snare of her own making. No, she decided, she would handle everything herself. She would continue to be strong for Alex, and she would find a way to make it work. She would never give up Belle Arbor — never.

A moan of exquisite pleasure escaped Suzanne Labadie as waves of passion swept through her. She clutched her lover more closely to her, reveling in the touch of his big hands upon her slim body and the feel of him penetrating the very depths of her need. Arching against him she offered herself to his ardor. In a heated mating, they came together — he big, dark, and fiercely male; she a golden goddess of sorts with hair the color of dark, spun gold reaching nearly to her hips and a small but lushly curved figure. None of her lovers had ever managed to stir her to such heights of sensual excitement, and Suzanne exulted in his demanding possession.

"Please, Shark . . ." she whispered in his ear as he thrust avidly into her. "Please, please, hurry!"

Her wanton response always aroused Shark, and he quickened his pace, seeking his own pleasure even as he pleased her. Bucking and writhing in a mad, passionate dance, they reached the pinnacle together then collapsed back on the wide comfort of her bed, sated.

Crushed beneath Shark's hot weight, Suzanne rested, enjoying the erotic sensations that still throbbed through her in the aftermath of their joining. He was the most powerful lover she'd ever had. There was an almost animal quality about his lovemaking, and it was that untamed savagery in him that brought out the equally wild side in her.

Their relationship had been a tempestuous one from the very first time they'd met. She'd been invited to one of the secret, illicit slave auctions that were held deep in the bayou country, and Shark had been one of the men in charge there. The attraction between them had been immediate, primitive and powerful. That she was the daughter of a wealthy planter hadn't intimidated Shark, and the fact that he was a smuggler and probably wanted by the law had meant nothing to her. It had been an elemental wanting that had transcended social lines, and now, several years later, they were still carrying on in secret.

Her widowed father had died shortly after they first began to see each other, and her inheritance had been substantial. At Shark's urging she had gone into business with him and invested a large portion of her cash holdings in his slave-smuggling enterprise. The demand for fresh, healthy slaves was tremendous in the south, and Shark's business had flourished. Now, even though the crops had failed numerous times at her plantation, Willow Bend, the return on her investment with Shark had made her an extremely wealthy young woman. She had no financial worries and probably never would have . . . all thanks to him.

Suzanne sighed at the thought. Not only was Shark brilliant at what he did, but he was also an excellent lover. A small, satisfied smile curved her kiss-swollen lips. Shark certainly knew how to stir her to shamelessness. Yet, even as she savored the memory of the delight of his touch, the image of another man intruded on her thoughts . . . *Adam Trent.* . . .

A perplexed frown replaced the smile as she visualized the tall, dark, handsome man who'd been courting her. At the thought of the dynamic Adam Trent, she found herself wondering what it would be like to have him in her bed and how it would feel to hold him tightly within her.

Shark's overpowering nearness suddenly left Suzanne feeling stifled. Moving away from the bed, she went to sit at her dressing table to brush out her hair. As she slowly drew the brush through the heavy golden mane, she was oblivious to Shark's glowering presence in her bed. In her mind, she was back at the ball that had been held at the Whitneys' home in New Orleans the previous weekend. It had been a magical night. She had spent almost the entire evening with Adam, dancing and talking. Toward the end of the evening they'd managed to elude her real escort for the night and disappear into the secluded gardens for a long moment alone. It had been heavenly. His kisses had left her breathless and aching for more.

Something about the rich planter from Charleston excited and intrigued Suzanne. She sensed he was different from all the other men she'd ever known. Certainly she knew that she had wanted him that night more than she'd ever wanted another man. It had been after their explosive embrace that she'd begun to think seri-

40

ously about marriage for the first time in her life. The thought of spending the rest of her days *and nights* with Adam left her breathless in anticipation, and she vowed to figure out a way to get him to the altar.

"Come here, Suzanne. We've little enough time together, and I have no desire to waste any of it," Shark commanded, interrupting her reverie. He was annoyed by her withdrawal from him.

Suzanne glanced up to meet his black-eyed gaze in the mirror before her. "No.," she replied simply, comparing him mentally to Adam and, despite the sensual hold he had on her senses, finding him wanting.

"No?" Used to having his every order blindly obeyed, Shark chuckled in disbelief as he got up and started across the room toward her. "I told you to come to me. Shall I drag you back to the bed?"

All at once, Suzanne found his caveman tactics boring. She couldn't imagine Adam ever treating her this way. She was sure he would be perfect, even in the bedroom.

"No one tells me what to do, Shark. I choose when and with whom I make love. You would do well to remember that," she told him haughtily.

"Oh, I'll remember that all right," he murmured as he came to stand behind her. There was no tenderness in his touch as he encircled her throat with his hands and squeezed in an almost threatening gesture. "But you should remember that without me your fortunes would be lost. You need me, Suzanne."

"I don't *need* anyone." She gave him a scathing look in the mirror.

"You *need* me. It's my business that keeps this plantation of yours running."

"That's only money," she scoffed. "There are men who've died for me, you know."

"They were fools," he derided, believing that any man

41

who'd sacrifice himself for a woman was an idiot and deserved to be dead. "A dead man's no good to you, Suzanne. Can a dead man share your bed? Can a dead man bring you gold?"

She was wearing the crescent necklace he'd given her months before, so to emphasize his point he grasped the chain and pulled it tight. The golden chain bit into her tender flesh. "You do love what I give you, don't you, Suzanne?"

Suzanne stiffened in protest. She didn't want to respond to him and tried desperately to resist, but when he moved his hands lower to cup her breasts and tease the taut peaks, she felt a hungry heat flush through her again. There was something about Shark . . . something about his touch that always set a fire in her blood.

"Yes, yes . . . oh yes!" she gasped as she watched their reflections in the mirror.

Shark knelt and drew her back tightly against him, allowing her to feel the rising strength of his need. He, too, stared at the mirror images of them, but soon his need for her was too powerful to deny. Pulling her from the chair and onto the floor, he took her quickly. His mouth settled hungrily over hers to silence any last protest she might have made, but she made no protest. Already her desire equaled his. Already she was moving restlessly against him. All thoughts of Adam Trent were temporarily banished from Suzanne's mind as she returned Shark's passion with abandon. She was a woman who lived for the moment, and the moment was now . . .

Chapter Four

"Engaged again!" Beau nearly choked on his beer at the news. He slammed his tankard down and stared aghast at Adam across the secluded table they shared at the Samson Saloon near the riverfront in New Orleans. "Are you crazy!"

Adam gave his friend a measured look as he drank slowly from his glass of bourbon. Though it was still early in the day, he felt in need of its reinforcing strength.

"There have been times during the past five months when I thought I was going crazy, but this is not one of them," he replied with cool precision.

"But what about Elise?" Beau demanded in a hushed, yet aggressively outraged voice.

Thoughts of Elise in her trancelike state seared through Adam, and a jolt of emotional agony shook him.

"Just why the hell do you think I'm doing all of this?" he came back sharply, draining the rest of his drink in one deep swallow.

"I don't understand," Beau admitted, confused. "How could your marrying another woman possibly help Elise?"

"I didn't say anything about marriage, Beau," he pointed out.

Beau's expression suddenly brightened. "You're on to something?"

"I think so," Adam began to explain as he signaled

the barmaid to come and bring the bottle. Directing her to leave the bourbon, he poured himself a full draft of the potent liquor. "There's a young woman here in town named Suzanne Labadie—"

"You think she might be the one?" He jumped ahead of Adam's explanation.

"It's possible. The plantation she owns upriver supposedly provides her only means of support. For two of the last three years, though, the crops have failed, and yet she still manages to live in a very expensive style. I made some inquiries—discreet, of course—but I couldn't uncover anything conclusive. All I could find out was that she's not in debt to any of the banks, and she hasn't mortgaged any of her land. I thought if I got a little closer to her . . ."

"She won't suspect anything, will she? I mean, since you're not really in love with her . . . ?"

"No, she doesn't suspect a thing, and she's not going to. As far as Suzanne Labadie is concerned, and the rest of the town for that matter, I'm a planter from Charleston who's in town on a combined pleasure and slave-buying trip."

"I knew it was a good plan when you suggested it. I only hope it works."

"It has to work, Beau. God knows we haven't had any success trying to find Shark any other way."

They both fell silent for a moment then as they thought of the frustration of the past months.

"How's Becky doing?" Beau inquired.

"Fine, now. You know how nervous she was in the beginning about all the deception, but she's handled it really well.

"That's good," he said, remembering how Becky had insisted on accompanying Adam on his trip to New Orleans after she'd learned of his scheme. She'd been determined not to stay behind in Charleston, never knowing what was happening.

"I decided not to confide in her about Suzanne," Adam confided. "For right now, it's better if we're the only ones who know of my suspicions and my plans."

"And Elise?" Beau wanted to know. Since Odile had died in the attack, Adam was the closest thing Elise had to family. He took his obligation to her very seriously, despite the fact that there was probably no hope for a future for them together.

"The doctor in Charleston was right. Elise had no trouble adapting to the change in environment," he answered. "I rented a house in the American section and hired a private, live-in nurse. I engaged Dr. David Williams, the specialist the doctor back home recommended, and he's been seeing Elise regularly"

"Did you tell the Whitneys about her?"

"No. No one knows about Elise's presence here, and I want to keep it that way. Becky and I made sure that she was comfortably settled in with the nurse before we even went on to the Whitneys. As far as they know, we're here on business with some time for pleasure. So far, no one's doubted it."

"Has the new doctor been able to help her at all?"

"I visited Elise the day before yesterday," Adam began, his expression growing strained as he thought of the painful visit. "There's been no change."

Elise had been sitting in a chair, staring out the window in her bedroom. Adam had carried on a one-sided conversation with her, speaking of nonsensical, personal things, but she had seemed completely unaware of his presence. When he'd left her, he'd been more upset than ever.

"I'm sorry, Adam. I know how difficult this must be for you."

For just an instant all of Adam's anguish was mirrored in his dark eyes. But he quickly recovered and shuttered the emotion from view.

"It's been so long, Beau . . . At first, I had hope. Then I thought the change of scenery might help her, but now I'm starting to believe all those doctors' damning predictions. I'm beginning to think that she'll never get better."

"I wish there was something more I could do," he offered.

"There's nothing," Adam stated grimly, taking another drink of bourbon. "I'm going to see her again this afternoon."

"Why in God's name do you keep torturing yourself?"

Adam was taken by surprise by his friend's question. "Beau . . . damn it, man! Don't you understand? It's my fault! All my fault! If only I could have—"

Before he could say more, Beau cut him brutally off. "If only you could have what, Adam?" he demanded furiously. He had watched Adam torment himself with guilt ever since the attack. No longer was his friend easygoing and happy. During the past months he'd become increasingly bitter, frustrated, and angry. Beau knew it was time to try to convince him of his own innocence. "If only you could have died? You're lucky you're still breathing! Hell," he swore vividly as he remembered the dangers they'd faced and the odds against them, "we both are!"

"I should have done something more . . . tried to make a run for it . . . something . . ." he argued.

"You can't change what happened, Adam, and second-guessing only makes it worse."

"I don't know, Beau. Sometimes the rage I'm holding back within me is so great I thing I'm losing my mind." Adam rubbed his forehead in a tense gesture. "I've got to find Shark. I've got to hunt him down like the animal he is and pay him back for all the misery and death he caused." He raised his fevered gaze to meet Beau's. I

46

have to, even if it's the last thing I ever do!"

Adam descended from the hired coach in front of the sedate home he'd rented for Elise.

"You want me to wait?" the driver asked.

"No, there's no need," he answered as he paid him in full.

Even after the conveyance had moved away, Adam remained standing in front of the house, staring up at it expressionlessly. Elise was here . . . He knew he should be glad to see her, but his heart was heavy in his chest. This lack of feeling filled him with even more guilt, as he convinced himself that he was betraying the love he and Elise had shared. Miserable, Adam mounted the stairs and knocked on the door.

"Mr. Trent, come in." Nurse Halliday pushed the door wide to allow her employer to enter. "Dr. Williams is still here. He's with Miss Clayton right now."

"Good," Adam said as he walked into the parlor. "I was hoping to have a chance to speak with him."

"As soon as he's finished, I'll send him to you."

"Thank you."

"Would you care for some refreshment?"

"No. That'll be all for now."

"Fine, sir."

Alone, lost in a haze of misery and frustration that threatened to overwhelm him, Adam began to pace the room.

"Mr. Trent . . . Nurse Halliday told me you were waiting to speak with me." David Williams paused just outside the parlor door.

Adam looked up to see the physician standing there. "Yes, Dr. Williams, please join me." He gestured for him to come in and take a seat.

"Thank you." Of average height and weight, there

seemed nothing out of the ordinary about the dark-haired Williams. It was only when you met his aquamarine gaze squarely that the true depths of his strength of character were revealed. He did not accomplish things in life through brute force, but through the force of his dynamic personality. David judged people instantly by what he read in their eyes and seldom in his thirty-five years had he been wrong. He had known from the beginning that Adam Trent was troubled man, tortured by his own personal demons of the past, but he knew that the planter wanted no advice from him. He had been hired to try to help his fiancée and that was what he was going to do.

"Elise . . ." Adam spoke hesitantly. He wanted to know if she was better, yet he was fearful of hearing only bad news.

"I've made no progress yet, Mr. Trent," he informed him. "The trauma she suffered was so catastrophic to her sense of well-being that she has no desire to return to reality. It's my understanding that in this type of case, where there's evidence of psychomotor retardation, the patient has managed to find peace somewhere in the innermost regions of his or her mind. It's a soothing contentment that cocoons them and allows then to deny all pain."

"So Elise is lost in a dream world?"

"Lost is not the word. She's chosen to be there. Where's she's existing in her mind, she's insulated and protected. Hidden there, she does not have to cope with the agony and humiliation that reality has trust upon her."

"But doesn't she realize that it's over, that she's safe again?" Adam had difficulty understanding.

David sensed his confusion and wished there was more he could say to comfort him. The trouble was that no one understood the workings of the human mind and spirit. Even after years of intense study, he still did not know the exact method that would draw his patient out of her self-imposed, mute exile.

"In her mind it may never be over, Mr. Trent." At Adam's stricken look, he continued, "All I can do is keep trying to break through to her."

"But you've been seeing her for almost a month and there's been no change."

"I wish I could offer you a guarantee, but I can't. With your permission, though, I'll continue to try everything I know to help her."

"Of course, Dr. Williams. I've been told by many that you're one of the best in handling these cases. As long as there's hope, I'll never give up trying."

"Good. I'll carry on with my daily sessions as we've agreed."

"Whatever you think best, Doctor."

When the physician had gone, Nurse Halliday returned to speak with Adam. "Miss Clayton is in her room if you'd like to visit her, Mr. Trent."

Adam nodded solemnly and started slowly up the stairs. He paused briefly before her partially closed bedroom door and then knocked softly. He waited hoping for a response, but when none came, he pushed it wide and entered.

"Elise?" He saw her sitting in a high-backed wing-chair by the window staring out at the sun-caressed garden below. "Elise, darling, it's me . . . Adam."

He came to stand before her. She didn't acknowledge his presence in any way, but continued to look out the window, her face blank, her once-dancing eyes dull and lifeless. When Elise didn't respond, Adam knelt in front of her and took her hands in his.

"Elise."

Adam wanted to plead with her to return to him, but the words wouldn't come. He waited there for long minutes before leaning forward to press a tender kiss upon her cheek, but even that action brought no answering response. Disconsolate, he got to his feet and strode quickly from the room.

Giving Nurse Halliday only a departing nod, Adam escaped the torture chamber the house had become. A sense of wretchedness gripped him as he fled. In dire need of some time alone, he signaled a passing conveyance and directed the driver to take him to the saloon-gambling house known as Hewlett's Exchange. He would have a few drinks and try to relax for a while before heading back to the Whitneys'. Adam knew that Becky would be waiting with an endless barrage of questions about Elise's condition and his meeting with Beau, and he was in no mood to discuss anything.

A short time later, he was downing a stiff shot of Hewlett's best whiskey in the upstairs bar of the establishment. The potent liquor burned as it went down, and Adam welcomed its heat.

"Sir, care to join us in a friendly game of poker?" a gray-haired, distinguished-looking man called out from where he sat with two others at a nearby table.

The distraction of a low-stakes card game appealed to Adam, and after refilling his near-empty glass, he joined them.

"I'm Jacques Chenier. This is Paul Michel and Antoine Ducharme," Jacques made the introductions.

Adam shook hands all around as he introduced himself, and he studied his opponents with casual interest as he sat down. Paul Michel was a thin, nervous man with bright blue eyes that darted constantly about the room. The dark-haired Antoine Ducharme, on the other hand, was not a particularly big man, but he was heavyset and rather untidy in his dress. He was already well into his cups, and Adam wondered if he should even be playing.

As the game began none of the men seemed to be particularly avid in their gambling, and Adam was glad, for it would make the game that much more enjoyable if no one took their losses too seriously. Play continued for over an hour. In the beginning, they were well-matched and the hands were challenging. The pots that were won and lost were not exceedingly large, and no one player lost any more than the rest. Then, as Antoine Ducharme continued to drink excessively, his awareness began to slip and his playing became sloppy. Again and again he bet on poor hands, and again and again he lost.

"My hand," Adam said with some satisfaction as he laid down his cards for all to see.

Jacques and Paul acquiesced easily, but Antoine, in his drunken stupor, grew annoyed. He glanced down at his rapidly dwindling pile of money and felt more than a little panic-stricken. Though the amounts he'd lost would not have been considered large by a rich man's standards, Antoine's finances were in such dire straits that he could not afford to lose any more at all. His drunken, gaming ways had not been serving him well lately, and during the last few months he had lost nearly all of his young niece's and nephew's inheritance. Even his own funds were running dangerously low, and he was desperate for a chance to regain what little he'd lost.

Jacques dealt the next hand, and Antoine was almost exultant when he glanced at his cards and discovered that he'd been given two pairs—threes and eights. Confident of a win, he bet heavily. When Paul and Jacques dropped out, he grew even more assured, and when Adam called, Antoine gladly spread his cards out before him. He was so wrapped up in his seeming triumph that he did not notice Adam's reaction. Eagerly, he reached out to rake in what he thought were his winnings.

"Well, gentlemen," he gloated, "I think I shall call it a day."

"Wait." Adam snared the drunken man's wrist as he started to scoop up the money. When he had Antoine's attention, he laid down his own hand.

Antoine was in shock as he stared at Adam's three kings. He flushed in pained embarrassment.

"Now, If you will excuse me?" Adam sensed that things were getting a bit too serious with Ducharme, so he pocketed the winnings and started to leave.

Outrage filled Antoine as he watched the stranger stand. "I demand another chance!" he challenged.

"Antoine!" Paul spoke up, knowing of his quick temper and wanting to avoid trouble at all costs.

"Antoine, you haven't lost that much," Jacques cajoled. "Besides, you're temporarily out of funds. Perhaps you should call it a day?"

He stiffened in insult at his friends' interference. Meeting Adam's gaze, he said, "One more hand, Trent."

Adam had no desire to be drawn into a confrontational situation. "Sir," he began politely, "since you're short of funds, there's no point in playing. Perhaps another time?" He wanted to give the drunken man a graceful way out, but Antoine refused to take it.

"No, now," he insisted. "I may be short of funds, but I do hold the title to Belle Arbor."

Jacques and Paul exchanged surprised looks.

"Belle Arbor?" Adam asked.

"The Ducharme plantation," he bit out in terse explanation. "I demand one final hand to clear the slate." His liquor filled him with false bravado.

Now Adam was the one cornered. With pretended ease he returned to his chair. "One hand of poker?" he inquired quietly.

"One hand, five-card stud," Antoine snarled, determined to win back his money. Writing out a makeshift deed to the plantation, he tossed it casually on the table.

So it began. The tension in the room was thick as all present gathered to watch. The cards were dealt, yet, when both men examined their hands for the first time, they betrayed no emotion.

Again Antoine felt victorious as he stared at his pair of jacks. This time the fool had definitely dealt him a winning hand.

"It was your challenge, Ducharme," Adam prodded, his expression stoic. "Show your cards."

It seemed all the spectators held their breath as he spread out his cards. A murmur of approval swelled through the crowd as they saw the jacks. When Adam didn't visibly react, Antoine again reached for the pot.

"I believe the pot is mine," Adam declared, as he laid down three fives.

A collective gasp came from the onlookers, and all eyes focused on Antoine.

He was sitting rigidly, staring at Adam's cards in numb disbelief. A shock of realization rushed though him. He felt himself go pale in awful acceptance. *He had lost the damned plantation.* . . . He knew there was no recourse, so he stood up slowly.

"Indeed, it is your hand, sir," he agreed stiffly. "I shall send the deed to you late this afternoon.

"I'm staying with the Whitneys in the Garden District."

"I'm acquainted with your host." Antoine gave a curt nod and then made an unsteady exit as the crowd moved in closer to congratulate Adam.

Chapter Five

The coach moved down the back road at a measured pace as the driver, a heavily built black man named Harlan, directed his team around the ruts and bumps with sure-handed expertise. As they neared a slightly overgrown side road, he slowed and made the turn, pulling to a halt just past the intersection.

"This is it," Harlan announced to his passengers.

"*This* is Belle Arbor?" Becky asked excitedly, clutching at her brother's arm as she got her first view of the magnificent house. When Adam had told her that he'd won a plantation in a card game, she certainly hadn't expected this. Their family home in Charleston was lovely, but it couldn't compare to the majesty of this pillared mansion. "Why, it's beautiful." Her soft tone reflected the amazement that shone in her warm, brown eyes.

"Yes, ma'am, it sure is," the driver agreed.

"Ducharme must be a total idiot," Adam remarked scathingly, wondering at what kind of fool would gamble away such an outstanding estate. "Let's drive on up. I don't know if anyone's expecting us or if anyone is even here. He was very vague when I spoke with him about it."

"Yes, sir," Harlan replied respectfully as he slapped the reins lightly against the horse's backs and headed up the long drive toward the main house.

The sound of a carriage coming up the drive interrupted Lianne as she labored in the flower garden near the reflecting pond. She straightened up from her arduous task and cast a curious glance at the approaching conveyance. Lianne could see a dark-haired man and woman in the carriage, but did not recognize them. She was not expecting company and wondered who they were.

As Lianne hurried down the house to meet her unexpected visitors, she paused, suddenly realizing that she was in no condition to be greeting anyone. Because she'd known she would be working outside all day, she had chosen her oldest dress to wear that morning and had tied her thick, lustrous hair back in a tight, school-marmish bun. She looked down at her mud-, grass-, and sweat-stained clothing in dismay. Several buttons at the bodice of her gown were undone against the humid heat, and her skirts were heavily soiled from kneeling on the damp earth. Brushing what grime she could from her gown, she quickly rebuttoned the bodice and continued on her way. Lianne knew she bore no resemblance to the lady of Belle Arbor. In fact, with her dirt-smudged face and the loose tendrils of hair escaping the practical knot at the nape of her neck, she appeared more the unkempt servant than the mistress of her home, but at this point little more could be done about it.

Harlan pulled the carriage to a halt before the front door, and Adam climbed down and turned back to help Becky out. Harlan began unloading their baggage as they stood staring about the grounds.

"It's rundown, Adam, but I think with a little investment on your part and some hard work, it could be as wonderful as we first thought it was." Becky confirmed what Adam had been thinking. As they'd drawn nearer to the house, they had been slightly distressed to discover that all was not as perfect as it had seemed from a distance.

"It's perfect for what we need," Adam remarked. Belle Arbor's location near the river and its easy access to the bayous provided him with just the outlets he needed to maintain secret contact with Beau should the need arise.

"I wonder why no one's come out to meet us yet? Do you suppose there's no one here? Surely Ducharme sent word to let them know what happened."

"I'm sure there are at least a few servants around somewhere. The house is open. We might as well go in and announce ourselves."

They had just started up the front steps when Lianne came around the corner of the house. The sight of the driver unloading luggage gave her pause, and she frowned. *What was going on? Who could possibly have come here for a visit?*

Then she saw the two strangers going up the stairs of her home. The man was tall and leanly muscled. His broad shoulders filled out his expertly tailored, bottle-green jacket, and his long, powerful legs were encased in fawn-colored trousers that fit him to perfection. Lianne knew she had never met him before, because if she had, she would have remembered. He was without a doubt the most handsome man she'd ever seen.

The woman at his side was as beautiful as he was handsome. Her hair was long and dark, her figure slim. She was wearing a very rich looking, royal blue traveling suit that fit her superbly.

The contrast between their sophisticated appearance and her own current state of dress was so marked that Lianne felt even more painfully aware of her own woeful condition. Still, she knew that there was no time to even consider changing, for, whoever these two were, they looked as if they were about to make themselves completely at home in her own house.

"Pardon me, but may I help you?" Lianne asked as she emerged from the shadows.

The feminine voice that called out to Adam was cultured and refined; the woman he found it belonged to left him staring in surprise. He turned, expecting to see a lady approaching, and instead had found a very dirty, very disheveled young woman standing at the bottom of the stairs. She looked downright filthy. Some of her long, red-gold hair had escaped confinement and was scraggling limply about her dirt-streaked face. Only her wide, sparkling emerald eyes revealed anything positive about her, and Adam found himself caught up in that flashing green gaze.

"Hello," he greeted her with a smile.

At his smile, Lianne's breath caught in her throat. Never in her life had she felt such a sudden, overpowering attraction to a man. He was absolutely gorgeous! Her heart lurched in an unfamiliar rhythm, and for a long moment, she was speechless. She made an effort to pull herself together. Though it pained her to think it, she realized that the lovely woman at his side was no doubt his wife, for they certainly made a striking couple.

Adam continued to speak. "Yes, you can help us. I'm Adam Trent . . ."

Lianne's usually practical brain was disconnected as she mused . . . *Adam Trent . . . what a wonderful, strong, masculine name . . . it suited him. Yes, he definitely looked like an Adam Trent . . .*

"And I'd appreciate it if you could tell whoever is in charge here that the new owner has arrived," he finished.

His statement left the already light-headed, daydreaming Lianne in shock. *What!* She crashed back to reality. *New owner? What was this idiot talking about? Belle Arbor wasn't for sale. It had been in her family for generations, and it was going to stay that way. Surely he must be mistaken. It wasn't Belle Arbor he was claiming. It had to be another plantation.*

Adam, thinking he had explained everything clearly, continued on up the stairs with Becky.

Lianne watched them in total confusion. Then, just as they were about to enter the house, she recovered enough to follow them. Hiking up her skirts in a very unladylike fashion, she bolted up the steps after them.

"Wait a minute!" she called out, confronting them as they were about to go inside. "There must be some mistake."

"This is Belle Arbor, isn't it?" His response held a note of impatience.

"Well, yes it is, but . . ."

Adam scowled, annoyed that Ducharme hadn't notified anyone here of his imminent arrival. The man had had over a week and yet had not sent word of the change of ownership. As he turned to face her, he discovered that the woman was standing there with her skirts still in hand. Her indiscreet pose revealed much, and his dark-eyed gaze was drawn to her very shapely legs and trim ankles. An unexpected jolt of sensual appreciation startled him, and his scowl darkened as he forced himself to look away. His open regard brought an unwelcome blush creeping into her cheeks, and she quickly dropped her skirts.

"Then, tell the person in charge that I'm here," he repeated sharply, aggravated with himself for the sudden awareness he'd felt for this unkempt, seemingly slow-witted chit. Certain that he'd made his point this time, he didn't pause, but turned and walked on inside the house with Becky.

Lianne was tired. Sleep had eluded her for days, and her nerves had been stretched taut as her worry about the fate of the plantation had consumed her. But all thoughts of weariness fled as she stared after the couple. *Just who in the hell did this Adam Trent think he was, turning his back on her and walking right on into her own house that way! Did he really think he owned it?* She frowned.

Rooted to her place on the porch, Lianne struggled to understand exactly what was happening here, but no rational explanations came to her.

"Where should I take this trunk?" Harlan asked as he came up the steps behind her.

His question broke through her consternation.

"You can put it back in your carriage and be quick about it!" she snapped.

Spurred to action by the thought of someone actually trying to take over her home, Lianne charged inside leaving a stunned Harlan behind. She dashed into the study where the guncase was located. With shaking hands she pulled her father's best shotgun from the case and loaded it. Belle Arbor was hers and Alex's. It would never belong to another!

Lianne thought of Adam Trent's casual, demeaning dismissal of her, and her blood began to boil. How dare he speak down to her so! How dare he think that Belle Arbor was his, the arrogant ass! Her mouth thinned to a grim, determined line as she stalked toward the study. She was going to show him just who was in charge of Belle Ardor. She was!

Adam and Becky were standing in the middle of the spacious parlor admiring their surroundings when Lianne's icy command cut through their conversation.

"Hold it right there, Mr. Trent!"

They looked up together to find the woman they'd just spoken with outside holding a shotgun on them. In a protective move, Adam immediately stepped in front of Becky to shield her from possible harm.

"I want you out of my house right now!" Lianne ordered, motioning with the gun for them to head outside.

Adam was puzzled. *Her house?* "This can all be explained very simply if you'll just let me . . ." He started to reach into his inner coat pocket to retrieve the deed, but at the sound of her next threat he froze.

"I wouldn't do that if I were you. I'm a dead shot at this range."

"Look, miss . . ." He was growing exasperated.

"Don't 'look miss' me! I don't know who you are or what you're doing here, but you'd better get back outside real fast!"

Adam tensed as he stared at her in disbelief. Her eyes were glittering dangerously, and her breasts were heaving in indignation beneath the soft, cotton fabric of her gown. He wondered distractedly why he'd noticed. He didn't know who this woman was, but he knew he didn't like anyone holding a weapon on him. He was tempted to try to wrestle the gun away from her. Becky, however, knew her brother very well and placed a light, restraining hand on his arm to stop him.

"I think we'd better do as she says, Adam," Becky said in a calm tone.

Lianne gave a tight nod in approval of her sentiment and backed up into the hall so they could pass her without coming too close.

Adam kept himself between Becky and Lianne as they retreated outdoors. As they emerged from the house, they came face to face with Harlan, who was waiting there with their trunks.

"Mr. Trent, I wasn't—" His explanation was cut off as he saw Lianne coming outside behind them, shotgun in hand. His eyes rounded, and he backed away from the confrontation. "I thought you said you owned this place!" he said accusingly as he hurried down the steps before them.

"I do!" Adam bellowed, furious at being so humili-

60

ated. "Miss, if you'll just let me show you—"

"Get down those steps after your driver, mister. Lady, you'd better tell him to do as I say or you might end up a widow!" Lianne stood unmoving just beyond the front door, her legs braced apart, her eyes glowing with a fervent inner fire of rage. She trained the gun squarely upon the hesitating Adam.

Though Becky knew their situation was serious, a bubble of amusement filled her. It was interesting enough to see this woman standing up to Adam without fear, but that she thought them man and wife struck her as truly funny.

"I don't think there's any danger of that," Becky replied easily. "Come, darling." She drew Adam with her as she led the way down the stairs. Her eyes were twinkling with good humor. Adam slanted her an outraged look. He was not used to backing down in any confrontation, and he found nothing the least bit humorous about their current position.

Stopping at the bottom of the steps, he turned around to glare at Lianne. Even though he was infuriated by the situation, he couldn't help but admire the sight the woman made as she stood so proudly on the porch, guarding the house. He couldn't imagine how, moments before, he'd thought her slow-witted. She looked like some avenging Valkyrie . . . fierce, protective, passionate. The last thought disturbed him, and he pushed it from his mind. *Who the hell was this woman?*

"Miss Lianne . . . have we got company?" Sarah came out of the house and stopped dead in her tracks the instant she saw Lianne, gun in hand, facing down the strangers. She'd been working at the back of the house and realized they had visitors when she heard strange voices.

"They were just leaving, Sarah," she answered without taking her eyes off Adam.

"You're Lianne Ducharme?" Adam demanded in surprise. The Whitneys had told them that Antoine was the guardian for his young niece and nephew who were named Lianne and Alex. He hadn't really paid much attention at the time, thinking the history of the Ducharme family unimportant. Now he wondered why Antoine was living in such style in New Orleans while his ward was living here on this rundown plantation in what appeared to be an obvious state of poverty.

Lianne stiffened at what she perceived as sneering disbelief in his tone. "I am," she replied with dignity.

"Miss Lianne, what's going on here?" Sarah interrupted uneasily.

"This man claims he's the owner of Belle Arbor."

"What!"

"Miss Ducharme . . ." Adam began as he slowly reached into his pocket to draw out the papers. "If you'll just take a look at this, I think it will clear everything up." He held out the neatly folded title.

"See what he's got, Sarah," Lianne directed.

The servant hurried to take the papers from Adam and then handed them to her mistress. Lianne kept the gun on Adam as she glanced down at the document. Fear and anger jolted through her as she recognized the legality of the title and her uncle's handwriting. Belle Arbor now belonged to one Adam Trent. It was signed by her uncle and dated a week ago.

Lianne's hands began to tremble as terrible, soul-shattering emotions tore her apart. Everything he'd said was true . . . but how? How could this be? What had Uncle Antoine done?

"How?" was the only word she could choke out.

"I would have thought that your uncle would have notified you, but obviously he didn't," Adam said levelly. "He lost the plantation to me in a card game."

"In a card game . . ." Lianne repeated flatly as she

62

stared at him. Bitter, galling tears burned her eyes, but she refused to show any sign of weakness.

Becky could see that the young woman was in complete shock from the news that she was losing her home, and her heart went out to her. Wanting to try to ease her distress, she spoke up gently, "Miss Ducharme, perhaps we could discuss this inside . . . without the gun?"

Lianne looked at Becky and, seeing no malice in her earnest gaze, lowered the shotgun. Without a word, she walked back inside. The crumpled title fell from her benumbed fingers as she reentered the main hall and wandered into the parlor.

"Miss Lianne, let me take the gun. You don't need it," Sarah coaxed, feeling her pain as her own.

For a moment, a flare of passionate hatred lit her emerald eyes. "If Uncle Antoine was here, I'd need it. I'd use it, too!" she vowed angrily as she reluctantly handed the weapon over.

Sarah said nothing, but Lianne knew her silence meant complete agreement.

"Adam," Becky spoke his name softly as she held him back from immediately following Lianne back inside.

"What?"

"What do you intend to do now?"

"I intend to take possession of my plantation," he stated firmly as he started to move off again, but once more Becky held him back.

"Adam," she said in exasperation, "it's obvious that she knew nothing about any of this."

"So?"

"So this must be very traumatic for her."

"That's not my problem, Becky." His voice hardened. He had no time to concern himself with the misfortunes of the Ducharme family. The girl was not his concern. "I can't help it if Ducharme's a bastard."

The cold indifference of his tone confirmed what she'd suspected, and she protested vigorously, "You can't just throw her out of her own home!"

Adam gave his sister a strained look as he headed up the stairs to the porch. "It's no longer *her* home. *I'm* the owner now."

Becky stared after him incredulously. Less than a year ago Adam would never have been so heartless in dealing with anyone, but ever since the raid on the *Windwood,* he'd changed. He'd become callous to any goals but his own, and it broke her heart to think that he would never again be the loving, caring man he once was. She hurried after him, wanting to buffer any confrontation he might have with Lianne Ducharme.

"You needn't worry that we'll be a burden, Mr. Trent," Lianne was managing to say as Becky joined them.

"We?" Adam asked.

"My brother, Alex, and myself," she clarified, facing him. "He's out riding in the fields somewhere, but he'll return soon."

"We aren't worried about you being a burden, Miss Ducharme," Becky put in before Adam could say any more. "I'm sure this has all come as a horrible shock to you."

"Yes, it has," Lianne agreed. "Belle Arbor is our heritage . . . our birthright. It's been in my family for generations, and I'd hoped to keep it that way . . ." She paused and drew a ragged breath before glancing at Adam. "I'll travel to New Orleans and meet with my uncle this very afternoon to see what kind of arrangements can be made. I hope you won't mind our staying on for a short while until things can be worked out, Mrs. Trent."

"Miss Trent," Becky corrected. "I'm Adam's sister."

"Oh . . ." Lianne's surprise was evident as she

glanced between the two of them, and she wondered why she felt so oddly pleased by the news.

"And, we won't mind your staying on until your affairs are settled," she went on.

"Thank you. I appreciate your kindness," Lianne told her, although she was still finding it difficult to believe that she was now a guest in her own home.

Adam's expression grew thunderous as he listened to his sister calmly invite Lianne to remain in residence. The last thing he'd wanted or needed was the Ducharmes staying on at the plantation. He'd been pleased with winning Belle Arbor, for it provided him with a private base to continue his pursuit of Shark. Becky offering the Ducharme girl and her brother sanctuary, though, complicated an already difficult situation. Besides, he admitted to himself reluctantly, there was something about Lianne that attracted him, and he couldn't afford the distraction.

"You're welcome here for as long as it's necessary," Becky assured her, completely ignoring her brother. She admired Lianne for the way she was conducting herself under the most trying of circumstances, and she knew for a fact that if their situations were reversed, she would not have been taking everything quite so calmly.

"I'll go upstairs and get ready to make the trip into town. If I set out in the next hour, I should be able to reach Uncle Antoine's before evening. I'd like to make the trip alone, so will you object to Alex staying here? He won't be any trouble to you. Sarah can take care of him."

"That'll be fine," Becky assured her.

"Well, if you'll excuse me then?"

"Of course."

Lianne left the room, her shoulders proudly squared, her chin held high. Adam watched her as she walked out, taking in the gentle sway of her rounded hips and the soft swell of her bosom. When he realized what he was doing, his mood grew even blacker. He had only one reason for being there and that was to seek his revenge. Nothing else mattered to him — nothing.

Becky had been watching her brother with interest, and she found his obvious annoyance over Lianne's staying on strange. It seemed to her that he was over-reacting for some reason.

"I don't think she'll be staying here long," she offered. "I'm sure they'll want to move out as soon as something can be arranged."

"Good," he responded almost too quickly. "I've got no time to waste worrying about whether the Ducharmes are going to find out what I'm doing."

Once she was sure that Lianne had gone upstairs and was out of earshot, she probed quietly, "She's quite a lady, though, don't you think?"

In answer, Adam only shrugged. Then, spying the liquor cabinet across the room, he strode purposefully to it and poured himself a stiff shot of bourbon. It was a move that completely surprised his sister. She knew Adam was not normally a heavy drinker, and she wondered just what was disturbing him so deeply.

There was nothing Lianne wanted to do more than to linger in the tub of hot, steaming water and pretend that all was right with the world, but she knew she couldn't. There could be no pretending. The worst had happened and now she had to deal with it.

Snatching up the scented soap, she quickly began to scrub herself. She had to hurry if she was to make it to New Orleans this afternoon. Bathing completed, she stood up and grabbed the oversized towel Sarah had laid out for her. She stepped from the tub as she dried herself and wandered toward her wardrobe to select the clothes she would wear into town.

Out of the corner of her eye she caught sight of herself in her full-length mirror, and she paused there, towel in hand, to study her reflection. With critical intent, she took inventory of her own attributes . . . high, firm breasts, not too big and not too small . . . a trim waist . . . curving hips . . . long, slender legs. Assessingly, Lianne regarded her own face, and she decided that her thick mane of shiny burnished hair and her green eyes were definitely her best features. Though she judged herself no raving beauty, Lianne knew she already looked infinitely better than she had when she'd come from the garden.

Remembering the scene that had just taken place downstairs left her dispirited. Her shoulders slumped in defeat as she turned away from her mirror image to begin to dress. There was a knock at the door as she was struggling to button the last few buttons at the back of her gown.

"Yes? Who is it?"

"It's me, Lianne," Alex called out.

"Come on in, sweetcakes," she invited, glad that she would get to see him before she left.

The door opened, but instead of bustling in as he usually did, Alex was very subdued as he entered. His eyes were huge in his face as he looked up at her solemnly.

"Is it true?" he asked uncertainly, his fear showing.

"Is what true?"

"Is it true that the man and lady downstairs now own Belle Arbor?"

Lianne hedged, wanting to give him an easier explantation, but none was forthcoming. There was no use in trying to soft-pedal it. Resignedly, she told him what had happened.

"I'm leaving to go into New Orleans right away, so I can see Uncle Antoine and try to straighten this all out," she concluded. "Sarah will be here to take care of you while I'm gone, but I shouldn't be away any longer than late tomorrow. All right?"

Alex looked confused as he tried to grasp how his uncle could have given away their home to a stranger. "Bella Arbor will be ours again when you get back, won't it, Lianne?" he ventured.

"I hope so, Alex . . . I hope so."

Her answer seemed to satisfy him for the time being. "Good." Alex smiled in relief and then was back to normal. He gave her a quick kiss and a hug before dashing from the room in boyish abandon.

Lianne's eyes burned as she watched him go, and she prayed with all her heart that she would be able to come up with a way to get her family's home back.

Chapter Six

It was near dusk as the Ducharme carriage made its way through New Orleans heading for Antoine's house in the French Quarter. Within the confines of the vehicle, Lianne rode in silence. To all outward appearances, she seemed very much the genteel young lady — her expression was schooled to blandness, her hair was done up in a sedate style, and her deep green traveling suit was high-necked and quite modest. Only her hands clinched tightly in her lap betrayed the truth of her inner turmoil.

Lianne had alternated between violent anger and wracking despair during the long trip to town. Things had been difficult for her before, but nothing matched the humiliation she'd felt when faced down by that . . . that Adam Trent. She tried to think of a suitably disparaging reference for him, but her limited knowledge of such colorful language left her stymied. A sneer of contempt curved her lips as she thought of him. The arrogant ass! His condescending attitude had made the awkward situation even more traumatic for her, and she knew she would hate him forever for his cavalier treatment of her. Not that he cared what she thought, Lianne reflected bitterly. He'd shown absolutely no compassion for her plight. Only his sister, Becky, had seemed to understand the devastating impact of what had happened to her, and Lianne would always remember her sympathetic kindness.

Lianne was glad that she hadn't run into Adam again before she'd left for town. The farther away she stayed from him the better. She scoffed at herself now for ever having thought of him as handsome. There was nothing really attractive about the man . . . Why, he was just like the black panther she'd seen one day in the bayou. It had been sleek and mesmerizingly beautiful, but there had been something very cold and very dangerous about it. It had been an amoral predator concerned only with its own survival, its own territory . . . just like Adam Trent.

As the carriage swung around a corner and pulled to a stop, all thoughts of Adam fled her mind. She was there—at Uncle Antoine's. The time had come for the real confrontation. When the driver opened the door for her, she descended with her usual grace and then paused for a moment on the walkway to glance up at the building. It was a cold-looking house, devoid of warmth, and she fought down the feelings of dread and panic that threatened. She wanted to face her uncle down, but she was truly afraid of what she was going to discover. If he'd gambled away her home, what else had he done? Marshaling her dignity, she continued up the walk. She knew Antoine wouldn't be pleased to have her show up on his doorstep unannounced, but at this point, she didn't care. She had to learn the truth.

His butler, Benjamin, answered the door. "Miss Lianne . . . this is a surprise. Come in," he invited though there was no warmth evident in his tone.

"Thank you, Benjamin. I've come to see my uncle. Please tell him I'm here." Lianne tried to sound as confident as she could as she faced the servant.

"I'm sorry, ma'am, but he's out for the evening."

"Oh." The discovery that she would not be able to meet with him immediately left her feeling oddly deflated, and a wave of disappointment swept through her.

"Miss Lianne, where shall I put these bags?" The driver entered behind her carrying her things.

"You'll be staying on?" Benjamin queried, puzzled. Mr. Antoine rarely welcomed his niece or nephew into his home. He wondered why he hadn't been informed of the visit.

"I'll be staying, probably just for tonight," she answered.

"And your brother?"

"He did not accompany me."

"Well then, just take her things upstairs to the second bedroom on the left."

"What time do you expect my uncle to return, Benjamin?" Lianne asked as she moved into the parlor.

"I'm not sure. He didn't say."

"I see. Well, I'll have dinner while I wait. See to it, please."

"Yes, ma'am."

Adam had spent the afternoon touring his new plantation, and he'd been most satisfied with what he'd seen. The crops appeared to be doing well, the stables were well-stocked, and, though some repairs were definitely needed, the house would easily become a showplace again. All that had been good news, of course, but the information that he'd come across concerning their neighbors had pleased him even more. He'd known that the Labadie plantation was in this general area, but he'd had no idea that Suzanne's home bordered Belle Arbor. The discovery had encouraged him tremendously. The closer he was to Suzanne, the easier it would be to court her and win her trust.

Later that evening, after Alex had gone on to bed, Adam sat alone with Becky in the dining room savoring his after-dinner brandy. He was excited that things were turning out so unexpectedly well, and he knew exactly what he had to do next.

"I want to give party . . ." he began, drawing his sister's immediate attention.

"A party? Here? Why?"

"A housewarming, of sorts," Adam said casually enough though his thoughts were far from casual on the subject. He hadn't yet told Becky of his plan to marry Suzanne, and he didn't intend to. The less she knew about things, the better. "I think it would be a good way to meet the neighbors."

"And possibly make some contacts?" she shrewdly finished for him.

"I'm going to find Shark, Becky, one way or the other." His response was terse. "I'm going to do whatever it takes."

"I know," she answered sympathetically, not understanding at that time the real meaning of his words. "I'll do all that I can to help. How soon did you want to have this party? The house and grounds need a lot of work, but it shouldn't take much more than a month to get it done."

"We'll plan on six weeks, then. Everything should be ready by then. . . ."

Though Becky thought Adam was referring to the house, he was really thinking about Suzanne. He felt certain that he could win her by the time of the party, and he knew it would be the perfect time to announce their engagement. It rankled Adam that he had to be so patient in his pursuit of her, but he had no intention of destroying his chances of success by rushing things. He felt certain that he was on the right track. He would catch Shark, and when he did, he would make him pay.

* * *

72

Antoine's mood was black as he entered his home in the wee hours of the morning. He'd felt good when he'd gone out earlier. It had almost been as if the debacle at Hewlett's the week before hadn't happened. His confidence had returned, and he'd felt sure that it was his night to win. He snorted in self-derision. The night that had begun with such promise had ended miserably. He'd lost again, badly.

Still, while Antoine hated to lose, he felt no remorse over losing more of Lianne's and Alex's money. The fact was that even in losing he felt an almost triumphant satisfaction. He had always hated his brother, Richard, even from the very beginning. As a child, Richard had always been the perfect one who could do no wrong. Later, when their parents had died, Richard had inherited the bulk of their estate while Antoine had been given a mere stipend. He had never forgiven his parents, and he had never forgiven Richard.

Antoine had not shed a tear at his brother's and sister-in-law's deaths and, in fact, had relished taking on the role of guardian to Lianne and Alex when Mark had died. It was in that position that he hoped to achieve some satisfaction for the unfairness life had dealt him. Antoine smiled drunkenly to himself, knowing that he'd certainly done that. He'd lost the plantation and now he'd lost most of their ready cash. All his niece and nephew had left were two trust funds that had been set up by their mother, and that could not be touched until they reached their majority. Though that meant he was temporarily running short of funds, it did not distress him unduly. He would think of a way to win some of it back. Antoine Ducharme had never gone completely broke yet, and he was sure he never would.

His senses were so dulled by drink that he paid no attention to the unusual fact that lamplight glowed from his parlor. Instead, he staggered on down the hall

73

to his study where he knew his amply stocked liquor cabinet awaited him. His hands were shaking as he lighted the lamp on his desk, but they steadied just as soon as he had taken a deep swig directly from the half-full bottle of bourbon. Though the potent liquor burned, he relished every moment of it, and he gave a deep sigh of almost sensual gratification as he tilted the whiskey to his lips once more.

Lianne had been dozing in a chair in the parlor when the sound of his drunken entrance had awakened her. She'd hurried to follow him, afraid that he might retire for the night before she'd get the chance to speak with him.

"Uncle Antoine?"

The sound of her voice came so unexpectedly in the stillness of the room that it frightened Antoine, who'd thought he was completely alone. He whirled abruptly about, his eyes wide and wild.

"You! What are you doing here!" he demanded as he quickly strove to regain his composure.

Lianne felt only disgust as she stared at him. "I'm sure you know why I've come," she told him angrily. The long hours of waiting for him had not dampened her wrath. "I want to know how you came to bet my family's home in a card game! Although looking at you now, I can easily see how it might have happened."

Her words were so sneering and degrading that Antoine reacted immediately. He had been forced to tolerate such slurs from his father and brother, but he would not stand for it from this little chit. He slapped her hard, bloodying her lip.

"You will not speak to me in that manner, miss! I am your guardian whether you like it or not, and you will show me the respect due me in that position."

Lianne had never known violence before, and she was stunned by his abuse. She wanted nothing more

74

than to flee the scene, but she knew she couldn't back down now, not when her whole future was at stake.

Girding herself, she wiped the blood from her mouth as she spoke. "I know Father left Alex and me quite well-fixed, and I want you to take our money and re-purchase the plantation. I don't care what it costs. I just want you to buy Belle Arbor back from Adam Trent."

Antoine regarded her with a faintly amused expression. "Saying that I could buy it back, why should I?" he demanded. "The place has been losing money ever since your brother died. You've proven you can't run it," he belittled her, "and I certainly have no interest in becoming a farmer." He said the last with clear distaste.

Lianne was furious. He was refusing to right a wrong he'd done, and she was helpless to wield any kind of power to force him to do it.

Antoine continued. "Not that it matters, my dear. You see the money your father provided for you is lost . . . just as Belle Arbor was . . ."

"What are you saying!" She stared at him aghast, no longer feeling the pain from her cut lip. "You can't mean it's all gone?"

"That's exactly what I mean." His grin was nasty.

"But how? Why?" Though she'd never completely trusted him, it came as a shock to discover the truth of his grasping, evil nature.

"Your father claimed everything that was rightfully mine," he told her with hatred dripping from his words, "and now I've returned the favor. I've lost it all at the gaming tables, my dear little niece. It seems you and your brother are quite the paupers, and if you think I'm going to pay your bills and take care of you out of my pocket, you're wrong."

Lianne regarded him with loathing. This was the man fate had put in charge of her life—this was the man who'd controlled everything, lost everything, and

75

now was almost laughing about it! Anger still filled her, but the complete hopelessness of her situation was drawing her deeper and deeper into a vortex of agonizing despair. If her home was gone and her money was gone, what would she and Alex do? Where would she and Alex go?

One thing Lianne knew for certain, Antoine didn't have to worry that she would ever come to him for anything again. She would spend the night only because the lateness of the hour prevented her from leaving immediately. First thing in the morning, she was going back to Belle Arbor. She didn't know what they were going to do to survive, but she knew she would rather beg on the streets from strangers than to approach him for help. When she left his house tomorrow, she hoped she'd never have to see him again for as long as she lived.

"I don't want or expect anything from you. I will be leaving in the morning," Lianne said as calmly as she could before turning her back on him and hurrying from the room.

Antoine smiled as he watched her go. He was rid of them at last. He didn't know what she was going to do, and he didn't care. Lifting the bottle to his lips, he drank deeply in a toast to his own brilliance. He was rid of them, and he was glad.

Adam stood at the window of the bedroom he'd chosen as his own, looking out across the moonswept grounds of Belle Arbor. Though it was well after midnight and he was tired, he found sleep elusive. After so many months of endless chases and frustrations, the prospect that he might be on the verge of a breakthrough in locating Shark left him tense. He was eager to be on with it, although logic told him to bide his time, and it was that conflict that left him restless and yearning for his final satisfaction.

Still on edge, but resigned to waiting, Adam strode back to the wide four-poster bed and stretched out upon it. Folding his arms beneath his head, he stared about the darkened, unfamiliar room. Thoughts of Suzanne remained with him as he courted sleep. He hoped with all his heart, mind, and soul that she was Shark's connection in New Orleans. He had to find the pirate, for only then would he ever be able to find peace with himself. Until that time he would remain a man driven by an unquenchable need for revenge.

Eventually the strain eased from his body, and his eyes closed in slumber. It was not a restful sleep that claimed him, though, but one riddled with memories of Elise and their short period of time together before the attack. In the dream, Elise's face swam before him . . . Elise laughing . . . Elise telling him of her love for him . . . and finally Elise after the assault—mute, withdrawn, an unwilling participant in life. His heart ached for her and for what they'd lost. Yet even in his sleep, he knew it was gone forever, and with that subconscious acknowledgement, her image faded, and for a brief moment before he fell into a deep, mindless slumber, another woman played through his mind—a fiery, spirited woman with eyes the color of brilliant, sparkling emeralds.

Lianne paced the bedroom, her expression serious as she contemplated what to do next. She knew she should have been despairing over what she'd learned about her uncle's underhanded maliciousness, but she refused to succumb to that emotion. Instead, a renewed sense of pride and self-respect filled her. No longer did she feel responsible for the way things had been going at Belle

Arbor. The plantation hadn't been losing money while she'd been running it! Her uncle had been losing the money! His taunts that she'd been incapable and should give it all up had just been vicious attacks designed to hurt her and undermine her will to succeed.

A shiver traced down Lianne's spine at the realization of the power of his hatred. She had had no idea that he felt that way about them, and she was glad now that they were done with him forever.

With as much cool-headed logic as she could muster, Lianne labored to think of a way to turn things in her favor. There had to be a way! There had to be! Her mind was racing, seeking answers to her troubles, when a glimmer of hope surfaced. The trust funds! She remembered the trusts that her mother had set up for each of them. If Uncle Antoine hadn't managed to steal them too, there would be enough money in those accounts to at least begin repurchasing her home.

A surge of excitement pulsed through Lianne. She would be able to do it! First thing in the morning, she was going to meet with the banker. If the money from the trusts was still there, she planned to make Adam Trent an offer for Belle Arbor and use it as a down payment. Now, she prayed that Adam Trent would be willing to sell.

Adam Trent . . . the man loomed forth threateningly in her thoughts, and a feeling of apprehension shook her. Lianne wondered why just the thought of him could disturb her. She knew Adam for what he was—an arrogant, chauvinistic opportunist—so there should be no problem in dealing with him. She would be prepared. After they'd concluded their deal, and he was gone from Belle Arbor, life would get back to normal again.

At the thought of her beloved home, a heavy gloom descended upon Lianne. She tried to force herself to think positively, but she failed miserably. What if Adam wouldn't sell? The fear was a very real one, but she refused even to think about that possibility. No, she was going to buy her plantation back, and she was going to make it successful all by herself. Her hopes and dreams for Belle Arbor were back intact. She could do it—she knew she could.

A feeling of deep-seated contentment filled her as she felt once more in control of her own destiny. Lying down upon the bed, she suddenly realized just how tired she really was. With the torture of her doubts eased, she gave herself over to rest. As she surrendered to the softness of slumber, the faint, disturbing memory of a dark-haired, broad-shouldered man flashing her a wide, warm smile taunted her and was gone. She slept.

79

Chapter Seven

Having reached the age of thirty-eight without being trapped into matrimony, Cyrus Shackelford was a man most pleased with himself. Handsome in a smooth sort of way, the banker was a little above average height and had medium brown hair and hazel eyes. Women generally found him attractive, and he was always quick to take advantage. Though many had tried to claim his heart, he had never fallen in love. In his opinion, a woman was to be used for as long as it suited him and then discarded in favor of a younger or more beautiful one.

Cyrus smiled as he thought of Lianne Ducharme, who was waiting for him now. She was quite lovely, and the thought of her gracing his bed sent a thrill of desire through him. Perhaps when they'd completed their business, he could encourage her to more enjoyable pursuits. Picking up the file he'd been searching for, he headed back to his office to speak with her.

Lianne's expression was schooled to one of mild interest as she awaited Cyrus Shackelford at the bank early the following morning.

"Ah . . . here we are, Miss Ducharme," Cyrus said as he reentered the office with the Ducharme file in hand. He closed the door, enjoying the thought of being alone with her for a time, and then went to sit at his desk before her. He opened the document and scanned the contents intently. After a long moment, he looked up.

"I'm afraid if ready cash is what you're after, the news isn't good."

"What do you mean?" Lianne stiffened, expecting him to pronounce the worst—that Antoine had spent every last cent including the trusts.

Cyrus cleared his throat nervously. It was obvious to him that Antoine Ducharme had been constantly raiding his wards' accounts and that there was little left. All that did remain were two trust funds that could not be touched as yet. "The main Ducharme account has been closed due to lack of funds."

Lianne knew this, so she displayed no outward shock. "I see. And the trusts?"

"The trusts are still engaged."

"Good. I'd like to take that money and put it in an active account, please."

"I'm sorry, Miss Ducharme, but that's not possible. The money is not available for your free usage. I assume you know the terms of the trusts your mother established?"

She had been afraid of this, for she knew of the stipulations. "Yes, I know the terms, but I had hoped, considering the circumstances, that they could be waved."

"Not in cases dealing with this type of trust fund," he informed her sympathetically. "You see, these trusts were set up so that they could only be touched when you and your brother reached your majority or you married."

"And there's no way to circumvent this? Not even if my uncle has stolen all the rest of my money, and Alex and I are nearly destitute?" Lianne demanded dramatically, angered by the absurdity of her position. She was having to beg for her own money!

"No. I'm sorry, but I'm bound by the law." His answer was final, but he did not want to leave it there for fear that she might reject him as a possible suiter later because of hard feelings. "There are other ways to raise capital, though, if you find yourself in need of immediate cash. Have you ever considered mortgaging Belle Arbor?"

"No, I could never do that," Lianne answered hastily as she got to her feet. There was no way she could tell this man or anyone that her uncle had lost Belle Arbor, too. "I'm sorry to have taken up so much of your time, Mr. Shackelford."

"It's been my pleasure, and if I can ever be of further help to you, please let me know."

"I will, and thank you."

As Lianne left the bank, frustration filled her. The money was there, but she couldn't touch it until she turned twenty-one and that was many long months away. Again anguish and despair threatened. Her best chance to buy her home back had ended in disaster.

There was only one thing left for her to do. She was going to return home and make an offer to Adam Trent. It was only a matter of ten months until her twenty-first birthday. If he would accept the proceeds from whatever she could make selling her mother's jewelry and the few family heirlooms she possessed, she could still try to make a go of it. As she climbed into the carriage, Lianne silently estimated just how much money all her more precious personal possessions would bring, and she prayed that Adam would deem it enough.

"This bayou connects to a couple of the other plantations and then on down to the gulf," Alex explained to Adam as they rode up to Belle Arbor's small dock early that afternoon.

"Which plantations?"

"Bonne Cherie, the Martin place, and Willow Bend, the Labadie plantation."

The discovery that the bayou connected with both the gulf and Suzanne's home served to reinforce Adam's belief of her involvement with Shark's smuggling operation. The bayou provided the perfect shelter for the pirate and his illegal merchandise. It would be a relatively simple matter for her to keep her partnership with Shark a secret as long as they used the dark, dangerous bayous to carry out their business.

Adam grew determined to learn every inch of the area. If Shark was in there, he was going to find him.

"I'll bet it's tricky trying to find your way through," he coaxed, hoping to learn more from the youngster.

"It sure is." Alex's grin was one of childish superiority as he offered, "But I could show you if you really want me to. Once you learn it, it's easy to remember."

"I'd like that." It was the offer Adam had been hoping for. He wanted to learn the passage, and he wanted to learn it quickly.

Starved for male affection, Alex beamed as Adam quickly accepted his offer.

"Come on, I'll take you now. We've got time," Alex urged. During their hours of riding the plantation together that day, he had found himself coming to like this man who had so suddenly appeared in his life.

They settled in the skiff and pushed off from the Belle Arbor dock. In silent trespass, they moved through the darkened swampland, and Adam listened in earnest to all the boy told him. Alex had been raised in these bayous, and Adam trusted his every word. He committed to memory each clue and direction he gave him. When Alex pointed out Willow Bend's dock, Adam directed him to tie up.

"But why do you want to stop here?" He asked with barely disguised hostility. He hated Suzanne just as fiercely as his sister did.

"Miss Labadie is a friend of mine."

"She is?" Alex's idealized opinion of Adam shattered.

"Yes," Adam affirmed, unaware of his feelings. "I think I'll go up and see if she's at home."

"I'll wait here."

"You're sure?" He was puzzled by his sudden change of mood, but knew of no reason for it. At his nod of agreement, Adam said, "I won't be long."

Alex was sullen as he watched Adam disappear up the walk from the landing. He wanted to hate him for liking Suzanne, but he couldn't. All he could hope was that his newfound idol wouldn't get involved with her and end up dead like his brother.

Though it was mid-afternoon, Suzanne was still wearing her dressing gown as she lingered lazily in the cool, shaded quiet of her bedroom. The night she had just passed with Shark had been one in which she'd gotten little rest. It had been his last night before sailing again, and they had spent the black velvet hours of the darkness sharing heated passion. Dawn's first light had drawn him from her side, and he'd left her reluctantly with a promise to return as quickly as he could.

Suzanne had slept most of the day away, and now, with no pressing social engagements, she could see no good reason to be up and about just yet. Stretching in an almost feline movement, she settled herself among her pile of pillows as she focused her thoughts on the man she'd really been desiring the night before . . . Adam Trent.

The thought of the tall, debonair planter sent shivers of delight coursing through her. She missed him, she decided almost petulantly. She'd been forced to leave New Orleans rather abruptly the week before, because

84

Shark had arrived and it was necessary for her to meet him at the plantation. Now that he was gone and not due to return for some weeks, her time was her own to do with as she pleased . . . and she pleased to pursue Adam.

The prospect of seeing him again encouraged her to get up and get moving. Just as she was about to use the bellpull to call her servants to her, a knock sounded at her door.

"Yes, what is it?" she demanded, throwing the door wide.

"There's a gentleman downstairs, Miss Suzanne. He says he'd like to see you." Rosie, the slender, attractive, young black woman who was her maid, informed her.

"A gentleman?" She was surprised by this news, for she hadn't heard a carriage come up the drive. "Who is it? How did he get here?"

"He says his name is Adam Trent, and I guess he came the back way. I saw him walking up from the dock."

"Adam? Adam is here?"

"Yes, ma'am." She read the excitement in her mistress's expression. "Shall I tell him you'll be right down?"

"Yes—of course. Make him comfortable, and then get back up here and help me dress!"

"Yes, ma'am, Miss Suzanne." Rosie hurried off to do as she'd been told, marveling at her reaction to the gentleman's presence. She had never seen Suzanne act so excited before, and she wondered if the good-looking man waiting in the parlor was someone special.

Suzanne was thrilled at the thought of Adam waiting for her below. She could hardly believe that he'd made the trip all the way from New Orleans just to see her. While the romantic in her rejoiced at seeing him again, the practical woman in her breathed a deep sigh of relief that Shark had already set sail. They would be all alone for the first time since she'd met him many weeks ago.

As Suzanne scurried about the room pulling out the clothes she wanted to wear, she found herself remembering the last time she'd been with Adam. It had been at the Whitney's party, and the night had been absolutely heavenly. Though Adam had not been her escort that evening, they had managed to slip away to the garden for a very passionate encounter before being interrupted. Her pulse quickened at the thought of his devouring kisses. She longed to be held in his arms once more and this time to learn the complete thrill of his possession. Her fantasies urging her on, she began to struggle into her clothes even before Rosie's return.

Alone, Adam stood at the parlor windows staring out across the fertile fields of Willow Bend. Though he felt badly about leaving Alex to fend for himself down at the dock, the maid had assured him that Suzanne would be joining him in just a few minutes, so he'd decided to wait and take the opportunity to look around.

Willow Bend had all the outward appearances of being a very successful operation. The house, a pillared brick mansion of royal proportions, was in perfect condition. The lawns were lush and perfectly manicured. The outbuildings he'd seen on his walk up to the main house were equally well-kept, and the fields looked as if they were flourishing. No where was there any clue that the crops had failed miserably the last few years. There was absolutely no hint of poverty or despair.

Adam glanced about the parlor with a jaundiced eye, wondering bitterly if any of the exquisite, expensive furnishings had been paid for with money made off the raid on the *Windwood*. With an effort, he forced the thought away. He had to play the ardent lover when he greeted Suzanne. He could not afford to give any clue to his real feelings or motives. He was too close now. There was no way he was going to allow himself to fail.

Suzanne took one last look in her mirror, checking to make sure that she looked her absolute best. The blue-sprigged muslin daygown was modest enough even if the bodice hugged her breasts enticingly and the full, flowing skirt emphasized the smallness of her waist. She'd had Rosie style her hair down so it tumbled about her shoulders in a riot of soft, golden curls. Once Shark had told her that there was no man alive who could resist the temptation to run his hands though her hair when she wore it that way. She hoped will all her heart that he was right. She wanted Adam and she meant to get him. With the utmost of confidence in her appearance, she headed for the door.

"I want to be alone with Adam. See to it." The order was curt.

Rosie recognized her tone and was quick to agree. "Yes, ma'am."

With that, Suzanne swept out into the wide hall, ready to pursue the man of her dreams.

"Adam?" she called out as she descended the curving staircase.

Hearing her call, Adam strode from the parlor to greet her. As he watched her coming down the steps, he knew there could be no denying she was a beautiful woman. Gracefully elegant, her blond hair and blue eyes made her many a man's dream. But though he appreciated her loveliness, he suspected that there was far more to Suzanne than just a pretty face.

"Suzanne, you look more lovely every time I see you." He smiled in greeting, but it was not a smile that reached his eyes. He moved forward to meet her at the bottom of the stairs.

"Why, thank you, Adam," she preened as she took his

arm and led him back into the parlor. "I just can't believe you're here! It's so wonderful to see you."

"It's good to see you, too," he answered huskily, playing his part to the hilt.

As Suzanne drew him down on the sofa beside her, she asked archly, "What in the world brings you all the way out here to Willow Bend?"

"You, of course," Adam answered gallantly. "I missed you . . ."

The intimacy of his lowered tone sent a tingle of delight through Suzanne. "Oh, Adam . . ." she sighed as she leaned slightly toward him in open invitation.

Adam wasted no time drawing her in his arms to kiss her, and her response to him was as wild as it had been in the garden of the Whitneys'. With cold calculation, he deepened the exchange, deliberately wanting to arouse her, deliberately trying to make her want him.

Suzanne was unaware of anything except that Adam seemed to desire her as much as she desired him. She melted against him, surrendering to the power of her own passion for him. No other man's touch had ever ignited such fires of need within her. She was certain that this had to be love.

Adam was the one who broke off the embrace. "I have something to tell you . . ." he began.

Adam sounded so serious that Suzanne feared he was returning to Charleston. "You're not leaving New Orleans already, are you?"

"In a manner of speaking, yes," he answered cryptically and went on before she could voice a protest. "But I'm not returning to Charleston yet. My business here hasn't been completed."

"That's good." she smiled up at him flirtatiously. "But if you're not going to Charleston . . . ?"

"You are looking at the new owner of Belle Arbor," he announced. "I'm moving in next door, so to speak."

"What?" She was stunned, but recovered quickly. "I mean that's marvelous! We can see each other so often now . . ." She was elated at the news.

"As often as you like," Adam affirmed, giving her a quick kiss.

"But how did you manage it? I would have sworn that Lianne would do everything in her power to keep that place." Suzanne said the last disparagingly.

"It wasn't Lianne I had my dealings with. It was Antoine Ducharme."

"Her uncle?" Her eyes grew round at the realization of what must have happened. "So, he sold the plantation out from under her, did he? I always knew he was a sly one."

"He didn't sell it. I won it in a card game."

Suzanne was struck by the absurdity of it all. She knew how hard Lianne had been working to make the plantation succeed, and she thought it highly amusing that the other woman had now lost everything because of that drunken uncle of hers. Suzanne had hated Lianne ever since the incident with her brother, and she was glad that such a run of bad luck had befallen her. She gave a chortle of malicious glee.

"I take it you're pleased with the arrangement?" Adam gave her a questioning look.

"Oh, yes, and in more ways than one. I have no use for Lianne Ducharme, and it pleases me no end to see her get her comeuppance. But that doesn't matter. All that matters is that we can be together more often now . . ." She paused for effect. "That is, if you're interested?"

Adam was wondering why she felt so vindictive toward Lianne as he responded, "Suzanne, there's nothing I'd like more than to spend as much time as possible with you." At last, something he'd told her wasn't a lie. The more he was around her, the more likely it was that he'd find the proof he was seeking about her involvement with Shark.

"I'm so glad." Suzanne felt marvelous. Not only had one of her old enemies gotten what she deserved, but now she would have ample opportunity to work on winning Adam's love. She went into his arms again, pressing herself fully against him, wanting him, needing him, hoping he would take her then and there.

Suzanne actions left no doubt in Adam's mind about what she was after. The thought of making love to her did not appeal to him at all, but he knew that if she forced the issue there would be no easy way for him to refuse. With all the inner enthusiasm of a man going to the gallows, he acted the ardent suitor.

Suzanne knew that she was being brazen with Adam, but she didn't care. All she wanted was to have his hands upon her bare flesh as he moved hard and strong between her thighs. She'd been imagining the potency of his full lovemaking for days, and now that she had the chance to fullfill that dream, she was not about to deny herself. As his hand sought her breast, she pushed him slightly away.

"Wait . . ." she murmured breathlessly, getting to her feet and going to close the parlor door. She pivoted to face him, her back pressed against the portal, and turned the key in the lock, "I don't want us to be interrupted like we were the last time in the garden." A purely sensual smile curved her lips.

Adam's gaze was hooded as he watched her move sinuously back across the room to stand before him. He felt cold inside, as if nothing could touch him emotionally at that moment. Continuing with his masquerade, he reached up and took both of her hands to pull her down across his lap. His lips sought hers. Adam put all else from his mind as he trailed hot kisses down her throat. Going on animal reactions alone, he quickly worked at the buttons of her bodice to free her bosom to his touch. He had just parted the soft fabric and moved to press his lips to the tops of her breasts where they swelled above the edge of her chemise when he saw it.

Adam froze . . . unable to move . . . unable to think. Revulsion filled him as he stared down at the necklace, the golden crescent, that lay nestled between her breasts. He knew immediately that it was the same as his own, which even now burned coldly against his chest beneath his shirt in a deadly reminder of his true purpose. His jaw tensed as he let the shock ease from him, and his breathing became ragged. He had his proof. This was it. He needed nothing more. There was no other way Elise's necklace could have come to Suzanne except through the pirate. A powerful feeling of victory filled him. At last he was close. Now it was only a matter of time until Shark showed up.

"Adam?" Suzanne didn't understand why he'd suddenly stopped, and she worried that she'd done something wrong.

"I'm sorry, darling." He shifted her from his lap and turned to face her.

"Sorry? What is it?"

"I want you so much, but I don't want to take advantage of you."

Take advantage! Please take advantage! Suzanne was screaming willingly in her mind as she struggled to come to grips with what he was saying.

"Adam, you are such a wonderful man . . ." She was so dumbfounded by his statement that she could think of nothing else to say at the moment. He respected her? The idea appealed, but it did nothing to ease the throbbing desire that still pulsed through her.

"Suzanne . . . will you marry me?" Adam knew he could wait no longer to try to claim her.

"Oh, Adam! Marry you!" She stared at him in open

delight. She had never expected him to propose this quickly. Her every dream was coming true! "Oh, yes, yes! I'll marry you!"

He was rather startled by her hurried acceptance. From all that he'd heard about her in the past, she'd never seriously considered marriage before, but he did not pause to question his good luck. She'd said yes, and that was all that mattered.

"You've made me very happy, Suzanne," he told her honestly as they embraced again. When he drew away, he took her hand in a confiding gesture.

"I can hardly wait to make our announcement!" Suzanne gazed up at him adoringly.

"I feel the same way. Why don't we plan a big party and announce it then?"

"A surprise?"

"Yes."

"It sounds wonderful."

"I'd like the party to be at Belle Arbor," he said smoothly.

"That would be fine, darling."

"Good. It may be a few weeks until we can get things together. Becky feels the house is in need of some work. Let's not tell anyone of our engagement for a while. I'd like to make it a special night for the both of us, and I can think of no better time to announce it than at my new home with you at my side."

"Sounds heavenly," Suzanne told him, "but I must admit I'm so thrilled that it's going to be difficult keeping it a secret."

"It should only be a matter of a few weeks . . . six at the most," he explained. "Then, my darling, we'll tell the world."

"I can hardly wait!" She launched herself into his arms. "I love you, Adam. I have for some time now."

Trapped, not wanting to declare a love he didn't feel,

Adam kissed her deeply. It was a long, lingering kiss designed to assure her of his feelings. "And now, though I don't want to, I have to go . . ."

"So soon?" Suzanne pouted prettily.

"There's nothing I'd rather do than stay with you, but I didn't make the trip here alone. I came over in a skiff with Alex Ducharme, and he's still waiting for me down at the dock."

"Alex is still living there with you?" She frowned, wondering what the boy was still doing at Belle Arbor.

"Yes. They're staying on until they can make some other arrangements."

Jealousy flared in Suzanne's heart. "Surely they've got somewhere else to go. I don't see why they have to impose upon you."

"Becky seemed to think it was the least we could do." Adam shrugged as he stood and pulled her up with him. "Anyway, I'm sure they'll be gone soon."

"Good," she declared as she linked her arms around his neck. "Now, when am I going to get to see you again?"

"Are you staying here or going back into town?"

"Now that I know you're near, I'll be staying."

"Good. There's a lot of work that needs to be done at Belle Arbor, but I promise I'll try to get away to visit as often as I can."

"I'll be waiting to hear from you," Suzanne told him as she pulled his head down to kiss him one last time.

Chapter Eight

Shark waited and watched. He had wanted to set sail earlier that day, but the sighting of an unknown clipper plying the coastline had held him at bay. He'd been forced to cool his heels and hide out in the bayou since early morning.

"Whoever this is," Will Johnson began as he kept careful watch at his captain's side, "he's looking for something."

"Or somebody," Shark growled, remembering what he'd heard about the mysterious Captain Spectre who was searching the Gulf for him and wondering if this was him.

"Do you think it's the law?" Will asked.

"There's no reason why the law would suddenly be looking here for us."

"Then Spectre? We've all heard about him . . ."

"Shut up." Shark's eyes narrowed as he considered what to do. If this was Spectre, and somehow, instinctively, he knew it was, he had half a mind to confront the ship and have it out right here and now. Common sense held him back, though. The risk of exposure was too great. He didn't want to jeopardize his smuggling trade. Besides, the *Banshee* was the fastest ship on the high seas. No one could catch her. All he had to do was keep outrunning this Spectre, and then perhaps one day soon the mysterious captain would tire of his search and go back to wherever it was he came from.

"What are you gonna do?" Will finally asked.

"It'll be completely dark soon. We'll make a run for it then, before the moon rises."

"Aye, aye, sir." He hurried off to begin their preparation to sail.

That Beau was frustrated in his effort to locate Shark was nothing new. What was new was the unusual conviction he felt that he was close . . . very close for the first time in all the months they'd been looking. Since his meeting with Adam the week before, Beau had begun systematically searching the maze of coastal waterways for some sign of the pirate. He'd found nothing definite yet, yet somehow he sensed he was near. As dusk faded and the inky blackness that was night enveloped the land and seas, Beau was just about ready to call the search off for yet another day when the call of his lookout alerted him to possible trouble.

"Ahead, sir!" the mate called excitedly.

In the darkness only the ghostly outline of the ship's white sails could be seen. The sails were full to catch the brisk night breeze, and it was obvious to those aboard the *Sea Shadow* that the vessel meant to move and move fast.

"Make full sail and be quick about it! We may have something here!" Beau bellowed. "Stay with them, men!"

The *Sea Shadow* seemed to spring to life in the water as she immediately took up the chase. Beau was tempted to bring his guns to bear, but he was not certain of the identity of the other boat and could not take the risk. Hurrying to stand beside the helmsman, he watched and waited.

Aboard the *Banshee*, Shark nervously paced the deck. This was the first time since he'd begun smuggling slaves that anyone had even come close to catching him, and he didn't like it. He didn't like it at all.

Shark was tense as he barked out a continual stream of orders to his men. Though they were at full sail, they were not pulling away. The unknown vessel was staying with them and possibly even gaining ground.

On through the night they sailed. As the *Banshee* took evasive maneuvers, the oncoming, threatening boat matched them. Shark knew that the hours of total darkness were limited and that, as fleet as the other ship was, they would have to break away from them soon or be prepared to fight it out.

"Head due west!" Shark ordered, a plan he hoped would work forming in his mind.

Will heard his command and knew immediately why he'd ordered the change in course. They generally steered clear of that area, for it was not unusual for cloud banks to form there. This trip, however, the shielding curtain of fog might be just what they needed to aid them.

Time seemed suspended as they raced on through the night, and when the cloud of devouring whiteness loomed suddenly visible in the darkness, Shark smiled.

"Take her in!"

Even though Beau was not overly familiar with the waters up until this point, he'd managed to hold his own with the other ship. Now, however, as the fleeing craft disappeared directly into the fog bank, he knew he had to slow down. A frustrated curse echoed across the *Sea Shadow*'s desk as he ordered his crew to slow their own racing vessel and steer away from the white oblivion that lay dead ahead.

"But, sir!" a mate protested. They'd searched long and hard for Shark, and this was the closest they'd ever come to catching up to him. If indeed it was him.

"I know, I know." Beau, too, mourned the lost opportunity.

"Do you think it was him, Mr. Hamilton?"

"It was him," he concluded firmly, "and the next time, he's not going to get away."

Even though night had fallen, the shutters in the study at Belle Arbor were still closed as they had been all afternoon against the day's brilliant intrusion. The study door, too, remained closed against unwanted interruptions. Adam had made sure that Becky knew he needed to be alone. He had declined to dine with her and had secluded himself there to think. As the darkness claimed the room, he'd lighted the lamp on the desktop, and now he sat staring into its flickering golden flame, trying to sort out his thoughts.

His mood was black. When he'd first returned from Willow Bend, though, he'd felt victorious and in need of a little personal celebration. He'd toasted his success alone, feeling very confident. Everything had turned out just as he'd suspected it would, and his plan was working perfectly. In a few more weeks, Shark would be his!

Adam had not told Becky any of what had taken place. All Becky knew about Suzanne was that she was a lovely woman he'd been courting lately, nothing more. She would learn of the 'engagement' when everyone else did at the party.

He'd felt almost jubilant when he'd settled in at the desk earlier. When he saw the letter from Dr. Williams on top of the stack of papers before him, he'd grown sober and then a bit hopeful. Setting his tumbler of bourbon aside, Adam had ripped open the envelope and begun to read. There had been no change. Elise was still the same.

Adam's sense of triumph and possible hope had vanished as completely as if it had never existed. In that poignant, painfilled moment, he'd realized that no matter what kind of victory he achieved over Shark, it would not be enough. It would never bring Elise back. He would never be able to recapture those times before the raid.

Now, as Adam got up from the desk to refill his glass at the liquor cabinet, his grief turned to anger. His hard, driving need for justice would not let up. He might not be able to restore the past, Adam swore to himself, but at least he could make the one responsible pay for it. He filled the glass to the brim, tossed it down, and then poured another.

Suzanne crept into his thoughts then . . . conniving little Suzanne. Knowing that he was going to have to continue to treat her as his beloved until Shark showed up repelled him. She was partially to blame for what had happened to Elise! Adam shook his head in amazement as he recalled his quick recovery from the shock of finding out that she was wearing Elise's necklace. It pleased him that he'd been able to carry on with the charade so convincingly after such a devastating blow, and it left him feeling much more confident about his dealings with her in the future. If he could handle a shock like that, he knew he could handle just about anything. He took another deep drink.

A knock came at the door and it annoyed him. He didn't want to speak with anyone right now. He'd told Becky specifically that he wanted to be left alone tonight.

"What is it?" he demanded impatiently. He expected it to be Becky, and he was surprised to find it wasn't.

"It's Lianne. I've just returned. I'd like to speak with you now, if you have the time. It's important." Lianne stood rigidly in the hall awaiting permission to enter a room in her own house. The thought only fueled her resolve to convince him to sell it back to her. She was glad now that she'd had a snifter of brandy before coming to speak with him. It took the edge off the humiliation she was feeling.

Adam was not concerned with Lianne Ducharme or any problem she might have. He figured she was just coming in to tell him that she and Alex would be leaving shortly, and that suited him just fine. The sooner she and Alex were gone, the better.

"Come on in." Adam invited as he swigged again from his glass, draining it. He paid little attention to Lianne as she entered the room behind him and closed the door. "Please, take a seat," he directed, not even bothering to look up at her as he added more liquor to his glass.

"Thank you." Lianne said to his back, irritated by his obvious indifference. She bit her lip to keep from making a snide remark. Up until yesterday, she had been the owner. Yesterday, she would have been the one asking him to sit down.

"I take it you've seen your uncle and—" Adam turned around to face Lianne who was seated behind him, and his words drifted off as an unexpected, explosive charge of sensual awareness raced through him. He had instinctively known that she was a beautiful woman, but he'd had no idea that she was really this lovely.

As controlled as Adam usually was, this time his composure slipped for an instant, and his amazement showed clearly on his face. His appraising gaze raked heatedly over her. Her hair had been pulled up and away from her face on the sides, emphasizing the loveliness of her features, and then left to fall freely to her shoulders in a thick cascade. The simple dress she wore was by no means anything fancy, but it fit her slender figure to perfection, and the loden green color highlighted the glory of her eyes.

It was then, caught up in that challenging emerald gaze, that Adam realized he was openly staring at her. Moving quickly to mask his interest, he told himself that it didn't matter to him that she was even more attractive than he'd ever imagined. She would soon be out of his life forever, and, judging by his reaction just now, that was for the best. There was no time for an entanglement. He had to concentrate on Suzanne.

"Yes, I did meet with my uncle." Mezmerized once again by his rakish good looks, Lianne had found herself staring openly back at Adam. How handsome he was in snug-fitting dark pants and a white shirt that was unbuttoned at the neck just enough to reveal the beginnings of a dark mat of chest hair. Lianne had to force herself to look away and refocus on the real reason she was sitting there before him . . . Belle Arbor.

"And?" As he spoke, Adam leaned one hip against the desk in a nonchalant posture directly in front of her, the gesture inadvertently drawing her gaze to the way the material of his pants stretched tautly over the leanness of his hips and muscular thighs.

Lianne swallowed and dragged her gaze upward to meet his eyes. She wished he would move away and put the barrier of the desk between them. He was far too close. She had never reacted to any man this way before, and she found that his nearness disconcerted her. She wanted to think about Belle Arbor and the future, not about how attractive he was.

"And I've come to make you a business proposition," Lianne finally managed, girding herself to make her proposal. This had to work . . . it just had to!

"You have?" This took Adam completely by surprise. He'd expected her to merely fill him in on the details of her exit from the house and his life. Instead, she was now claiming that she wanted to discuss business with him, and he couldn't imagine what it could be.

"Yes. I want to buy Belle Arbor back." There, she had said it. She took a deep breath as she awaited his response.

"No," Adam replied without hesitation. "Belle Arbor is not for sale."

His answer came so quickly that she was astounded. "You aren't even interested in hearing my offer?" She couldn't believe that he had refused so abruptly. Any good businessman would at least listen to a profitable proposal!

"No. I've no interest in selling Belle Arbor." He was firm as he answered. He was not about to let go of the plantation now that he knew of its connection to Willow Bend and the Gulf. It enabled him to make direct contact with the *Sea Shadow*. The setup was perfect, and he was going to take full advantage of it.

Lianne flushed with fury. She wanted to attack him physically and force him to agree to her offer. She was irate as she demanded, "Why not? You've only been here a day! It can't mean anything to you!"

"Oh, but Belle Arbor does mean a lot to me. I've found I like it here," Adam said with cool precision. "I plan to stay for some time."

"But I can pay you . . ." she said quickly, ready to present him with all her calculations, willing to plead with him.

"Don't even waste my time or yours bringing up figures." Adam waved her next statement aside with a casual, dismissing action. "Belle Arbor is not for sale at any price." His gaze hardened upon her as he emphasized his point. He would not be deterred from catching Shark.

Lianne could not control the rage that exploded within her. She had been ready to beg him to listen to her, but he'd refused her even that! She would not quit! She would not be forced to give up! Not by her uncle and certainly not by him! How dare he ruin her life, and with such nonchalance!

"I hate you, Adam Trent!" She launched herself at him in a futile attack, ready to strike out at him in any way she could. "I hate you for everything you've done to us! Somehow, someway, I'm going to get my home back! I will, you'll see!"

Adam was totally unprepared for her assault, and her actions shocked him. She landed one glancing blow to his face before he managed to get his defenses up. As furious as she was, Lianne was fighting him with all her might, and Adam had to trap her arms behind her back to stop her.

Adam's cheek was smarting and his pride was bruised as he brought the squirming vixen tightly against his chest, pinning her there. For just an instant at that first intimate contact, it seemed to Adam that all time had stopped. A charge that was almost electric jolted through him as he stared down at her in bewilderment. His gaze went hungrily over her flushed face. He saw the anger flashing in her emerald eyes and wished, suddenly and perversely, that she was looking at him with passion instead of fury. His gaze shifted to her mouth, and he knew a gut-wrenching longing to claim those tremulous lips and devour their sweetness. He wanted to probe the honeyed darkness of her mouth and feel her return his kiss full measure. Her breasts were crushed to his chest, and they felt soft and full. Adam longed to bare them to his gaze, to touch them, to weigh their softness in his palms. He wanted to —

The direction of his thoughts jarred Adam, and he gave a slight shake of his head to try to clear it of such foolish notions. Lianne Ducharme was not for him, no matter how enticing he found her to be. With a sneering condescension meant to degrade, he responded to her taunts of hatred.

"Don't waste your hate on me, sweetheart," he sneered, tightening his hold on her in an almost threatening manner. "Hate your uncle. He's the fool who gambled away your precious Belle Arbor."

Lianne was aware of the heat of his lean, manly form against her and had the circumstances been different, she might have enjoyed being in his arms. As it was, she was too angry to feel anything but fury. She struggled valiantly against his overpowering strength, pushing ineffectually against the rock-hard wall of his chest in an effort to free herself, but it was a useless endeavor. Realizing that she could not possibly escape him until he chose to let her go, she hated him even more.

"Let me go!" she hissed. She was seething. He had totally humiliated her and all she wanted to do now was escape. Tears of frustration threatened, but she refused to show Adam any weakness.

Adam realized then that he had to let her go. He released her abruptly, as if burned by her touch. Lianne was so surprised by his unexpected compliance to her demand that she stumbled. Adam kept his features schooled into a mask of indifference as he casually resumed his position, leaning negligently back against the desk. Standing before him, Lianne glared up at him, her hands clinched into fists of frustrated fury at her sides. Adam regarded her levelly and was again struck by how desirable she was. He knew a very real yearning to taste of her passion in his bed, and it was only through a supreme effort of will that he pushed that distracting thought from him. He gave her a cool, tight smile.

"Is there anything else you feel we need to discuss?" he queried with an outward calm that revealed nothing of his inner turmoil.

Lianne wanted to shriek her rage! Oh, how she despised him! He was so smug—so infuriatingly self-confident! Someday she hoped he got exactly what he deserved! She mustered what little control she had left.

"No." It was a shaky, tight-lipped answer.

"If you'll excuse me then?" He turned his back on her, dismissing her completely.

Again she wanted to attack him, but it was no use. Her last hope had been dashed. It was truly over now. Lianne felt her heart sink. She was helpless. With her innate, ladylike grace, she swept from the room, unaware that behind her Adam was watching her exit, his dark-eyed gaze hooded, his expression unreadable.

Lianne closed the door as she stepped out of the study and then stood indecisively in the shadowed hall. Though she appeared composed, deep inside of her all she wanted was to run away and hide. She had failed. What was she going to do now? She wasn't just worried about herself. Her responsibility for Alex weighed heavily upon her. She had to provide for him, too, and she wouldn't have any money for nearly a year. Where would they go? How would they live? She wrung her hands, the only outward display of her upset.

Glancing nervously about, Lianne knew she had to get away by herself. She needed time to collect her thoughts. She couldn't even conceive of facing Alex right then, so she hurried down the hall and through the kitchen seeking an avenue of escape.

For the first time in her life, Lianne could see no alternative course of action open to her. She was out of options. The end had come. There was no hope of ever getting Belle Arbor back, Adam had certainly made that clear, and there would be no money to support them even minimally for nearly a year. Despair gripped her in an almost physical embrace.

Lianne hurried through the kitchen and then paused at the edge of the porch. She glanced about wildly, trying to think of a safe haven from the desolation that hounded her. A small cry escaped her, and she bit her lip to stifle any further cries. Rushing from the porch, she ran blindly off through the night in search of a place of solace and of peace.

Though Adam had managed to keep his expression impassive as Lianne had fled the study, he couldn't stop watching her. It seemed that he was mesmerized by her, and his dark-eyed gaze had followed her every movement. Adam frowned as he remembered the excitement that had rocketed through him when he'd held her, and he wondered what it was about her that could affect him that way. Not even Elise had had such power over his senses.

Adam picked up his tumbler of bourbon and took a deep drink, welcoming the burning heat of its potency as he tried to push all thoughts of Lianne from him. But even as he tried, he found he was putting himself in her position and looking at things for the first time from her point of view. It was then that he came to realize what she was feeling.

Suddenly, Adam swore violently to himself as he gave a rough, denying shake of his head. Annoyed, he again tried to put all thoughts of Lianne and her situation from his mind. It was not his concern! He was not going to get involved with her! Just the fact that she could drift into his thoughts, showed how much trouble she could potentially prove to be. At this time in his life, he needed full concentration. There could be no distractions from his purpose, and catching Shark and making him pay was his purpose.

Adam had never had much of a problem controlling himself before in any area of his life. He felt reasonably confident now as he took a sip of his bourbon that he could suppress the disturbing attraction he was feeling

105

for Lianne. He was certain that it was a purely physical thing and that he would be able to master it. Why, even on the *Windwood* he'd managed to keep a tight rein on his desire for Elise, and he had *loved her.*

The thought of Elise brought a deep sense of guilt and forced him to face up to the faint, tormenting question he wanted to ignore. If their love had been so true and so wonderful, why was he able to feel this desire for Lianne? Even though Elise was ill, shouldn't his love for her have remained strong and vital? The more Adam considered it, the more upset he became.

Adam moved to refill his glass and told himself that this would be just one last drink. Yet, when he came back to sit at the desk again, he brought the bottle with him. As he savored the potent bourbon, it occurred to him distantly that Lianne hadn't told him when she and Alex were leaving.

Chapter Nine

Lianne didn't know how long she had wandered list-
lessly through the flower garden before heading toward
the reflecting pond. She was near collapse, mentally
and physically. All the fight had gone out of her, and
she felt empty and drained. She had done her best, but
it had not been good enough. She had lost.

Lianne drew a shuddering breath as she dropped
down on the pond's grassy bank. Hugging her knees to
her chest, she stared sightlessly out across the small
lake's black, glossy surface seeking the comfort that this
view often gave her. Yet tonight, instead of soothing
her, the inky darkness offered only cold, harsh emptiness.

Her very soul grew numb as she contemplated all
that had happened. Always before there had been a
thread of hope . . . something she could hang on to
until things got better, but now there was nothing.

When she'd vowed never to return to Antoine, she'd
meant it. He had openly declared his hatred for Alex
and her, and Lianne knew he would find pleasure in
seeing them suffer. She wouldn't give him the satisfaction. Set upon the path she'd chosen, she would not go
back.

The moon had not yet arisen, and the night was
silent and breathlessly hushed as if waiting in anticipation of its coming.

Surrounded by the blackness, Lianne felt really

107

alone for the first time in her life. It was a moment of supreme vulnerability, and it broke the last of her control. A sob of defeat tore from her throat as she acknowledged her loss. Tears she'd long denied fell freely, and she didn't even bother to wipe them away. She had been broken. It was useless to fight and struggle any more . . .

It was late. Becky and Alex had long since retired, having come by the study to bid Adam good-night an hour or so before. Still seated at the desk, Adam was staring thoughtfully at the half-empty bourbon bottle. It fascinated him to think that he could have possibly drunk that much liquor tonight. He didn't feel drunk. If anything, he felt even more tense and on edge that he had before he'd begun drinking in earnest. Annoyed, Adam wondered belligerently if he would ever be able to find a measure of peace. He knew he certainly wasn't finding it at the bottom of a bottle of bourbon.

It suddenly seemed stuffy and overly hot in the study, so Adam got up and opened the shutters to let the night breeze cool the room. He paused at the window to take in the beauty of the summer night. In the distance, he could see the moon's first light paling the midnight blue of the sky. The scent of cut grass and blooming flowers perfumed the humid evening air. Adam breathed deeply hoping to clear his head a little bit as he massaged the taut muscles at the back of his neck.

All seemed serene, and he wished he felt as calm and tranquil. Adam was about to turn away from the window, when he heard a faint disturbing sound. He frowned, concentrating, but the elusive cry had faded and died on the breeze. Adam had almost dismissed it as his imagination, when it came to him once more. Somehow, he knew instinctively that it was a woman weeping. She sounded lost, alone and in great pain.

Some unknown need compelled Adam to investigate. He left the house and moved quickly through the gardens trying to figure out from which direction the cry was coming. He made his way along the winding paths, following the plaintive cry that only occasionally drifted his way.

The siren's song of sorrow led Adam to a small rise overlooking the pond. He paused at the crest, and it was from there that he caught sight of her for the first time. The moon had just made its full appearance, frosting the land in silver light. Lianne, sitting on the bank before him, looked like some magical, gilded goddess as she wept, her head bowed in supplication to some unseen deity.

Adam stared at down at her, startled. His heart wrenched at the keening sound of her mournful cries. A spear of pain stabbed his liquor-sodden conscience at the realization that he was the one responsible for her distress. He had taken her home, he had refused to sell it back and he was in the process of virtually throwing her off the place.

Adam wanted to ignore the guilty feelings that were assailing him. He could no longer afford to be a gentle man who was concerned with others' thoughts and emotions. That part of him had died when Elise had been injured. He told himself that he had to be cold and callous if he was to succeed in what he was doing.

Still, Lianne's obvious grief touched him as nothing else could at that moment. He recognized that her dreams had been crushed just as completely as his had been all those months before. No longer was she the invincible Valkyrie holding him off with a shotgun or attacking him with a vengeance for crimes she imagined were his. Now she was woman . . . vulnerable . . . fragile . . . in need of help . . . in need of protection.

109

A warm surge of tenderness washed through him. Suddenly Adam wanted to comfort her. The hard protective shell he'd built around his more gentle emotions crumbled, destroyed by Lianne's tears.

He spoke her name, his voice hoarse. "Lianne . . ."

Lost in the dark world of her own misery, Lianne heard a man's voice, but thought she was imagining it. There was no one who would come to help her. No one who cared. She gave a soft sob, not yet aware of Adam's presence.

"Lianne," Adam repeated, drawing nearer.

Her head snapped up as she realized she was no longer alone, and she got quickly to her feet, angrily dashing the tears from her cheeks. "You! What are you doing here?"

"I heard you crying."

"I'm fine." Lianne lied, trying desperately to pull herself together, but it was useless. Her defenses were down.

"Lianne, you're far from fine." Adam watched her as she attempted to regain her composure, and when she failed he took a step closer. "Can I help?"

His offer of help struck her as tremendously ironic. Why did he want to help her now? "Sell my home back to me," she demanded flatly.

"I can't do that."

"Can't or won't?" Lianne interrupted him angrily.

The tenderness that filled him refused to let him be drawn into a pointless argument with her. She was in no condition to fight with him or he with her, he realized.

"Lianne . . ."

His tone was gentle and coaxing as he said her name, and it went over her like a velvet caress. A thrill of sensual shock ran through Lianne as her gaze collided with Adam's. In the moonlight, his handsome features

110

appeared even more so. She stared at him in confusion. She wanted to deny the breathlessness that threatened. She hated him! How could she feel this way about him when she despised him completely? Lianne argued with herself not to be fooled by this caring, comforting disguise he was presenting. Didn't she know what he was really like? Didn't she hate him for all that he'd done?

But in this moment of total vulnerability, her heart was ruling. For once, she wanted to believe that a gentle and tender side really did exist in Adam. Her gaze explored his, reading in its depths a degree of warmth she'd never before believed possible for him.

Lianne grew totally bewildered. Dazedly, she wondered how it would feel to rest her head against the broad width of his shoulder, to feel his arms protectively around her instead of threateningly. A coil of emotion tightened deep within her, and a single tear coursed down her pale cheek.

"Lianne, let me help," Adam said huskily as he reached out and wiped the tear from the soft curve of her cheek.

It was a simple, yet intimate contact, and Lianne felt it to the depths of her being. It was the first time Adam had ever touched her in kindness, but she knew she would remember it forever. She was mesmerized by the power of that caress.

The almost casual action sent a lurch of excitement surging through Adam, and he gazed down at her, unsettled. The desire he'd known when she'd been fighting him in the study had been fiery and powerful, but the desire that filled him now was different and somehow even more overwhelming. It pulsed through him creating a burning hunger for her, urging him to draw her close and hold her in his arms.

"Lianne . . ." He lifted his hand to cup her cheek

111

fully in a loverlike gesture.

The searing heat of his touch burned its way to the very center of her resistance.

"No . . ." Lianne murmured in protest. She knew she should move away and break the contact, but the strength of the attraction she was feeling held her immobile. She was helpless to deny herself that which she needed most . . . a moment of affection . . . a moment with someone who cared about her . . .

Adam was moonstruck as he gazed down at her. In the delicate shadows of the night, he found Lianne even more lovely than ever before. Her hair tumbled about her shoulders in glossy, silken disarray, and Adam longed to comb his hands through the red-gold mass and feel the glory of it against his skin. Her emerald eyes were wide, and he could read the fear and confusion there in the tear-sparkled depths. It only made him want her more. He wanted to erase those fears. He wanted to soothe the sorrow he felt responsible for. His gaze dropped lower to the sensuous curve of her mouth, and he noticed the trembling there.

"Ah, Lianne, you are so beautiful . . ." The words escaped him in almost a groan as he raked his hands back through her hair at her temple and tilted her face to his. He sought her lips with his own, capturing their soft sweetness in a kiss that was surprisingly gentle considering how badly he desired her.

Lianne's first reaction was to draw back. This was the arrogant Adam Trent . . . the man who'd taken her home and who'd treated her in such a condescending manner. The man she hated. Even as she fought inwardly to deny what was happening, his lips broke down the last fragments of her resistance. She gave up her struggle to refuse his kiss.

Adam knew the instant she stopped fighting him, and he slipped one hand down to the small of her back and urged her fully against him.

Lianne gasped at the unexpected sensuality of being pressed so tightly to the alien hardness of his hips. Her pulses were racing and a strange inner excitement began to build. "Adam . . ." She whispered his name in hushed wonder as a shudder passed through her.

Adam claimed her lips once more, this time parting them and delving into the dark, honeyed sweetness of her mouth. Lianne's knees threatened to buckle beneath her at this previously unknown intimacy. She clutched at his shoulders for support. Crushed to his chest, her senses were reeling.

Adam could feel the firm thrust of her hard-tipped breasts against his chest even through the layers of their clothes. The desire to caress those satiny orbs was near to overpowering, but he held back. He did not want to frighten her. He had only meant to comfort her. Yet, as his mouth continued its exploration of hers, tasting and teasing, taunting and arousing, Adam's passions spiraled. As much as he gave, she returned full measure. Her eager response fired his already flaming need. He wanted her—oh, how he wanted her.

Lianne felt transported as she gave herself over to Adam. His devouring kisses had driven all thoughts of reality from her. In this moment of her life, this was all that she wanted . . . to be held and loved by him. It felt good to be in his arms, to feel cherished. When he sought the softness of her breasts, she was stunned by the unexpected sensations the caress provoked. Currents of desire coursed through her.

"Adam . . ." Mesmerized by her feelings, she cried out his name.

At her encouragement, Adam lifted her into his arms and lay her upon the bed of grass. Some distant vague part of Adam called out a hushed warning, telling him that this was wrong, that there was something he should remember, but he paid it no mind. Lianne's beauty, plus the moonlight and bourbon, had conspired to render him a creature of instinct.

With infinite care, he continued to press kiss after passionate kiss on her waiting lips as his hands began a foray over the inviting curve of her bosom. Lianne arched into his touch, and Adam groaned in excited anticipation of finally seeing those pale, succulent mounds. His hands were unsteady as he unfastened the bodice of her dress and parted the fabric. Impatiently, he pushed her chemise aside to bare her breasts to his gaze.

Adam's breath was hot and strangled in his throat as he looked upon her tender, burgeoning woman-flesh for the first time. Her alabaster breasts were full and ripe, and the dusky pink peaks were a taut reflection of her desire. He gave a gutteral moan as he bent his head to capture one pert bud with his lips.

Lianne had been lost in the web of sensual excitement. Adam had woven about her. Willingly, she'd lain in his arms matching him kiss for ardent kiss, craving his heated caress. When he'd unbuttoned her gown, she'd closed her eyes in embarassment. No man had ever taken such liberties with her before. Yet even as she knew a maindenly shyness over his boldness, she was anxious to know more of his lovemaking. It was only as his hot, wet mouth closed over her nipple that Lianne went rigid with shock. She had never known a man would do such a thing, and she was torn between bewilderment and wild, erotic joy.

"No . . . please . . ." Frightened by the intensity of what she was experiencing, Lianne tried to push him away.

"What is it, love?" he questioned huskily as he drew back for a moment. "Am I going too fast for you?"

"No . . . I—I never felt this way before."

114

"Relax, sweet. Let me love you. Let me show you how beautiful it can be between a man and woman . . ."

When Lianne went still and made no further protest, Adam lowered his head again and trailed fiery kisses down her throat, pausing briefly at her pulse point and then dipping even lower to reclaim the swollen, throbbing rosebud. Pleasure radiated to the very core of her as he suckled erotically at her breast.

Innocent that she was, Lianne was helpless before his practiced expertise. Swept away by passion for the first time in her life, Lianne was his to do with as he pleased. When Adam stripped off her clothing, she murmured no protest, but gloried in the heat of his big body over hers. As he teased her to greater and greater heights, her timidity faded, and she began to return his caresses.

Adam's hands were everywhere, tracing patterns of fire upon her willing flesh. He stroked her legs and hips, readying her for his even more intimate caress. Moving ever closer to the center of her need, he lifted his head to watch her expression as he finally sought that womanly sweetness.

Lianne tensed as he would have explored her innermost self, and she closed her legs against his intrusion.

"Easy, love, easy. I won't hurt you."

His tone was so earnest and sincere that she forced herself to relax a bit. She remained still as he gently breached that which no man had ever touched before. With knowing pressure, he searched out her pleasure point and began a rhythmic massage that left her panting and writhing beneath him.

"Adam!" It was a hushed cry that broke from her lips as she reached that which she'd unknowingly craved. She clung to him as the ecstasy of her release took her to bliss and beyond. Nothing mattered but being in Adam's arms. Nothing mattered but the explosive joy he'd just given her. Nothing mattered . . . She lay breathless and pliant in the haven of his arms.

Knowing that he'd pleased her only heightened Adam's own need. With deliberate intent, he began to arouse her again, seeking out her most sensitive places with his ardent touch. To Lianne's complete surprise, she found herself responding, and this time she held nothing in reserve. With a hunger that amazed her, she drew his head down to her for a flaming kiss. Compelled by her age-old womanly desire, she began to unbutton his shirt, anxious to feel the heat of his hard chest against her bared breasts.

Adam broke away only long enough to shed his shirt and then returned to cover her body with his. It was a scorching, heart-stopping contact, and they were so caught up in the moment that they could only gaze into each other's eyes in awestruck wonder.

"I want you, Lianne," Adam confessed. He kissed her again with explosive delight, his tongue meeting and dueling sensually with hers.

Lianne knew there had to be more, and she threw caution to the wind in her need to learn of completion. "Please, Adam . . ." she encouraged him.

That little urging was all he needed to destroy his last thread of restraint. He moved slightly away to free himself from the rest of his clothing and returned to her.

Lianne had never seen a completely naked man before. Shamelessly, she regarded Adam with open interest. His shoulders were broad and strongly muscled, his chest wide and deep and covered with a dark mat of curling hair that tapered to a V at his navel and lower. His hips were slim, his belly flat, his legs long, straight, and thickly muscled. Her gaze lingered with obvious curiosity on that which made him a man, and she wondered in virginal confusion whether all men were

116

so well-endowed. She thought him most magnificent, and her heartbeat quickened at the thought of being possessed by him. When Adam came back to her, she welcomed him with open arms.

Adam was moving in a liquor-ladened haze of sensuality as he knelt before Lianne and then moved possessively between her soft, parting thighs. She was perfect, every inch of her. In the moonlight, her skin glowed with a pale translucence that seemed to beg for his touch. Her breasts were swollen and throbbing, their darker crests taut with desire. In her passion, she was responding to him as no other woman ever had, and he knew he had to possess her fully. He wanted to bury himself in the tight, hot sheath of her. He wanted to love her.

Positioning himself, Adam thrust forward into her wet, welcoming warmth. The slight barrier that was her innocence was rent asunder by his powerful move, and Lianne could not prevent a cry of agony at the sudden, shooting pain. She had not known there would be pain.

Adam was stunned by this proof of her virginity, although he realized that he should have known. He thought briefly of stopping, but knew it was too late. He was beyond control, his body demanding satisfaction. He began to caress her once more even as he started to move in a sensual tempo.

Lianne had been too taken aback by the agony of his impalement to respond immediately. Yet as Adam kissed her and touched her again with gentle, arousing persistence, her reluctance disappeared. In its place, a hot, throbbing desire blossomed.

Although the coolness of the night surrounded them, they moved together in blazing inferno. Striving for the pinnacle, aching for completion, they soared to the peak of love's delight. Passion exploded, shattering the glory of their cresting ecstasy. Waves of pulsing pleasure surged through them both as they lay wrapped in each other's arms, their limbs intimately entangled. Their joining was a sharing, a moment of perfect joy.

Adam had never known such ecstasy. He cradled her close, savoring the sensations that remained with him in the aftermath of their soul-shattering lovemaking. He closed his eyes, blotting out all that might threaten this moment. He felt blissfully at peace. He was for that instant content.

Lianne, too, remained unmoving in his embrace. She had never known complete sensual satisfaction before, and it left her dizzy with the ecstasy of it. She felt cosseted and safe, wonderfully warm and totally protected. She wanted to stay in the refuge of Adam's embrace forever.

Lianne closed her eyes, refusing to think, allowing herself only to feel. A great sense of tranquility filled her, and she sighed. Open and vulnerable, she started to drift off to sleep, thinking only of how perfect their lovemaking had been and how marvelous it felt to be held this way.

Chapter Ten

The forlorn call of a single water thrush split the night's silence, and at its call the protective liquor-induced haze that had enveloped Adam's senses suddenly vanished. In confusion, Adam went rigid as he found himself still linked with Lianne in passion's most precious embrace. Reality returned with a vengeance, burning the truth of all that had happened into his soul. *What the hell had he done!*

Adam wanted to deny it all, but the cold, hard, undeniable fact of Lianne lying passively in his arms smashed any protests he might have uttered. A tangle of guilt-ridden emotions filled Adam. What had he been thinking of? How could he have betrayed Elise this way? The serenity that had been his for that brief period was gone.

At his sudden movements, Lianne murmured his name softly. The sweet, love-husky sound of her voice sent a thrill through Adam, and he stifled a groan of renewed desire. Lianne opened her eyes to look up at him adoringly, and their gazes met and held.

For just an instant as he stared down into her eyes, Adam almost succumbed to the temptation to remain here in her arms. He found that he didn't want to leave her. Her nearness was intoxicating, and it was that jarring realization that drove him from her arms. Adam knew he had to get away. His movements were jerky and awkward as he tore his gaze from hers and disengaged himself from her warm, willing embrace.

"Adam? What is it?" Her voice reflected bewilderment as he shifted his weight from her and released her from that intimate bond, all the while refusing to look at her again. She watched in confusion as he snatched up his clothing and began to dress.

"Nothing. Just get dressed," he bit out tersely, keeping his head averted. He didn't want to look at her for fear that the wildfire of desire that had erupted between them might reoccur. There was something about Lianne that affected him as no other woman ever had. She meant trouble, and he vowed to himself to stay as far away from her as he could from this moment on.

"But Adam . . . have I done something wrong?" was all Lianne could say, for she was stunned by his coldness. She suddenly felt chilled to the bone. Was this the man who just a short time before had cradled her in his arms and taken her to the heights of ecstasy? The beauty of what had happened between them was a rapidly fading memory. It its place came doubts, and confusion, and finally anger when he didn't respond right away.

Adam wished he had the bottle of bourbon with him. At this moment his need for a strong drink was overpowering. He girded himself as he turned to face Lianne. He kept his expression stony as he stared down at her, ignoring the hurt shining in her luminous eyes. He had to sever this intangible thing that existed between them, and he had to sever it now.

"Everything is wrong, Lianne. I'm sorry. I never meant for this to happen. What happened here tonight was a terrible mistake." There, he thought, it was out. Though making love to her had been the most exciting encounter he'd ever experienced, he knew it could never be repeated.

Terrible mistake! The words echoed hollowly through

Lianne, and the night lost all of its magical glow as she stared up into the coldness of his gaze. The warmth she'd thought she'd seen reflected there earlier was gone. The tenderness she'd imagined in his manner had been just that, her imagination. In its place came the harsh truth — at the lowest moment of her life, when she'd been hurt and defenseless, Adam had used her. He'd known exactly what to say and what to do to encourage her to surrender to him, and she'd fallen into his trap like the naive innocent that she was. She'd been willing, and he hadn't hesitated to take that which she'd given.

Lianne was furious with herself, and she berated herself silently for having forgotten just what a rotten bastard Adam Trent really was. She grabbed up her clothing and began to dress. When she'd finished, she turned on him.

"You're right, Adam. This was a mistake! A big mistake! But you needn't worry that it will ever happen again. Believe me, the last thing I'd ever want is a repeat of tonight!" She finally managed to vent some of her wrath as her pride began to return.

Her words cut Adam to the quick, but he refused to acknowledge the hurt. This was what he wanted. He wanted her to avoid him and now she would. He knew he should have felt victorious, but he didn't. Instead, as Adam watched her disappear into the house, he felt empty and hollow.

Adam waited several minutes before following Lianne back indoors. He made his way slowly to the study and went straight to the bourbon. Adam skipped his glass altogether now and drank directly from the bottle, wondering all the while why his need for revenge suddenly seemed so jaded to him.

* * *

121

It was a dark and quiet night in New Orleans. Settled in for the evening, Nurse Halliday was startled by the unexpected knock at the door. She hastened to answer it, thinking that it was probably her employer. She'd known that Mr. Trent had been out of town for the past week and had missed his regular visits to Miss Elise.

"Dr. Williams!" She was surprised to find the doctor paying a call at such a late hour. He had already made his regular call earlier that morning, and she had not expected him back until the following day.

"Good evening, Nurse Halliday. May I come in?" the good doctor asked.

"Of course, Doctor. Please." She held the door wide for the physician and then closed and locked it securely behind him. "Is something wrong? Is that why you've come?"

"No, Nurse. Everything is fine," he reassured her. "I just thought I'd stop by and see how my patient was doing. Has she retired for the night yet?"

"No, sir. She's in her room."

Nurse Halliday led the way upstairs to Elise's quarters.

"Miss Elise . . . Dr. Williams is here to see you," she called out as she knocked softly on the partially closed door and then went in.

Elise was sitting in the wing chair and appeared to be staring out the window. She did not respond in any way to their entrance into her room.

"I'll leave you with her now, Dr. Williams. If there's anything you need, just send word."

"Thank you."

David Williams remained standing near the door, studying his patient. He thought her case a particularly tragic one. She was beautiful and had everything to live for . . . a bright future with a loving fiancé . . . and yet

122

here she was, trapped in a mute, wasted existence.

The tragedy of Elise Clayton's illness, however, was not what had brought David here tonight. It had been something else. Something that had happened at their session that morning, and it had been haunting him ever since. It had seemed to him, for just an instant during the course of his talking to her, that there had been a flicker of awareness in her lovely, blue-eyed gaze. It had come and gone so quickly that, at the time, he'd thought he had imagined it. But the more he'd dwelt on it as the hours had passed, the more he'd become convinced that something had happened. In fact, the feeling had become almost obsessive, and David had found himself canceling a dinner engagement just to return to see her again.

"Elise?" David said her name in a questioning, conversational tone as he drew a straight-backed chair along with him and sat down before her. "Elise, it's me, Dr. Williams. I thought I'd come back and see you again."

She gave no recognition that she was even conscious of his being there.

"You see, I've been thinking about you all day, and I wanted you to know that I really believe you're going to get better."

David waited. Nothing.

David tried to remember exactly what it was he'd been talking about that morning that had seemed to touch a chord of response within her, but he could recall no one particular subject. He had just been making idle, yet encouraging conversation, much as he was now. At a loss to duplicate his earlier efforts, he just began to talk with her as he would a good friend, pausing in his monologue every now and then to wait in patient silence, in hopes that she might be moved to speak up.

David watched her face intently as he spoke, studying her delicate features for some sign of change. He noticed, not for the first time during his long weeks of treating her, how lovely she was in spite of her withdrawn state. His heart ached to be able to heal her. He wanted her to improve. He wanted to hear the sound of her voice, of her laugh. He found himself wondering what she liked and what she disliked. In a moment of unprofessional desperation, he took her hand in his and pressed it to his lips.

"Elise . . . talk to me . . ." he commanded in a strained voice.

Somewhere in the distant recesses of Elise's mind something stirred, beckoned by a soft, urgent call. A part of her urged her to respond to the call as a seedling does to the warmth of the sun, but another part of her shrieked a fearful warning. There was no gentleness in the real world. There was only pain and death! Memories of her Aunt Odile being raped and killed and of her own attackers swarmed through her mind and cut off the sound of the coaxing male voice. Quickly, her consciousness dissolved into forgetfulness, safe and protected from life's gruesome ugliness.

It was several hours later when David finally gave up. It had been a long day, and an even longer evening, for Elise hadn't shown any improvement. He was exhausted. In a weary motion, he raked his hand through the darkness of his hair and then rose from the chair. He paused only long enough to touch Elise's cheek in a light caress before quitting the room. Though his spirits were low over his lack of success, he knew even as he left the house that, in the morning, he would begin again. Somehow, he was going to find a way to release her from her self-imposed prison and set her free.

* * *

Lianne paced her room impatiently waiting for Sarah to bring her bath. She was anxious to scrub every inch of her body so she could erase all memory of Adam's touch from her flesh. When the knock came at her door, she answered it eagerly, expecting it to be Sarah.

"Come in, Sarah. I—" She started in surprise to find Becky standing there in the hall wearing her wrapper. "Oh . . . Becky . . ."

"I heard you moving around in your room, and it's so late, I was wondering if something's wrong?" Becky had not had the opportunity to speak with Lianne since she'd returned from her visit to her uncle's. "Did things go all right in town?"

Still not adept at hiding her emotions, Lianne's expression gave away her concern. Before she could say any more, Becky spoke again.

"Something is wrong, isn't it?" she asked, her dark eyes suddenly filled with sympathetic worry. "Why don't you tell me about it. Maybe Adam and I can help you in some way."

"I don't want or need your help," Lianne answered stiffly, not wanting anything to do with Adam Trent ever again. All she wanted to do was to somehow survive.

"I'm sorry I intruded, Lianne. I just thought you might need a friend," Becky told her softly as she turned to go.

When she saw the hurt suddenly reflected in the other woman's gaze, Lianne realized how wrong it had been to strike out at her. Becky had been nothing but kind to her and Alex, and she knew her curtness had been uncalled for.

"Becky . . ." Lianne stopped her from leaving. "You're right. Things aren't turning out quite the way I thought they would."

"Do you want to talk about it?" Becky was not going to force Lianne to confide in her. If they were to become friends, it would have to be something they both wanted.

Lianne nodded and she opened the door wider to allow Becky to come into her room. "It might help."

"What happened in town? Did you get everything straightened out with your uncle?"

Lianne's eyes clouded as she explained her predicament. "So, in effect, Alex and I are destitute until I come of age in ten months." She gave a heavy sigh. "I'm not sure what I'm going to do next. Uncle Antoine is the only family Alex and I have, but there's no way I could ever go back to him."

"Of course not!" Becky was outraged by all that she'd heard. "You shouldn't ever have to go back to him! Why, if I were a man, I'd call him out for what he's done to you!"

"Please! Don't say that!" Lianne quickly protested at the thought of dueling. "It wouldn't be worth it."

Becky flushed, realizing her mistake as she remembered the story of Lianne's older brother's death. "I'm sorry. I didn't mean to upset you. It's just so unfair that he's managed to steal your inheritance and get away with it!"

"I know, but there's nothing more I can do. Our trust funds are still intact, but I can't touch them until I turn twenty-one."

"Then I see no problem at all," Becky said cheerfully.

"What do you mean?" Lianne stared at her puzzled, wondering how she could be so confident when the future looked positively bleak.

"You and Alex can just stay on here with us. There's plenty of room, so I see no problem. What do you say?"

Her offer was so generous that Lianne was taken aback. But as much as she wanted to stay in her home, she knew she couldn't. Adam would never stand for it. She was sure he wanted her gone just as soon as possible.

"No, Becky. We can't do that."

"Would you mind telling me why not?" Becky felt certain that it was her pride standing in her way, and she refused to allow Lianne and Alex to end up on the streets. "It's only a matter of a few months."

"I know, but . . ."

"But what?"

"Your brother."

"What about Adam?" Becky asked shrewdly, thinking of his unusual reaction to Lianne.

"I'm sure he doesn't want us to stay on." Lianne knew that for a fact, especially after what had happened between them tonight.

"Nonsense. Adam won't mind." She would not be deterred from her purpose. "He's got too many other things on his mind to concern himself with what we do. Besides, he and Alex are getting along famously."

"They are?" This news came as a complete surprise and nudged her closer to accepting Becky's offer. Lianne struggled to make her decision. What Becky was offering her amounted to her salvation. She and Alex desperately needed a haven for the few months until her trust matured.

Yet, while Lianne argued with herself to accept for Alex's sake, her instincts were telling her to run as far and as fast as she could to escape from Adam's devastating nearness. She hated him, but the fact remained that he had only had to touch her and all her vows of despising him had disappeared. Lianne groaned inwardly as she remembered how willing she had been, and she fought hard not to blush in Becky's presence.

Still, Adam's cold-hearted claim that what had happened between them was a mistake, and that it would never happen again, reassured her somewhat. That danger dismissed, Lianne realized she had to accept. They had nowhere else to go, no one else to turn to for help. Her pride was a fine thing, but it wouldn't feed Alex or keep a roof over his head.

"But I don't want to be a burden to you," she ventured hesitantly.

"A burden? Hardly," Becky scoffed. "I'm going to need your help."

"You will? For what?"

She explained how Adam wanted to have the party and how he had already directed her to refurbish the house. "What do you say? Will you stay on and help me restore Belle Arbor? I would really value your advice. Besides, since you know everyone around here, you can help me plan the party, too."

Having no alternative, Lianne finally assented with as much grace as she could muster. "Thank you, Becky, Alex and I would love to stay. But are you sure Adam won't object?"

"Don't worry about Adam. I'll take care of him."

Becky sounded so confident that she could influence her domineering brother, that Lianne couldn't suppress a smile.

"There, that's much better," Becky teased, pleased at seeing Lianne smile for the first time, and then impulsively she gave her a warm hug. "We're going to get along just fine, you'll see. Now, don't worry about a thing."

Sarah's knock interrupted them. As Sarah and her helper entered carrying the hot water for Lianne's bath, Becky started from the room to give Lianne her privacy.

"Becky?"

"Yes?" She glanced back just as she would have disappeared through the door and saw Lianne staring at her a bit wistfully.

"Thank you."

It was a heartfelt thanks, and Becky felt tears come to her eyes. "You're welcome."

As she returned to her own room her heart ached for Lianne. She admired her tremendously for how well she was holding up under the strain of her circumstances, and she knew she would do everything in her power to help her all she could.

Lianne locked the door once the servants had gone and then made short order of stripping off her clothing. She couldn't wait to get into the tub of steaming water and scrub away all memory of Adam's possession.

It was then as she stepped into the bath that she noticed the smear of blood on her inner thighs. The relative calm that had been hers for such a short time shattered. Guilt and rage filled her. How could she have been so stupid? How could she have given away her most valuable gift to Adam, of all people? She knew him for what he was. He was an opportunist who took what he wanted when he wanted it. And that was just what he'd done tonight. She had been there, and she had been willing. Lianne groaned at the thought of her own eager actions. No wonder he'd claimed it had all been a mistake when the moment of passion had passed. He hadn't really wanted her. He had just used her. How could she have doubted all that she knew about him even for a moment?

Fiercely she began to wash. Lianne prided herself on being a woman who learned from her mistakes. Her encounter with Adam had been just that, and it would never happen again. When at last she felt clean, she rose from the heated water in dripping splendor and quickly began to towel herself dry. She stepped from the tub meaning to pull on her nightdress immediately, but curiosity drew her to her mirror. Lianne stood before her reflection studying herself to see if there was any visible proof of the changes this night had wrought on her body. She was relieved to find that she looked exactly the same outwardly. Only her eyes revealed the sadness that she kept hidden deep within her and would never share.

Satisfied that no one else would ever learn of her indiscretion, she donned her nightgown and slipped into the welcoming comfort of her bed. A deep, quieting sleep claimed her quickly.

Adam could not rest. In the wee hours of the morning, he sought out the peaceful solitude of his bedroom, but it was not peace and solitude he found there. Instead, as he lay still fully clothed upon the wide, four-poster bed, he was hounded by the memory of his time with Lianne. She had been so excitingly responsive. Even now, just the remembrance of her freely given love could stir him.

With chilling brutality, he told himself that Lianne was just another woman like the many he'd known before Elise. There had been nothing really special about her. He'd been lonely and she'd been all to available. That was all. Yet, as he tried to convince himself of that, he could still remember the silken length of her pressed fully against him, and the way her hot, hungry body had taken him deep within the womanly heart of her.

Adam grimaced into the darkness. No matter how much he logically tried to deny what had happened, his body knew. He had desired Lianne from the start, and he still wanted her. Callously, he attempted to tell himself that it had been necessary to hurt her the way he had, but his conscience still prodded him with the cruelty of his words and actions after having loved her.

130

Adam cursed out loud into the darkness of his room as he practically threw himself from the bed. Knowing he would find no peace there tonight, he strode to the window and remained there, staring out across Belle Arbor's fertile acres, until the sun's first light caressed the eastern horizon.

Chapter Eleven

It was late morning as Lianne sat with Becky at the dining room table deep in discussion over the work that needed to be done to the house. Intently, they went over the list of repairs that needed to be done and the supplies they would need from town to accomplish their tasks. It was a labor of love for Lianne, for it had pained her greatly during the past year to watch her home fall into disrepair because of her own lack of funds. She felt vindicated now that she knew it was all Uncle Antoine's fault, and she was eager to help Becky bring Belle Arbor back to its original magnificence.

"You'll go into New Orleans with me, won't you?" Becky invited.

"You want me to help you shop?" Lianne was stunned by her offer.

"Of course," she insisted, her eyes alive with good humor. "You could show me all the right places to go for what we need."

Lianne hesitated, unwilling to help spend someone else's money, even if it was going for her beloved home. "But, Becky, you know I'm not really a part of any of this."

"What do you mean?" she was puzzled.

"You own Belle Arbor now, not me. I'm only still here by the grace of your friendship. By rights, Alex and I should be —"

"Right here!" Becky refused to listen to her any

more. "You're here because I've invited you to stay, and I don't want to hear any more about it."

Lianne was surprised by the ardency of her statement. Becky Trent was proving to be one formidable woman. The thought made her smile. Maybe Becky really could handle Adam.

"That's better," Becky teased good-naturedly. "Now, you absolutely must help me with all of this. I don't see how I can possibly accomplish all that needs to be done in the short time Adam's given me."

"How much time did you say we have?" Lianne got serious about their discussion again.

"Less than six weeks."

"It'll be difficult, but we can do it."

Adam had just returned to the house and was striding down the main hall heading toward the study. A serious lack of sleep and a whopping hangover from his overindulgence the night before had rendered his mood less than easy-going. He was just about to enter the study opposite the dining room when he overhead the very last of Becky's and Lianne's conversation. Listening to their chitchat, he realized with great consternation that Lianne would be staying on, and he grew furious. How had this happened? Becky knew that he needed no interference in order to pursue his goal. Adam wanted to march into their midst and demand an explanation from his sister as to why Lianne would be helping her with the redecorating, but he controlled himself with an effort.

"Rebecca!" he bellowed from where he stood in the hall. "I'd like to speak with you in the study, please!" With that he stormed inside the study to await her.

Becky had not heard him come inside, and she was surprised by the anger in his tone. "I wonder what's got his dander up?" she remarked with no outward display of worry as she got up to go see what he wanted. "Why don't you finish making that list while I go talk to Adam?"

"Fine," Lianne agreed, hiding her nervousness as she watched her newfound friend leave the room. She knew exactly what was troubling Adam. He'd probably heard what they'd just been discussing and was outraged to find out that she and Alex were staying on for a time. Drawing a deep breath, she started in on the task at hand. Lianne tried to concentrate, but she found it difficult, for at any moment she expected Adam and Becky to emerge from the study with the news that she would indeed have to leave Belle Arbor.

Adam had escaped from the house early that morning just as soon as things began to stir. He'd had no desire to see Lianne again and, in fact, had been silently hoping that he would return home and discover that she and Alex had already packed up and left. He found it unsettling, to say the least, to hear Becky going over her future plans for Belle Arbor with Lianne and asking for her help. He wanted to find out just what his sister was doing.

"Yes, Adam, what it is?" Becky asked as she entered the study to speak with him. There was a definite touch of annoyance in her tone as she eyed him disdainfully. He looked terrible, almost as if he hadn't slept at all the night before, and she wondered what his problem was.

"I want to know why she's still here?" Adam demanded curtly. "Didn't she make plans to move into the city with her uncle or something?"

"No. That didn't work out, so I've invited Lianne and Alex to stay here with us."

"You what!" Adam stared at her in total outrage. "How could you make such arrangements without consulting me? Don't you realize what I'm trying to accomplish here? I can't be worrying about strangers living in the house with us when I'm making my plans."

134

"I'm sorry, but there was no other way," Becky replied firmly, undaunted by his anger.

"Of course there's another way. Find it."

"No, Adam. You don't understand. You see, Lianne and Alex have nowhere else to go."

"What the hell are you talking about?" he snapped. He did not want Lianne living in the same house with him. "They've got their uncle, let them go live with him."

"It's not that simple," Becky began as she went on to explain their predicament. "So, you see, they're in the direst of straits right now, but everything will be fine when Lianne turns twenty-one."

Adam gave his softhearted sister a strained look. "And just how soon is that?" Silently, he was praying for Lianne's birthday to be next week.

"In about ten months," Becky supplied easily as she cast him a glance from beneath lowered lashes. She knew Adam was deeply involved in his plot to trap Shark, but she felt certain that Lianne's presence here wouldn't hamper his efforts in any way. There was no reason why Lianne would even be aware of his business.

Still, as she watched her brother closely, Becky wondered if there wasn't more to all this. Adam had reacted strangely to Lianne the first time he'd met her, and now this outraged response to the discovery that she'd be staying on seemed out of character for him.

A muscle twitched in Adam's jaw as he fought to control his fury. "I see."

"Good, I knew you would." She went to him where he stood by the window and gave him a quick kiss on his cheek. "Lianne thought you might want her and Alex to leave anyway, but I told her you wouldn't mind them staying on. She's going to help me with all the work around here, and I can certainly use the help."

135

"Wonderful," he croaked harshly.

"Well, if that's all you wanted, I have to get back to my planning." Becky headed for the door. "By the way, Adam, you look terrible this morning. I know you were working hard last night, but didn't you get any rest at all?"

At his exasperated look, she quickly hurried from the room, leaving him scowling toward the heavens in search of help.

The following days passed in a whirlwind of activity for all of them. Lianne was so caught up by Becky's enthusiasm for their redecorating plans that she hardly had time to think, let alone worry about Adam. The only time they were together for any extended period was at the evening meal. Adam was unfailingly polite to her, but there was a cold indifference behind his actions that somehow had the power to hurt her.

Lianne knew she should have been thanking her lucky stars that he was behaving in such an exemplary manner, but for some reason his lack of interest in her stung. She felt strangely annoyed when he carried on animated conversations with Alex and Becky, and then turned grudging attention to her whenever she joined in.

It was painfully obvious to Lianne that their encounter had meant absolutely nothing to Adam. Though they had made love, he could dismiss her easily now, as if what had occurred between them had been of trivial importance. She had to admit that his aloofness made it easy for her to go on as if nothing had happened, and she knew she should have been relieved. Yet a part of her still ached over his casual dismissal, and she wondered why.

* * *

"I'll be traveling into New Orleans tomorrow," Adam announced at dinner. "I have some business that I must attend to."

"That's perfect, Adam," Becky chimed. "Lianne and I will come with you."

The thought of spending long hours in a carriage with Adam unnerved Lianne, and she quickly tried to withdraw from the trip. "That's all right, Becky. Why don't you go into town, and I'll stay here and see to things."

"Nonsense." Becky refused to allow her to stay at the plantation. "You know how much I need your help with the merchants. You have to come with me." She glanced surreptitiously at her brother and noted the sudden tenseness in his expression. Keeping her expression carefully blank, she turned to Adam. "You don't mind, do you? How long did you want to stay?"

"Probably just one day. I had planned to return the day after tomorrow." Adam was angry at his sister's interference, but could think of no good excuse to get out of taking them along.

The prospect of spending so much time in such close proximity with Lianne irritated Adam. He'd barely been able to control himself around her since the day they'd made love, and he'd been looking forward to a day away from the torture of her nearness.

His heart ached as he regarded her now. He wanted her badly. She was so strikingly beautiful, and all he could remember was how exciting it had been to possess her. She had been a firebrand in his arms, and they had melded so perfectly.

At the memory, Adam felt the familiar tightening in his loins and had to force the remembrance of their time by the pool from his mind. It annoyed him that just the thought of holding her and kissing her could

137

arouse him so. Sitting there in the dining room, he reaffirmed his vow never to touch her again.

"That'll be just fine," Becky was saying as Adam wrestled, unbeknownst to them, with his raging desire for Lianne.

"What am I going to do?" Alex chimed in, hoping that he was going to be included.

"You're going to stay right here," Lianne ordered.

"Aw, Lianne, please let me come along. Please? I promise to be good."

"Sweetie . . ." she began, ready to refuse him, but Adam spoke up.

"Of course you can come," he invited expansively. Having Alex along in the carriage with them for the long drive, he knew, would provide some relief from being in such close quarters with Lianne.

"It's settled, then," Becky said, eyeing Adam suspiciously. He was certainly acting rather strangely. She could have sworn that he'd been irritated by her plan to join him on the trip, and now he had invited Alex along, too. Strange. Very strange. Especially since it was not a pleasure trip. Becky knew that he'd received a note from town that afternoon, and it was probably news from Beau.

The thought of Beau sent a thrill of excitement through her. She hadn't seen him since they'd arrived in New Orleans, and she longed for the chance to be with him again. Becky had loved Beau ever since she was a little girl. Being Adam's best friend, he had always treated her with a brotherly indulgence, and up until several years ago that had been enough for her. Now that she'd become a woman, she wanted him to recognize her as an attractive female, not just as Adam's little sister. So far, she hadn't had much success in getting his attention. His reputation as a ladies' man was well-founded, but she wasn't about to let that stop her. She

138

was going to marry Beau Hamilton, he just didn't know it yet.

"I want to get an early start, Becky, so be ready to go about seven," Adam told her.

"We'll be ready," she assured him, delighted that she would soon get to see Beau again.

Two hours into the journey to town, Adam sat in almost grim silence with his arms folded across his chest, staring out the window of the carriage. He had known that it was a bad idea when Becky had insisted on coming with him, but he'd had no idea that it would have turned into this much of a torturous endeavor for him.

Adam had thought that bringing Alex along would distract him from what he was feeling toward Lianne, but he'd been wrong. Instead of being diverted, Adam had found himself sitting directly across from Lianne. Not only did he have to look at her continually, but at every bump and turn of the carriage their legs touched. He kept trying to shift away from even that little bit of contact, but short of climbing up on the seat like an idiot, there could be no escape.

Their eyes had met only once. Briefly, Adam had seen a flare of emotion reflected there, but Lianne had quickly shuttered her feelings. Then she had gazed at him with the same cool disdain he'd come to expect from her since that night. Miserable over his inability to control his conflicting emotions, he bided his time. Eagerly, he anticipated their arrival in New Orleans.

Lianne managed to maintain her composure even though she longed to flee the confines of the carriage and escape Adam's overpowering closeness. She had made a point of keeping her distance from him ever since that night. Now, trapped as she was in such close quarters, she was forced to admit to herself that Adam was a devastingly handsome man. It was difficult for her to acknowledge the physical attraction she felt for him. Lianne harbored no doubts at all that she despised him, and it left her completely perplexed to discover that she could desire him even as she hated him.

Her gaze had accidentally met his just once early in the trip, and Lianne had felt the jolt all the way to the very depths of her soul. It had seemed that he could read her most intimate thoughts, and since that moment, she'd masked all her feelings. She would not let him see how deeply he affected her. She would not reveal it to him or to anyone else. She wanted nothing more to do with Adam Trent . . . nothing.

They elected to stay at the elegant St. Louis Hotel while they were in town. As soon as they'd checked in and were safely ensconced in their rooms, Adam made his excuses and left. Becky was a bit surprised by his hasty exit, but made no remark to Lianne. She wasn't sure if he was in a hurry to take care of his own business or if he was just in a hurry to get away from them.

Becky had been very aware of the thread of tension that had existed between her brother and Lianne during the trip to town, and she couldn't help but be curious about it. She had known from the very beginning that Adam was attracted to Lianne, but she had no idea what could have happened between them to create such a strain. One way or another, she planned to find out.

Adam slammed his fist down on the tabletop in testimony to his complete frustration. "Damn! To be so close . . ."

"I know," Beau agreed, as they met later that day at the Samson Saloon. "But there was nothing more we could do at the time. The way I figure it, these are the areas we need to keep searching." He pointed out the strategic points on the charts he had.

"The only trouble I see is that we don't know where Shark's gone or how long he's going to be away. It's going to be a long tedious wait, I'm afraid," Adam remarked. "Judging from what you've told me about your location when you saw the ship, it looks like his home base is somewhere near the backwater exit from Suzanne's plantation."

"And yours," Beau added with a confident smile. "Your winning the plantation was certainly a coup for us. For once, we got a break."

"I know," he agreed. "I could hardly believe it myself when I first found out. It'll be a simple matter for me to slip away now. I'll start making runs with you now that we're so close."

"Good. We'll go out on short runs, a day or two at a time."

"I'll be able to manage that with no problem."

"When did you find out that Suzanne was one of your neighbors? I mean things couldn't have worked out more perfectly."

"I found out from the Ducharme boy, Alex. He was showing me the way through the bayou. That was when I stopped to visit her . . ."

"It must have been difficult for you, finding her wearing the necklace and all." Beau met his friend's gaze and saw the torment there.

"Keeping myself under control at that moment was one of the roughest things I've ever done in my life. All I wanted to do was strangle her, Beau. To think that she's involved with Shark and all his bloodthirsty ways . . ."

"But you did propose."

"I had to. Once I'd seen Elise's necklace, I knew I had to keep an eye on her. What better way than as her

141

fiancée?" Adam took a deep drink of the ale before him. He had sworn off bourbon ever since that night with Lianne.

"Have you told Becky?" Beau asked.

"No, and I'm not going to, not yet anyway."

"That's for the best, I guess, but how have you managed to convince this Suzanne to keep it quiet?"

"I'm planning a big party at Belle Arbor in a few weeks. I told Suzanne that I wanted to announce our engagement then, and she agreed to keep it a secret for the time being."

"Have you been to check on Elise yet?"

Adam rubbed the back of his neck in a weary gesture as he thought of her. "I went there first before coming here to meet you."

"And?"

His bleak expression told it all. "No change."

"I'm sorry, Adam. I wish there was something I could do to make this easier for you."

"I'm afraid there's nothing anyone can do, Beau."

The two men fell silent for a while as they finished off their drinks. Beau signaled the barmaid to bring two more mugs of ale, and the buxom wench hurried to comply.

"Here ya go, darlin'," Katie, the barmaid, cooed, sidling up to Beau as she set the drinks before them. They were both good-looking men, and she was eager to have either one of them in her bed. "Can I get you anything else?" Her tone said it all as she managed to rub the side of her bosom against Beau's shoulder.

The long months of celibacy at sea had taken their toll on Beau, and he was more than a little interested. The girl was comely enough and clean-looking.

"See me later," Beau told her as he gave her a particularly dashing smile and a huge tip.

"You bet." Katie smiled and winked as she moved off

to finish waiting on her other customers.

When she'd gone, Adam grinned knowingly. "I was hoping you could join me for dinner tonight, but if you're going to be otherwise occupied . . ."

"I won't be busy that long," Beau returned his grin. "What time are you planning to eat?"

"Probably around seven. We're staying at the St. Louis."

"So, Becky came along?" For some reason, he was pleased with the prospect of seeing her again.

Adam nodded and then added less than enthusiastically, "The Ducharme girl, Lianne, and her brother, too."

"You mean they're still living on the plantation with you?" Knowing Adam's desire for secrecy, he was astounded by this news.

"Becky's behind it all," Adam remarked, trying to sound offhand about it. He quickly went on to explain the loss of Lianne's inheritance and how they wouldn't have any money until she came of age and could claim her trust.

"I hope they don't get in our way," Beau said grimly, his usually easygoing nature suddenly serious. "They're not thick with Suzanne, are they?"

Adam frowned. "I don't think so, but it wouldn't matter. There's no way anyone is going to find out what we're doing. We're far too close to finding him to take even the smallest risk."

Satisfied that things were finally working out, they drank a silent toast to their progress and then sat back to enjoy the rest of their ale.

Chapter Twelve

The last thing Lianne wanted to do was to have dinner with Adam and one of his business associates. Her spirits sank at the thought as she waited in Becky's room while she got ready. Alex was taking dinner in the room he and Lianne were sharing and then was going to retire early. Lianne tried to plead tiredness, so she could stay closeted with Alex, but Becky refused to believe her.

"What is going on between you and Adam?" she asked shrewdly, her eyes narrowing as she tried to gauge Lianne's reaction to her bold, assessing statement.

Lianne blanched at her newfound friend's perceptiveness, fearing that somehow Becky had learned what had happened. But as quickly as she had the thought, she discarded it. No one knew, and it was going to stay that way.

"I don't know what you mean," Lianne replied with as much casualness as she could muster.

"I mean," Becky drawled for effectiveness, "when I first asked you to stay on, you seemed certain that Adam was going to force you to leave."

"Oh." She was almost relieved that that was what this was all about. "Well, I just thought he didn't like me, that's all. I mean, I did threaten him with a shotgun and all."

"And," Becky went on with emphasis, "every time

you two are around each other, you're both jumpy and nervous."

"Really?" Lianne tried to sound surprised by this observation. "I hadn't noticed."

Becky studied her for a long, silent moment before continuing to brush out her hair. "It doesn't really matter, I guess." She looked up in the mirror to watch Lianne's reaction. "It's just that I've never seen Adam react to another woman the way he does to you. And, believe me, I've seen Adam with a lot of women."

It's probably because he can't stand the sight of me and wishes I was gone! Lianne thought caustically.

"I imagine women do flock to him, don't they?" She couldn't stop herself from asking.

"Oh, yes. He's always had a way with the opposite sex, but then he's a very attractive man." Becky wanted to goad Lianne into a revealing conversation.

"I suppose he is," Lianne responded noncommittally, refusing to meet Becky's gaze in the mirror. *If you like arrogant chauvinists,* she completed the thought silently. "Who is this other man who's joining us for dinner tonight?"

"It's Beau," Becky's tone softened as she said his name.

Lianne noticed the slight change in her and quickly took advantage of the opportunity to change the subject away from Adam. "You like him, don't you?" she remarked insightfully.

Becky glanced up at Lianne, and this time their gazes met. "Can you keep a secret?"

"Yes, if you're sure you want to share it."

She put down her brush and turned to face her, her expression conspiratorial. "I'm in love with Beau."

"Becky! That's wonderful!"

"I'm glad you think so, because I sure don't."

"Why? Is there a problem?"

145

"He doesn't love me."

"How do you know? Has he ever told you that?"

"No. You see, he's Adam's best friend, and it's almost as if I've known him all my life."

"So?"

"So, Beau thinks of me as a little girl . . . you know, Adam's little sister," Becky's heartache was obvious.

"Then you have to do something about that," Lianne told her firmly.

"What? I know all about Beau and Adam. They're two of a kind. They like beautiful, sophisticated women."

"And you don't think you're beautiful and sophisticated?" She looked at her friend incredulously.

"No."

"Then take another look in that mirror, Becky. You're absolutely gorgeous."

Becky considered that a high compliment coming from Lianne, for she thought her a fantastic combination of beauty and bravery. Turning to stare at her own reflection, she tried to see the woman Lianne was talking about, but she couldn't. Instead of noticing the loveliness of her own unblemished, fair complexion, Becky saw only the smattering of freckles on her nose. Instead of appreciating the thick, rich, mahogany tresses that swung past her shoulders now in glossy waves, she saw the curls as too wild and unmanageable. Instead of admiring her own petite figure, she thought herself too short and too thin to be lovely enough for Beau. She had seen some of the women Beau had courted, and she knew she fell short of their tall, buxom beauty.

"You've never seen the women who attract him. Why, Beau can get any woman he wants," Becky mourned, feeling relieved to at last be sharing her deepest, most precious secret with someone. She had never dared tell Adam, so she had kept her love to herself all these years.

"Then all we have to do is to convince him that you're the one he wants. Right?" Lianne prompted, feeling pleased that Becky had confided in her. It made her feel less like an unwelcome guest and more like a true friend. In fact, watching Becky's eyes light up at the thought made Lianne feel almost young and carefree again. It seemed so long since she'd had time to think about such things.

The twinkle was back in Becky's eyes as she gave Lianne a wide, confident grin. "Right." Stalking to her trunk she started to sort through the pile of fashionable gowns she'd brought along. She snared a deep rose satin one and held it up for Lianne's inspection. "What do you think?"

"I think you're on the right track." She returned her smile and began to help her dress.

When they had finished, Becky posed before the cheval glass to admire their handiwork. The dress was simply cut and plain in style, but its lack of ornamentation made it perfect for the petite Becky. The bodice was modestly cut, but hinted at the tempting fullness beneath. The full skirts emphasized her tiny waist, and the rose color complimented her beautifully. Becky looked very chic.

"Watch him not even notice!" she grumbled, afraid to get her hopes up.

"Shame on you, Becky Trent! As easily as you handle your brother, you'd think this Beau Hamilton would be simple for you."

"All right. I'm as ready as I'll ever be, but what about you? What are you going to wear?"

Lianne realized then that she had no gown that could even compare to Becky's. "I've got a very nice one in my room. Let me go change, and I'll be right back."

"I'm coming with you. You were kind enough to help me. Now I'm going to return the favor, but we've got to hurry. It's almost seven now, and I promised we'd meet Adam downstairs in the lobby no later than seven."

They hurried to Lianne's room. Shooing Alex out of the way, Becky took charge, brushing out Lianne's long hair and then leaving it down, about her shoulders.

"Don't you think I should style it up?" Lianne asked.

"Absolutely not. If I'm wearing mine down, so are you. Here, we'll use this ribbon . . ." Artfully, Becky wove the ribbon through her hair. "There. Now for your dress and we're ready."

Lianne drew out the only gown she owned that was suitable for dinner at the St. Louis. It was a sedate dinner dress that was several years old. Though not as stylish as Becky's, Lianne knew the deep emerald color suited her. The bodice was square-cut, and the sleeves were long and puffed. A wide band of ivory lace trimmed the cuffs and neckline, enhancing her pale, creamy complexion even as the rich green color drew attention to her eyes.

If Becky was disappointed in the dress, she said nothing. Instead, she heaped compliments upon her, telling her how beautiful she looked. Standing back to look at Lianne, she nodded approvingly.

"You look marvelous," she told her with pride, and then mumbled to herself under her breath, "I just hope someone notices."

"Did you say something?" Lianne asked as she dabbed a bit of perfume at her pulse points.

"Oh, no . . . nothing."

Becky didn't know if there was anything happening between Adam and Lianne, but she knew her brother needed some encouragement to go on with his life. She knew, as he did, that his future with Elise was doubtful. In all these months, no doctor they'd seen had given them any hope. Adam needed to feel like a man again, and Becky felt certain that if there was a woman alive who could help Adam forget Elise, it was Lianne.

"Lianne you look real pretty." Alex beamed at her. He couldn't remember the last time he'd seen his big sister dressed up and looking so lovely.

"Why, thank you, darling." Lianne gave him a quick hug.

"You even smell pretty!"

Lianne gave a lighthearted laugh as she ordered him under the covers. "To bed with you, young man. I'll kiss you again when I get back from dinner."

"Oh, all right." Alex was less than enthused about being left behind this evening, but Lianne had explained to him earlier that tonight it was adults only.

For the first time in ages, Lianne was feeling almost carefree as she descended the main curving staircase with Becky. All that ended abruptly, however, when she looked up to see Adam standing at the foot of the stairs, one arm resting casually on the newel post, watching her. There was another, blond-haired man at his side, but she had eyes only for him. Clad in basic black, his shirt and cravat a vivid snowy white contrast, Adam was remarkably handsome.

Lianne's heart swelled in her breast, and her pulses raced as her eyes met his. Annoyed that just the sight of him could affect her so, she quickly looked away. She silently cursed the thought of having to spend the entire evening in his company. With fierce insistence, she reminded herself that she hated him.

Adam didn't want to feel this attraction to Lianne, but he found he couldn't take his eyes off her as she came down the grand staircase with Becky. The dress she was wearing was not of the latest fashion, but the style was becoming to her. The décolletage was not by any means revealing, but the slight swell of her breasts above the square neckline sent a shaft of desire through Adam.

Though Adam had been making a deliberate effort to try to forget that night, it all came back to him in a powerful surge of sensual recognition. He remembered Lianne's passionate response to his touch. He remembered her long, slender legs wrapped tightly about his waist as they were locked in love's embrace. He remembered the satiny softness of her breasts in his hands and the heat of her abandoned kisses as they sought bliss together.

Adam bit back a groan as he struggled to keep his physical urges under control. He couldn't want her. He wouldn't want her. What had happened between them had been a terrible mistake. He'd been drinking, and she'd needed someone to comfort her. He'd had the misfortune of being in the wrong place at the wrong time. It wouldn't happen again, he repeated his vow to himself. No matter how drawn to her he was, he would not give in to this weakness. He turned away from the sight of Lianne to say something to Beau, but to his dismay, Beau was staring up at the two women, and he appeared just as entranced as Adam had been.

"What the hell are you staring at?" Adam demanded a little too harshly.

Beau cast him a questioning glance, wondering at his friend's reaction. "Is that Lianne Ducharme with Becky?"

"Yes," he snapped.

"From the way you've always spoken of her, I assumed that she was a young girl," Beau ventured, watching him with interest, trying to read his response. Ever since the attack, Adam had displayed absolutely no interest in women. Beau could tell that Adam's interest was reluctant, and he could well understand it. It wouldn't be easy to forget his memories of Elise, but Beau knew he had to if he ever wanted to rebuild his life. At least, he was glad that his friend was starting to feel things again. "And I had no idea she was so gorgeous."

"She's pretty enough, I guess." Adam attempted to sound nonchalant as he went along with him.

"What does your Suzanne think about her staying on at the plantation with you?" Beau asked, quirking one expressive brow.

"She had no objection." He was tired of discussing Lianne already and wished Beau would drop it.

"Understanding woman, your Suzanne," he said dryly.

"She's not *my* anything!" Adam snarled under his breath just as Becky and Lianne reached them.

"Good evening, ladies," Beau greeted them expansively.

"Hello, Beau, Adam," Becky returned, her eyes only for Beau. She thought him the most magnificent-looking man in the whole wide world. She longed to throw herself in his arms and kiss him, but she knew he'd probably never recover from the shock.

"You two are looking most lovely tonight." Beau turned on the charm. "Don't you think so, Adam?" he goaded with carefully disguised good humor.

"Yes, you both look very nice."

They accepted the compliments with good grace as the two men ushered them forth into the main dining room. Lianne could understand why Becky was in love with Beau. Not only was he very handsome, but he was interesting to talk to and had a great sense of humor. She liked him immediately and knew she would do all she could to help Becky further her cause.

Beau carried most of the conversation as the meal progressed. Adam sat in an almost sullen silence. He refused to join willingly in their light repartee, and he answered only those questions that were posed directly

151

to him. As Beau flirted openly with both women, Adam's expression grew more and more thunderous. Beau found Lianne a very intelligent, witty young woman, and, he had not sensed that there was more to his friend's reaction to Lianne then just aggravation at having her still in residence at Belle Arbor, he would have considered courting her. To Becky, Beau gave little real thought. She looked pretty, as she always did, but she was Becky. She had always been there, and she would always be there. She was cute and fun and Adam's little sister.

Becky was growing frustrated. She knew she looked her absolute best tonight, and yet she was getting no more attention from Beau than she normally did. He was being his usual charming self, as always, but there had been no spark of sudden, male recognition in his eyes when he'd looked at her. It was just like it always was when they were together. He was nice to her, he was sweet to her, but he was not loverlike to her, and she wanted to strangle him.

Adam thought the night would never end. Except for the news from Beau that they had almost caught up with Shark in the Gulf, the entire day had been a disaster. First, the damned, miserable carriage ride to town . . . Lord, he'd thought it would never end . . . then the visit to Elise, and now here he was, forced to sit and listen to Beau carry on with Lianne like some besotted fool. He wished he could just get up and leave. He wished he was anywhere but there. He wished this whole thing with Shark was over, and he was back home in Charleston. He wished—

"Shall we go for a walk around the rotunda?" Beau asked, interrupting his somber musings.

"I'd like that." Becky was thrilled at the chance to spend more time with Beau. She wanted the evening to go on and on and on.

"I think I'll pass," Adam said curtly. He needed to get away by himself for a while, and a visit to the hotel's well-stocked bar seemed most appealing.

"Me, too." Lianne quickly declined, for she wanted to give Becky time to work her wiles on Beau. "I need to get back upstairs and check on Alex."

"Perhaps we'd better go upstairs with Lianne to make sure she gets to her room all right," Becky said slowly, disappointed that she was going to miss her opportunity to take a walk with Beau. "It is rather late, and no lady should be unescorted at this time of night."

"Nonsense." Lianne hurried to discourage her friend. "I'll be fine. You go on ahead. There's no reason why I should ruin your evening."

"Better yet, Adam can see you to your room," Beau suggested, pointedly ignoring the black look Adam shot his way.

Having been put on the spot and seeing no way out of it, Adam agreed. Lianne wanted to argue that there was no need, but she didn't want to stand in the way of Becky having some time alone with Beau. Girding herself, she smiled her thanks politely and bid Becky and Beau good-night.

As they left the restaurant, Becky and Beau wandered off across the rotunda while Adam and Lianne started up the staircase toward their rooms. They did not speak as they mounted the sweeping stairway. The tension between them was an almost palpable thing, but they both tried to ignore it. When they reached the floor where their rooms were located, Lianne tried to rebuff Adam.

"Thank you so much for seeing me this far. I'm sure I'll be fine from here," she said with pretended coolness. All through dinner she'd been trying to dismiss the strange excitement that filled her from just being near him. Now, as they stood here alone in the deeply shadowed privacy of the hall, the faint, fresh, manly scent of him sent her senses reeling. Lianne knew she had to get away from him as quickly as possible. She turned and started off down the hall.

Perversely, Adam refused to let her go. Reacting without thinking, he snared her by her arm, stopping her. "I agreed to see you to your room, and I will."

Lianne's expression was guarded as she looked from his hand up to his face. "There is really no need," she told him as she tried to ignore the feel of his touch.

"Lianne . . ." Adam's tone was husky as he gazed down at her in the duskiness of the dimly-lighted hallway. The simple contact of his hand upon her arm was electric. There was only Lianne and him, here, alone . . . Adam couldn't stop himself from slowly drawing her closer.

Lianne was caught up in the heat of his dark-eyed gaze. Entranced like a moth before a flame, she didn't resist as he pulled her near.

Her thoughts grew chaotic as she struggled with her own reactions to his touch. She tried to remember that this was the man who'd refused to sell her her home . . . the man who'd taken her innocence and then told her he was sorry and that it had all been a mistake! She hated him! She knew she did! Yet . . .

Adam bent to her then, his mouth descending to seek and find hers. Somewhere deep in the recesses of Adam's mind, he knew he shouldn't be doing this. He knew he should steer clear of Lianne. She was already a fire in his blood, and he knew it would only get worse if he tasted of her love again. Yet somehow, now that he was alone with her, he couldn't stop himself. It didn't matter to him that they were standing in the center of the hall and could easily be discovered at any moment. All that mattered was that he had to kiss her. He kissed her deeply, devouringly then, wanting to stir her to the heights again as he had that night.

A flush of fevered passion pulsed through Lianne as his mouth moved over hers. As much as she wanted to believe that she didn't desire Adam, that she hated him, her body responded wildly to his. Lianne clutched at his shoulders as she swayed toward him.

Adam broke off the kiss to gaze down at her. His eyes were a glittering reflection of the strength of his own desire. He kissed her again tenderly and felt her willing response. He drew back slightly as he slipped a supporting arm about her waist. With the gentlest of encouragement, he started to guide her toward his room, all the while pressing her close to his side.

Chapter Thirteen

For a moment Lianne went along with Adam. His kiss had been a very potent reminder of the ecstasy she had found in his arms. There was nothing she would have liked more than to forget everything and lose herself in the sweet heat of his embrace, but with the torrid memory of his loving also came the soul-chilling memory of the aftermath and his cruelty.

"No, Adam . . . no, we can't do this." With the last of her willpower Lianne stiffened and pulled away from him.

"You're a fool if you think you can deny this thing that exists between us," Adam declared hotly, trying to draw her back into his embrace.

"You said yourself that what happened between us was a mistake!" she countered, thinking of his betrayal.

Adam knew she was right. Logically, what was happening was all wrong, but he was beyond caring. Lianne was all he wanted, and he would not be denied. He gazed down at her, his dark eyes aglow with the fever of his desire.

"Lord, I know this is wrong . . . a mistake . . . but I want you, Lianne . . ." He groaned as he crushed her to his chest and kissed her. His hands tangled in the thickness of her hair as he held her close.

Adam's kiss started off almost forcefully, as if he sought to subdue her objections, but abruptly he changed. With the lightest of caresses his lips explored hers teasingly, seeking to coax from her that which he couldn't demand. He wanted her to give herself to him freely. He did not want to take her against her will.

Had Adam continued to be forceful with her, Lianne would have fought him, but when he became gentle, her resistance crumbled. Her slumbering passion stirred to life. As his lips left hers to seek out the sensitive cords of her throat, her need for him was stoked to a fever pitch.

"Oh, Adam . . ." Lianne sighed. She had fought this physical need for as long as she could, but she couldn't refuse him any longer. She was afire with the yearning to be his again. Willingly she looped her arms about his neck and returned his kiss fully.

Adam knew the moment Lianne surrendered. Without further hesitation, he lifted her into his arms and kissed her. Mindless to all but the need to be alone with her, he strode purposefully to his room and entered, closing and locking the door behind him.

The light from the lamp he'd left burning cast a golden glow about the room as Adam moved to the bed and lay Lianne upon it. He followed her down, not giving her time to think or protest. He wanted her too much. He needed her too much.

Protest was the furthest thing from Lianne's mind as she welcomed Adam to her with open arms. All rational thought had fled. Her response to him was elemental. Lianne was woman and Adam was man. As he moved over her, she eagerly caressed him, tracing the hard-muscled planes of his back and shoulders. She lifted her lips to accept his kiss, and she returned it full-measure. Her tongue boldly sought his in a hungry, challenging exchange.

Lianne's caresses thrilled Adam, and he gave full rein to his own desires. With a quiet sense of urgency, he unfastened her gown and slipped it from her shoulders.

He managed to untie the narrow ribbon at the top of her chemise, but the buttons gave him a moment of trouble. Lianne wanted nothing more than to feel the touch of his lips upon her aching breasts and so she brazenly helped him.

Adam held his breath as he watched her loose the three tiny buttons. When she finished she looked up at him and smiled a heated, seductive smile of invitation. His gaze shifted from her passion-flushed face to the partially exposed, creamy swell of pale flesh.

"You're beautiful, Lianne," he murmured thickly as he stared down at her in sensual appreciation. He kissed her once, softly, briefly, and then shifted his weight lower. It seemed to Adam that he was moving in almost slow motion as he bent to press his lips to the partially exposed tops of her breasts.

"Adam . . ." Lianne gasped as he brushed the delicate fabric aside and captured one pert peak with his lips. As he suckled erotically at her breast a surge of excitement jolted through her, centering and coiling deep in the womanly core of her body. Feverishly, she began to move against him, wanting him to fill the aching emptiness within her.

In answer to her unspoken demand, Adam pressed himself intimately to her. Moving his hips seductively against her, he let her feel the proof of his own matching desire.

Lianne caught her breath as hot, glorious warmth flooded her loins. She held his head to her, enraptured by the glorious feeling of his kisses upon her bosom.

Adam moved to claim her lips again as his hands worked at freeing her from her gown. They parted only briefly to divest themselves of their clothing and then came back together in an explosive embrace. Their need for oneness rendered them mindless. Hands touched and caressed, trailing patterns of fire over their already feverish bodies. Their lips met and lingered in arousing exchanges that incited their passions to even greater heights.

No longer willing to be separate from her, Adam parted her thighs and settled between them. Lianne could feel the heat of his manhood pressing against her, and she reached down to caress him and urge him on. The emptiness she was feeling was far too painful. She needed to be a part of Adam, to hold him deep within her body and to once more know the fullness of his love.

Adam needed no further encouragement. Covering her hand with his, he guided himself to the secret heart of her and sheathed himself in her body. Lianne arched to him, loving the feeling of being joined in such intimacy. When he began to move, she matched his rhythm.

No longer completely innocent of love's ways, Lianne wanted to try to please Adam. Her hands were never still as she explored the strength of his driving hips. Writhing beneath him in rapturous splendor, she could feel her own peak of excitement building. With each kiss and touch, she grew closer and closer to that tumultous release only Adam could give her. As the frenetic pace of their joining quickened, her desire crested. Wave after wave of heart-stopping ecstasy washed through her, taking her to the ultimate joy and beyond.

Adam knew Lianne had reached the pinnacle, and the knowledge that he'd taken her to the heights sent his own passions spiraling out of control. He joined her in that delirious perfection, peaking in a throbbing, soul-stirring climax. Clasped together, their breathing ragged, their bodies damp from the exhaustive exertion of their mating, they lay silently enthralled.

Lianne's eyes were closed as she hugged Adam fiercely to her. Never in her wildest dreams had she imagined that anything could be so completely overwhelming. She felt drained, yet she also felt sated. It made no sense, yet it made perfect sense. This was where she wanted to be . . . where she felt safe and protected and shielded from all of life's ugliness. She drifted off to sleep then, borne away by a heavy velvet drowsiness that momentarily cloaked the terrible truth from her.

Adam lay perfectly still, his arms holding Lianne cradled tightly against him. He did not want to let her go. He wanted to hold her forever. In all his experience, Adam had never known such ecstasy. What he found with Lianne surpassed anything he'd ever known, and he didn't want it to end. He wanted the serenity and peace he found only in her arms. He needed it. . . . The thought faded as exhaustion claimed him.

Lianne opened her eyes and blinked in stunned disbelief. She was in Adam's bed, wrapped securely in his most intimate embrace. Sleepy confusion filled her as she fought to remember how she'd come to be here. She stared at Adam, thinking that in repose he looked much younger, almost boyish. Lianne smiled to herself as she thought him the most handsome man in the whole world.

Adam must have sensed that she'd come awake, for he too stirred and opened his eyes. He was relaxed in her arms for a moment, but then he suddenly tensed. With a stricken conscience, he realized that once again he'd been weak in letting his passion for Lianne overrule his common sense. He had no business letting his emotions get out of hand like this. The complications that could result would be too far-reaching.

Yet, even as he knew that he had to stay completely away from her for her sake and for his own, Adam didn't want to leave her. She was so warm and giving.

He felt as if the circle of her arms was a rare haven in the storm of his life, but that was a tempest into which he dared not bring her.

Cursing himself for his weakness, Adam released her and moved away. He hardened his heart as he went. At whatever cost, he had to put Lianne from him mentally and physically and keep her from him. This would be the last time he ever allowed himself a lapse of control.

Adam sat up on the edge of the bed, taking care to keep his back to her. He didn't want to look at her. He didn't want to gaze upon her lovely body and remember the glory of her limbs entwined with his and the ecstasy of possessing her. He wanted to forget everything about her. He had to get control of himself and this crazy desire he had for her. Nervously, he raked a hand through his hair.

"Adam . . ." Lianne almost sighed his name as she watched the fascinating play of muscles across his back.

With a caressing hand, Lianne reached out to Adam, and it shocked her when he flinched at her touch and stood up. His reaction jarred her to the depths of her soul. He had claimed in the hall that they couldn't deny what was happening between them, yet now that they'd made love, he was coldly dismissing her. Lianne suddenly felt cheapened, used.

Fury filled her. Uncle Antoine had used her, taking what he could from her estate without giving any thought at all to her well-being. Now, Adam had used her, too, but in a different, even more devastating way. He had wanted her, and he had taken her. It had been a purely physical thing for him. What made her even angrier was that she had allowed it. A firm resolve stiffened Lianne. She would not be used by him or any other man ever again. Without further hesitation, she flew from the bed and began to dress.

"Damn you!" Lianne cried as she pulled on her clothing. Tears stung her eyes, but she refused to let them fall.

Adam reacted instinctively. In a flash, he was in front of her, grabbing her by the wrist as she would have stormed from the room. "Where do you think you're going?"

"What do you care?" she challenged viciously. "You got what you wanted, didn't you!"

Adam's stony expression didn't change at her accusation, and he made no effort to deny it.

A torrent of emotion welled up inside of Lianne. It was true . . . all of it . . . She glared at him furiously. "This is the last time I'll ever let you use me, Adam Trent!" Snatching her arm free of his grip, she rushed from the room without looking back.

Becky and Beau strolled together around the massive rotunda of the hotel, wandering idly though the galleries and arcades.

"What's going on between Adam and Lianne?" Beau asked in his usual point-blank manner.

"Why do you ask?" Becky paused in their walk to give him a curious look. She had begun to think that she was imagining things between them.

"Adam was acting strangely tonight. I mean, we had met earlier in the day, and his mood seemed regular enough, but tonight . . ." Beau shook his head in puzzlement.

"I know," she agreed, giving credence to his suspicions.

"She's a gorgeous woman," he said, "and yet when he spoke of her this morning, I got the impression from the way he was talking that she was just a young girl."

Beau's first remark annoyed Becky. Why did he notice how pretty Lianne was and not pay any attention to her? Becky put the thought from her as quickly as she thought it. She had absolutely no reason to be jealous of Lianne. Lianne was her friend.

"I think Adam may be attracted to her and doesn't know how to handle it. It's not as if things are normal for him right now," Becky confided.

"No. They're not, are they?" Beau was talking more to himself than Becky.

"Did Adam tell you how Lianne tried to run us off with a shotgun the first time we met her?"

Beau threw back his head and laughed at the thought. "No, but I'll bet that was something to see."

"It was." Becky laughed lightly as she remembered Adam's frustration. As she went on and told him the whole story, Beau listened intently.

"So, not only is Lianne beautiful, she's smart, too." He paused as he considered his friend's predicament. Adam might be attracted to Lianne and forced to live in close quarters with her, but his responsibility as he saw it was to Elise and to his mock, unannounced engagement to Suzanne. Adam was trapped. It was no wonder his mood had been black. Poor Adam.

"I like her a lot. She's going to help me fix up the house and grounds so it'll be ready for the party we're giving." Becky was pleased that she'd managed to bring their conversation around to something other than Adam and Lianne. "Are you going to come?"

"This is the first I've heard about it. When are you having it?" Beau asked, pretending not to know anything about the upcoming party.

"Probably in about a month. I'm sure it'll take me that long to get everything in order."

"If I'm in port, I'll make it a point to be there."

"Good." Becky couldn't prevent the happiness she felt from reflecting in her voice. Her mood was so lighthearted as they headed back upstairs that she took

Beau's arm without a second thought. It almost felt like her dream come true as she walked beside him. With childish delight, she let her imagination run away with her, pretending to be his and his alone, pretending that they were on their honeymoon and were going to live happily together for the rest of their lives. Had she known of Beau's real thoughts, she would have been hurt and angry.

Beau was wondering how to spend the rest of the night. He'd thoroughly enjoyed his lively assignation with Katie earlier that evening, and since he wasn't due back at the *Sea Shadow* until daybreak, he was seriously considering returning to the saloon to see her again. The thought appealed.

"Which room is yours?" he asked as they reached the correct floor.

"It's down near the other end," Becky told him, all the while trying to think of a way to make him take notice of her. Brazenly, she considered inviting him into her room, but she quickly discarded that idea. Once she got him in there, she wasn't sure exactly what to do with him. Oh, she had a glimmer of an idea about what went on between a man and a woman, but since she'd never done more than kiss a boyfriend when she was sixteen, she had no idea of how to go about seducing a man as worldly as Beau. She realized with some despair that this was not going to be easy, but, she decided silently, whatever it took, she was going to do it. She was going to marry Beau Hamilton. "This is my room," she admitted reluctantly as they reached the correct door.

Gentleman that he was, Beau took her key from her, unlocked the door, and then handed it back. "Good night, Becky."

"Good night, Beau." Becky repeated dutifully, and then knew a moment of consternation as he gave her a quick, brotherly peck on the cheek and headed off down the hall.

She almost screamed her frustration. Beau was getting away! All her efforts to look beautiful for him, all her flirting and planning, had been for nothing! Beau was leaving, and she wouldn't get to see him again for weeks and weeks!

"Beau!" she called out to him before she realized what she was doing. "Beau, wait!"

"What is it?" Beau paused to look back, puzzled by her call.

It was then that Becky ran to him and, without preamble, threw her arms around his neck and pulled his head down to hers for a kiss, full on the mouth. Becky put every ounce of knowledge she had about kissing into that exchange. With the utmost of loving enthusiasm, she pressed her lips to his in her best effort to communicate all the emotion she felt for him.

For a moment Beau was stunned and stood stock-still with his arms akimbo. The sudden awareness of her as a woman full-grown left him perplexed. He wasn't quite sure how to react to the soft feel of her very enticing curves against him. This was Becky, for heaven's sake! Beau finally had enough sense to gently grip her upper arms and move slightly away from her.

"Becky," he began firmly, intending to tell her that her behavior was not quite proper, but the look in her eyes stopped him. "Good night, Becky."

Becky had put her all into that kiss, and she was mortified that Beau could end it so easily and with such coolness. A painful flush stained her checks, and she was grateful for the shadows in the hall that hid her embarrassment from him.

"Good night, Beau," she whispered, then turned and fled to the safety of her room.

Beau watched her go, feeling slightly bewildered. He

had never thought of Becky as a mature female before, and the recognition troubled him. Of course she was lovely, but she had always been lovely. Even as a young girl, she'd had the looks of an angel, and her beauty had only improved with her maturing. He gave a slight shake of his head. Ladies' man that he was, he wondered why he'd never noticed her before. She'd grown up right before his eyes and, until this moment, he'd never realized it.

Still, he reminded himself, Becky was Adam's sister. She was not fair game. She was sweet and pretty and completely untouchable. Beau knew there was no point in even thinking about tempting himself, and he knew he'd have to be more careful not to be alone with Becky in the future.

The hotel's bar was doing a booming business as Beau entered and glanced around. His encounter with Becky had left him feeling in need of a drink, but the thought of returning to visit Katie at the other saloon had faded in appeal. He was surprised to see Adam standing alone at the far end of the bar nursing a drink.

Adam noticed someone heading his way and cringed inwardly when he realized it was Beau. He'd needed some time by himself to sort out his thoughts, but it was obvious he wasn't going to get any.

"I wondered what you had in mind for the rest of the night," Beau chided as he joined him.

"Now you know," Adam responded brusquely.

Immediately Beau sensed that his tense mood at dinner had not lessened. If anything, his friend seemed even more on edge. He ordered a beer and drank most of it in silence, waiting for Adam to speak first. When he did, Beau was surprised by his request.

"I want to start sailing with you as much as possible once everything is set up with Suzanne," Adam said as he drank the last of his bourbon.

Beau was tempted to question him, but waited. "All right."

"I figure now that I know the way, it'll be relatively easy to slip in and out through the bayous. We can set up a rendezvous point and specify meeting times."

"No problem."

"Good."

"After our meeting earlier, I made plans to head out again tomorrow. Do you want to sail with us?"

The prospect of being back on his boat out on the Gulf lifted his spirits. He'd been away from the sea for far too long. He needed to feel the roll of the deck beneath his feet again and the sea breeeze in his face.

"I'll leave word for Becky at the desk that I've been detained here in town on business. She'll understand. They were planning on going back to Belle Arbor tomorrow anyway. There's no reason why they can't make the return trip without me." Adam turned away from the bar. "I'll go pack and meet you in the rotunda."

Chapter Fourteen

As the carriage made its way toward Belle Arbor the following afternoon, Lianne and Becky sat silently while Alex napped, curled on the seat next to his sister, his head resting on her lap. For the women, the trip home seemed to be taking forever. They were both exhausted, for they had passed a restless night. Haunted by thoughts of what had happened to them respectively, neither had been able to sleep.

Lianne's night had been interminable, for she'd been unable to excuse herself of partial guilt in making love with Adam. She could have refused to go with him, but she hadn't. He had only had to touch her, and she'd fallen willingly into his arms. Even now in the carriage with Becky and Alex, the memory of Adam's glorious possession set her pulses to racing.

Lianne cursed the desire she felt for Adam and renewed her vow of hatred. All night she had dreaded facing him this morning, knowing it was going to be miserably awkward. She had also loathed the prospect of the trip home in such close quarters with him. Yet, when Becky had informed her that Adam wouldn't be joining them today or returning to the plantation with them, she found herself irrationally angry. She supposed she was lucky that she didn't have to see him. Certainly, she had nothing left to say to him, but his very absence infuriated her. She found herself wondering just where he was and what he was doing.

Becky sat lost in thought as the carriage rumbled on over the rough roads. She had been longing to tell Lianne how she'd kissed Beau so brazenly ever since they'd met early that morning for breakfast, but with Alex along, she'd had to keep it to herself. Now that the youngster had finally fallen asleep, she could keep still no longer. She had to tell Lianne everything that had happened.

"I think I may have ruined any chance I ever had with Beau last night," Becky finally admitted to Lianne.

Lianne looked up at her friend in concern. "What happened?"

A slow flush crept into her cheeks as she answered, "We had a lovely time, just Beau and I. We walked all through the arcades and talked and laughed." She paused, remembering, and then sighed. "But then, when he walked me up to my room . . ."

At Becky's hesitation, Lianne's heart sank. She hoped and prayed with all her might that her friend hadn't succumbed to Beau's lethal charm.

"Well . . . well, I kissed him!" she blurted it out. Once she'd said it, her reserve was gone, and she started to cry.

"That's wonderful!" Lianne tried to bolster Becky's feelings as she searched her reticule for a clean, lacy handkerchief. "Here." She handed it to her and then asked, "Now, tell me, why are you crying? You wanted him to kiss you, didn't you?"

"Of course," Becky managed, trying to bring her tears under control. "But, you see, he didn't kiss *me* . . . *I* kissed *him!*" The thought of her humiliation renewed her crying.

"So, you kissed Beau?" Lianne repeated, confused. "Was it that terrible?"

"Oh, no," she answered quickly, still sniffing. "It was wonderful, but it was awful, too, because Beau didn't

169

really kiss me back. I mean, he didn't feel a thing. He broke it off and just stood there. I was so embarrassed."

"What did he say?"

"Not a thing, except a very firm 'Good night, Becky.' "

"That's it?"

She nodded in response. "I mean, I put my everything into that kiss, and he just stood there! I could have died."

"Now, don't give up yet," Lianne encouraged.

"How can you say that?"

"You can never tell what a man is thinking," she lectured, knowing from her own personal experience just how true that was. "Who knows? Maybe he broke it off because he did feel something. You'll just have to wait and see. How soon until you see him again?"

"Not for weeks and weeks." Becky mourned the thought of endless days without seeing Beau. "He said he'd come to the party if he's in port."

"Good. Then all you have to do right now is put him from your mind and start concentrating on the party. Before you know it, all those weeks will be over, and Beau will be back." As Lianne advised Becky, she also took her own words to heart. If she just managed to keep herself busy, the months until her birthday would pass much more quickly.

"We do have a lot to do," she agreed, her expression turning more thoughtful as her crying stopped. "Where shall we start first?"

The balance of the ride passed quickly as they immersed themselves in planning the restoration of the house. It was only when their carriage turned up the main drive that they realized they'd made it home already.

"Look, Lianne." Becky was pointing out her window toward the unknown carriage that was tied up in front of the house. "We've got company. Do you know who it is?"

Lianne leaned over slightly to get a better view and suddenly went rigid. She recognized the carriage all right! It was Suzanne Labadie's! What was she doing here? Lianne had hoped she would never have to see her again as long as she lived.

"Lianne?" She'd noticed the tenseness in her manner and was puzzled by it.

"Yes, I know who it is," she replied flatly. "It's Suzanne Labadie."

"Oh, Suzanne must have come over for a visit . . ." Becky was not especially fond of the woman, but held no great dislike for her, either. "She's got a plantation nearby, doesn't she?" When Lianne didn't answer immediately, she glanced over at her to see what was wrong. Becky was shocked to see that Lianne had gone deathly pale. "Lianne? What is it? What's the matter?"

"Nothing," she said quietly as she drew a deep breath and girded herself to face the woman she hated most in the whole world.

Before Becky could ask anything else, their carriage drew to a halt. Lianne woke Alex, and leaving him to get out at his own sleepy pace, she hurriedly descended from the conveyance and started up the steps into the house. Suzanne had no business being here, and Lianne wanted her out of the house and off Ducharme property! She stormed through the door and came face to face with Suzanne.

"Ah, here they come now, Sarah. I won't be needing you anymore. You can go," Suzanne dismissed the servant coldly.

Sarah looked from Lianne to Suzanne and quickly backed from the hallway.

"Hello, Lianne."

"What are you doing here?" Lianne demanded

171

sharply, her color high as her fury grew unbounded. She didn't want this woman defiling her home with her presence. "I told you never to set foot on Belle Arbor again! How dare you show up here!"

"It's my understanding, Lianne, that you're no longer the owner of Belle Arbor." Suzanne's look was smug as she delivered the cutting setdown.

Lianne blanched at her deliberate cruelty.

"Suzanne . . ." Becky made a sweeping entrance just then. She'd heard Suzanne's vicious remark and wanted to save Lianne from further embarrassment. "How wonderful that you've stopped by!" she greeted the other woman with pseudo-warmth.

"Becky, dear. It's so good to see you," Suzanne moved past Lianne to give Becky a social hug.

"It's good to see you, too, and you're timing is just perfect," she went on. "Lianne, Alex and I have just this minute returned from a trip to New Orleans. If you'd been any earlier, you'd have missed us."

"I'm glad I didn't," she replied, quite pleased that she'd put Lianne in her place.

"Come on into the parlor so we can chat for a while." Becky realized that there was something desperately wrong with Lianne, so she played the gracious hostess to the hilt as she ushered Suzanne ahead of her.

"If you'll excuse me, I need to freshen up a bit," Lianne lied, really needing only to escape.

"Of course, Lianne," Suzanne purred as she moved on into the parlor. "It was lovely seeing you again, and you, too, Alex." She spoke to the youngster as he entered the house belatedly.

As soon as she was out of sight, Alex turned on his sister. "What's *she* doing here?" he demanded angrily.

"Visiting Becky, I guess," Lianne answered as she started up the stairs.

"Or Adam," he muttered as he trailed after her.

"What did you say?" Lianne stopped and took him by the arm.

"She probably just came to see Adam," Alex shrugged.

"Why would she do that?"

"'Cause they're friends. Adam told me so the day I showed him how to get to Willow Bend through the bayou."

Lianne felt her knees go weak. "Adam has visited Suzanne?"

Alex nodded. "I waited for him down at the dock. I didn't want to go see her. Adam sure was gone a long time."

His youthful honesty seared her already battered emotions. Adam was seeing Suzanne . . . The pain was almost unbearable. It had been terrible enough when Mark had fallen prey to her cunning ways, but the thought of Adam with Suzanne deepened her despair.

"I see . . ." Lianne kept her tone as indifferent as she could. She did not want Alex to suspect that anything had upset her. After all, what Adam did was Adam's business. She certainly had no interest in him, she told herself. "Tell you what, why don't you run down to the kitchen and see what Sarah's got for you to eat. I'm going to change clothes and get comfortable, and then I'll be down to join you in a little while. All right?"

"All right!" At the thought of food, Alex's eyes lit up. He charged off down the steps and disappeared toward the back of the house as Lianne moved slowly on up the steps, her shoulders slumped in weary defeat.

"I understand from Adam that you're planning to do a little fixing up around here?" Suzanne remarked cattily as she glanced around the parlor.

"Yes. In fact, that's why we went into town. I had

173

some things I needed to order before we could begin."

"Thank heaven," she sighed exaggeratedly. "This place is so run-down. Why, the Ducharmes have practically let it fall down around their ears. It was such a pretty place once."

Her observations stung Becky, for she knew just how hard Lianne had worked to keep the place going. "And it will be again," she told her firmly.

"Oh, I'm sure, now that Adam owns it," Suzanne returned. "Where is he, by the way? He sent me a note saying that he'd be back today."

This was news to Becky. She had no idea that her brother maintained that close of a relationship with Suzanne. "Adam was held up on business in town. I'm not sure how soon he's going to return. It could be as long as a few days, I suspect."

Suzanne was disappointed and it showed. "I had hoped to see him today."

"Is there anything I can do?"

"Oh, no. This was purely personal," Suzanne confided as she stood up. "Well, I suppose I'll be going since he isn't here."

"I'm sorry he didn't make it back, but I'll be sure to tell him of your visit as soon as he arrives."

"That'll be fine."

When Becky had seen Suzanne off, she went back inside and immediately went upstairs to Lianne's room. "Lianne!" she called out as she knocked on her door.

"What do you want, Becky?" came her tired answer.

"I think we need to talk."

There was a long, silent pause, and then the door slowly opened to admit her. Lianne felt almost betrayed by the Trents' association with Suzanne, and she held herself aloof as she faced Becky, forcing her to speak first.

"Lianne, do you want to tell me about it?"

"About what?"

"I heard what Suzanne said to you. She seemed quite pleased with your misfortune."

"I'm sure she is," Lianne answered bitterly as she crossed the room and stood before the window. She stared out across the fertile fields that had once belonged to her family, her body rigid, her hands clinched. "You see she's responsible for it all."

"What?" Becky was aghast at the news.

Lianne quickly explained how Mark had died. "I vowed that I'd never let that woman set foot on Belle Arbor again . . ." she finished fiercely.

"I can understand why," Becky sympathized. "I'll do my best to slight her from now on." As she spoke she could see the tension ease from Lianne.

"Thank you," Lianne said gratefully. It was difficult enough for her to assume the role of guest in what had been her own home, but the possibility of having Suzanne visiting there regularly would have been more than she could bear.

"How about coming back downstairs with me? We can get something to eat. It's been a while since we last ate." Becky wanted to lighten their mood.

"I think I'll just lie down for a while," Lianne declined. "I didn't sleep very well last night, and the trip back was tiring."

"Alex was the lucky one. He got to sleep practically the whole way. I'll see you downstairs later then."

When Becky had gone, Lianne did curl up on the comfort of her wide bed. The memory of her disastrous encounter with Adam along with Suzanne's snideness tormented her, and she closed her eyes, hoping to block it all out. If she never saw either of them again as long as she lived, she'd be happy. She drifted off peacefully, welcoming the blissful oblivion of sleep, for only in slumber was she safe from the hurt and anxiety of her real life.

Suzanne was in a spiteful mood as she slammed into her room and started to undress. Her excursion to Belle Arbor had been a wasted effort. Adam had not returned. In irritation, she rang for Rosie.

"I want my trunk packed immediately."

"Ma'am?" The servant stared at her in confusion.

"I said pack my things!" she snapped. "I'm going into New Orleans for a few days!"

Recognizing the anger in her tone, Rosie rushed to do as she was told. Miss Suzanne's vile temper was legendary, and the maid knew it was wise to keep a very low profile whenever she was mad. With the utmost of efficiency, she arranged her mistress's things and then went to help her dress.

"Have the carriage brought around," Suzanne ordered after she'd changed into a traveling gown.

"Yes, ma'am."

"And if anyone should come calling while I'm away, tell them I should be back by the week's end."

Rosie nodded and rushed out of the bedroom to see to her wishes.

Later, ensconced in the comfort of her plush carriage, Suzanne thought back over the course of the afternoon and realized that it hadn't been a total loss. At least, she'd gotten to face down Lianne Ducharme and put her in her place. Suzanne gave a throaty laugh as she gloated over the other woman's misfortunes. She knew that ever since Lianne's brother had been killed in that ridiculous duel, Lianne had hated her. Now, it served her right to have lost everything. She was as stupid as her brother had been.

As quickly as she thought of the Ducharmes, she

dismissed them. Instead, she turned her full attention to thinking of Adam. Suzanne sighed. She hadn't seen him for a few days, and she missed him. Night after night she tossed and turned in her bed as she imagined having him there with her. She could hardly wait to announce their engagement, and she was even more excited about their wedding. She hoped that Adam wouldn't mind a very short engagement. She didn't want to wait a minute longer than necessary to become Mrs. Adam Trent.

That was precisely the reason for her trip to New Orleans. Since Adam was going to be busy for the next few days, she thought she would take the opportunity to visit her dressmaker and order the gown she wanted for her engagement party. She also decided to start looking at pictures of wedding dresses. Suzanne wanted the most beautiful gown ever created for her marriage to Adam.

A smile curved her lips as she pictured the ceremony in her mind. She would make sure it was the biggest and the best New Orleans had ever seen.

A vague sense of worry nagged at her as Shark entered her thoughts. She had no idea how he would react to the news of her engagement, and frankly, she told herself bravely, she didn't care. Adam was the man she loved. Shark had just been a passing fancy. Suzanne was certain that once she had Adam in her bed, she would never want or need another man.

The thought of making love to Adam sent a thrill through Suzanne. She wondered suddenly if there was any possibility that she might be able to casualy catch up with him while he was still in town. It certainly would be wonderful to spend a few days together dining out on the town and visiting friends. Surely there would be any number of social events they could attend together. Then perhaps, just perhaps, she could entice him into her bed. The fantasy appealed, and she passed the rest of the ride imagining how wonderful it was going to be to lie in Adam's arms.

Adam stood at the rail of the *Sea Shadow*, his legs braced against the rolling deck, his face turned into the wind. The salt spray stung, but he made no effort to look away. The sea had been the main driving force of his life for as long as he could remember. He loved it. This was where he belonged.

Adam's mood had been harsh when they'd come aboard, and Beau, not wanting to suffer his company any longer than necessary, had been quick to leave him to his own devices. Now, as he stared out across the blue-green waters, he could feel his perspective returning. Lianne had accused him of using her, and, as much as he wanted to deny it, he knew he had. He was 'engaged' to Suzanne, Elise needed him more than ever, and yet he'd been unable to stay away from Lianne.

Adam drew a steadying breath as he remembered the absolute ecstasy of her embrace. He realized then that making love to Lianne had been the most beautiful thing that had ever happened in his life, and with that thought came both guilt and remorse. He was bound in a web of intrigue and shattered promises. He was trapped in an existence that couldn't include Lianne. His future offered no bright tomorrow, no hope.

As painful as it had been to let Lianne go the night before, Adam admitted to himself that it had been for the best. There could be no doubt after the scene last night that Lianne hated him completely, and that was good. If she hated him, she would make it a point to avoid him.

Adam knew he'd done the right thing in leaving town with Beau. A few days at sea would help him get a better grip on his emotions, so he could follow through with what needed to be done . . . catching Shark. The memory of the pirate and the raid renewed his resolve to exact his revenge. Soon they would have him trapped and then it would be over—for everyone except Elise . . . Adam gripped the rail tightly, the dull ache of his despair clutching at his heart. Once his future had seemed so promising, and now, all his dreams had ended even before they'd had a chance to begin.

Turning away from the sea, he started back across the deck to seek out Beau. It was best to keep constantly busy. There was less time to think that way.

Chapter Fifteen

David Williams leaned forward to rest his elbows on his desktop. In a bone-weary motion he rubbed the back of his neck and then rotated his broad shoulders to loosen the cramped muscles there. He was tired, so very tired. He had just spent hours going over his notes regarding his treatment of Elise Clayton, and still he could find no clue to the secret of unlocking her terror and freeing her from her mute existence.

Usually a very patient man, David found himself growing more and more angry over his lack of success. Frustration gripped him, and he was beginning to suspect that he'd imagined that one moment of sanity he'd seen reflected in Elise's eyes weeks ago. He wanted to believe that it had happened, but he'd made no progress with her in all this time.

In a moment of totally uncharacteristic fury, David lost control and slammed his fist down on the desk. "Damn! There's got to be a way! There's got to! I can't let her go on like this . . ."

Only when he became consciously aware of the pain in his hand did David realize for the first time the power of his fury and how personally involved he'd become in this case. The recognition of the depth of his feelings of Elise gave him pause. He'd always made it a rule never to allow himself any personal feelings where his patients were concerned. Yet the thought of the young beauty, silent for so long now, touched him deeply. She was so lovely . . .

David resolved firmly that no matter what the other experts said, he would never give up hope. Some day, some way, he was going to reach her.

Though it was late at night, a single lamp was burning at full brightness on the dresser in Elise's room.

Lying on the bed, Elise stared about the strange bedroom in supreme confusion. She was certain that she wasn't at home. Her room was pink and white. This room was done in shades of pale yellow and gold. *Where was she?* She sat up a bit too abruptly, and a wave of dizziness forced her to lie back down. Lifting a shaking hand to her forehead, Elise frowned as she tried to remember.

Distant, hazy memories came to her slowly at first — memories that were warm and soft and gentle . . . memories of home and her aunt . . . memories of a man's voice . . . tender, coaxing, soothing. *Did she know someone named David?* she wondered, and then, at that instant, everything in her mind sharpened to crystal clarity. A shaft of ultimate terror jarred through her. There was no one named David. There was only Adam, the ship, and those men!

To keep herself from screaming, Elise bit down on her hand so hard that she drew blood. She didn't want to remember. She didn't want to relive those horrible events that had devastated not only her body but also her very soul. *Why hadn't she died too, just like Aunt Odile?* She cursed the fates that had treated her so cruelly. If she had died, at least then she would have been at peace.

With all the strength she could muster, she frantically withdrew from the horror. The black veil of protection that shielded her from the agonizing torment descended, blotting out the savagery that haunted her. Surrendering willingly to the comfort of its forgetfulness, Elise let herself slip away from the pain. It was so easy to do . . . to just let go . . .

The sun was up. It had been for over an hour. The birds had already ceased calling out their morning greeting. The new day was well under way.

Huddled in her bed, Lianne lay in quiet misery. Normally, she was the first one up in the morning, but today, as for the past several days, she'd been unable to muster even the most elemental energy. The last thing she felt like doing was getting out of bed. She was completely worn out. Lately, it seemed as if she couldn't get enough sleep no matter how early she went to bed.

As she remained curled up under the covers, Lianne wondered if she was getting sick. She felt terrible, and along with being tired all the time, her stomach had started to act up. No matter what combination of foods she ate in the morning, nothing seemed to agree with her. This morning, she was feeling so awful that she decided not to even think about food. But in trying to not think about it, she thought about it and her stomach churned madly.

Dragging herself from the bed, she had just enough time to make it to the chamber pot. Wretchedly she clutched her arms about her waist as her body was wracked with spasms. When nature had resolved itself, Lianne leaned weakly against one bedpost. Her limbs were quaking as she tried to steady herself. Her face was ashen.

The knock at the door startled Lianne, though she didn't know just why. Surely everyone was wondering where she was by now. "Who is it?"

"It's Sarah, Miss Lianne."

"Oh . . ." She had no strength left to say any more.

When Lianne had not appeared for her usual early breakfast, Sarah had been puzzled. Lianne hadn't been acting herself for a long time now, not that she could blame her young mistress for being upset over the loss of her home. Yet as well as she knew Lianne, Sarah felt it was more than that.

Ever since Lianne had returned from that short trip to New Orleans five weeks ago and run into that no-good Labadie woman, she had become more and more quiet. The fact that Suzanne Labadie now made regular calls on Mr. Adam whenever he was in residence had only deepened Lianne's withdrawal. She rarely laughed anymore. She was eating less and less, and she often chose to skip dinner with Miss Becky and Mr. Adam.

As Sarah pondered Lianne's actions, she slowly came to realize that the only time her mistress acted anything like her normal self was when Mr. Adam was away on one of his business trips. The connection surprised her. She knew Lianne had no use for Belle Arbor's new owner, but she had not thought that she hated him so much it would cause her to lose her appetite. Certainly, neither one of them went out of their way to speak to the other. It seemed to Sarah that they just tolerated each other.

Still, Sarah suspected that there was something very serious troubling Lianne. After waiting nearly an hour for her to come down to eat, she finally decided to check on her. She wasn't sure how to help Lianne, or even if she could, but she wanted to let her know that she was there if she needed her.

Sarah opened the door and came face to face with her mistress. One look at her pale face and frightened eyes sent her rushing to her side.

"Miss Lianne, honey, what's wrong?" She helped her

back into bed.

"I guess I'm sick, Sarah," Lianne answered as she lay back down and pulled the covers protectively up to her chin.

"From what I can see, there ain't no guessing about it," Sarah hustled to help make her comfortable. "Have you been sick all night?"

"No. It's just in the mornings . . ." she replied faintly as she closed her eyes.

At her words, Sarah went still. *In the mornings?* "You mean you've been sick like this on other mornings?" She fought to keep the sharpness out of her tone.

Lianne nodded slowly. "For about a week now, I guess, but usually by afternoon I'm feeling all right."

"Why didn't you tell me sooner?" she asked soothingly.

She shrugged slightly. "I kept thinking it would go away, but it hasn't . . ."

"No, it sure hasn't," Sarah agreed as she picked up the chamber pot. "I'm going to clean this up, and then I'll be back with a cup of tea for you. That should help settle your stomach."

Again, Lianne only gave a nod and didn't even open her eyes when Sarah left the room. She trusted her friend completely. If anyone could help her to feel better, it would be Sarah.

As the servant bustled down to the kitchen to prepare the tea, her mind was racing. *Lianne was sick, but only in the mornings . . . She always felt better by the afternoon.* The symptoms were there, but how could it be? She'd had no men callers. Adam was the only man Lianne had had any contact with, but her dislike of him was plain. She avoided him like the plague. Surely there was no way . . .

Sarah stopped what she was doing and frowned. Her smooth brow furrowed at the thought of Lianne pregnant with Adam's child. She shook her head in confusion and denial. Picking up the tray, she headed back upstairs, wanting to believe in her heart that her mistress just had a touch of sickness that would soon pass.

Sarah didn't bother to knock when she reached Lianne's room. She entered quietly, and then took care to make sure the door was closed firmly behind her. She kept her expression blank as she approached the bed with the tea.

"I want you to sit up and take a few sips of this for me," she instructed. "It should help settle your stomach real quick."

Lianne hadn't had the strength to move while Sarah was gone, and she'd barely acknowledged her return. The hope that something just might help her feel better encouraged her to at least make the attempt. Biting her lip to fight back the threatening nausea, she levered herself up to a sitting position.

Sarah had already set the tray on the bedside table and she hurried to position Lianne's pillows supportively behind her. "There now," she spoke comfortingly. "Just try a little of this. That should be all it'll take."

"Do you really think it'll help?" Lianne lifted her gaze questioningly to Sarah's.

"We'll know real soon now, won't we? Go on, have a drink." Sarah tried to lighten the mood with her casualness, but all the while she wanted to tell Lianne that the special tea she'd prepared for her had worked wonders for her mother when she'd been pregnant with Alex.

Lianne took a small sip from the delicate china cup, grimacing slightly at the brew's hot bitterness. "Ugh . . . what is this?" she asked.

"It's an herb tea. It should help settle your stomach, but you're going to have to drink more than that."

Dutifully, Lianne swallowed another mouthful and then sat back and waited. At any minute she expected her stomach to rebel at the intrusion, but if anything the magical potion seemed to ease her distress. She drank again, a little more deeply this time.

"Does it seem to be staying down?" Sarah ventured as she moved about the bedroom straightening things.

"It really does seem to be helping," Lianne confessed to Sarah, her expression reflecting her delight at the discovery. "I feel much better already. Where did you learn to make it?"

"I always fixed it for your mama," Sarah told her easily as she kept picking up the room. "When she was pregnant, her stomach would act up, and this tea was the only thing that helped."

When she was pregnant . . . Lianne had heard no more of Sarah's explanation than that. She sat stunned, the tea cup poised in midair, halfway to her lips. Could it be? *No . . . No . . . No . . .* she screamed silently.

Yet even as Lianne tried to logically refute the possibility, she was suddenly aware of a myriad of things that had changed in her body. Lianne had paid little attention when her monthly flux was late. It was not unusual for her times to be erratic, and, considering the stress she'd been under, she hadn't really thought it that surprising. Now, however, the absence took on a whole new significance. How late was she? A week? Two or three? A quick mental calculation sent a shiver through her. She was more than three weeks overdue.

Lianne swallowed nervously. She glanced to where the older woman stood openly regarding her now. It occurred to her then that Sarah had known right away while she had been so unaware.

How could it have happened? They had only been together those two times. Lianne's hands began to shake so badly that she was forced to set the tea cup down. She blushed painfully as she met Sarah's eyes.

"Have you been with a man, Lianne?" Sarah's tone

was not condeming. It was warm and encouraging and filled with understanding.

It took Lianne a long moment to find her voice. "Yes, but I can't be pregnant! I mean . . ."

"How long ago?" Sarah tried to find out more.

"Weeks . . ." Shock settled through her as she recognized the new heaviness in her breasts.

"Have you had any other symptoms? Your mama's waist always got big on her first . . ."

Suddenly Lianne had to know the truth. Throwing off her covers, she left the bed to stand before her cheval mirror. The flowing, long-sleeved, high-necked nightdress hid her figure from view, so she stripped it off. She felt no embarrassment as she stood completely nude before Sarah. Sarah had been with her since she was a baby and knew her body as well as Lianne did.

With avid, fearful interest, Lianne studied her slender curves. The thickening about her waist was minimal, but it was there. Their gazes met and held in the reflection. The acknowledgment silent. Slowly, Sarah picked up the hastily discarded gown and handed it back to her.

"What are you going to do?" She wanted to help, but knew her place. This was something Lianne would have to handle in her own way.

"I don't know." Lianne slipped back into the gown and retreated to the bed. "I never thought anything like this would happen. It never entered my mind. I mean there were only two times when we were together . . ."

She looked up guiltily, feeling the burdensome weight of her indiscretion. Suddenly, she needed to tell Sarah everything. She had kept all her heartache and disappointment bottled up inside of her all this time, and it was too much to bear alone any longer. Her voice was strangled as she began to explain, "It was awful, Sarah. The whole thing . . ."

"What happened, child?"

Lianne moved off the bed to wander around the room. "It was that first night after I came back from seeing Uncle Cyrus . . . Adam and I . . ."

"So it was Mr. Adam?"

At Lianne's nod, Sarah found she was actually shocked to find out her guess had been correct. She had harbored no particularly strong feelings for Adam one way or the other since he'd taken over Belle Arbor. She'd thought it had been decent of him to allow Lianne and Alex to stay on at the time, but she suddenly wondered if Lianne had been blackmailed into being with him in order to remain in her home.

"He didn't force you, did he?" she demanded in a quick display of protective anger.

"Oh, no!" Lianne put her suspicion to rest. Though she hated Adam and thought him arrogant and cold, he was not a man who had to force a woman to make love to him. Adam Trent was the kind of man women could not resist. Wasn't her own weakness around him proof of that? That he had destroyed her will so easily had only made her hate him more. "No, it was nothing like that . . ."

"Then, you're gonna have to tell him, you know, and the sooner the better."

"Tell him?" The thought terrified her. She didn't want anything more to do with him. She had deliberately avoided him ever since they'd returned from the New Orleans trip.

For his part, since returning to Belle Arbor, it seemed that Adam was completely unaware that she went out of her way to avoid him. He had gone on about his business without giving her a thought. When they did run into one another, he'd been cold and distant. He had never made any effort to seek her out or to speak with her alone. Adam was a man who took what

188

he wanted without care or thought about the consequences. He had used her and discarded her. It had been a momentary thing for him.

Lianne hated Adam and wanted absolutely nothing more to do with him. Never in her wildest dreams would she ever have thought that she would be anxious to leave Belle Arbor. Since returning from New Orleans, she'd been waiting anxiously for the weeks and months to pass so she could get what little remained of her inheritance and move away with Alex.

Now, however, fate had intervened. Her entire existance was in upheaval again. Instead of being able to leave and begin a new life, she found herself irrevocably bound to the very man she despised by the child nurturing inside her.

"Yes, tell him," Sarah was saying. "He's the father of the baby you're carrying. You have to tell him."

Lianne couldn't think. A few minutes ago, she'd thought herself ill. Now, all of a sudden, her whole world was in a shambles. The problems in her life before seemed trivial compared to what she faced now.

"You don't understand. He doesn't care about me, Sarah," she admitted.

"He made love to you, didn't he?" she came back.

Lianne's eyes glittered feverishly as she remembered their fervent matings. Caught up in the desire that had exploded between them, they had both been helpless to deny its power, but was that love?

"I need to be alone, Sarah." It was all too freshly painful for her to go on talking about it. "I need time to think . . ."

Sarah understood, but she also recognized the urgency of the situation. "You can't take too long, Lianne."

She glanced up at her, her agony clearly showing on her expressive features. "I know."

When Sarah had gone and she was alone with her thoughts, Lianne sank down on the bed and hugged her pillow to her. Pregnant . . . she was pregnant . . . She touched her still flat stomach with a gentle hand, and for a moment, she indulged herself in a childish fantasy. She was loved, and the baby was wanted. Adam was thrilled with the news, and they were married right away. Their lives would be perfect, and they would live happily ever after. A small smile touched her lips.

In her imagination it sounded blissfully wonderful and uncomplicated, but the reality of the situation was something else. Adam did not love her, and she couldn't picture him being thrilled with the discovery.

Still, she had to tell him, she knew that. With the big party only a day away, Lianne decided to wait until afterward to approach him. Things would be calmer then, and it would be easier to find time to speak with him alone. Just the thought of being alone with him again left her tense, but with a major effort of will, she faced up to her responsibility. Adam had to be told, and she would do it just as soon as she could get up the nerve.

Chapter Sixteen

The musicians began to play, and the lilting strains of the music drifted through the open windows out into the velvet night. Belle Arbor was ablaze with lights, and to the late arriving guests it appeared almost castle-like in its newly renovated splendor.

In the hall at Adam's side, Becky was filled with excitement as she greeted their guests. She couldn't believe the long weeks had passed so quickly. Tonight was the night she would get to see Beau again! Her heart thumped wildly at the prospect.

Becky knew that Beau and Adam had been in contact. Several times during the past five weeks Adam had been called into town on 'business,' and she knew that 'business' was with Beau. Still, Beau had never found the time to come to Belle Arbor as she'd hoped he would.

Becky worried continually that her bold kiss at the hotel had ruined the very special relationship that existed between them, fir having him as a friend was far better than not having him at all. She missed him terribly and planned to act as though nothing had changed between them when he arrived. Her determination faltered, however, as her lively imagination conjured up a worst-case scenario. What if Beau was angry with her? What if he shunned her now because of her brazenness? A shadow of fear shown in Becky's eyes, and the tension within her became even more sharp-edged. Things had to work out tonight. They just had to.

Adam's deep voice as he spoke to some new arrivals forced her back to the present, and Becky smiled her most charming smile as she turned to welcome more of their friends from New Orleans.

As the party got in full swing below, Lianne lingered in Alex's room. She had little desire to go below and join the celebration.

"The music's started, Lianne." her brother pointed out. Aren't you gonna go downstairs?"

"I guess it is time, isn't it?" She gave him a small, half-smile as she leaned over the bed and kissed him good-night. "You stay in bed now and get some sleep, love"

"Do I have to?" Alex protested, not at all pleased with missing out on all the fun. It had been years since there had been a party at Belle Arbor, and he wanted to go.

"Absolutely." She suppressed a smile as she started from the room.

"Lianne, it's not fair, you know," he argued, pouting. "You're going to have fun, while I'm stuck staying up here."

Lianne gazed back at him adoringly. He was still so innocent and precious. He had no idea how difficult it was going to be for her to go down there and act like she was having a good time. If she'd ever wondered about a career on the stage, tonight would be the test. She would have to greet old friends and pretend that life was wonderful, when in truth things had never been worse.

"Sometimes I think I would rather be up here with you," she told him honestly.

"You would?" Alex's eyes widened in surprise.

"Yes, but, unfortunately, tonight is not one of the

times when I can stay. Becky's expecting me now, and I have to go, Alex. I'm a little late already. Be good for me?"

He looked decidedly grumpy as he gave her a slow, less-than-enthusiastic nod.

"Promise?" she challenged, not completely trusting him until she heard the answer out loud.

"Yes." His expression was sullen, and his bottom lip stuck out.

"Then I'll try to find Sarah and have her sneak you up a treat. How's that?"

"Gee, thanks, Lianne!" All semblance of disappointment vanished, and he grinned at her. "And, Lianne?"

"Yes?"

"I like your new dress. You look real pretty."

"Thank you, sweetheart." She went back to the bed to give him one more hug and then left his room smiling. Even when things appeared the darkest, she could always count on Alex to brighten her mood.

Wanting to check one last time to make sure she did look her best, Lianne stopped off at her own bedroom for a minute. She paused before the mirror over her dressing table to check her hair. Sarah had styled it up away from her face on the sides and then fashioned the back into a loose flowing cascade of curls. At her ears, she wore her mother's diamond-and-pearl earbobs. She was pleased that she still looked fine even after all of Alex's hugs and kisses.

Lianne was still troubled over the gown she wore, though. When the seamstress had come to the house to take Becky's measurements for a new ballgown, her friend had insisted that she take Lianne's statistics, too. She had tried to discourage it, reminding Becky when they'd had a moment of privacy that she had no funds for a new dress. Becky had simply pooh-poohed her arguments, telling her it was a gift for all her help in restoring the house. She had continued to protest, but finally quit when Becky threatened to order a dress she liked for her without her approval. After having convinced her to accept the gown, her friend had enlisted her help in choosing the style and materials. Now she stood arrayed in the most beautiful dress she'd ever owned in her life.

The gown itself was elegant perfection. Created of the finest watersilk, it shone white, but shimmered and appeared to change colors in the light. Simply cut, it was off the shoulder in style with a fitted waist and full, flowing skirts.

Lianne stared in dismay at her bosom. The measurements for the dress had been taken before her pregnancy had begun to affect her, and though her waistline hadn't been affected that dramatically to alter the fit, her fuller breasts were now swelling dangerously above the décolletage. The three-strand choker of pearls she wore only seemed to enhance that expanse of creamy flesh.

For a moment, Lianne thought of changing, of finding something less daring to wear, but it was too late. Becky had gone down to greet the arriving guests half an hour ago, and she had promised her that she would be right down.

Lianne squared her shoulders and held her head high as she swept from the room. Many of those Adam and Becky had invited were longtime acquaintances of her own family, and though she dreaded facing them, she knew she could not appear cowed or helpless before them. She was a Ducharme, and if nothing else, she had her pride.

The gentle, soothing rhythm of the music touched her battered soul in a way nothing else had in a long time, and she felt young and almost carefree as she started down the staircase. The feeling lasted only a moment, though, as she was Adam standing near the foot of the steps with Becky at his side. At the sight of him looking so utterly handsome, her heart swelled painfully in her breast. His white shirt was a vivid contrast to the dark suit he wore and his cravat was, as always, perfectly tied.

Adam hadn't seen her yet, and Lianne hesitated in her descent. She thought about turning around and fleeing back upstairs to wait until he'd gone to join his guests in the parlor-turned-ballroom. She had avoided him totally since discovering her condition, and she wasn't ready to talk to him yet. She was afraid she'd betray herself and reveal the torrent of emotions that were troubling her before she was fully ready to discuss them with him.

"Lianne . . ."

Just as Lianne was about to retreat, Becky caught sight of her, and it was too late to seek refuge.

"Adam, look. Lianne's finally coming down to join us," Becky announced to her brother, pointedly drawing his attention to her.

Since there were no other guests to greet, Adam had no choice but to look up as Lianne made her grand descent of the staircase. He had thought he had conquered his attraction to her. He'd thought that all these weeks of staying away from her had cured him of the compelling need he'd felt for her or he'd thought what had happened between them had been an aberration that would never happen again. He had been wrong.

As Adam stared up at Lianne, he felt a lurch of excitement within him. She was a vision of loveliness as she seemed to float toward him. Her gown was heavenly, its pale shimmering color enhancing Lianne's emerald eyes and perfect complexion. Adam's gaze dropped from her face to her bosom, and he froze at the sight of her creamy breasts swelling so temptingly above the bodice.

The memory of their loving hit him an almost physical blow. He remembered the feel of her long, silken limbs wrapped around him. He remembered the taste of her satiny flesh, and the velvet clasp of her body sheathing his. He remembered, and he desired, and he cursed himself silently as he forcefully brought his surging passion for Lianne under tenuous control.

With supreme effort, he shuttered his emotions behind a mask of hostlike politeness. Turning to greet her, he reminded himself that tonight was the night he and Suzanne would become officially engaged. It wouldn't do for him to be leering at Lianne while he pledged his undying love to another woman.

"Good evening, Lianne," he spoke with little emotion.

Lianne felt her soul go cold as she met Adam's cool gaze. She had hoped to see some warmth in his expression, but there was none. She forced a smile as she returned his greeting.

"Good evening."

"Lianne, you look absolutely gorgeous," Becky said enthusiastically. "That gown is perfect on you, but then we knew it would be!"

"You look pretty wonderful yourself," she remarked, admiring Becky's dress. Basically white, it was trimmed with turquoise ribbons and rosettes. The bodice was low, but not nearly as daring as Lianne's had turned out to be, and the skirts were full. At her throat and ears, she wore a matching set of sapphire and diamond necklace and earrings. Her hair was done in an unswept style with a coordinating turquoise ribbon woven through.

"Do you really think so?" Becky asked under her breath, needing her reassurance.

"Yes," Lianne answered firmly, and then lowered her

voice to inquire, "Is he here yet?"

"No. Not yet."

"Well, don't worry. He'll come."

"I hope so, Lianne," she said wistfully.

Adam had turned away from them, and as he did he saw Suzanne's carriage draw up. He went forth to greet her, pushing Lianne from his thoughts as he prepared himself to play his part as adoring fiancé.

"Suzanne, I'm glad you're here." He helped her down from the carriage and kissed her quickly. "You look stunning."

Suzanne glowed under his compliment. She had worked for hours to look her very best, for tonight she would announce to the world her intention to become Mrs. Adam Trent. Her excitement knew no bounds. She had been anticipating this night for weeks and could hardly wait for the announcement to be made.

She'd had her hair arranged up in an artful style that emphasized the graceful lines of her neck. The deep rose satin of her gown highlighted her glowing complexion, and the dress itself was magnificent. The décolletage was nearly as revealing as Lianne's, but strangely, when Adam regarded her, he felt no uncontrollable surge of desire. Her tiny waist and swaying hips beneath the full, bell-shaped skirts would have enticed many a man, but he felt completely unmoved.

Adam said a silent prayer that he could succeed in carrying off his plan. If pretending to love her would net Shark for him, he would do it. Damn it! If he had to walk through the fires of hell to catch Shark, he'd do it! Camouflaging his grim determination, he escorted her inside.

Lianne was still in the hallway with Becky when Adam entered with Suzanne on his arm. She saw the way they gazed at each other. When Adam spoke, it was to her and her alone. Lianne felt her spirits sink into an abyss of pain. Only her Ducharme pride kept her from running from the hall is distress.

"I think I'll join the others," Lianne said to Becky as she disappeared into the ballroom.

Becky, understanding her hatred of the other woman, let her go without a word. After a moment, she went to greet Suzanne.

"Suzanne, I'm so glad you could come."

"I wouldn't have missed tonight for the world, Becky," Suzanne responded, giving Adam a knowing look as she squeezed his arm more tightly to her breast.

Becky watched Adam's reaction, and she couldn't believe that he actually seemed to enjoy Suzanne's clinging ways. She didn't understand what was going on with her brother, but she planned to find out. How could he pay so much attention to someone like her? Becky had known instinctively that Suzanne was a cold, calculating female. She'd felt that way about her even before she'd learned of her dealings with Lianne, and she couldn't figure out why Adam didn't recognize it, too.

Though she had done nothing to encourage Suzanne, she had still occasionally dropped by unannounced to see Adam. Becky had tried her best to be cordial during those visits, but it had been difficult, especially since she knew how much it hurt Lianne to have the woman on Belle Arbor property. It made her feel slightly sick to know that Lianne was going to have to put up with Suzanne's presence all evening.

The music began again and Adam glanced at Becky. "Shall we go on in?"

"I suppose."

Adam and Suzanne went on ahead of Becky as she lingered in the hall to take one last look outside for Beau.

* * *

Cyrus Shackelford drank deeply of his bourbon as he watched Lianne enter the room. He'd always thought her attractive, but tonight she was positively ravishing. Seeing that she was alone and knowing that she wouldn't remain that way for long, he set his glass aside and headed straight for her.

"Miss Ducharme, it's so good to see you again," he greeted her smoothly, his gaze lingering on her bodice. "You look marvelous tonight."

"Why, thank you, Mr. Shackelford," Lianne returned, feeling uncomfortable under his avid gaze. She suddenly wished she could hide somewhere.

"Cyrus, please," he encouraged, "and may I take the liberty of addressing you as Lianne?"

"Of course," she replied distractedly as she saw Adam enter the room with Suzanne on his arm. She watched as he swept the blond beauty out onto the dance floor, holding her close.

Lianne expected anger, but all she felt was a deep, abiding hurt. One hand moved instinctively to her waist to hover protectively there over the new life that was nestled deep within her. Determined not to reveal any of her inner turmoil, she smiled brightly as she turned to Cyrus.

Cyrus felt warmed by the sudden change in her. Tonight just might be the night he cracked Miss Lianne Ducharme's icy reserve. She had always been a bit standoffish with him, but maybe her attitude was different now that she'd lost her money and her plantation.

Working in the bank had helped him develop the instincts of a predator, and he suspected that Lianne was vulnerable right now. Confirmed bachelor that he was, he had no interest in marriage, but thought perhaps that an arrangement could be made between

199

them. From her financial situation, he knew she was in desperate financial straits and would remain so until her trust funds came payable the following year. Since she wasn't living with her uncle in town, he suspected that she was relying on the goodwill of the Trents to see her through until such time as she was once again able to support herself. He smiled to himself. He had wanted Lianne for a long time, and it looked like he was finally going to get her.

"Would you care to dance?" he offered, eager to begin his seductive pursuit.

"Yes, please," she accepted, and moved into his arms.

The banker squired Lianne about the dance floor. He enjoyed the slight press of her body against his and the fresh, delicate scent that was her. He had always imagined that she would be an excellent dancer, and he'd been right. They moved easily together following the ebb and flow of the music. Cyrus knew without a doubt that they would be equally perfect together in bed. The heat of his true thoughts shone briefly in his pale eyes, but Lianne was not looking at him at the same time and missed it.

Adam was managing to keep a smile on his face despite Suzanne's endless chatter as he manuevered her about the room.

"Darling, how soon are we going to make our announcement?" she badgered.

He groaned inwardly at the thought, but then bolstered himself by remembering his purpose. "I felt mid-evening would be appropriate. What do you think?"

"That sounds perfect," she cooed. "I can hardly wait, Adam. I want everyone to know just how much I love you, and how happy we're going to be together."

"They'll know, my darling," Adam pledged.

Adam made the mistake of looking up just then. He caught sight of that brief flash of revealing emotion on

Cyrus's face as he danced Lianne around the room and felt murderous with unexplained rage. He had heard about Cyrus Shackelford and his reputation with women, and he didn't want his slimy hands anywhere on Lianne. Lianne glanced up at Cyrus and laughed lightly at something he'd said. When Adam saw this, he wanted to lunge at them and tear them apart. He barely managed to continue to dance with Suzanne and maintain his outward calm. Only his darkened eyes and tense jaw gave away his inner turmoil, and only someone who knew him very well would have noticed.

For a lack of nothing better to do as she danced with one of the older married men in attendance, Becky was gazing about the dance floor watching the other couples. She heard Lianne's lighthearted laughter and at the same moment saw the fleeting change in Adam's expression. She blinked in stunned surprise, not believing what she'd seen, confused by it.

Could Adam possibly be jealous of Lianne? In the beginning, when they'd first come to Belle Arbor, she'd had hopes that Lianne would be the woman to free Adam from his emotionless exile, but it had seemed that he wasn't interested. He'd paid little attention to Lianne, and, in fact, often made it a point to deliberately avoid being near her. Becky had slowly been forced to give up her hope that they would fall in love.

Now, however, Becky thought there might be more to his ignoring of Lianne than she'd originally suspected. Perhaps his cold indifference was really a protective shield against caring for someone again. Perhaps he really did feel something for Lianne, but didn't want to show it. Perhaps . . .

Of all people, Becky had understood what Adam had suffered in losing Elise as he had. She'd also known that he couldn't spend the rest of his life trapped in the same self-imposed nonexistence that held Elise. His life had to go on. The doctors had told him that. Common sense dictated it. Endless mourning would achieve nothing. He had done all he could for Elise. It was time to get on with his life.

Having seen his face just now, Becky was convinced that Lianne was the woman who could help break through that hard, brittle shell that encased Adam's heart, yet she didn't know how to convince him of that. Somehow, she hoped to get the two of them dancing together tonight. Perhaps that little bit of contact would do some good. At least, Becky thought, it couldn't hurt to try, and then maybe, by the end of the evening, things might be different in Adam's life.

Little did Becky know as she dreamed about uniting the two, that fate had already intervened, and that by the following day Adam's life would be unalterably changed forever.

Chapter Seventeen

When the music ended, Adam kept covert watch as Cyrus escorted Lianne off the dance floor and guided her to the refreshment table. He dipped her a cup of punch and remained close by her side, acting the ardent suitor.

As the bachelor fawned over Lianne, Adam felt unexpectedly protective of her. He found he wanted to warn her about Cyrus. He wanted to tell her not to trust him, to tell her that he was known for using women and then leaving them without a thought.

However, Adam realized it would be ridiculous gesture on his part. After all, hadn't he been the one who had really taken advantage of Lianne? He had used her for his own selfish reasons. He had taken her sweet innocence and given her nothing in return.

The recognition of his own coldhearted actions stung. Only the thought of his ultimate goal reaffirmed his reasons for all that he'd done and eased his guilt. He dismissed the idea of interfering, knowing it would be better if he minded his own business and stayed far away from the lovely Lianne.

Leaving Suzanne with a group of friends, Adam excused himself and went into the study to pour himself a stiff drink. He was both pleased and irritated to find it deserted. He was glad for the time alone to calm down, but alternatively he had hoped to stall in returning to Suzanne's side. Her smothering presence was wearing on him, and he did not relish spending the night dancing attendance.

Adam drained his drink and then poured another. The burning liquor helped soothe his tautly stretched nerves, and he drew a deep, steadying breath. Calmly he told himself that if he focused his thoughts solely on catching Shark, it would make the rest of the night bearable. Soon, very soon, the pirate would return to contact Suzanne, and when he did, he and Beau would be ready and waiting.

At the thought of Beau, Adam wondered where his friend was. He should have been here long ago, and he began to worry that something might have happened aboard the *Sea Shadow*.

Aware that he'd delayed his return to the party for as long as politely possible, Adam stepped from the study taking his tumbler of bourbon with him. Then, almost as if he conjured him up, Beau arrived.

"Glad you could make it," Adam drawled sardonically as he strode down the hall to meet him.

"Sorry I'm late, but I had some unfinished business to take care of," Beau offered his excuses.

"What did she look like? Katie, the barmaid, maybe?" Adam teased good-naturedly as he led him down the hall and into the study to get him a drink.

"Ah, the lovely Katie . . ." Beau gave a tight laugh. He hadn't seen the barmaid since that afternoon weeks ago, and he wished it had been something as simple as an assignation with a woman that had put him behind schedule. "No. I'm afraid this was business."

"Trouble?" Adam was instantly concerned.

"There was some damage to the rigging, and I wanted to make sure it was completely repaired before I left."

"Good. Everything's in order, then."

Beau nodded. He helped himself to the fine bourbon. "Suzanne's here?"

"Yes." Adam's tone was less than enthusiastic.

"And you're ready for tonight?"

"Yes," he answered tersely, "our plans are made. We'll be making the announcement in another hour or so."

Beau lifted his glass in a toast. "To our ultimate goal."

"Right." Adam saluted him, too, and then they both downed the potent liquor.

Becky had been making the rounds of the ballroom, visiting with all the guests while she tried to find a moment to speak with Lianne alone. She'd found that nearly an impossible task, for Cyrus Shackelford seemed intent on monopolizing her company all night. She was about to deliberately interrupt when she caught a glimpse of Beau walking past the ballroom doorway out in the main hall, and all thoughts of getting Adam and Lianne together vanished.

Beau was here at last! Becky's pulses leapt at the sight of him. She wanted to run to him and throw herself in his arms, but she fought down the urge. Sedately, without drawing undue attention to herself, she left the small group she was chatting with and started from the room to greet him. Becky got as far as the door and was about to go out into the hall when the sound of their voices reached her.

"Sorry I'm late, but I had some unfinished business I had to take care of . . ."

"What did she look like? Katie, the barmaid, maybe?"

"Ah, the lovely Katie . . ."

Beau's answer and the laugh that followed were all that Becky needed to send her temper soaring. How dare he! Here she was practically making herself crazy trying to think of ways to attract him and entice him, and here he was out running around with barmaids!

Becky stopped at the door too angry to go out and greet Beau. Backing away from any confrontation with him, she struggled to control her fury. Her kiss had meant nothing to him! He had been with another woman even before coming to the party!

Pain tore at her heart. All her plans and worries were for nothing. There had been no change between them, because in Beau's eyes nothing existed between them to begin with. He probably thought of her as nothing more than a nuisance. Certainly, he wasn't attracted to her or he would have responded that night when she'd kissed him.

Her dreams were shattered. If Beau didn't want her, then she would find someone who would. There were any number of single, attractive men there tonight. She was going to set her cap for the best-looking one with the best prospects. She was tired of hoping and praying that Beau would notice her.

Becky moved to the refreshment table and took up a cup of the champagne punch, drinking it thirstily. It surprised her to find it went down so easily, so she took another. She turned around to face the crowd in the ballroom then, eyeing all the eligible men in attendance. One by one she studied them with detached interest. Of course, there was Cyrus Shackelford, but Becky found him more obnoxious than attractive, especially since he was so much older than she was. She wondered how Lianne had tolerated him for so long tonight. Then there was Michael Randolph and Lyle Beaumont, but she found neither of them particularly exciting.

It was then that she spied the devilish Edward Courtois as he flirted with several of the other young ladies across the room and knew instantly that he was the one she wanted. Ed was by far the handsomest of all the young wealthy bachelors with his wavy, light brown hair, dark eyes, engaging manner and easy grin. Lianne had told her all about him. She knew that he came from an excellent family, and she thought him just about the most charming, outrageous man she'd ever met. He could outdance, outdrink, and outtalk almost anyone. Rumors of his reckless gambling ways were rampant, but Becky didn't care. She wanted to have fun tonight. She wanted someone to help her forget Beau, and she believed Edward was the one. Setting her cup aside, she headed across the room to talk to him.

It was only a short time later when Adam and Beau finally came to join the merrymakers.

"Fine party you're having here," Cecil Whitney told Adam as he clapped him on the shoulder.

"Thank you, Cecil," Adam responded, and then quickly made the necessary round of introductions since Beau was a stranger in their midst.

"Adam, darling . . ."

At the sound of Suzanne's drawl, Adam stiffened, but only Beau noticed his reaction.

"Hello, sweet." Adam allowed her to take his arm as she came to stand at his side.

"I missed you," she complained in saccharine tones. "You were gone so long."

Adam was not the sort who dealt with petty jealousies and possessiveness well. Any other woman, at any other time, would have risked losing Adam forever by a display of such petulance, but this was Suzanne and the circumstances were different. Adam gritted his teeth and smiled.

"Beau just arrived, Suzanne. Have you two met yet?" He distracted her and made the appropriate introduc-

207

tions.

"It's a pleasure to meet you, Beau Hamilton." She smiled sweetly at him. "Any friend of Adam's is certainly a friend of mind."

While finding her helpless Southern-belle routine effective, Beau could see the spark of cagey intelligence in her eyes. This woman was no fragile flower of womanhood. There was much more to her than most people realized. "It's my pleasure, Miss Labadie. I've heard only wonderful things about you from Adam."

Suzanne gazed up at Adam adoringly as she responded, "Please call me Suzanne, Beau. I have the feeling we're all going to be great friends from now on."

The music began again, and Beau took the opportunity to ask Suzanne to dance. She was pleased with his offer, and they soon joined the crowd of dancers circling the ballroom floor.

Adam stayed with the group of men and continued to talk with them about business. Caught up in the conversation, his dark head was bent toward them as he concentrated on what they were saying. Through the music and the discussion of crop prices, he heard her. It was a soft laugh, a laugh of genuine amusement, he thought, a laugh of delight that brought his head up to seek her out.

Swirling around the dance floor, locked in Cyrus Shackelford's arms, Lianne was trying to maintain an air of gaiety and nonchalance. She kept telling herself that it would soon be over, that she only had to keep up the charade of having a good time just a little while longer. But the intensity of Cyrus's courtship this evening was leaving her decidedly ill at ease. She was growing tired of fighting him off. His hands were on her at every opportunity, and Lianne could hardly wait for the meal to be served so she could politely make her excuses and get away from him.

Lianne would have loved for some other man to come and cut in on them as they danced, but she knew few of the other bachelors at the party were up to the challenge. Cyrus had more money, power, and prestige than almost anyone else in attendance. If she was going to get away from him she was going to have to do it all by herself.

Lianne knew exactly what kind of man Cyrus really was. He went after the woman of his choice and, because of his social position and good looks, was seldom denied. Tonight, she mused confidently, would probably be one of the few times he would not succeed in making a conquest. The last thing she wanted or needed was an involvement with a man, any man.

"Shall we slip outside for a breath of fresh air?" Cyrus's question was rhetorical, for he'd had already danced her out one of the french doors onto the wide porch, and it was too late to protest.

The night was dark. The moon had yet to rise, but the sky was rife with millions of twinkling stars. The delicate, sweet scent of honeysuckle was borne on a faint breeze. It was a lovers' night. It was a night for romance.

Cyrus had been anticipating this moment since he'd first seen Lianne earlier that evening. He wanted to make her his, and he didn't intend to fail.

"Lianne, my darling," he spoke huskily as he drew her near.

Lianne held herself rigidly in his arms as he would have embraced her. "Cyrus, I hardly think this is proper."

"Come, sweetheart, don't fight me. We've known each other for a long time now." He tried to kiss her, but she twisted slightly and the kiss landed harmlessly on her cheek.

"Just because we've known each other in a business

209

sense, and occasionally socially, doesn't give you the right to take such liberties with me."

"Lianne, there's no reason to be so upset," Cyrus cunningly tried to soothe her and put her fears to rest. He lifted one hand to tilt her face up toward his. "We'll be perfect together." His mouth descended taking hers in a hot exploration.

Lianne felt as if she was going to gag. Cyrus's kiss was nothing like Adam's. There was no explosion of desire, only revulsion.

Lianne pushed with all her might against his chest, managing to break off the contact. "We're not going to be anything together! Let me go!"

Cyrus knew then that she was not some simple miss who would give herself to him without a thought. His voice hardened as he prepared to make his offer. "What is it you want, Lianne?"

"I want you to let me go," she repeated, missing his point.

"Look, there's no reason to play so hard to get. We both know how poor you are and how you're living here at Belle Arbor strictly on the Trents' charity." His words were cold and hard.

Lianne gasped at his blunt cruelty. "What are you saying?"

"I'm saying that I'm willing and prepared to offer you everything money can buy. Just name your price."

"What?" Lianne couldn't believe it.

"I'll set you up in town in your own house, and you won't have to worry about your finances ever again." He leered at her as he slipped one hand higher to cup the underside of her breast. "All you'll have to worry about is pleasing me."

Lianne almost couldn't believe what she was hearing. She stood stunned for an instant and then reacted instinctively, slapping him soundly. "Get your hands off me, Cyrus Shackelford!"

Cyrus was outraged, and instead of releasing her, he bruisingly tightened his grip on her. "Oh, so you like it rough, do you?" He crushed her against his chest and again he kissed her, this time with demeaning force. His tongue raped her as he slid one hand into her bodice and brazenly fondled her.

Lianne was fighting for real now, twisting and turning as she tried to escape his brutal treatment. "I'd live in the streets before I'd consent to be your mistress!" she hissed when the kiss finally ended.

Cyrus chuckled viciously as he pinched at her tender flesh. When she winced and continued to struggle, he smiled thinly. "That's just where you may end up, my dear, but first I'm going to—"

"No!" she moaned as his touch grew even more hurtful. "I'll scream!"

"Go ahead. No one will hear you over the music," he remarked confidently, not thinking that anyone would have followed them.

As Lianne started to cry out, Cyrus raised a hand to strike her. It was then that the deep, threatening voice boomed from the shadows.

"I wouldn't do that if I were you, Shackelford." Adam's voice was taut with rage as he stepped forward.

Adam had been trying his best to ignore Lianne and Cyrus while they were dancing, but when he saw the banker maneuver her outside, he'd been driven to follow. After making a quick excuse to Suzanne, he'd disappeared into the study and then gone out onto the porch through the doors there.

Adam was immediately glad that he'd followed them, for he found Lianne in the middle of a desperate struggle to escape from Cyrus's clutches. The sight of the other man's hand on her breast sent his fury soaring. He had no right touch Lianne! As Adam moved closer, the urge to throttle Cyrus to within an inch of his life was strong within him. He kept his fists clinched at his sides in a desperate effort not to lose what little control he had left.

"You heard the lady, Shackelford. She doesn't want anything to do with you." There could be no mistaking the steely edge in his tone. "Now, why don't you just back off."

Cyrus was livid, but he knew better than to make a further scene. In disgust, he let his hands drop away from Lianne's soft curves and stalked off into the darkness, muttering vicious curses under his breath.

Adam stared down at Lianne in the muted light. She looked fragile and frightened as she hurried to straighten her disheveled clothing, and he wanted more than anything to take her in his arms and hold her. He wanted to reassure her that everything would be all right. Hell, he admitted angrily to himself, he wanted to sweep her up into his embrace and carry her upstairs to his room and make mad, passionate love to her. He took a small step closer, lifting one hand slowly, meaning to to tenderly touch her cheek.

Lianne couldn't believe Adam was there. A part of her wanted to rejoice at his nearness, yet another part of her warned her to be careful, that he couldn't be trusted, that he was as bad in his own way as Cyrus was. Still, the look in his eyes was soft and gentle . . . When Adam moved to touch her cheek, she almost took that last step toward him.

"Adam, darling?" Suzanne's voice was hard and clear and severed any warmth that had existed in that one delicate moment with the force of an arctic wind.

As Suzanne came out of the ballroom and moved purposefully to his side, Adam dropped his hand away from Lianne as if he'd been burned.

"So this is where you slipped off to," she said sweetly. "Good evening, Lianne." She linked her arm possessively through Adam's, her expression smug. "It's an absolutely glorious night, isn't it?"

Lianne's pride was the only thing that saved her. Squaring her shoulders, she lifted her chin in defiance of the misery that would have claimed her. "Yes, it is, but I think I've had enough fresh air for now. If you'll excuse me?"

Adam was stoic as she walked past him. His wooden expression did not betray his inner turmoil. Only when she'd disappeared around the corner of the house and Suzanne tugged at his arm did he react.

"Now that we're alone, let's go for a walk in the garden."

"Of course," he managed to reply, and he escorted her down the steps and out along the shell-lined paths.

When they'd moved far enough away from the lights of the house that they couldn't be seen, Suzanne stopped and turned to Adam. In a single, sinuous move, she wrapped her arms behind his head and drew him down for a long kiss. Her mouth was hungry beneath his as she pressed herself fully against him.

"Oh, Adam, I've waited all evening for the chance to be alone with you," Suzanne sighed.

In no mood to talk, Adam didn't bother to answer, but kissed her instead. He knew Suzanne would accept that as a sign of his love. Yet while he was kissing her, his mind was still focused on Lianne.

The jolt of emotion he'd experienced when he'd witnessed Cyrus's hands on Lianne had been more powerful than anything he'd ever known before. For a moment, even his need for revenge had been eclipsed by his desire to protect her from the other man's degrading advances. The realization shook him.

213

Adam knew he couldn't let anything get in his way. He was too close to success now. Nothing could interfere! He held Suzanne closer at the thought and returned her kiss with increased fervor.

Chapter Eighteen

"Beau! I'm so glad to see you. When did you get here?" Becky's cheerful greeting came to him as he stood alone at the refreshment table, and he looked up to see her approaching on the arm of a handsome young man.

"I was delayed and only arrived a short while ago," he told her as he bent to kiss her cheek in a very brotherly fashion.

Becky was seething at his lame excuse, and she only barely managed to keep still as she accepted his kiss. "Beau, I'd like you to meet Edward Courtois. Edward, this is Beau Hamilton, an old friend of my brother's."

Beau shook hands with the younger man. "Good to meet you, Edward."

"Nice to meet you too, sir," Edward returned keeping one arm about Becky's tiny waist.

Beau wondered why he suddenly felt so old. Becky's use of the term "old" in introducing him and Edward's calling him "sir" faintly disturbed him somehow. He also wondered why the sight of Edward holding Becky so intimately bothered him.

The music began again, and just as Beau would have asked Becky to dance, Edward beat him to it. He swept Becky up into his arms and guided her out onto the floor. In frustration, Beau scowled blackly as Edward whisked her away.

To his amazement, Beau found himself silently wishing that he was the man holding her and dancing with her as he watched them move gracefully about the floor.

The intensity of the thought surprised Beau as he followed Becky's progress around the room. In the virginal, white gown and with her hair done up, she looked the true innocent and, at the same time, undeniably, enticingly lovely. She was the kind of woman a man wanted to take to wife, the type of woman who bore a man's children and made his life worthwhile.

Beau stared openly, mesmerized by this vision of Becky, the woman. He remembered that night in the hotel and her effort at playing the seductress. He'd known that he'd handled it badly, but, at the time, he'd been too shocked by his reaction to deal with it properly. Beau thought now of all the excuses he'd used to stay away from her during these past weeks. He'd put off coming to Belle Arbor for as long as he could, but he hadn't been able to avoid it tonight.

Feeling once more in need of a stiff drink, Beau turned away from the dancers and left the room. He headed down the hall to the study to refill his bourbon glass. He was standing at the liquor cabinet in the corner of the room when Lianne came hurrying back inside from the veranda. She did not notice him right away, and as he watched her, he saw how agitated she was. Beau realized that something must have happened to her outside. Ever the gentleman, Beau made his presence known.

"Lianne?"

Lianne jumped guiltily. She had not expected anyone to be in the study and had hoped for a short time alone to gather her wits about her. She had come far too close to falling prey to Adam's enthralling nearness again there in the warm, caressing darkness of the night. "Beau . . ."

"Is something wrong?" He set his tumbler aside and

216

went toward her.

"Oh, no . . . nothing's wrong. Everything's fine now."
It was a lie. She knew it and he knew it.

"You look wonderful," he complimented, knowing
when it was wisest to change the subject.

The last thing Lianne was concerned about right
then was her appearance, but she managed to make all
the correct responses.

"I was just about to return to the ballroom. Would
you like to dance?"

"I'd love to, thank you."

They spoke of inconsequential things as they re-
joined the others. Deciding to wait for a new melody to
begin before dancing, they stood on the sidelines in
companionable silence. It was then that Beau overheard the three older ladies who were seated along the
wall.

"My, my, Camille, dear, have you ever seen your
Edward so taken with a young lady before?" René
Mansard questioned as she kept an eagle's eye on the
antics of the young roué.

"This *is* unusual for my Edward," Camille Courtois
answered, a bit bewildered.

"Do you suppose he might be getting serious about
someone?" Judith Anderson asked. She'd know Edward
ever since he was a young boy, and she, too, was surprised by the undivided attention he was lavishing on
Becky Trent tonight.

"I don't know. It is out of the ordinary for Edward to
spend the entire evening with only one young lady."

"I guess we'll just have to wait and see what develops.
She certainly is a lovely girl, and the Trents do have
money," Judith pointed out.

"They make a handsome couple, don't you think?"
René sighed romantically.

"Just because he's danced exclusively with her to-

217

night, doesn't mean he's going to marry her, René," Camille said tartly.

"She seems such a lovely girl, though, I hope she doesn't go the way of all his other loves," Judith remarked.

"Judith!" Camille gave a little gasp of indignation.

"Well, Judith is right, you know," René defended her outspoken friend. "Your Edward isn't known for his devotion to any one girl. Why, you know the scandal that almost erupted last summer over the Douglas girl."

Camille grimaced at the memory. "Maybe this time it will be different."

"Maybe . . ." The other two agreed.

Beau had kept his back to the three ladies, and it was a good thing that he had, for his expression was nearly murderous when their conversation finally drifted on to other things. So, Edward was quite the womanizer was he? Beau regarded the laughing couple through a red haze as they danced about the floor. There was no way Beau was going to stand by and let Becky get involved with someone like him. If she didn't get away from him soon, he was going to take matters into his own hands.

Even though she flirted happily with Edward, Becky had eyes only for Beau. She had told herself that she was going to completely ignore him tonight, that she didn't care any more what he did or who he did it with, but the truth was, she couldn't stop loving him. Every chance she got, she covertly glanced his way. The vivid color of the deep scarlet jacket he wore set off his blondness, and the contrasting white shirt and form-fitting dark trousers also enhanced his male beauty. She thought him the most handsome man in the room, but she was careful to disguise her feelings.

Becky hoped that she'd be able to continue her act of indifference all night. Not that it mattered, she thought wearily, for she knew that he had no real romantic interest in her. But just for her own self-pride, she would not throw herself at him again like a lovesick schoolgirl.

When the dance ended, Edward stayed right by her side, guiding her to the refreshment table to join some of the others. Beau refrained from going after them. Instead, he turned his full attention to Lianne as the next melody began. Taking her in his arms, they moved out onto the floor.

When Adam and Suzanne returned to the ball, she was smiling quite smugly and high color stung her cheeks. Adam's kisses and caresses were breathtakingly exciting as usual, and she was anxious for their announcement to be made so she could gloat before all the other envious women. Adam was going to be hers and hers alone!

At Adam's insistence, they joined the other dancers, but the music ended soon after they'd started. Suzanne was disgusted to find that they were standing next to Beau and Lianne on the dance floor. As a waltz began, Beau took the initiative.

"Suzanne, may I have this dance?"

Suzanne did not want to leave Adam, especially not with Lianne. She had never thought Lianne a very attractive woman, but tonight the gown she wore was definitely an eye-catcher. It irked her that Lianne was still living at Belle Arbor, and it had disturbed her greatly when she'd found Adam alone with her out on the veranda. Suzanne wondered what had transpired between them before she'd shown up, but didn't concern herself too much. Adam's fervor in the garden had been so convincing that she truly believed she was the only woman in his life.

"I'd like that, Beau." She gave Adam a look that promised much as she went into Beau's arms.

Adam stood riveted to the floor. He knew etiquette

219

demanded that he dance with Lianne, but he wasn't quite sure he could stand it. It would be hell holding her close and moving in such a seductive rhythm with her. *Why,* he thought crossly, *couldn't this damn song have been a schottische?*

"Lianne?" He quirked one brow in invitation as he held out his hand to her.

Lianne wanted to run. She had managed to avoid Adam all night except for that one time out on the porch that had almost ended in disaster. She had been glad and relieved when Suzanne had shown up, for she had definitely felt herself weakening toward Adam as he'd touched her cheek. The sight of Suzanne taking his arm had reminded her forcefully of just how much she hated the both of them.

Lianne wished ardently that she could walk away from him now and never look back, but she knew she couldn't. In the back of her mind, a taunting voice told her over and over again that she would never again be free of Adam once he learned the truth of her condition.

Lianne's eyes met Adam's as she reached out to take his hand, and she found herself nearly swallowed up in their black, fathomless depths. His expression was carefully guarded so she could read nothing of his thoughts.

Lianne didn't want to dance with him. She didn't want to be held in his arms. She didn't want to be reminded of the mastery he had over her senses. She shivered as he drew her into the circle of his arms and began to waltz with her.

Adam felt her reaction to his touch and thought it was revulsion. He knew she hated him, and he believed she had every right to do so. He regretted that she had been forced into the dance by circumstances, but there had been nothing either one of them could do without drawing notice.

At first, they were stiff and unbending with each other. They held themselves apart. They did not want to relax and enjoy the dance, but the melody was a haunting one, and it possessed them almost from the very start. A sweet enchantment flowed around them as they dipped and swayed in perfect rhythm. Around and around they spun, completely caught up in the waltz, unmindful of the onlookers who thought they danced as if they were made for each other.

Their eyes were locked in timeless combat as their bodies moved in unison. The dance was as thrilling as their lovemaking had been, and Lianne felt almost transported by the ecstasy of it. She wondered faintly how she could react this way physically to him when the rational part of her was warning her of the danger. She thought if she could just start talking she could break the spell that held her, but she found she didn't want to. This was ecstasy, and in tormented shock, she realized she didn't want it to end.

Adam, too, was caught up in the wonder of the moment. Why did this woman, of all women, have such an impact on him? He knew she despised him. He knew there could never be anything between them, but for right now, for this instant, he didn't care. Soon he would have to publicly announce his love for Suzanne, but now there was only Lianne, here in his arms.

The music ended. Forced back to reality, both feigned ordinary behavior as they moved together to find Suzanne and Beau.

"I wanted to thank you for what you did outside," Lianne said coolly as they walked slowly across the dance floor.

"He hasn't come back, has he?" Adam asked tautly. He didn't want to think about Cyrus or the abuse he'd tried to wreak on Lianne. Adam felt it was far better if

221

he put the memory of his wild, nearly uncontrollable fury from him.

"No. I haven't seen him. I'm sure he's left."

"Good."

"What's good, darling?" Suzanne questioned quickly as she picked up on a part of their conversation and wanted to know more of what they were talking about.

Adam adroitly avoided her inquiry. "Nothing important, sweet." His words cut Lianne to the quick. "Have you seen Becky?" he continued.

"I saw her in the hall with Edward a few minutes ago," she offered, "but I'm not sure where they were going."

"I'll check," Beau volunteered abruptly, and he strode off into the main floor hall as Lianne quickly absented herself from Adam and Suzanne's company.

"I thought you said you wanted some bourbon . . ." Becky asked, puzzled when Edward set aside the glass of liquor she'd just handed him.

"That was just an excuse, Becky," Edward confided with a grin as he approached her and took her into his embrace. "What I really want is something far more intoxicating . . ."

With easy confidence, he bent to her and kissed her. His mouth moved over hers in a heated exchange unlike anything Becky'd ever known before. For a split second, she wondered what it would be like to kiss Beau this way, but quickly put the thought from her. She was with Edward. He was the man she wanted. Everything was working out very well.

Emboldened by her open response, Edward pulled her closer as his hands began a restless exploration. Becky was intrigued by his actions.

She had never known even the slightest taste of a

man's passion before, and she was finding it quite pleasant. The closer he came to touching her breast, the more she found she wanted to experience that caress. Had she known how to urge him on, she would have. As it was, she wrapped her arms around him and pressed herself to his chest.

Edward sensed her eagerness and was thrilled with it. Becky was quite beautiful, and he'd been longing to hold her all night long. He trailed hot kisses down her throat and shoulders and knew a feeling of triumph when she swayed weakly against him.

"Oh, Edward . . ." Becky sighed. She'd never experienced anything quite so delightful as the touch of his lips at her throat. Shivers of pleasure coursed through her as she clung to him.

Swept away by the feeling of what he thought was her surrender, Edward crushed her to him. He wanted to feel her slender body next to his as his mouth claimed hers in a devouring exchange. Locked in the passionate embrace, he did not hear the footsteps in the hall or the sound of Beau entering the study. Had he been aware of the intruder, he would not have chosen that particular moment to possessively settle his hand over the sweet swell of Becky's breast.

Beau thought that Becky had gone outside for a walk with Edward, and he only glanced in the study as a second thought. What he saw there sent his temper raging.

He reacted without thinking as he stormed into the room and grabbed Edward by the shoulder, spinning him completely around. "What the hell do you think you're doing?"

Edward was stunned by the interruption as Becky cried out in dismay.

"Beau! What are you doing here?"

"I'm protecting your honor, Becky. That's what I'm

223

doing!" He stated furiously as he eyed Edward with supreme distaste. He wanted to hit the younger man. He wanted to take him outside and beat the living daylights out of him.

"Becky's honor needs no protection from me," Edward offered gallantly. He started to draw Becky back to his side when Beau turned a vicious glare on him.

"It looked like it to me, Courtois," Beau snarled.

"My intentions are strictly honorable."

"Your honorable intentions are going to be lying on the ground in the middle of the dueling field at sunup if you don't get the hell out of here. Now, why don't you just take a nice walk outside and cool off, before I cool you off personally . . . and permanently."

Edward was confused by his fury. Certainly, what he and Becky were doing was nothing out-of-bounds, and Beau Hamilton was not her brother or any relative at all for that matter. He looked to Becky.

Embarassed, humiliated, outraged, and, along with all of it, more than a little pleased, Becky gave Edward a curt nod. "You'd better go, Edward. I'll speak with you later."

"Are you sure you'll be all right?"

"Courtois . . ." Beau's tone was deadly as he took a menacing step toward him.

Edward hesitated no longer, but hurried from the room. Becky seemed to be following him, and Beau spoke up.

"Wait a minute. I want to talk to you," he commanded, and he watched in amazement as Becky closed and locked the study door behind Edward.

"Don't worry, Beau. I'm not going anywhere." Becky turned on him, her arms akimbo, her temper flaring. "I want to talk to you, too!"

Becky stalked back across the room to stand right in

front of him. She didn't want to think about how handsome he looked. She didn't want to think about how wonderful it was that he thought he was protecting her virtue. She didn't want to think about the urge she had to throw herself into his arms and taste his impassioned kiss and wild touch. Becky struggled to stay angry with him.

As Beau watched her come, his thoughts were a mess. Lord, she was so gorgeous! Even now, in her self-righteous anger, she looked like some avenging angel. He wanted to be furious with her for taking the risk of compromising herself with that fool Courtois, but all he could think of was how unbelievably lovely she was and how much he wanted her. His gaze missed nothing . . . the flashing blue eyes . . . the way her breasts were heaving in indignation . . . the seductive sway of her skirts as she came toward him. The stirring of desire deep within his loins could not be denied. Beau wanted her. She was woman, all woman, and he was going to make her his.

As Beau had the thought, he realized the extent of her fury and grimaced. Becky was angry, and when Becky got angry she was not easy to deal with. If anything she could be as determined and hard-headed as her brother. He knew calming her wasn't going to be easy, and as for the rest . . .

"Beau Hamilton, you pig-headed, overbearing lout!" Becky raved, waving a finger in his face. "Just who do you think you are coming in here like that?"

"I didn't want to see you make a fool out of yourself," Beau said and immediately realized it was the wrong thing to say.

"Make a fool out of myself?" She stared up at him in disbelief. "The only one who made a fool out of himself was *you!*"

"He had his hands all over you, Becky. Surely, you

know about his reputation." Beau was suddenly on the defensive.

"Edward's reputation? No, I'm afraid I don't know about his reputation. Why don't you enlighten me?" she snapped, her hands on her hips, her eyes boring accusingly into his.

"He's a womanizer . . ."

"That's certainly the pot calling the kettle black!" she interrupted snidely.

"He's never settled down with any one woman before," Beau went on, trying to remember everything he'd overheard from the conversation those three women had had.

"Neither have you."

"Well, I wasn't the one you were making love to, damn it!" He was losing the thread of control he had on his temper now.

"I'd hardly call a few simple kisses 'making love,' Beau Hamilton! You have a dirty mind."

She started to spin around to turn her back on him, but Beau caught her by her arm and forced her to look at him.

"You're right about one thing, Becky. I'm just like Courtois, and that's why I know him so well. You may not have thought anything would have come of that little interlude I just put an end to, but let me tell you, you're wrong. Dead wrong." At the thought of the other man taking her innocence, Beau unknowingly tightened his hold on her.

Becky's eyes widened as she felt the bite of his grip on the tender flesh of her arm. "Beau, you're hurting me," she spoke the words softly.

Beau blinked, and slowly realized what he'd been doing. "I'm sorry," he murmured as he loosened his hold somewhat. "The last thing I'd ever want to do is hurt you, Becky."

As if spellbound, Beau slowly drew her closer until she was in the circle of his arms. His eyes caught and held hers. There was a flare of some emotion in the depths of her gaze, but he could not quite grasp its meaning.

Becky was afraid to speak. She was afraid something might break the magic of the moment. Beau was holding her! Beau was being tender with her! Beau had been jealous! She'd never suspected a slight flirtation with Edward would bring such marvelous results. Vaguely, she wished she had tried that tactic long ago.

"I know, Beau," Becky finally whispered huskily.

Beau groaned as he gave up the fight to refrain from kissing her. Damn, but she was the most confusing woman he'd ever known. One minute she was spitting at him like a fiery she-cat, and the next she was hot velvet surrender in his arms. Pushing all thoughts from him, he lowered his head to hers, claiming her mouth in a firebrand of excitement.

Becky met him willingly in that exchange. This was what she'd always wanted. This was the man she'd waited her whole life for . . . Beau . . . Looping her arms about his neck, she clung to him. He was the essence of her being. He was the love of her life. Now was her chance to show him just how much he meant to her.

Beau felt his desire rage out of control as she melted against him. He had never known such ecstasy. She was a vibrant flame in his embrace. Her innocence lured him, but her passion branded him her own. He caressed the length of her back, bringing his hand to rest at her hips and urging her closer to the proof of his need for her.

Becky gasped at the contact and then settled more tightly against him. He felt so big, so strong, and so good to her. She wanted to stay in his arms forever. She wanted to taste of his love. She wanted to make him hers in all ways, to bind him to her for all time. She loved him.

When Beau lifted a hand to caress her breast, she shifted position to allow him freer access to her womanly curves. Her willingness sent his passion soaring. Slipping his hand within her bodice, he caressed the satiny orb.

Becky felt her knees buckle as rapture flooded through her. Edward's caress, though pleasant, meant nothing compared to Beau's. Beau's touch was pure power, sapping her strength until she was trembling helplessly against him.

"Beau . . . Oh, Beau. . . ."

"I know, love," he told her gruffly as he picked her up into his arms and kissed her. He was about to lay her down upon the loveseat in the corner when a knock came at the study door, freezing him in midstride.

"Beau?" It was Adam.

"Yes, what do you want?" he asked, the annoyance in his voice easy to discern.

"Is Becky with you? Edward said you two were in there talking. . . ."

Beau glanced down at her as he slowly set her back upon her feet. Her eyes were sparkling with wicked humor. Becky was glad that Edward had only thought they were talking. With a self-possession she little felt, she walked to the door and opened it for her brother.

"You wanted me?"

"Yes . . ." Adam was disconcerted as he glanced from his sister to his best friend. Having heard the turn of the lock, he wondered what had been going on in here between the two of them. Becky looked radiant, though, and since he trusted Beau implicitly, he didn't worry.

"Well?"

"I was about to make an announcement, and I'd like you to be there."

"An announcement? What kind?" Becky was instantly curious.

"You'll see." Adam came into the room and filled up his glass with another large portion of bourbon. "Coming?"

Becky glanced back at Beau and then started from the room after her brother. When Beau reached her side, she gave him a brilliant smile.

"I think there's some unfinished business between us, Beau Hamilton," she said in low tones for him alone to hear.

Beau suddenly became nervous. Adam's interruption had tempered his passion, and cool-headed thinking had returned. The realization of what had almost happened in the privacy of the study startled him. "Becky —" he began.

"No, don't say anything." She paused at the ballroom door to face him squarely. "I love you, Beau. I always have and I always will."

With that, Becky swept on into the room ahead of him to hear what her brother had to say.

Chapter Nineteen

A small smile curved Lianne's lips as she saw Becky reenter the room looking ecstatically happy and then saw Beau following right after her. When Edward had returned to the ballroom a short time before he had seemed quite flustered about something. At the time Lianne hadn't paid much attention, but now, noticing the way Beau was hovering near Becky, she wondered just exactly what had transpired between the three of them.

For Becky's sake, Lianne hoped that Beau had finally come to his senses and recognized what a beautiful young woman she really was. If anyone deserved the happiness of getting the man they really loved, it was Becky. Lianne loved her like a sister and wanted only the best for her.

Lianne was surprised when Becky came to her. Her friend's face was alight with an inner joy. She looked radiant, happy and loved.

"You'll never guess what happened . . ." Becky whispered excitedly before Beau joined them.

"Oh, I think I have a good idea." Lianne smile widely. "Are you happy?"

"Beyond all my wildest dreams," she confided just as Beau came to her side.

"I'm glad for you, Becky. I really am."

It was just then that Adam raised his voice above the din of mellow conversation in the ballroom.

"Excuse me, everyone. I'd like to have your attention for a moment, if I may?"

A hush fell over the room, punctuated by only a few curious whispers.

"I have an announcement to make tonight . . ." he began, casting a fond look toward Suzanne.

Lianne frowned at this, trying to figure out exactly what it was Adam could be announcing.

"Becky? What's this all about?" She tried to sound casual, but something intuitive inside her warned her to get control.

"I don't know," Becky answered honestly. "The first I'd heard about it was when Adam came to get us in the study a minute ago."

Adam took Suzanne's hand then as they all looked on and drew her close to his side. "I'd like to let everyone know," he said in calm, measured tones, "that Suzanne Labadie has accepted my proposal and has agreed to become my wife."

The pain that sliced through Lianne at his proclamation was unbelievable, and, though horror stabbed at her heart, her only betrayal of emotion was in her eyes as they widened in soul-wrenching disbelief. *Adam was going to marry Suzanne . . . Adam was going to marry Suzanne . . .* she repeated over and over to herself as she stared at him in mute confusion. Lianne tried to deny what she'd heard. She tried to tell herself that this couldn't be happening, that the man who had fathered the child she was carrying was not going to wed her most hated enemy. But when Adam took Suzanne in his arms and kissed her warmly before the gathered crowd, it was burned into her consciousness forever. A part of her shattered as the bleakness of her life engulfed her. Complete and utter despair threatened her very sanity.

When Adam released Suzanne from his lover's embrace, she looked for Lianne in the crowd of now-cheering well-wishers. Their eyes met across the width of the room, and Suzanne gave her a very smug, self-satisfied smile.

Suzanne was thrilled with what she perceived as her victory over Lianne. Not only had she made Adam hers, she would also ultimately be the mistress of Belle Arbor, and the first thing she was going to do when she moved in was to throw the Ducharmes out. Her smiled widened at the thought.

When Suzanne looked away, a violent wave of nausea drained all the color from Lianne's face. *Suzanne was going to be the mistress of Belle Arbor. Suzanne was going to marry Adam.* Suddenly, the room seemed to be closing in on her, and Lianne was desperate to escape. She had to get away. She had to think!

Becky was standing beside Lianne, stunned by her brother's completely unexpected announcement of impending nuptials. She couldn't believe it. Adam was going to marry Suzanne? She turned on Beau, her expression reflecting both outrage and hurt. She knew Beau was aware of just about everything Adam did, and she was ready to demand an explanation from him when she noticed the direction of his gaze. For some reason Beau was intently watching Lianne.

"Becky . . ." he said softly, nodding toward Lianne.

Becky glanced at her friend and realized immediately that something was terribly wrong.

"Lianne?" Becky spoke her name, but, even as she did, Lianne fled the room through the french doors without a backward glance.

As Adam, with Suzanne clinging to his arm, was surrounded by those offering their congratulations, he suddenly, perversely, needed to see Lianne. He looked up, his gaze combing the crowd for her, but he could find no trace of her. Reluctantly, he returned his attention to Suzanne and the lavish felicitations being bestowed upon them by his guests.

In her flight, Lianne paused on the veranda and looked wildly around. She had to get away . . . she had to escape. Shivering uncontrollably, she dashed down the steps and out into the garden. She was thankful that everyone was inside, for the last thing she needed was to run into anyone right now.

Lianne ran madly down the winding garden paths without thought to her dress or hair. Branches from the shrubbery seemed to be trying to reach out and snare her, but she ignored the scratches and the tugging at her clothing. She ignored everything. Crushed . . . shattered . . . despondent, she charged on. Her breathing rasped painfully in her throat and her chest tightened in agony, yet she kept going.

Only when Lianne reached the reflecting pool did she stop her headlong flight to stare about herself in horrified disbelief. The pool! Her mindless escape had taken her back to the scene of her greatest degradation, to the scene of her greatest heartache. It was here that she had given Adam her most precious gift, and it was here now that she had to face the humiliation of her folly.

"Lianne!"

Becky's distressed call came to her through the night, but Lianne refused to answer. She didn't want to be found. She didn't want anyone to know her shame.

"Lianne, where are you? I know you're out here somewhere, and I'm going to find you."

Still, she remained silent.

"Lianne . . ." Becky's tone turned pleading. "I know how difficult this must be for you . . ." She emerged from the garden to see her friend sitting at the water's edge. Without another word, she rushed to her side and dropped to her knees beside her. "Lianne, I'm sorry about all this. Really, I am. I had no idea that Adam planned to marry Suzanne. In fact, the very thought of it leaves me furious. I wish he had warned me so I could have tried to talk him out of it."

Lianne didn't speak for a long time as she stared out across the pond with unseeing eyes. She was so still, so quiet, that she seemed almost a marble statue in the silvery moonlight. Only when she began to tremble visibly and drew a deep, shaking breath did she appear alive again.

"It doesn't matter, Becky. Really it doesn't," she lied, still not looking at her friend. She wished she would go away and leave her alone. What she had to face now, she could only face alone.

"If you think I believe that for one minute, you're wrong," Becky replied firmly. "If it didn't matter to you, you wouldn't have run out of the ballroom that way. I saw your face, Lianne. I know how badly this hurt you."

"You really have no idea, Becky. None . . ." Lianne's whisper was strangled.

"Can I help? Can I make this easier for you somehow?" Becky felt helpless in the face of her desolation.

"No." Her answer was flat. "No one can. What I have to do is take Alex and leave here as quickly as possible." Lianne turned to her, her emerald eyes wild.

"I thought we'd agreed that you were staying here until your money became available." Becky could understand Lianne being a little upset over finding out that Suzanne would be the mistress of Belle Arbor, but she didn't understand why her friend was reacting with such complete panic. "Adam and Suzanne haven't even announced a wedding date yet. There's no reason for you to leave now."

"You don't understand, Becky!" Lianne cried, and then could have cursed herself for revealing too much.

"I don't understand what, Lianne?" Becky demanded. "Tell me what it is I don't understand."

234

"If I don't leave here right away, there might not be any wedding."

"Now I'm really confused. Why would your staying on here affect Adam's plans for marriage?"

Lianne's gaze darkened as she faced her fully. "You must promise me that you'll never reveal to another soul what I'm about to tell you . . ."

"Lianne . . ." Becky was incredulous. "What is going on?"

"Promise me, Becky, or so help me I'll get up from here and walk away and never look back."

"Lianne . . ."

"Swear to it, Becky. Promise you'll keep my secret!"

"All right, I promise," she answered in exasperation. "Now, what are you talking about?"

Lianne twisted her hands nervously in her lap as she gathered her courage to tell Becky the truth. Finally, lifting her chin in a regal move, she spoke. "I'm pregnant, Becky. I'm pregnant with Adam's child."

She could only stare at her in shock. "My God . . ." Lianne—pregnant? All of her earlier suspicions had been true. Adam had been attracted to her, but what had happened? "But how? When?"

At Lianne's strained look, Becky realized how ridiculous her first question had been.

"There's no need to go into any of the details. What happened was a mistake." Lianne hated herself for using Adam's own words to describe their loving. "We both know it was wrong. We both know it should never have happened."

"How can you say that it was just a mistake?" Becky asked urgently as she took her hand supportivly. "You're carrying my brother's baby. A baby's no mistake! A baby is a blessing!"

Lianne wanted to feel that way . . . she loved children. But there had been no love in her dealings with

Adam, there had just been irresistible desire and then hate.

"Becky, I shouldn't have told you." Lianne suddenly regretted sharing the news.

"No, no! I'm glad you did. Now that I know . . ." Her mind was racing as she tried to figure out what to do next.

"Now that you know, you'll do nothing."

"Then you'll do it. You have to tell Adam," she declared.

"I meant to. I really did. I was going to talk with him tomorrow. But don't you see, Becky, it's pointless now. He doesn't love me. It's Suzanne he wants . . ."

Becky's anger over Adam's engagement to Suzanne had mellowed to more confusion than anything else now. She wished she knew exactly what had precipitated his proposing to her, but Adam had not chosen to confide in her about this at all. That in itself hurt, and she tried not to think about it.

"All I want you to do is to help me get away," Lianne was saying. "I know I don't have the right to ask this of you, but if you could just loan me enough money to last me until the trusts are paid, I swear, I'll pay every cent back with interest." She was earnest in her plea as she tried to plot her escape from the misery of her current situation. "Alex and I could leave town. No one would ever have to know. I'm sure Suzanne wants us out of here anyway, and probably the sooner the better. We won't be missed, Becky."

"I'd miss you," she stated fiercely.

Lianne felt tears burn her eyes. "Thank you."

Impulsively, Becky threw her arms about her and hugged her tightly. "Don't worry, Lianne. I'll think of something." When she let her go, she smiled. "You sneak on upstairs and try to relax. If anybody asks me where you are, I'll just tell them you weren't feeling well."

"Thanks Becky. I don't know if I could handle going back in and facing everyone after the way I ran out of there."

"No one saw you but Beau and me. The rest were too busy offering their congratulations."

Lianne nodded, glad that she hadn't made a fool out of herself. They got to their feet and headed back to the house. Lianne entered the back way and went up the rear stairway to make certain that she didn't run into anyone, while Becky brushed her skirts clean and went back inside to find Beau. She was definitely going to need his help to solve this problem.

It was late. The last of the guests had departed some time before, and Suzanne rejoiced in being alone with Adam. He was standing at the open french doors in the study, sipping from a tumbler of bourbon as he looked out across the moonlit countryside.

"It's going to be all ours one day soon," she said throatily as she set her drink aside and rose from the loveseat.

Adam was feeling tense. Ever since the engagement had been made official, he'd felt trapped, and he didn't understand why, because the trap was of his own making. This was his plan. It was working beautifully, and it was only a matter of time now until it was over.

Suzanne came to stand behind him and slipped her arms about his waist. "Together we're going to do great things with these two plantations, Adam. I can hardly wait to move in here with you . . ."

She pressed herself against his back in hopes that he would lose the masterful control he had on his desires and take her off to his bed. She wanted to spend the night here with him. She wanted to love him fully . . .

now . . . tonight.

Adam automatically stiffened at her words and her touch. He had to force himself to relax.

"It'll be sooner than you think," he told her as he drew her into his arms and kissed her.

"We haven't talked about a date for the wedding yet. Do you care how soon it is?"

Girding himself, he tried to sound enthusiastic. "How long will it take you to plan it?"

Suzanne slanted him a wicked smile as she raised her face to his for another kiss. "We could run away tomorrow."

Adam didn't doubt for a moment that she was serious, but he pretended not to believe her as he chuckled good-naturedly. "You know you want a big wedding. This will be a one-time thing for the both of us, so I think we should do it right. Spare no expense." He offered the money as a diversion.

"All right." She pouted prettily. "If I can't convince you to elope, I'll just have to make ours the most ostentatious ceremony this parish has ever seen."

"Whatever pleases you, my sweet." Adam kissed her again, faking passion.

"You please me, Adam," she said huskily.

"And I'll please you more once you're mine, Suzanne."

"I could be yours now . . ." Suzanne kissed his throat as she moved sensually against him.

Pretending it was an effort to tear himself from the excitement of her embrace, he stepped back to gaze down at her. "No. I want to wait until we're man and wife. I want everything to be perfect the first time we make love."

She signed at his romantic intentions as they started moving toward the front door and her waiting carriage. "You're everything I've ever wanted in a man, Adam.

We're going to be so wonderful together."

He kissed her one last time, lingering with just a suitable amount of regret, and then handed her into her conveyance. When it had disappeared down the drive, Adam ran a hand wearily through the dark thickness of his hair and then turned to go back inside.

The house was quiet. It had an almost deserted feeling to it as he reentered, and in a way, he was glad. He needed some time alone, some solitude.

Adam hadn't had a chance to speak privately with Becky since he'd made the announcement, and, judging from the angry looks she'd slashed his way during the balance of the evening, he knew there would be hell to pay once she finally cornered him. She was used to being included in every portion of his life, and — no doubt — she was angry with him for not confiding in her.

Adam wondered if he should tell her the whole story now that everything had gone according to plan. Beau had decided to spend the night rather than make the return trip to town, and Adam considered seeking him out and asking his opinion. Adam didn't get the chance, however, for as he stepped back into the study, he was confronted by a very angry, very resentful Becky.

"Hello, Adam," she bit out tautly. "I'm glad you made it back from saying good-night to your *fiancée!*"

"Becky . . ." His tone had a warning edge to it as he closed the door to insure their privacy.

"Don't you dare 'Becky' me, Adam Trent!" Becky exploded. "Do you have any idea of what you've done?"

Adam had never seen his sister in such an uproar, and he knew then that he had no choice but to tell her the complete truth.

"Of course I know what I've done," he returned, "and if you'll just shut up, I'll explain the whole thing."

"Yes, please. I'd like to hear this." She glared at him, her blue eyes glacial. Her manner was still furious, but more controlled now.

"This whole thing is not what you think," he began quickly, wanting to straighten everything out so she'd understand.

"Then you're not engaged to Suzanne Ducharme?" Becky asked with saccharine sweetness.

"Well, yes, but—"

"I thought you were going to explain everything, Adam. So far you've explained nothing."

He gave her a very pained look. "Becky, I'm 'engaged' to Suzanne for one reason and one reason only."

Becky thought of the sickening display he'd put on all evening, dancing with Suzanne and kissing her. Her stomach turned as she thought of Lianne being a witness to all that. "Because you love her, right?" she asked bitterly.

"Hell no!" Adam bellowed. "I don't love Suzanne!"

His sudden burst of outrage surprised Becky, and her expression of frosty disdain faltered. "Really?"

"Becky," he began earnestly, ready to disclose everything he knew, "Shark's partner is a female. Suzanne's plantation has failed to produce a paying crop for several seasons now, but she still continues to live a lavish lifestyle. She is in debt to no one. She has not mortgaged her land."

"And you believe Suzanne is Shark's partner on that little bit of evidence?" Becky's eyes were wide and accusing.

"No, Becky. There's one thing more I haven't told you." Adam went suddenly still as he remembered.

"What?"

"You know the crescent medallion I wear."

"Yes."

"I had one made for Elise as an engagement present,

240

too." He grew hoarse. "It was taken from Elise during the raid."

"Yes, so?"

"Suzanne has it. I've seen her wearing it."

"Oh, my God! Are you sure it's the same necklace?"

"I'm positive. I had it made especially for Elise." His jaw tensed as he struggled with his emotions.

Becky went to him then and put a sympathetic hand on his arm. "But why this engagement?"

"I have to stay close to her, and this seemed the easiest way. Hopefully, Shark will make an appearance before I'm forced to go through with the wedding." He grimaced at the possibility.

Becky thought of Elise and Adam's torment over the raid. She thought of Lianne and the baby. She realized the terrible web of intrigue that held Adam bound, but she also knew this was something she could not withhold from him. She had to tell him, and she knew that when she did, his whole world, all his plans, were going to be destroyed.

"Adam . . ." She spoke his name softly, tentatively.

He looked up at her. His whole body was tense, his dark eyes were burning with a fervent, inner fire. "I'm going to get that bastard, and when I do—"

"Adam, stop—there's something I have to tell you. There's something else you need to know."

"What?" he questioned. Noticing her grave expression, he sensed uneasily that this was the real reason for her visit to his study tonight. "What is it, Becky?"

"It's Lianne . . ."

This caught Adam totally off-guard.

"Lianne?" He frowned. He hadn't seen her since before the announcement. Memories of their intimate moment on the porch and then the ecstasy of their one waltz began to overwhelm him, but he pushed them away.

"Yes, Adam. Lianne is . . ." She hesitated, unsure how he would react, started at the beginning. "Lianne was very upset by the announcement of your engagement."

"So?" Adam snapped.

Quickly Becky explained. "So, Suzanne was responsible for Lianne's brother Mark's death. Lianne hates her for it, and she was devastated when she heard that you were planning to marry her . . . doubly so." She was growing frustrated, for somehow the news she'd wanted to impart wasn't coming out in the way that she'd intended.

"Doubly so? What are you talking about? Why should I care if my engagement upsets Lianne?" Adam demanded callously, focusing only on his goal to get Shark.

His words angered Becky, and she quit worrying about how he would react to the news. She forged ahead.

"Adam . . . you should care. You have to care."

"I don't *have* to do anything, Becky, except find Shark."

"Lianne is pregnant, Adam. The baby is yours."

Chapter Twenty

Adam's expression remained curiously blank as the shock of her revelation penetrated his very soul. He stared at his sister without really seeing her. His thoughts were chaotic. *Pregnant? Lianne was pregnant?* But how? Angrily, he berated himself for the stupidity of the thought. He knew how.

At his continued silence, Becky became slightly unnerved. She had never expected him to react this way. She had expected anger . . . outrage . . . but never this.

"You're denying it, then?" Becky challenged. "You're denying the child is yours?"

"I'm not denying anything." His voice was hard and filled with bitterness.

"Lianne wouldn't have lied to me, Adam. Lianne—"

He cut her off abruptly, demanding, "Where is she?"

"In her room, I guess . . . I—" She would have said more, but Adam had already stalked from the room leaving her very much alone. Becky rushed after and watched in silence as he took the stairs two at a time and then disappeared down the upstairs hall.

Lianne couldn't sleep. She'd tried everything . . . a hot bath . . . a snifter of brandy . . . but nothing had helped to settle her nerves. Wearing a pale green silk gown and wrapper, she paced her bedroom endlessly, wondering what to do next. A part of her wanted to wake Alex and flee with what little they had left. She wanted to escape Belle Arbor and Adam before her condition became apparent, but Becky's promise that she would help kept her from running.

Lianne was only now realizing what a great risk she had taken in confiding in Becky. Still, she trusted her and knew that her friend would come to her aid. After all, it wasn't as if she was begging for charity, she reassured herself. She would repay every cent Becky loaned her.

The soft knock at her door startled her, and she jumped at the unexpected intrusion. She thought perhaps it was Becky and, nervously clutching her wrapper around her, she unlocked the door and started to open it. At the sight of Adam, his expression murderous, she tried to slam the door shut again, but he forced his way into the room.

Lianne backed away from his threatening presence. "What do you want?" she whispered, frightened. She prayed desperately that Becky had not told him of the baby. She didn't want him to know. She only wanted to leave.

"What do you think I want?" Adam consciously kept his voice down and his eyes never left her as he shut the door behind him.

Lianne's eyes grew round as her worst fears were realized. Becky had told Adam. "She's told you . . ."

"Yes, she told me," Adam snarled as he moved closer. His gaze raked over her with humiliating familiarity.

Lianne read what she thought was disgust in his eyes and grew angry. She hadn't planned this! She had been just as surprised as he was! With a prideful lift of her chin, she met his gaze bravely.

"I asked Becky to keep the secret, Adam. Had I known she would go to you right away with the news, I would never have confided in her."

"Oh? And just how much longer did you think you

could keep this a secret?" he asked sarcastically.

"I had planned to tell you," she defended herself quickly.

"When, Lianne? When I was at the altar with Suzanne?"

"I had no idea that you were going to get engaged to her!" Lianne was furious with him for even suggesting such a thing. "I was going to tell you after the party . . . sometime next week."

"I see," he said shrewdly, "but this worked out even better for you, didn't it?"

"What are you talking about?" she snapped, thinking him quite crazy.

"I'm talking about your plan," Adam countered, trying not to look at her breasts and the way they were heaving in her supposed indignation.

"Plan? What plan?"

"It all makes sense now. It's just a shame I wasn't wise to you before all this happened." He was growing increasingly angry as he felt desire for her heating his loins.

Lianne didn't know it, but she looked enticingly beautiful in the silken negligee. Her hair was loose and flowing about her shoulders . . . her skin had a translucent beauty that begged for Adam's touch . . . and her breasts were perfection themselves, their peaks clearly outlined as they teasingly pressed against the satiny material.

Damn! Adam swore violently to himself. He couldn't allow this to happen! It had been this damn fool weakness he had for her that had gotten him into this horrendous mess in the first place. The last thing he needed to do was worsen the whole thing by giving into his desire for her again.

"I don't know what you're talking about." She would have turned away from him, but he snared her wrist in a viselike grip. "Let go of me!"

"That wasn't what you said the night you seduced me!"

"Seduced you?"

"Of course. How perfectly you had it all worked out, and so quickly, too. Seduce him, get pregnant, force him to marry you. Perfect! In one masterful move, you had your home back and a rich husband to boot. Not only that, but your deceitful ways have also managed to wreak the perfect revenge upon Suzanne." Adam leered down at her.

It hadn't occurred to her before that her dilemma would affect anyone except her and Adam, but the thought that she had now gotten back at the vicious Suzanne filled Lianne with a searing, burning joy. Adam saw the change in her expression and grew even more furious.

"Did you think it up on the spur of the moment, or did you plan the whole thing on your way back from seeing your uncle after you found out that you were dirt poor?" Adam continued, his voice cold and lashing.

His stinging accusation jolted her and left her seething. "Why you . . . !" She hadn't planned any of this! She wasn't like that! She wasn't!

"I've got just one question for you. What if you hadn't gotten pregnant right away? What would you have done then? Continue to surrender to me, even while you pretend to 'fight' it?"

"You're disgusting!"

He laughed viciously. "I am, am I? I'm not the one who would stoop to such lengths as to sell my body to get what I want!"

"I hate you!"

"Oh, I'm sure you do, but you're probably overjoyed at the prospect of being mistress of Belle Arbor, aren't you? What would you say if I refused to marry you?"

Adam tightened his hold on her as he dragged her against his chest, pinning her there.

"I never asked you to marry me! I've never asked you for anything except to sell my home back to me!"

"And when I wouldn't, you decided get your home back another way!"

As he held her pinioned in a steely embrace, she pounded on his chest in a futile gesture.

"No! You've got to believe me! I didn't plan any of this!" Lianne protested, tears streaming from her eyes. How could he think her so vile? What had she ever done that he could think she'd do such a thing?

Adam gave a short, scoffing laugh, his heart hardening in the face of her tears. He'd let them affect him once, but never again. Lianne was a conniving witch. She'd plotted this whole thing and ruined all of his own plans. His scheme to trap Shark was in a shambles, and it was all because of her.

"Don't worry, my dear," he drawled coldly. "We'll marry."

"I'd rather die!" she shot back defiantly.

"Don't tempt me, Lianne," Adam said tersely as he tightened his hold upon her.

Helpless in his grasp, she shivered at the intensity of his words.

"No child of mine will be born a bastard. We'll be married tomorrow."

"But what about Suzanne?" The words were out before she knew it.

Adam gave her a chilling smile. "Just because we have to marry to give the child a name doesn't necessarily mean that my relationship with Suzanne will have to change."

Lianne's eyes reflected her tender shock at his declaration. He planned to keep on seeing Suzanne even after they married.

"Ours will be a marriage in name only, my dear," he proclaimed, denying the physical attraction he felt for her that was even now surging through him. The fact that he was reacting to her nearness this way angered him. She had used that sweet little body of hers as a tool against him once, and he would never allow that to happen again. Abruptly, Adam released her and turned away. "I hope you sleep well." With that he strode from the room, pledging only to give a name to his unborn child.

Lianne stared after him in heart-numbing agony. She hadn't known until that moment that the romantic dreamer in her had been hoping for a happy ending to her trauma. She had hoped that Adam might find joy in the knowledge that he was to be a father, but it wasn't to be.

Shattered, she collapsed on the bed. She cried endlessly until there were no more tears to be shed. Frightened and lonely, she passed the balance of the long, black night staring into the darkness, her heart aching and heavy.

Becky had desperately wanted to go to Lianne, but she knew now that it was none of her business. Still, she worried. A year ago, she would never have doubted Adam's integrity in such a situation. He was an honorable man. But he had changed so much since the raid that she feared his obsession with catching Shark would overrule his honor. She was nervous as she awaited his return.

Adam was livid. He considered retiring to his room, but knew any quest for sleep would be futile. The power of his useless rage filled him with restless energy. There were too many things to be considered, too many things he had to work out.

Downstairs, Adam headed once again for the study. Unaware of Becky's presence, he crossed the room to the liquor cabinet, poured himself a very generous portion of bourbon, and then stopped to inhale a deep breath. His grip on the crystal tumbler tightened until his knuckles showed white. The tight rein he'd held on his anger broke. In a violent, savage action, he threw the glass and its contents across the room and watched with little satisfaction as it shattered against the far wall.

"Do you feel better now?" Becky's voice cut through the heavy silence.

Adam didn't bother to look at her. Instead, he merely picked up the bottle of liquor and took a deep drink.

"Do you really think that's going to help?"

"It certainly can't hurt, my darling little sister." He thought of Elise. He thought of Suzanne and Shark. He took another drink.

"Adam . . . is it really all that bad?" Becky went to him and put her hand on his arm, but he shrugged off her touch and dropped down negligently into the chair behind the desk. Still, she persisted. "Lianne's a beautiful woman, and you could learn to love her. She is the mother of your child."

Leaning back, bracing his long legs up on the desktop, he lifted his narrowed eyes to hers and froze her with an ice-cold glare. "The wedding will be tomorrow."

"All right." At least she was relieved to her that.

"You might as well go ahead and take charge of it," he directed with little interest. "I don't know if Lianne's in any condition to do it."

"You didn't hurt her, did you?" Becky asked sharply, ready to run to her friend's aid.

"Hell, no, I didn't hurt her!" he snapped, wondering how his sister who knew him so well could even think of such a thing. "She's fine. In fact, she's probably up there right now gloating over her success."

"What are you talking about?"

"I'm talking about her devious little scheme to hold onto Belle Arbor. You know how badly she wanted to keep this place. Well, when she couldn't buy it back, she decided to get it back another way," he sneered.

Becky was jarred to the depths by his allegation. She knew Lianne. She had seen her friend's very real distress. This had not been a planned occurrence.

"You're wrong about this, Adam. You don't know—"

"*I know,* Becky," he stated harshly. "*I know.*"

His hate-filled conviction destroyed Becky's usually mild temperament. "Did you know that she made me promise not to tell you? Did you know that she only wanted me to loan her enough money so she could get away from Belle Arbor before you married Suzanne?"

"Lianne's cunning, Becky. She probably knew you'd run right to me with the news," he pointed out maddeningly, "and you did. It worked perfectly."

Becky gritted her teeth in frustration at his blindness. "Don't you realize how it must have affected Lianne to hear you announce your engagement to Suzanne while she was standing there pregnant with your baby?"

"I imagine my soon-to-be bride was quite delighted," he returned bitterly, still assured in his belief that Lianne had deliberately gotten herself with child.

"Why do you have such a low opinion of Lianne?" Becky challenged. "What has she ever done to you to make you feel this way about her?"

"I'll tell you what she's done!" he exploded as he slammed out of the chair. "She's just destroyed everything I've worked for, everything I've tried to do."

"She didn't get pregnant by herself, Adam!" Becky nearly shouted at him. She understood the rawness of

250

his anger, but she knew he was also to blame for what had happened.

His expression turned murderous as he scowled at his sister. He cursed the wild desire he'd felt for Lianne that had led to this. "What the hell am I supposed to tell Suzanne? I can't let this opportunity slip away when I'm so damned close to nailing Shark!"

"Adam, you've admitted that the baby Lianne is carrying is yours. That's the important thing. That's what really matters. Does revenge against that damned pirate carry more importance to you than protecting your own flesh and blood?" Realizing that she'd pushed him as far as she was going to be able to, she moved to the door. "Think about it, Adam."

He did not watch her leave the room, but he heard the door close quietly behind her. He looked down at the bottle he still clutched in his hand and in disgust set it aside. He didn't need any more liquor tonight. He needed a clear head.

Sitting back down at the desk, Adam leaned forward to rest his elbows on the desktop and rest his head in his hands. He didn't want to think about it, but Becky's admonition to think of his child stayed with him. A baby . . . his own . . . The thought was rather awe-inspiring.

Adam's mouth twisted into the closest thing to a smile he could manage at the moment. He loved children. He got along wonderfully with Alex and imagined briefly having a son of his own. Yet as he was envisioning riding and sailing with a male offspring who looked suspiciously like himself, the image of a tiny emerald-eyed vixen stole into his thoughts.

His smile started to widen at the vision, and suddenly, seeing the direction of his own thoughts, he froze. Why had he felt such joy at the image of a little girl who so closely resembled Lianne? She had no hold on him. She meant nothing to him. She was only the mother of his child, nothing more. Still, even as he convinced himself that he didn't care for Lianne, something in the back of his mind reminded him of the overpowering attraction he felt for her and that tomorrow she would be his wife.

"I now pronounce you man and wife. What God has joined together, let no man put asunder," intoned the priest as the small group stood gathered rather solemnly in the parlor early the next afternoon.

Lianne blanched when she heard his last declaration, and she trembled. The whole ceremony had been a travesty. They had pledged to love, honor, and obey, but it had all been a lie. Adam had already told her that he had no intention of parting with Suzanne. Obviously, he considered their marriage just a slight inconvenience, necessary because of the baby. It came to her that he might very well divorce her once the child was born, but the thought was so painful that she quickly put it from her mind. She would think only of the baby, and maybe that would help temper the desolation she felt over Adam's cruel accusations.

At his closing words, Adam turned to his bride and stared down at her with an enigmatic expression. His gaze was dark and unreadable as it raked over her upturned, pale face and then down to her left hand that now bore his ring. She was his. Knowing that it was expected, he took her in his arms and kissed her.

After the way they had parted the night before, Lianne had not expected any kind of display from him. The ceremony had been essentially sterile, and she expected the rest of her life to be that way, too. When his gaze met hers, she felt suddenly trapped, and when he crushed her to him, she started to protest. Before she could speak, though, his mouth swooped down to claim hers in a possessive, passionate exchange.

Lianne felt her knees threaten to give way as he ruthlessly plundered the sweetness of her mouth. It was almost as if he was trying to prove something to himself and somehow punish her at the same time. Shivering uncontrollably, she clung to the broad width of his shoulders, thankful for the support.

"Adam?" It was Beau who dared to speak up.

At the sound of his friend's voice, Adam's sanity returned. He broke off the embrace, releasing Lianne as abruptly as he'd taken her in his arms. With all the manner of a man unaffected by what had just transpired, he coolly turned to thank the priest for performing the wedding on such short notice.

When Adam finished speaking with the priest, Alex could no longer control his enthusiasm. With all the excitement that only a youngster can exude, he launched himself into Adam's arms and hugged him fiercely.

"Adam! I'm so glad you married Lianne! That means we're brothers now, huh?" He gazed up at Adam with open, youthful adoration.

"Yes, Alex. We're brothers now." For some reason, Alex's uncomplicated wonder and excitement touched Adam deeply, and he hugged him back with equal enthusiasm.

"Boy! You had me scared for a while there," Alex reported with a laugh.

"I did?" Adam looked down at him, his curiosity evident.

"Did you ever! I was really worried," he confided seriously. He remembered Mark and how his involvement with Suzanne had ended in tragedy. "I was afraid that you liked Suzanne better than Lianne!"

It was awkward for a moment as a stunned silence

descended. No one had told Alex of all the intrigue that had occurred regarding the wedding. He just thought that marriages happened this way.

Having dealt with Alex's candid observations for many years now, Lianne recovered first. "He had to like me best, Alex, because I'm so much like you," she teased with a feigned lightheartedness.

"That's right," Adam agreed. Lianne looked up in surprise at his statement, but his eyes were flat, hard, and passionless as they met hers.

Announcing that there were refreshments there for all to enjoy in honor of the celebration, Becky led the way into the dining room. Alex darted happily ahead to sample of the tasty array of treats with the others following. Only Adam and Beau lingered behind.

"When are you going to see Suzanne?" Beau asked.

"Today, as soon as I can get away," he answered curtly.

Beau nodded. "It won't be pretty."

Adam snorted in disgust, not at all looking forward to the encounter.

"What are you going to tell her about Lianne?"

"Whatever I think she'll believe," he said gravely. "Shark's got to return soon. It's been weeks since you saw him sail out. He's due back at any time now. I can't afford to lose the one sure connection we have to him!"

"I wish you luck."

"I'm going to need it. When are you planning on sailing again?"

"I'll be returning to the ship tomorrow."

"Good."

"Adam? Beau? Aren't you coming to join us?" Becky's invitation was a carefully veiled command.

Both men exchanged troubled glances and then went in to join the others in celebrating the marriage.

Chapter Twenty-one

Suzanne stared at Adam, her face as white as a sheet, her blue eyes burning wildly with explosive wrath. "You've *what!*"

"Lianne and I were married this afternoon, Suzanne," he repeated the news bluntly as he stood stiffly before her. He expected and was prepared to take whatever abuse she decided to heap upon him.

"I can't believe it. How could this have happened? Last night you pledged your love to me before all those people, and today you tell me that you've married another woman . . ." She was distraught at the thought of losing him, yet the humiliation she knew she was going to suffer when word of this spread took precedence over all else in her mind.

"It was necessary, Suzanne," Adam said flatly. "Lianne is carrying my child."

"She's what!" Suzanne cried, horrified.

"Lianne's pregnant. We married only to give my child a name."

"Your child? Your child!" she raged, her fear of embarrassment lost in a sea of roiling anger. "You tell me that you want to wait to make love to me until we're married, and all the while you're bedding Lianne!"

"It wasn't like that," Adam told her with as much calm as he could muster.

"And I'm supposed to believe you just because you

say it's so?" She got up from the sofa where they'd been sitting and moved away from him when he would have held her.

"Suzanne, I didn't bed you, because I respected you and wanted to save our lovemaking for our wedding night." He hoped he sounded earnest in his explanation.

Suzanne believed what Adam was telling her. He was everything she'd ever wanted in a man, and she didn't want her dream of having him to end. Adam Trent was to be hers!

"This thing with Lianne just happened," Adam went on to explain.

Suzanne had always known Lianne was no good, and this just proved it. Not only was she as stupid as her brother had been, but she was a slut, too.

Obviously Adam's encounter with her had occurred some time ago for her to be able to announce a pregnancy now. Probably, Suzanne figured, Lianne had thrown herself at Adam. Red-blooded male that he was, he wouldn't turn down a willing female, especially since this happened before their own engagement. Suzanne's lips curled into a snarl as she imagined the great joy Lianne must have taken in announcing her impending motherhood to Adam after he'd already openly proclaimed his love for her.

"I want to believe that, Adam, but what am I supposed to do?" she asked, her fury giving way to calculated tears she hoped would affect him. "You're the only man I've ever loved, and now I've lost you."

This time when he tried to embrace her, she did not resist but melted in his arms. She hid her face against his chest, hiding her smile of triumph at his next declaration.

"You haven't lost me, darling," he promised as he bent to kiss her.

Suzanne's heart swelled at his unspoken promise of continued devotion, and she thrilled to the touch of his lips on hers. This was Adam, the man she loved. A stupid little chit like Lianne wouldn't be able to hold a man like him. He was hers!

Suzanne found the thought of taking Adam to her bed on the day he married another woman perversely exciting. What better way to get back at that Ducharme bitch! She pressed herself willingly against Adam, wanting him to know that she would offer him anything. She was his for the taking. She wanted him more than anything in the world. Yet as she tried to deepen the embrace, Adam drew away.

"I have to go, darling."

"I want you, Adam. I don't want you to leave. Stay with me. Love me, please," Suzanne invited without reservation. "There's no reason to deny ourselves any longer."

Adam gave her a quick, silencing kiss. "There is a reason to deny ourselves, darling. I don't want to risk your reputation. I've already paid the price for one mistake, and it's a price I can't pay more than once."

"Oh, Adam . . ." She sighed ecstatically as she realized that his true concern in not making love to her was protecting her. "What will I do without you?"

"You won't have to do without me, darling. That will never change."

"You mean we can still see each other?" Suzanne was filled with hope.

"Every chance I get," he vowed honestly. "Do you really think I could stay away from you?"

At his confession, Suzanne kissed him wildly. "I'll wait for you, my love. Forever, if I have to . . ."

Despite the traumatic events of the day, Adam felt some satisfaction at her words. Perhaps all had not been lost. . . .

It was late as Lianne sat in the parlor with Becky, Beau, and Alex. Dinner had already been served and the dishes cleared away, but still Adam had not returned. Though he had not told her where he was going, she had known. He'd gone to Suzanne's, and now he'd been away for hours.

The pain in her heart was excruciating, but Lianne didn't really understand why. She rationalized that it was the humiliation she was suffering at being abandoned here before the others that hurt her so badly. She certainly didn't love Adam, she reminded herself. She hated him. She had been forced to marry him because of the baby, nothing else. What did she care if he spent their wedding day with the one woman she despised above all others? Suzanne had cheated her of Mark, and now she would take Adam from her, too. Unconsciously, at the thought, Lianne's hands clinched tightly in her lap.

Looking for a way to escape and be alone with her thoughts, she finally decided to put Alex to bed. "Alex, sweetheart, it's time for you to go to bed now."

"Not yet, Lianne. I want to see Adam again before I go to bed," he argued.

"Well, you'll just have to wait until morning, young man," she answered with a smile.

"But when's he coming back, Lianne? He's been gone too long." Alex put plainly into words what everyone else had been thinking.

Lianne flushed, but managed to answer coolly enough. "He had some important business to tend to that couldn't wait, love. He'll be back soon, you'll see."

"Yeah, but you said it's my bedtime already, and I wanted to tell him good-night before I went to sleep," he went on. "I wanted to tell him again how glad I am that he's my brother! I like Adam, Lianne. I'm glad you married him."

"Well, I'm sure you'll see him at breakfast, Alex. Now, no more arguing, it's bedtime."

"Good night, Alex," Becky and Beau said in unison as they watched Lianne usher him from the room.

"Are you coming back down?" Becky asked.

"No, I think I'll go on to bed, Becky. It has been a long day, and I am rather tired."

"All right," she agreed, understanding her need for some time alone. "We'll see you in the morning."

"Good night." Lianne followed Alex from the room as calmly as she could, although her first instinct was to run madly from their sight. She couldn't bear their looks of sympathy any longer.

When she'd tucked Alex snugly in bed and kissed him soundly, she returned to her own room to get ready for bed. Sarah was there already waiting for her with a hot bath and fresh linens.

"Thanks, Sarah. How did you know?" Lianne asked wearily as she began to strip off her clothing.

"Miss Becky told me that you were going to bed, so I got your bath ready."

"You're going to spoil me," Lianne said as she stepped into the steaming, perfumed water and sank down in its soothing comfort.

"You could use with a little spoiling," she retorted happily, not in the least bit distressed by her marriage to Adam Trent.

Lianne didn't answer as she closed her eyes against the bite of threatening tears. She didn't want to think right now. She just wanted to enjoy the scented bath and pretend for a little while that everything in her life was wonderful.

"I'll start moving your things into Mr. Adam's room first thing in the morning," Sarah told her as she tidied up after her.

Lianne's eyes snapped open at her statement. "You'll do no such thing, Sarah! My things will remain in here and so will I."

"What are you talking about, Miss Lianne?"

"I'll be remaining in my own room, Sarah. I'm sure Adam won't mind.

Sarah gave a snort of disbelief. "He married you, didn't he? I'm sure he's expecting you in his bed."

"And I'm equally sure that he's not!" Lianne shot back, embarrassed at having to reveal the nature of Adam's proposal. "Now, I don't want to hear another word about it, Sarah! Just do as you're told!"

Sarah didn't know exactly what had happened between Adam and Lianne, but she knew now it hadn't been the happy joining she'd thought it was going to be. In all her life, Lianne had never raised her voice to her or spoken to her in such a manner. For her to respond that way, something had to be terribly wrong.

"What is it, child? What's wrong?" She tried to coax her into talking about it, hoping it would help her.

But Lianne didn't want to share the humiliation of her "marriage in name only" with anyone, even though she knew that everyone would figure it out once they spend the first night apart.

"Nothing's wrong. Now, go on and leave me alone," she dismissed her. "I'll dress myself."

Adam rode slowly up the long drive to Bell Arbor. He had left Suzanne's long before sundown, but had not wanted to return home. The longer he stayed away from Lianne the better. He was not about to let her gloat over her masterful manipulations. She might be his wife, but his name was all she would ever have.

Adam tried not to think about the night ahead,

about sleeping in the same bed with her, about knowing she was his to take . . . No, he told himself furiously, as attractive as he might find her physically, there was no way he was going to allow himself to make love to her.

His mood was black indeed as he handed his mount over to a waiting servant and then strode inside. He was pleased to find that everyone else had gone to bed, and he decided to take the time to have a drink before going upstairs to join his bride. The bourbon went down smoothly, and he welcomed the bolstering heat of it in his system.

Adam was tempted to spend the night in the study drinking, but thought better of it. Though he hadn't wanted this marriage, he was not going to let Lianne chase him from his own bed. He finished off his liquor and started upstairs.

As he mounted the staircase, he found himself wondering if Lianne was eagerly awaiting him in their marriage bed. A mental image of her anxiously anticipating his coming filled his mind. In his unbidden fantasy he pictured Lianne wearing a seductive negligee that bared her long limbs and the curves of her pale-hued breasts. The glory of her hair tumbled down about her shoulders, and her arms were reaching out for him . . .

A surge of heat flooded his loins, and with a vile, muttered curse, he forced the vision away. He was not going to give her the satisfaction of knowing he desired her. He was not going to taste of her incredible sweetness. He was going to stay clear of her. They might share the same bed, but that was as intimate as they were going to get.

The bedroom was dark when he entered. Obviously, Adam thought, Lianne had gone to sleep. He was glad. He hadn't wanted to deal with her tonight anyway.

Then the taunting thought came — *So much for the fantasy.* She had gotten what she wanted, and that was all that mattered to her.

Adam made his way to the dresser and lit the single lamp there, intending to turn it up just enough so he could see to undress. Adam kept his gaze averted from the bed. He did not look at its reflection in the mirror, and he did not turn around. Instead, he methodically unbuttoned his shirt, shrugged out of it, and threw it aside. He had just started to take off his pants when he glanced up for the first time and saw that his bed was empty.

He stared at it in confusion for a moment, his emotions a curious mix of disbelief and outrage. *Where the hell was she?* He looked around then and noticed that there was no sign at all of her presence. Without bothering to put his shirt back on, he stalked from the room.

Though she was exhausted, Lianne had not yet managed to fall asleep. Every time she started to drift off, the memory of Adam's passionate kiss after the wedding ceremony would return, and she would come fully awake again. She didn't understand him, that was plain. He had declared that he didn't want her in any way, and yet his embrace had been as exciting and irresistible as ever. Lianne shivered in remembrance, then struggled to put it from her once more. She would never know the ecstasy of being with him again.

Unexpectedly, her bedroom door flew open and banged loudly against the far wall. There, silhouetted against the brightness of the hall, stood Adam. He seemed larger than life and seemed to fill the entire doorway. Even in the shadowed darkness, she could tell that he was angry about something, for he stood there, hands on hips, glaring at her across the width of the room.

"What are you doing in my room?" Lianne demanded as she struggled to sit up in bed, clutching the covers over her bosom.

"The question is — *wife* — what are you doing in your room?" he returned, moving into the room and slamming the door behind him.

"I intend to keep my room, sir," she answered haughtily, lifting her chin in determination.

"Like hell you are!" Adam declared. In a fit of fury, he strode forward to the bed and snatched her up in his arms, blanket and all.

"What do you think you're doing!" Lianne shrieked as he opened the door and started from her room.

"You are my wife, and your place is with me." Adam didn't know why he felt so strongly about it. He just knew that he did.

"Oh no, it's not!"

She tried to throw herself from his arms, but Adam only clamped his arms more tightly about her. As he turned to kick his bedroom door closed behind them, she continued to struggle. Her efforts were useless, though. All she managed to accomplish was to lose control of the blanket she'd kept firmly wrapped around her. It fell from her grasp just as he moved toward his bed.

Adam knew that she'd dropped something, and he glanced down at her to see what it was. He knew immediately that he'd made a mistake. Lianne was wearing a shimmering creation of a negligee that put the one in his fantasy to shame. The material was a filmy fabric, gossamer in texture. Its pale peach color teased his senses, revealing all of her luscious curves. He could see the darker tips of her breasts where the material stretched taut over her bosom. In her struggles, the gown had pulled up, leaving her long, shapely legs bare to his gaze.

A flare of molten desire shown in his dark eyes as they raked boldly over her. Adam felt the tension building in his loins, but he fought it down. It took every ounce of willpower that he possessed not to act upon his raging passion. A muscle twitched in his cheek as he kept control. Beautiful though she was, he would not bed her again.

Lianne knew a moment of panic as the blanket dropped from her grasp. She stared up at him, her eyes mirroring the fear and uncertainty she was feeling at being so exposed before him. Her pulse raced in frantic rhythm as her emerald gaze met his. She held her breath as he carried her to the bed, not sure what to expect from him. When he dumped her unceremoniously in the middle of it, she was shocked.

"That, my dear bride, is where you belong," Adam stated arrogantly.

At being so manhandled, Lianne came to her knees to face him. "I won't stay here with you! I have my own room, and I intend to use it."

"You make one move to leave that bed, and I'll tie you to it," he said in a tone that left no doubt in her mind that he would do it.

"But why?" Lianne argued. "You've said yourself that our marriage is a farce. Why ask this of me? Why not leave me alone completely like you did all evening?"

Adam smiled thinly at her last statement. "What's wrong, dear wife? Were you jealous?"

"I'd never be jealous of you, Adam Trent!"

Her words angered him and he reached out to grab her arms, hauling her up against him. "Did you think of me pleasuring Suzanne as I pleasured you?" he taunted, releasing one of her arms so he was free to fondle her.

Lianne jerked away from his touch as if she was burned. "I hate you!"

"Oh, yes, how well I know that. You hate me for everything I've ever done to you. Tell me, wife, exactly what have I ever done to you to incur such hatred? Was it because I've managed to pull Belle Arbor back from the brink of financial disaster? Or was it because I planted my seed within you and gave you my child? Or was it because I married you to save your reputation and to give my baby his rightful heritage? Tell me, Lianne, just why do you hate me?" Adam sneered as he pushed her almost violently back down on the bed. He stood over her, regarding her coldly. "You will share my bed, Lianne, and not just tonight, but every night."

"But—"

His sharp look silenced her. "I won't have it publicly known that our marriage is less than it should be."

Lianne scrambled to grab the sheet on the bed and cover herself, but the look he gave her shamed her for her action.

"You needn't worry that I will force my attentions on you. There are many who would eagerly ease my manly needs. I won't be troubling you, dear, and I will be discreet. Now go to sleep. It's been a long day and I, for one, am tired."

Lianne moved to the far side of the bed, still holding the covers tightly about her. As Adam turned away from her and began stripping off the last of his clothing, she wanted to ignore him, but she found herself watching him. She stared, mesmerized, as he stood naked before her, looking much like some sun-bronzed god. His body was sculpted muscle, his shoulders wide, his hips trim, his legs long and straight.

As Adam moved to put out the light, she thought he

moved with the grace of a beast of the wilderness . . . surefooted, quiet, ever ready to defend or attack. The comparison sent a feverish chill down her spine, and she closed her eyes tightly, wishing fervently for sleep to come, but knowing it would not.

She felt the bed sag under his weight and felt him move beneath the blankets. For some reason she was breathless and wary, but as the minutes passed and he made no move to touch her, she slowly relaxed. The next day she would be amazed to find that she'd fallen asleep so easily with Adam beside her.

Adam lay stiffly in his bed. His body throbbed with the need to take Lianne, to slake the passion he felt for her, but the iron-fisted rein he kept on his desires mastered his need. He would not make love to her, not tonight, not tomorrow night, never! It was near dawn before he finally managed to get a little rest.

David Williams had stayed on much later than usual with Elise this evening, hoping against hope for some small sign of improvement. Night after night, he'd come to sit with her, talking of anything and everything in an effort to encourage some kind of response from her. As he let himself out of the house and moved off down the darkened street, he felt as if all his efforts were for nothing. He had tried a whole range of approaches, but none of them had worked. Elise had not improved, and he was beginning to believe that she never would.

He'd even started to bring her small presents, little things like a single, fragrant blossom from the garden, but there had been no change. In a last, concerted attempt, he'd purchased a music box that played a sweet, light melody. Every night when he'd arrived, he had wound it up and played it to her as he sat with her. He had hoped that what conversation couldn't accomplish, music could, but again it had seemed to have no affect.

David's heart was heavy with a terrible sense of failure as he left Elise. His steps were slow and hesitant, and he found that he was actually dreading going home. His house, once his haven from his emotionally taxing work, now seemed lonely and almost barren. David frowned as he wondered at the change in himself.

It was during the wee hours of the morning that Elise came awake. She blinked sleepily and stared about the strange room, trying to remember what it was that had disturbed her rest. A tumbled twist of memories surfaced in her mind—scenes and faces, odd bits of conversations, none of them threatening, none of them exciting.

Only one memory carried any emotion with it. It was the memory of the music, of the haunting refrain that filled her with a firm sense of warmth and security. Now, in the dark of the night, Elise needed to hear that sweet, reinforcing melody again.

Elise sat up in her bed and looked around. In the dimness of the low lamplight she saw the object of her desire on the nearby dresser and gave a sigh of relief. Throwing off her blanket, she left her bed to claim the prize she sought. Her legs were trembling as she made her way back to the bed, the music box clutched tightly in her grasp.

Elise thought it odd that she should feel so weak, and she wondered about it. She was shaky as she sat down on the edge of the bed and placed the music box on the night table. With the utmost of care, she wound the spring and then sat enraptured as the lilting strains of the chime echoed sweetly in her chamber. She reached out with a finger to cherishingly touch the small treasure and then lay back on the comfort of her bed to listen.

Her last thought as she fell into a deep, restful sleep was of a gentle-voiced man named David, whose memory was indelibly interwined with that of the music. She sighed contentedly and slept.

Chapter Twenty-two

Becky could not sleep. For most of the long hours of darkness, she'd merely stayed in bed, alone with her thoughts. So much had happened and in such a short period of time that her mind was awhirl with the importance of all of it. She thought of Adam and Lianne and their forced marriage, and she said a little prayer that it would all work out.

The memory of Adam's confession concerning his real reason for being involved with Suzanne troubled her deeply, and his obstinate refusal to give up on his vendetta against Shark worried her even more. She wanted him to put it from him, to concentrate on his new wife and unborn baby, but there was no reasoning with Adam on the subject. Every time one of the messages from Dr. Williams came telling him that Elise still had made no progress, his mood turned black. He was held in the grasp of his obsessive need for revenge, and she wondered if it would ever end.

Becky was feeling overwhelmed as she thought of how complicated everything had become. Just a day ago at the party, she'd been trying to figure out a way to get Adam and Lianne together. For all her plans, she had never expected anything like this. Even Beau had been surprised by the speed with which it had all come about.

At the thought of Beau, Becky signed wistfully. He was so wonderful. Ever since the trouble had begun, he'd been there for her, helping her in any way he could. They had been so caught up in making all the arrangements of the wedding that there had been no time for them to have another private moment together. She had not had the chance to say any more about her true feelings for him.

Now that the wedding was over and life would be returning to some form of normalcy, she wished that she had more time with him. It was not possible this trip, though, for he was leaving early in the morning to return to the ship.

The prospect of not seeing him again for perhaps months on end left Becky feeling disconsolate. She yearned to be with him. She loved him, and she didn't want to be separated from him. She wanted to know his kiss once more and feel the exquisite joy of his touch. A coil of aching ecstasy built in the heart of her as she remembered their few minutes alone together in the study, and she wondered what would have happened had they not been interrupted.

For one wild instant, Becky considered stowing away on the *Sea Shadow* just to be near him, but she quickly discarded the idea. She was too old for such game-playing. No, if she wanted Beau, she was just going to have to go after him . . . and the sooner the better. For when he left Belle Arbor, he was going to return to New Orleans and that barmaid Katie . . .

The last realization drove her from her bed. Beau was still there. He hadn't left yet. This would be her last chance to be alone with him before he left, and she intended to take advantage of it. When he went back to town, he was going to remember what happened tonight and never go near the barmaid again.

Slipping into a long-sleeved silken wrapper, Becky quietly crept from her room and made her way to the far end of the hall where Beau slept in the guest quarters. A shiver of fear-tinged excitement tingled through her. Becky wasn't quite sure exactly what she was going to do once she entered his room, but she knew she couldn't let him leave without being with him.

Her hand was shaking as she reached out to turn the doorknob, and she drew a tremulous breath when it turned easily in her grip. Thrilled, yet still timid, Becky pushed on the heavy portal and opened it just wide enough to slip inside. With the skill of a thief, she shut it soundlessly behind her, and then stood with her back flush against it as she stared about the darkened room trying to get her bearings.

A breeze at the window ruffled the drapes and allowed the moonlight to penetrate the pitch blackness of the bedroom. She saw him then, lying on his back, asleep on the bed, a sheet drawn up over the lower half of his body. Beau seemed larger than life to her as she studied him. His blond hair, pale in its own right, was silvered by the moon's glow. His classically handsome features were relaxed now in slumber. Unguarded as he was now, Beau appeared young and carefree and looked much as he had during his late teenage years when Becky had recognized for the first time that she loved him.

Her gaze drifted over the wide expanse of his furred chest. The hair that curled crisply there was several shades of blond darker than the hair on his head. She lowered her gaze again, pausing painfully to linger on the vivid gash of a scar that marred his side.

A shudder wracked through her as she remembered Beau and Adam's return home after the raid and how desperately ill Beau had been. Adam had been well on his way to recovery by the time they'd made port in Charleston, but Beau's wound had been far more serious and potentially deadly. In a burst of determined will that she hadn't managed to equal since, she had taken charge of everything. She'd ordered him brought to their home, and personally nursed him through the crisis of the infection that had set in. Becky thought of those long nights when she'd sat up beside him, praying for his recovery. It had been touch and go for a while, but her prayers had been answered. Beau had recovered.

Now, as she gazed at him, she knew it was time for her to convince him of the truth of her love for him. Her fingers fumbled awkwardly as she untied the knot at the belt of her wrapper. She had never known it could be so difficult to get undressed! When at last the concealing garment fell away and she stood in the middle of the floor clad only in her gown, Becky felt decidedly silly. She did not know how to go about seducing a man . . . especially a man as worldly as Beau Hamilton.

Resolved not to back down now, Becky gritted her teeth and took off her gown. Beautifully nude, she approached her bed . . . tentative . . . more than a little frightened . . . yet filled with the heat of her passion for him.

"Beau . . ." she whispered his name in a husky voice as she came to stand at the foot of the bed.

Beau had been sleeping soundly, but only because he'd retreated downstairs after everyone else had retired to make good use of Adam's well-stocked liquor cabinet. Ever since his close encounter with Becky in the study had luckily been interrupted, he'd been suffering a major feeling of guilt. She'd been so gorgeous and so tempting . . . he hadn't wanted to stop making love to her. That had been the source of his torment ever since, that and her bold proclamation as she'd

272

entered the ballroom before him. She had said that she loved him, and for Beau, that made everything far too complicated. He cared for Becky a great deal, but love!

The sound of her voice came to him as if in a dream, and he frowned. Damn, but she managed to haunt him even in his sleep!

"Beau . . ."

Again he heard her softly call his name. This time it registered with him, and he realized that he wasn't dreaming of Becky. She was actually there. He opened his eyes, and in the gentle, filtered light of the moon, he saw her.

She stood motionlessly before him, his perfect vision of loveliness. Her breasts were round and full; their pink peaks were taut and begging for the arousing touch of his lips and hands. Her waist was slim and her hips gently curved, her legs long and shapely. In the contrast of the moonlight, her hair appeared ebony as it tumbled about her shoulders in a cloud of curls. Their eyes met then, his disbelieving, hers fearful, hesitant, questioning.

Beau's common sense was bludgeoning him with the truth of what was happening. *Becky had come to him,* the thought left him breathing hard. *But Becky is Adam's sister,* his rational side asserted with level-headed good reasoning. *Becky was standing totally naked at the foot of his bed.* He was still staring at her, enraptured by her presence. *Becky was a virgin and he was not to take her innocence under any circumstances,* logic presented itself.

"Beau?" she said his name again, this time even more hesitantly. She was terribly afraid that he was going to laugh at her or reject her outright, and if he did, she didn't think she'd ever be able to face him again. She had never done anything as brazen as this before, and she was frightened.

Beau heard the quality of fear in her voice and knew exactly what she was thinking and feeling. It tore through him, wrenching his vitals and filling him with emotion. Becky was here. Becky wanted him.

All his rational, sane reasons for not making love to her dissipated as wisps of fog before a fresh morning breeze. At that moment, nothing could have stopped Beau from taking her.

"Becky . . ." Beau held out his hand to her in invitation and was pleased when she took it. He knew of her inexperience with men and so drew her down beside him rather than rising up to meet her. Tenderly, he guided her to the mattress next to him. His eyes were an intense blue flame as they seared over her, committing to memory her every womanly curve.

Becky needed no further encouragement to let him know of her desire. Looping her arms about his neck, she pulled him down to her for a devouring kiss.

"I want you, Beau. I have for so long. Please love me tonight," she pleaded in a love-husky voice.

"Ah, love. You're so beautiful . . . so desirable . . ." He kissed her again and again, lost in the heady enthrallment of her embrace.

"Oh, Beau," Becky spoke his name reverently. She had been so afraid that he wouldn't want her, but now all those fears were laid to rest. He wanted her, he did! Hungrily, she raised her lips to his.

Beau knew he should go slowly with her and teach her the joy of love's ways, but his need for her was too fierce and too demanding. As their lips met, the sheet fell away and his hands began a sensual foray over her sensitive untutored flesh. He sought out all her most erotic places, exploring and arousing until she was mindless with her need and writhing beneath his caresses. His lips followed his hands as he brought her nearer and nearer to readiness for his possession.

Becky had never known passion could be so all-consuming. As he stoked the fire of her excitement, her world narrowed to only him. She felt aflame with raging desire. Every nerve in her body was tense and aching with the sweet agony Beau had created within her.

Becky reached for him, touching him boldly, marveling at the strength and power of him, and when she felt his response to her caress, she was filled with a great sense of womanly pride. She had never thought of herself as a particularly sexy woman, but Beau made her feel that way. Knowing that a simple touch from her could bring him such pleasure, she felt sensual and powerful.

Becky wanted to show him just how much she really adored him, to openly demonstrate for the first time in her life the fullness of her love. She drew slightly away from him. When he tried to take her back into his arms, she stopped him with a kiss. Rising above him, Becky trailed a teasing pattern of kisses down his throat and across his chest.

Beau was transported by her actions, and he tangled his fingers in the silky length of her hair. She moved even lower then to press her lips to his scar. The very tenderness of the act sent a jolt of heartfelt emotion through him, and the ultimate recognition dawned: *he loved her.*

In a powerful move, he reversed their positions, pulling her fully beneath him. Instinctively, Becky parted her thighs, and when he settled between them she gave a tiny gasp of excitement at the intimacy of the embrace.

Beau braced himself up on his elbows and smoothed an errant curl away from her cheek. His eyes were passion-darkened as he studied her face. Her lips were swollen from his ardent kisses, and her cheeks were flushed in proof of her desire. Her dark eyes were locked with his, communicating without words the depths of what she was feeling. The heat of his manhood was trapped between their bodies, and Beau remained still, fearful that he would lose all control if he continued to caress her.

"I want to love you, Becky," he told her.

"I want that too, Beau," she whispered, her eyes dipping to study the firm line of his mouth for a moment and then back. She thought he had a very sensuous mouth. "Very much . . ."

"Becky . . . I—" Beau began tentatively in a husky voice.

He wanted to profess his love, but he sounded so serious that Becky panicked. She was direly afraid that he was going to stop and force her to leave him. Remembering his reaction to her caress before and desperate to keep him from stopping, she reached down and touched him in what she thought was a completely shameless manner.

Beau's passion skyrocketed at her ploy, and a groan escaped him as he surrendered to the inevitable. "Ah, Becky . . . love . . ."

There would be no stopping now. They were past the point of no return. Beau rose up slightly and then guided himself to the heart of her heat. With unrelenting, passion-driven pressure, he moved against her. There was resistance, brief and sweet, and then he was buried in the hot silk of her body.

Becky had wanted this more than anything, and though there was pain in Beau's coming to her, she bit her lip to keep from crying out. Her eyes widened as she felt the hard length of him press ever onward and enter her fully. She was surprised by the sensation which seemed alien and strange.

"Easy, love," Beau said softly as he kissed her with

infinite care. "It'll be better in a minute. I promise . . ."

Becky returned his kiss, her tongue meeting his in a sinuous dance of desire. The pain of his invasion faded. as she was swept up in the glory of his kisses again. Forgetting everything but her need for him, she began to caress him again.

The feel of her eager hands upon him erased his effort at control, and Beau began to move. His motions were wild and penetrating as he sought that bliss of perfect joining with Becky. The rhythm was unknown to her, but she was an apt pupil. Matching him movement for movement, she was soon fully caught up in their lovemaking. The spiraling vortex of her passion grew unbounded as she responded to his learned expertise.

Beau kissed and caressed her continually. He wanted her to share in the fullness of completion, not to be an innocent bystander ignorant of love's joy.

A coil of excitement tightened deep within Becky's loins, and she found that she was holding her breath in anticipation of some wondrous revelation. When ecstasy claimed her in an explosion of rapturous delight, she cried out Beau's name. Wave after wave of pleasure flooded through her, and she arched against him in an effort to draw him even more deeply within her.

Beau read her reaction and thrust more avidly into her. He wanted to share the enchantment with her, and he did as he crested quickly. His body throbbed as he reached his pinnacle, and, when his peak had passed, he collapsed on top of her.

His breathing was hoarse and ragged, and sweat sleeked both of them. Neither spoke. There was no need for them to speak. After a moment, Beau shifted slightly to ease the bulk of his weight from her, but otherwise, he did not let her out of his grasp. Wrapped securely in each other's arms, they lay quietly, savoring the wondrous splendor of their joining.

Beau stroked her body in a long, gentling caress. Her skin felt like the finest satin beneath his touch, and he marveled at her softness. A moment ago she'd been an unquenchable flame in his arms, and now, she was quiescent, nestled against him in tender trust. It amazed him that they fit so perfectly together. She had been so responsive and giving. He'd never known another woman to be so loving. She was everything he'd ever wanted, and he knew he would never love another. As soon as this thing with Shark was over, they would return to Charleston and be married. The prospect please him enormously, and he smiled.

Becky was in heaven. Making love to Beau had been the most wonderful thing that had ever happened in her life. She had always known he was the man for her, and the perfection of their union had just reinforced that belief a thousandfold. With a small sigh, Becky lifted one hand to caress the furred width of his chest. She was startled when Beau reacted quickly and grabbed her wrist.

"Don't, love," Beau said little harshly.

Becky looked up at him, puzzled by his refusal. "Why, Beau? What's wrong?"

He gave a throaty chuckle as he saw the concern in her eyes. "Nothing's wrong, Becky. Nothing's wrong at all . . ."

"Then why won't you let me touch you? I like your chest and—"

He found her innocence so appealing that he leaned over her and kissed her soundly. "The truth is, my dear, that I'd like nothing better than to have you touch me—constantly, all day, every day. But we've got one thing to consider here . . ."

"What's that?"

"That is the tenuous hold I have over my desire when I'm near you like this," he told her in a gruff voice. "I still want you, darling, and it won't take much to encourage me to have you again."

"Who's stopping you?" she asked archly, wriggling against him with tantalizing effectiveness.

"I'm stopping me! Now quit that . . ." He held her slightly away from him. "You don't understand, sweetheart . . . This was your first time, and you'll be sore." Beau knew it was ridiculous for him to deny himself that which he desired the most, but this was Becky, not some saloon girl. He wanted everything to be perfect for her.

Becky couldn't believe what Beau was saying. He cared so much about her that he was afraid he'd hurt her if he took her again.

"Beau . . ." She said his name slowly, softly. "You're leaving me tomorrow, and I don't know when you'll be back. Please make love to me again, while there's time. Don't leave me like this . . . wanting you and needing you and loving you . . . please . . ."

At her words, all of Beau's honorable intentions disappeared. She wanted him. Nothing else mattered.

"I love you, Becky," he confessed earnestly, and then with a low, guttural growl, he moved to make her his again.

This time, their lovemaking was a wild, uncontrolled mating. Passions soared immediately as they came together. Becky knew what she had to do this time, and she displayed no shyness as she returned his caresses with equal and sometimes greater fervor. The quick fire explosion of their ecstasy shattered them both, and they lay clasped together, exhausted, sated, replete.

Much later, just before dawn, Beau quietly helped

Becky with her gown and robe and then carried her back to her own room. In the concealing darkness, he lay her upon the bed and kissed her tenderly. She pulled him sleepily down to her for one last kiss. When the kiss ended, he drew away to pull her coverlet over her. Beau told her softly that he loved her and that he'd be back as soon as he could, but Becky had already drifted off to sleep and didn't hear him.

Beau's regret was great as he left her. He found for the first time in his life that he was not eagerly anticipating going back to sea. The only thing that drove him was knowing that they couldn't be happily married until the revenge against Shark was complete.

The sun was edging above the horizon when he returned to his room, so rather than try to sleep, he decided to just stay up. He'd meet with Adam the minute he came downstairs and then be on his way back to the *Sea Shadow*. The quicker he and Adam located Shark, the sooner he and Becky would be together.

It was late morning when Becky finally awoke. She was stretching in a slow, feline manner when the glorious memories of the night just past came to her. She smiled brightly. Beau loved her . . . Beau loved her! Her heart was dancing, and she could hardly wait to see him again.

Becky was out of bed practically at a run. She washed up hastily and quickly brushed out her hair. She noticed that there was a glow to her cheeks and a sparkle in her eyes that hadn't been there before, and, with a light laugh, she admitted to herself that she knew why. Pulling on her most attractive daydress, she was on her way downstairs just as quickly as she could manage. Her steps were light as she made her way down the hall. When she heard Lianne's voice in the parlor, she went in to see if her friend knew where Beau was.

"Good morning," she greeted Lianne happily.

"Good morning, Becky." Lianne turned to her new sister-in-law, wondering at her good spirits.

"Is Beau around?" Becky asked avidly. She had no interest in making small talk this morning, all she wanted to do was to find Beau and kiss him.

"You didn't know?" Lianne asked, frowning.

"Know? Know what?" Becky paused, suddenly sensing that she was going to tell her something awful.

"He had to go back to New Orleans today."

"Yes, I knew that, but he didn't leave already, did he?"

"He left nearly three hours ago, Becky," she supplied reluctantly.

"Three hours ago?" Becky stared at her in hurt and confusion, and then had another thought. "Well, did he leave a message for me?"

"Not with me, he didn't, but he might have left one with Adam. They were closeted in the study for a long time."

"Oh. I see." She was crestfallen. Beau had told her that he loved her, and yet he had gone off and left her without a word.

"Why don't you check with Adam?" Lianne offered. "I'm sure if Beau was going to leave a message for you, it would have been with him."

Becky went in search of her brother. She finally located him out near the stables and asked him about Beau, but his answer was the same as Lianne's. Beau had left no message for her when he'd departed for New Orleans earlier that morning, and he hadn't known when he would be returning to Belle Arbor again.

Hurt mixed with anger as Becky returned to the house. Beau had claimed to love her. He had introduced her to the joys of love, and then left her without so much as a simple "good-bye." Becky was usually good-natured, but Beau's callous treatment of her stung. One way or another, she was going to see that he suffered greatly for going off the way he had. Still . . .

A small smile curved her lips at the memory of his loving. The tenderness and devotion he'd displayed reassured her that their night together had been special and that he wouldn't be forgetting her any too soon. She would get her vengeance, but when she did she would make sure that he loved every minute of it. Beau Hamilton was going to learn that she was not a woman who could be easily ignored.

Chapter Twenty-three

Tired though he was, Adam had tried to keep himself continually busy. Since Beau's departure that morning, he had resumed his normal activities around the plantation, working with the horses in the stables and riding the fields with the overseer, but he'd failed miserably in his efforts to keep himself occupied and his thoughts off Lianne.

He had awakened that morning to find her sound asleep, nestled against him. He thought Lianne quite beautiful when she was awake, but in repose he found her breathtaking. He'd wanted to kiss her awake, strip the gown from her body, and make love to her as was his right as her husband. Only by forcing himself to remember her cunning ways and devious schemes was he able to tear himself from the bed and escape the room.

Adam had welcomed the distraction of plantation work that day, for it had gotten him out of the house and away from Lianne. Still, as the hours had passed, he'd found himself thinking of her, and each time he'd cursed himself soundly.

Alex had sought him out while he was working in the stable and had spent the rest of the day at his side, asking intelligent questions about the running of the plantation and generally just enjoying being with him. Adam sensed that Alex was lonely and in great need of male companionship. He remembered his own youth and the time when he had been close to his father. He had spent every possible minute with him and had learned much of the ways of manhood during that time. Reflecting back, Adam came to appreciate more fully the influence his father had had upon him, and knowing that he had the opportunity to help Alex in the same way, he encouraged him openly.

The rest of the day passed pleasantly enough. Somehow he managed to keep himself from thinking of Lianne and the circumstances of their marriage. Instead, he concentrated on just trying to take care of the business at hand. Having good-naturedly answered all of Alex's inquiries all day, Adam was totally unprepared when the boy spoke up on their ride back to the house from surveying the south fields.

"Adam?" he began casually enough, just as he'd begun all his other queries.

"Yes, Alex?" Adam glanced over at the dark-haired boy who was looking at him, his expression serious.

"I know you and Lianne just got married yesterday and all that." He paused before going on. "But how come you and Lianne didn't go on a honeymoon? Aren't people supposed to go on a honeymoon once they get married?"

His question took Adam by surprise, and for a moment, he didn't have a good answer.

"Sometimes things just don't work out the way they're supposed to," he finally answered with more than a little honesty. "We didn't have time to plan this because everything happened so quickly. Maybe when the crops are in and the plantation's running smoothly again, Lianne and I will be able to get away." Adam hoped this answer would satisfy him, and when Alex seemed content with his reply, he was relieved.

"I know she'd like that," he told him firmly.

"She would?"

"Oh, yes. See, Lianne's talked to me about getting married. She told me she was going to wait until she found just the right man to love so she could be as happy as our mama and papa were."

Adam's cynical side found it hard to reconcile the Lianne he knew with the one Alex was describing.

"She told me when I got old enough to get married that I should wait for just the right girl, too," he went on.

"That's very good advice," Adam agreed solemnly as the memory of his engagement to Elise besieged him.

"And that's what you did, huh? You waited for Lianne." Alex sounded as if Adam was the wisest man in the whole wide world.

"Yes," he replied, trying to keep all the bitterness he was suddenly feeling out of his voice.

"She's pretty nice as sisters go, I guess," he concluded. "I'm just real glad that she married you, Adam."

Adam looked over at the boy and saw the love shining in his eyes. Unable to hurt him, not wanting him to know even the smallest unsavory detail about their marriage, he managed a warm smile.

"I am, too, Alex." He reached over and tousled his dark hair. "Real glad."

The moment was a poignant one for the both of them. They fell silent then as they finished the ride to the stables.

Adam was lost deep in thought as he considered all that Alex had told him. He found it vaguely disturbing that the youngster's view of his sister's actions would be so out of line with his own. He wondered at the change in character that must have occurred for Lianne to become the calculating shrew he believed her to be. Adam considered all that had happened to Lianne and attributed the change in her to that.

For just a moment, the thought occurred to him that Alex had been telling the truth and that he was the one who was wrong in his assessment of her motives. *Out of the mouths of babes* . . . As soon as the doubt entered his mind, Adam dismissed it. Lianne was no sweet innocent. Sure, she might have been a virgin the first time they'd made love, but it was all part of her scheme. When her plan to buy back her home had failed, she'd simply decided to use her body as a bargaining tool. She had planned and executed a plot to keep her home in her family. The bonus of double-crossing Suzanne had just been a casual stroke of luck for Lianne. She might not have known that would happen in the beginning, but Adam didn't doubt for a moment that she was enjoying the thought of having stolen Suzanne's fiancé.

By the time they reached the stable, Adam's anger with Lianne had returned, and his mood grew black. He sent Alex on up to the house, for he was in no hurry to see his bride again. It was some time later before he headed up the path.

Lianne had had a miserable day. She'd awakened early only to find that Adam had already gone. The discovery left her feeling oddly bereft. As usual, her morning sickness made its wretched appearance, but with the help of Sarah's knowledgeable nursing, she was soon up and around. When she'd come downstairs, Adam was in the study with Beau, and he had the door closed against intrusions. When Beau had departed for New Orleans immediately after their meeting, Adam had announced that he would be out working the plantation for the rest of the day and had left the house without even saying good-bye. Lianne had hoped that things would improve when Becky came down, but Becky had seemed somewhat distracted after discovering that Beau had already left. She had eventually pleaded the need to go up to her room to rest for a while, leaving Lianne alone once again.

Idleness did not sit well with Lianne. She had been carrying the entire load of running Belle Arbor for so long now that she felt foolish just sitting around doing nothing. Lianne knew she should be thankful that Adam was so proficient at taking care of the plantation, but actually she felt more than a little jealous.

Restless and determined not to sit around like an invalid just because of her pregnancy, Lianne went back upstairs to change into one of her plainer gowns and then went outside to work in the flower garden. It was hard work, but something she enjoyed doing. She got a great feeling of accomplishment from working with the soil and then watching the plants she'd nurtured grow and blossom.

The balance of the afternoon passed quickly for her as she worked. She lost track of the time and paid no attention at all to how she looked. She weeded and planted on her knees in the dirt. As the sun grew warm, she began to perspire. Lianne unbuttoned the top buttons of her bodice to help cool off a bit and wiped her brow with a slightly muddy forearm. Lost in the reverie of her task, she was oblivious to the lateness of the hour.

Adam started to enter the house through the front door, but decided against it. He was in no frame of mind to run into Lianne, so he skirted the house, intending to enter through the rear. It was then that he came across her as she labored in the flower garden.

Adam had expected to find his conniving wife playing lady of the manor and taking advantage of her newly secured position. He had not expected to find her working in the dirt like a common field hand. He was at once both stunned and outraged—stunned because he hadn't thought she would to continue to work so hard, and outraged because she was endangering the welfare of his child. The complex emotions bewildered him, so in typical male fashion, he reacted with blustering anger.

"What the hell do you think you're doing, madam?" he demanded as he stood glowering at her.

Lianne had been so absorbed in her work that she hadn't heard his approach. She looked up quickly and was disconcerted to find him standing over her, glaring at her imperiously.

"I am working with my flowers," she responded haughtily as she met his gaze without flinching.

Adam's condemning gaze was drawn irresistibly to her bodice where it was gaping open. He could see the beginning of her cleavage and one droplet of sweat trickling down into that dark, inviting crevice. He felt his loins tighten in response to the thought of kissing the dampness from that creamy flesh, and he quickly banished the thought. *Damn! Why was it that just looking at her could ignite his senses? What the hell was it about her that affected him so?*

"We have plenty of help. There's no need for you to be out here groveling around in the mud." He tried to focus on her face, but the smudge of dirt on her cheek made her look so appealing that he found himself wishing he could wash it away for her and then kiss the clean spot. Again he jerked his thoughts away from the sensuous and back to the matter at hand.

"I am not 'groveling around in the mud,' Adam!" Lianne was furious that he was ordering her around. She got to her feet and stood glaring up at him, her hands on her hips, looking much as she had the very first time they'd met.

"Just what would you call it, then?"

"I'd call it working in my garden! It's a little honest labor, something you obviously know nothing about," she threw at him accusingly, thinking of how he won the plantation so effortlessly in the card game and not of how he'd worked at improving Belle Arbor since taking over.

Adam wanted to take her by the shoulders and shake her. "You are now my wife and the mistress of my home. I will expect you to behave in a manner suitable to your position."

"Behave!" Lianne's tone was deadly. "Do you think I'm a dog you can order about or train to stay or go as you please? I'm a woman and I have a mind of my own!"

"Oh, yes, I know all about your devious little mind, Lianne. I've experienced its workings firsthand." His cut was cruel, and she gasped at the pain it caused. Adam smiled grimly at her reaction. He thought he would be glad to hurt her, but he'd gotten no satisfaction from throwing her scheming ways up to her. If anything, he found he was suddenly tired of the whole subject. What was done was done. "At least, madam, if you won't consider my wishes in the matter, think of the health of our child."

"The baby?" His sudden change of mood left her puzzled. What did the baby have to do with any of this?

"I'm sure it can't be doing the baby any good for you to be out here working in the hot sun, especially when there's no need for it. Please, if not for me, at least for the sake of our son, try not to exert yourself this way."

Our son? Lianne was staring at him in total confusion, not trusting him one bit. "I shall continue to do as I please, sir," she stated firmly, defiantly, "as you obviously are. You made it quite clear to me that this marriage of ours was a farce. I see no reason to respect the 'obey' part of our vows when we're ignoring the rest of them." Lifting her nose in the air in a regal demeanor, she started to move past him toward the house. "Now if you'll excuse me, I do believe it's almost time for dinner."

Adam watched her go feeling more frustration than he'd ever known in his life. The woman was maddening! Absolutely maddening!

It was nearly an hour later before they were ready to sit down to dinner together. Adam had avoided their bedroom until he'd been certain that Lianne had finished her toilette. As demanding as his desire for her had become, the last thing he wanted right now was to see her less than fully dressed. Sleeping in the same bed with her again tonight was going to be bad enough. He definitely didn't want to put himself at risk of losing control before he absolutely had to. He was going to resist the urge to take her if it was the last thing he did, and Adam was beginning to believe that it just might be.

The sound of horse's hooves drew their attention before they could even begin the first course. Adam frowned and then quickly got up from the head of the table to go see who was coming. Lianne, Becky, and Alex exchanged curious glances as they heard him greet another man, and though they tried to listen to the muted conversation, they were unable to discern anything that was said. After a moment, they heard the rider leave again, but Adam did not return to the dining room. Instead, he went into the study and locked the door.

Adam's hand was trembling as he stared down at the note from Dr. Williams. Never before had the physician sent him a note by special messenger, and he was almost afraid to open it. His chest felt tight and his eyes felt dry and burning. Then almost as if he couldn't stand not knowing, he quickly tore the missive open and began to read.

Dear Mr. Trent,
Please come to New Orleans. It is imperative that I see you at once. I will await your arrival at my office.
Sincerely,
Dr. David Williams

"Dear God . . ." was all Adam could say as he stared at the massage. *Something had happened to Elise* . . . He didn't even stop to tell the others that he was leaving. He simply left the study by way of the french doors and disappeared into the night without a word, taking the note with him.

Lianne, Becky, and Alex waited a considerable length of time before coming to the conclusion that something important must have happened to keep him away from the meal that long. Becky left the table to seek him out and find out what was wrong. It puzzled her when he didn't answer the study door, and, worried, she went around the house to the french doors to find the study deserted. She sought out one of the kitchen servants who told her that Mr. Adam had gone out to the stable and had ridden off a short time ago, and he had not told them where he was going.

Becky returned to the dining room, wondering what to tell Lianne. She suspected that Adam's abrupt departure might have something to do with Shark, but she could not discuss it with Lianne. She had to maintain Adam's secrecy.

291

"Did Adam say what was wrong, Becky?" Lianne asked when her friend returned, trying not to sound too interested.

"No . . . I—" Becky hesitated.

"What is it?" Lianne gave her a curious look.

"Adam's gone," she finally explained.

"Gone?" Lianne stiffened in her chair and went pale at her words.

Becky nodded. "Evidently whatever was in the note was very important. He rode out just a few minutes ago, and he didn't tell anyone at the stable where he was going."

In her heart, Lianne knew where he was going. "I see," she said tersely as she folded her napkin in a precise motion and laid it back on the tabletop. "If you'll excuse me, I think I'll go on up for the night."

Becky realized instantly that Lianne was thinking. She ached to tell her the truth about Adam's feelings for Suzanne, but she remained silent, respecting Adam's need for subterfuge. "I thought you were hungry?"

"I suddenly seem to have lost my appetite," Lianne told her as she pictured Adam with Suzanne . . . making love. The other woman had only to send him a message, and he flew to her side. Damn him! He'd spent most of yesterday with her, and now he'd gone to her again.

"Lianne . . ."

"Good night, Becky. Good night, Alex." She left the room with as much dignity as she could muster.

When she reached her bedroom, Lianne was very near tears. It annoyed her that Adam's behavior affected her so greatly. She had always prided herself on being able to control her emotions, but ever since he had come into her life that had changed.

Perhaps, Lianne rationalized, perhaps it was just

the pregnancy that was causing her to react to everything with such wild mood swings. The thought gave her some relief from the turmoil that was twisting and churning inside her like a living thing. *She didn't care what Adam did or who he did it with!* she told herself. *She didn't!* But as she curled up on her bed, she still couldn't stop the hurt that tore at her over the thought of him at Suzanne's, making love to her.

It was late when Adam finally reached Dr. Williams's office, and he was relieved to see that a light was still burning inside. He tied his horse to the hitching post and hurried up the steps to knock on the door. The doctor answered almost immediately.

"Mr. Trent . . . Thank you so much for coming so quickly. Please come in." David held the door wide to allow him to enter.

Adam was apprehensive as he came inside. "What's happened? Is Elise all right?"

David led the way into his private office and gestured for him to take a seat as he resumed sitting behind his desk.

"I think I may have hopeful news for you," he began, giving him a friendly smile.

"What?" Adam stared at him in disbelief.

David studied Adam's strained features and wondered at the cause. He had expected joy, not this despair he was reading so clearly in the other man's eyes.

"I think we've had a breakthrough of sorts," he told him.

Adam could not respond. He was stricken. In the beginning, he'd believed Elise would come back to him. Yet, as the months had passed, his hopes had all been dashed. In slow, painful resignation, he'd come to accept the prognosis. Adam knew that Dr. Williams had never stopped trying to reach her, but he had never really expected Elise to recover. Now, he was married to Lianne and had a child on the way . . .

"Sometime last night Miss Clayton got up from her bed and was moving about her room."

"Has she spoken yet?"

"No, not yet, but I'm sure it won't be much longer. Why, just the fact that she did get up on her own is very encouraging indeed," David finished.

"I see . . ." Adam's agony was clearly etched on his face as he met the doctor's gaze across his desk.

David saw the torment mirrored in his eyes. He wanted to help, but knew that it was up to Trent to take the initiative about discussing what was troubling him.

"Will you be staying in town tonight?"

"Yes. It's too late to head back now."

"That's good. Why don't you come by the house tomorrow to see her? A visit from you might be just the thing to speed up her recovery," David suggested.

"All right," he agreed soberly, thinking of how terribly he'd betrayed Elise and wondering how he would ever explain it all to her.

Chapter Twenty-four

Adam's mood was morose as he checked into the St. Louis Hotel, and it didn't improve when he was given the exact same room he'd had the last time he'd been in town. He almost protested and asked for another, but knew he would look ridiculous if he did. Memories or not, it was only a room, he told himself, nothing more.

Adam stopped in the bar for a stiff double shot of bourbon before retiring for the night. He was disconsolate as he sat alone at a secluded corner table in the saloon nursing his drink. Guilt weighed heavily upon him. He had no doubt in his mind that he'd ruined Elise's life before, and now . . . now that she was about to recover from that trauma, he was going to deliver a second, even more devastating blow to her well-being. This time he was afraid he would completely destroy her.

Elise was a beautiful, fragile, trusting woman. Adam cared for her deeply, and it tore him apart to think about telling her of his marriage to Lianne, but there was nothing else he could do. The thought of hurting Elise was almost too much for him to bear, and he drained the remainder of his drink in one fierce move.

Adam stared at the empty glass in his hand and then set it aside. When the barmaid would have come and refilled it for him, he waved her away. He knew that getting drunk wouldn't solve any of the problems he faced tonight. Lost in a tormented haze of misery, he headed upstairs to his room.

Everything was the same, he thought as he looked around the barren hotel room, except, in reality, nothing was the same. It had been six weeks since he and Lianne had made love in this room . . . in that bed. Adam stared at the soft, inviting four-poster as vivid memories of their heated joining assailed him. Their coming together that night had been glorious . . . wildly erotic . . . incredibly beautiful. Since then his entire existence had been indelibly altered.

Lianne . . . The strength of what he was feeling for her was so different from anything he'd ever experienced before that it left him troubled and confused. He had thought himself in love with Elise, but that emotion paled in comparison to the attraction that drew him to Lianne.

Every time he was near Lianne, he found himself wanting her. It wasn't just the simple physical need of a man desiring an attractive woman. He had had a great deal of experience with that type of involvement, and he knew this wasn't the same. No, this was something far more primitive, far more disturbing, far more difficult for him to handle.

His movements were jerky as he took off his jacket and shirt and then stretched out on the bed to try to sleep. Even as weary as he was and with the aid of the potent liquor, sleep could not overcome the burden of his anguish. In his mind, visions of Elise before and after the pirate attack blended with images of Lianne . . . Lianne with her flashing green eyes and fearlessness as she defied him at every turn, Lianne surrendering to him in love's dance, Lianne giving herself fully to the ecstasy of his possession, Lianne his wife now and one day soon her lovely body heavy with his unborn child. Once he had longed for Elise to be that woman, but now he couldn't imagine anyone but Lianne bearing his children.

The realization shocked him deeply, and he rolled over onto his stomach with a muttered curse. Tomorrow he would have to go to Elise and, if she was capable of understanding, he was going to have to tell her the truth. He closed his eyes against the wretchedness of the thought. He didn't want to hurt her anymore than she'd already been hurt, but lying to her would serve no purpose but to delay the inevitable.

Resigned, yet heavyhearted, he courted rest, but the night seemed to pass in slow motion, each minute an hour, each darkened hour a torturous eternity. By the time morning came, his nerves were stretched taut in anticipation of the meeting. He dressed in the same clothes with what care he could and then descended to take breakfast in the hotel dining room.

Adam was so deeply lost in his thoughts that he was oblivious to those around him as he settled in for his meal. Only when he heard someone address him did he look up and see Cyrus Shackleford sitting at the next table alone. The expression on the banker's face was sneering as he bid him hello.

"I understand you'll be coming to see me soon, Adam," Cyrus said with open contempt. He had not yet gotten over his anger at Adam's interference on the night of the party or the news of Adam and Lianne's sudden marriage the day after. Obviously if the rumors he'd heard were true, Trent had been courting Suzanne Labadie while bedding Lianne at the same time.

Nice arrangement, if you could get it, Cyrus thought scornfully. No wonder Adam had run him off Lianne on the night of the party. No doubt Adam had considered her his private property. It infuriated Cyrus all

297

the more now to know that Lianne had rejected him while she'd taken Trent as a lover. He'd vowed the moment he found out that if he ever got the chance, he was going to make her suffer for it.

"For what?" Adam gave Cyrus a coolly assessing look, wondering at the man's point.

"I handle all of the Ducharme finances, you know," he explained with disdainful precision. "I suppose you'll be wanting to put the accounts in your name now."

"I really hadn't given it much thought." His answer was brusque.

"Of course, you probably haven't even had time to discuss it. I mean, everything did happen so quickly," the banker sneered.

"Yes, it did, but I feel certain that my wife would approve of my transferring her accounts to the bank I do business with, Shackelford. I'll be in touch about making the necessary arrangements," Adam cut him off.

Cyrus was furious as he came to his feet. "Well, do give my best to Suzanne . . . and your wife," he drawled as left the dining room.

Adam sat rigidly in his chair watching the other man leave the room. He found it hard to believe that he'd managed to keep his temper under such firm control when all he'd really wanted to do was to throttle the fool for his snide remarks. Adam knew he should have suspected that the news of their hasty wedding would be the talk of the town, but he hadn't thought it would happen quite so quickly. No doubt Cyrus, in his jealousy, had been one of the primary ones responsible for the gossip. Adam was glad now that he'd gone though with the marriage as hastily as he had. He wanted to protect her reputation as much as possible.

The waitress brought his breakfast then, and though Adam tried to eat, his food seemed tasteless. He lingered over the meal for as long as he could, not wanting to arrive as Elise's too early, but the time finally came for him to go. Despairing, he left the hotel.

After his meeting with Adam, David had not slept all night either. He didn't know what it was that had been troubling the other man, but he could sense that it would have a profound effect on Elise. He left his home extra early the next morning just to have some time alone with her before Adam arrived.

"Dr. Williams!" Nurse Halliday greeted him excitedly when he arrived bearing a single red rose. "It happened again! I left the music box on the dresser as you'd directed, and this morning it was on the night table again."

David's spirits soared. It seemed as if it had taken an eternity, but he was thrilled that he'd found the key to unlock her emotions. Now, it would only be a matter of utmost patience and repeated reassurance to make the final, complete breakthrough. David could hardly wait. He wanted desperately to help her work through the terrors of her past. He wanted to hear her voice and to know what was truly in her heart.

"That's wonderful, Nurse," he told her. "Is she upstairs?"

"Yes, by the window."

He started up the staircase and then turned back. "I got in touch with Mr. Trent last night. He's in town and will be coming by today."

"Good." The nurse's face lit up at the prospect. "Seeing him may be the best medicine Miss Elise could have."

David realized that she was probably right, and it bothered him. "I'll be with Elise if you should need me."

"Yes, Doctor."

The sunshine was pouring in the window, bathing the room in bright, cheerful light. Elise was sitting in her wingchair looking out upon the garden below, much as she always did. David found himself hoping that some day he would find her watching the door for him instead of staring out at the scenery.

"Good morning, Elise," he said, his voice warm and gentle as he stared at her.

Elise looked lovely this morning. Her pale hair was shimmering about her shoulders in a sunbathed golden cascade, and the pale peach-colored gown she wore highlighted her perfect complexion. Though she had lost some weight during her long months of confinement, it had only enhanced the delicacy of her beauty.

David regarded her in silence for a moment. Even with all the trauma she'd suffered, she still had the appearance of a sweet innocent. He thought her quite the most beautiful woman in the world.

"I brought you a rose today," he finally said in a rather hoarse voice. It had never hit him quite so forcefully before, but David realized with something akin to sharp pain that if he helped Elise recover, he would lose her. Adam Trent was the man she loved. Adam Trent was her fiancée. Adam Trent would be the man she would run to when her perception of reality returned.

David was shaken by the torture of his thoughts, and moved to the dresser to put the single bud in the vase full of flowers there. Carrying the vase with him, he drew his chair up next to hers. David sat down beside her as was his usual morning routine.

"It's a gorgeous day outside." He made pleasant conversation as he placed the vase on the small table before them and picked up the music box from its place there. He wound it carefully and placed it deliberately in her lap. The day before when he'd done this she hadn't spoken, but she had responded openly for the first time by picking up the box and holding it close to her heart.

Though she didn't speak, Elise dropped her gaze from some faraway point to the treasure in her lap. The melody and the gentle man's presence filled her with a deep, abiding sense of security. She looked up, aware of the sun's warmth upon her and the man at her side. Her blue eyes, reflecting a clear moment of sanity, met David's unthreatening aquamarine gaze fully for the first time in all their months together.

The contact jolted David to the deepest reaches of his heart and soul, and as he continued to stare into her eyes, an unmitigated joy filled him.

"Elise . . ." he breathed her name in pure rapture as he took her hand in his. With slow, calm assurance, he lifted it to his lips and pressed a sweet-soft kiss to her palm, his eyes never leaving hers.

"David?"

It was a strained, tentative whisper, but to David it sounded like a chorus of angels.

"Yes, Elise. I'm David." He squeezed her hand reassuringly and then kissed it again.

"I'm glad you're here, David," Elise said slowly as if a great weariness possessed her.

"I'm here, and I'll never leave you," he told her fervently as he gazed at her. All the emotion he felt for her was showing clearly on his face.

Nurse Halliday admitted Adam to the house. She explained that the doctor was already there and with Elise now, but that he should go on up.

Adam did as she bid, but he was on edge as he approached the open door. He heard the muted sound of voices, and a shock ran through him as he recognized one as Elise's. *Dear God!* he thought in agony. He had prayed so long and so hard for her recovery, and now that she finally was getting better, he was about to destroy everything.

Adam drew a deep shaking breath and then stepped toward the door. He stopped, frozen in place as he watched the scene being enacted before him in the room. Elise was sitting in a chair at the window, her head bent toward the doctor as if considering something he'd said. She looked lovely, and he could tell by her movements that she was actually in possession of her faculties. Her features no longer bore that distant, detached expression he'd come to expect, but now reflected an awareness of her surroundings and a radiant adoration for the man at her side. David Williams was sitting with her, holding her hand to his lips. His expression openly reflected a love that, until this moment, Adam had never imagined existed.

Adam stepped back out of the doorway and out of sight. He felt like an intruder, watching the intimate scene. He was stunned by what that innocent, yet revealing moment had shown him, and he knew he needed time to think.

Retreating back downstairs, he told Nurse Halliday that the doctor had been busy, so he was going to wait for him there in the study. As he paced the room, his mind was racing. Could it have happened? Had Williams really fallen in love with Elise, and, if so, did she feel the same way toward him? This appeared to be the case, but he couldn't be sure.

Adam sighed and sat down heavily on the sofa. He

decided it was time for him to be perfectly honest with Dr. Williams. Perhaps then he could find the true answer to his questions.

A short time later David descended the stairs, his heart and professionalism on a collision course. He knew Adam Trent would be coming here to see Elise today, and he was desperately worried about how his visit would affect her. She had become so lucid, so open and responsive. It hurt him to think that seeing the other man again might cause her to regress to her previous, frightened behavior.

David hoped not. More than anything he wanted her to recover and live happily again. The trouble was, David wanted her to live happily with him. Acknowledging the completeness of his love for her had been difficult for him. He'd never been seriously involved with a woman before. His career had always come first. In the beginning, he'd dismissed what he was feeling for Elise as simply a manifestation of his own loneliness. He knew now, now that she was responding to him, that it was nothing that simple. He loved her, and he wanted to marry her as soon as she was well enough. He wanted to spend the rest of his life making her happy and helping her to forget all the tragedy she'd faced so far.

As he reached the bottom of the staircase, he saw Adam in the parlor. Totally disconcerted for a moment, he could only stand and stare at the other man—this man who, in reality, was his rival and yet who might be Elise's one and only chance for true happiness.

"Mr. Trent . . . I didn't know you were here. Why didn't you come upstairs to see Elise?" he asked as he went forth to greet him.

Adam's expression was enigmatic as he regarded the physician across the room. "I thought it would be better if we spoke down here."

"I see," David answered, frowning slightly. "What was it you wanted to talk about?"

"There was something I should have told you last night, but at the time I couldn't quite bring myself to be totally open with you."

David remembered the suspicion he'd had the night before that there had been something troubling Trent, and now he knew he'd been right.

"Would you like to talk about it now?" he encouraged.

"I think it's important that you know . . . I was married the day before yesterday."

"What?" There was no outrage in his statement, just plain, stunned disbelief.

"Lianne Ducharme and I were married."

David couldn't believe it. He wasn't sure if he should be happy personally or upset professionally. It thrilled him to think that the one man who stood between him and total happiness was now out of the picture, but he worried that this might hurt Elise.

"In the beginning, I hoped and prayed for Elise's recovery. You know yourself that I spared no expense in trying to find a cure for her . . ." Adam paused as he recalled those long, painful months of waiting for good news that he finally became convinced would never come. "But as time went on . . . well, things just happened between Lianne and me." He found himself balking at revealing too much about the circumstances of their marriage. Lianne was his wife now and deserving of his protection. "I never really believed that Elise would recover. If I had known . . ."

"Love cannot be controlled, Mr. Trent," David pointed out with a gentleness that was in no way a condemnation. In fact, he was thinking more in terms of himself than of Adam.

304

"I still care deeply for Elise, but . . ."

"I understand."

"Has she spoken of me yet? Has she said anything about the past?"

"No, not yet."

"I'm really afraid that if I see her now and tell her of all that's taken place I'll be undoing all the good you've accomplished."

"If Elise is half the woman you've said she is, I think, in time, she'll be perfectly capable of handling the truth," David assured him. "Life is not always fair in the way it deals with each of us. Everyone must learn how to cope in their own way, in their own time."

"Elise is a wonderful woman, Dr. Williams."

"I know," he said with a little more emotion than he'd meant to reveal.

"Well, I think it best if I go now. Will you notify me when you think the time is right?" Adam asked.

"Yes. I'll keep in touch just as we always have."

"Good. I want to know everything."

"I'll see to it."

Adam started toward the door to take his leave and then paused there to look back at David.

"You're in love with her, aren't you?" he asked point blank.

David's smile was slightly crooked as he met his gaze unflinchingly. "Yes, Mr. Trent, I am."

"Does she love you?"

"I don't know, but I plan on doing all I can to win her."

They regarded each other in open assessment for a moment before Adam responded. "I'm glad you've come to love her, and I hope it works out for you."

David only nodded in response and watched quietly as Adam left the house. Once Adam had gone, David headed back upstairs to spend the rest of the morning with Elise. Perhaps he could coax her from the seclusion of her room today for a walk in the garden, he thought with almost boyish enthusiasm as he climbed the steps. Now that she had opened up enough to start talking again, it was time to convince her to take another daring step back to reality, back to her life and her future.

As he entered her room, David found that she had heard his footsteps and was watching for him. He smiled spontaneously in a warm greeting and then said a silent prayer that he could find a way to insure that her future would be with him.

Chapter Twenty-five

Cyrus Shackelford was livid as he left the St. Louis's dining room. Adam Trent had insulted him again and this time publicly! No one ever insulted a Shackelford twice and got away with it! No one!

Without hesitation, he strode back to his office and canceled his appointments for the day. He ordered his carriage brought around and then headed straight for Willow Bend. He knew Suzanne had to be suffering from the humiliation Trent had just put her through, and he intended to make full use of her fury. *A woman scorned, after all,* he chuckled evilly to himself.

The ride to the Labadie plantation couldn't pass quickly enough for Cyrus, and he was relieved when he finally pulled up in front of the sprawling mansion. A waiting servant took the reins as he mounted the porch steps and hurried inside. He entered the house and instructed the maid to tell Suzanne that he was there before making himself comfortable in the parlor.

Suzanne was surprised by Cyrus's unexpected visit, and she wondered at the reason for it as she descended the stairs to join him.

"Cyrus, how nice to see you again," she greeted him warmly.

"Suzanne, you're looking as lovely as ever," he told her smoothly.

"Why, thank you," she preened, always eager for compliments. "To what do I owe the honor of your visit?"

"I have a business venture to propose and I'd like to enlist your help with it."

"A busines venture that requires my help?" Suzanne was really curious now.

"Yes, you see, Adam Trent has crossed me too many times lately, and I want to see him pay for all the trouble he's caused." Cyrus was bluntly honest with her. "I need your help to do it. Why with your contacts . . ."

"My contacts?" She gave him a measured look. "What contacts?"

"Don't play the sweet innocent with me, Suzanne. I'm your banker, remember? I know the state of your finances. I also know that the money you have is not coming from Willow Bend," he revealed, his eyes narrowing as he regarded her.

Realizing that he was far more shrewd than she'd ever given him credit for, Suzanne quickly decided to play along with his scheme just to find out what he was up to.

"I see," she stated with little emotion. "What exactly did you have in mind?"

"Look, we both know how embarrassed you must be after being thrown over by Trent just the day after he'd announced your engagement."

A telltale blush stung her cheeks, for she couldn't deny the truth of his statement.

"I have a plan that will make both of them pay . . ." he continued.

Suddenly Suzanne felt the need to put a stop to his erroneous thinking. "I don't think you quite understand the situation, Cyrus."

"What are you talking about?"

"The unfortunate timing of Adam's marriage hasn't really interfered in our plans. Adam still loves me, and as soon as he can, he's going to leave Lianne. We'll be married then."

"Has he told you that?"

"Of course," she answered, trying to remember Adam's exact words when he'd told her of their altered plans.

"I've never believed you to be a fool, Suzanne."

"What?!" she gasped at his insult.

"You'd better face the facts. There isn't a man in the world who wouldn't kill to get Lianne in his bed." He watched the color drain from her face at his brutal remark.

"So that's what your interest is in Adam and Lianne. What happened, Cyrus, did Lianne reject you?" Suzanne struck back just as cruelly.

Fury flared in the banker's icy blue eyes. "She's going to rue the day she refused me, Suzanne. You'll see."

"That may be, but it will have nothing to do with Adam and me." She refused to accept anything he was trying to tell her.

Cyrus was growing tired of her childishness where Trent was concerned. "You're wrong. Do you honestly think Trent will leave Lianne now that she's having his child? Can you deny that he was bedding her while he was courting you? Doesn't that tell you something?"

"No, Cyrus. You're the one who's wrong. I'm the one Adam loves." She tried to sound as convincing as possible.

Cyrus angrily came to his feet, aggravated at being thwarted by her refusal to see the truth of the situation. "Shall we just wait and see, my dear? I'm in no hurry to seek my revenge. When you realize that what I've told you is true, just let me know. You know where I am, Suzanne. All you have to do is send word. My plan is perfect, and working together we can both have our vengeance."

With that he was gone, leaving Suzanne to stare after him. Vehemently, she tried to deny to herself all that he'd told her, but still a niggling of doubt remained. Could it be true? Was Lianne the woman Adam really wanted?

Determinedly, Suzanne pushed the thought from her mind. Adam loved her, not Lianne. He'd told her so. Everything was going to work out just as she'd always hoped it would. Cyrus was wrong about Adam and Lianne, she was sure of it.

When Adam returned to Belle Arbor late that afternoon, Lianne and Becky were in the parlor. They exchanged meaningful glances as they heard him enter the house, but only Becky got up to go meet him.

"Adam?"

Adam was in no mood for a confrontation when he met his sister in the hallway. He was tired and he looked it. All he wanted to do was to get cleaned up and get some rest.

When Becky first saw him, she could tell right away that he'd been through some kind of terrible ordeal. Realizing the condition he was in, she said nothing about his strange disappearance the night before. Still, she couldn't help but wonder at the reason for his unannounced departure, and she worried that it had something to do with Beau.

Lianne followed Becky out into the hallway to greet Adam. Her reaction to his obvious exhaustion was completely different from her friend's. Instead of concern, she felt only disdain, blaming his weariness on a mad, passionate night spent in Suzanne's arms. The moment was tense and awkward and uncomfortably silent until Alex's excited greeting interrupted it.

"Adam! You're back!" the youngster whooped in

delight as he came charging down the steps to see him. Without pause, Alex launched himself into Adam's arms and gave him a fierce hug. "I missed you! I knew you wouldn't stay away too long!"

"I came back as soon as I could," Adam told him as he returned his hug.

Adam looked up then, and his gaze accidentally collided with Lianne's. It was a heart-stopping moment for Adam. He had thought of her almost continually for the entire time he was gone, but even his most passionate memories of her had not done her beauty justice. He was thinking of just how lovely she actually was when he was jarred to the depths by the scathing look of loathing she gave him. It was obvious from the glacial glare she shot him that she thought he was lying to Alex.

Adam was torn as he watched Lianne turn away from him and walk rigidly back into the parlor. He wanted to go after her, to explain all that had happened and erase that accusing look of disgust from her face, but he held himself in check. He owed her nothing. What did he care what she thought about him? He may have been forced to take her as his wife, but that didn't mean he had to answer to her. She didn't mean a thing to him, not a thing.

"Hey, Adam, do you want to go for a ride later on?" Alex piped in.

Glad for the distraction, Adam tousled his hair. "What do you say we ride together in the morning? I'm a little tired now."

"All right," Alex agreed happily, and he darted outside pleased with the promise of being able to spend some time with him the next day.

"I'm going to get cleaned up now. I'll talk to you later, Becky," Adam said. Once again he glanced toward the parlor where Lianne had gone and then went on up to his room.

As Adam entered the master bedroom, he was hoping that he would have a few minutes of peace and quiet, but the sight of Lianne's nightgown spread out carefully on the bed put an end to that hope. The delicate, feminine garment reminded him all too forcefully of the power of his desire for her. It angered him that she had such a firm hold on his thoughts, and his movements were agitated as he stripped to the waist and then stalked to the washstand to wash. A short time later, when the knock came at the door, Adam knew who it was.

"Come on in, Becky," he called out.

Becky did as he bid and then shut the door behind her. Before she could say anything, he spoke up first, offering what he knew she wanted to know.

"I was in New Orleans, Becky," he explained flatly as he grabbed a towel and began to dry himself. When he'd finished, he looped his towel around his neck and turned to look at her.

"New Orleans?" Becky frowned and then knew a moment of true panic. "Why did you have to go there? Has something already happened? I have to know, Adam, is Beau all right?"

"I didn't go because of Beau, Becky," Adam explained, a bit surprised by her show of concern for Beau. "I went because Dr. Williams sent for me. The note I received during dinner last night was from him." He moved to the wardrobe to get a clean shirt.

"Elise . . ." Her name was a breathless whisper. "Did something happen to Elise?"

Adam kept his back to her as he paused in his actions for a moment. When he did finally answer, it was without emotion. "Williams has made a breakthrough, Becky. It looks like Elise is going to recover."

"Dear God . . ." Becky sank down on the edge of the

bed, her mind awhirl with the implications of the news he'd just imparted. "What are you going to do?" She raised tormented eyes to his.

"I've already done it," he said as he shrugged into his shirt.

"What?"

"I told Dr. Williams the truth."

"But . . ." Becky's heart ached for her brother. For so long they had hoped and prayed for Elise to get better, and now . . .

"Don't worry about it," Adam remarked a bit coldly. "It seems that Dr. Williams has fallen in love with Elise, and she with him."

Becky didn't believe his attempt at indifference for a minute. She went to him and linked her arms around his waist to embrace him. "I'm sorry, Adam, so sorry."

"Why be sorry?" he asked. "Elise is going to be all right. That's all that matters."

"You still love her, don't you?" She looked up at him, trying to read behind the expressionless mask he had in place.

"It doesn't matter what I feel, does it? I mean, I *am* married now or have you forgotten?" he challenged bitterly, not wanting to examine his own emotions too closely.

"No, Adam, I hadn't forgotten." Becky felt chastised at his statement.

"Besides," Adam added, "Williams loves her. He'll make her happy."

"I just wish—"

"Wishing won't change anything. What happened, happened," he said flatly, interrupting her as he focused on what he was still driven to accomplish.

"But if Elise is going to be all right, then there's no need for—"

"There's every need, Becky!" Adam erupted, not

313

about to give up his vendetta against Shark. "My plans haven't changed. I'm not going to stop until I've found Shark and made him pay."

Anger consumed Lianne as she left the house to wander in the garden. How dare Adam leave without a word, stay away all night, and then return without an explanation? She was his wife and, as such, deserving of at least some reasonable justification for his absence. The memory of his insistence on a "marriage in name only" assaulted her. Evidently, he was showing her most plainly how he planned to live their lives from now on. Pain stabbed at her heart. Lianne didn't want to feel this hurt and humiliation, but she did.

Pausing amongst the fragrant, blossoming flowers, she stared out toward the reflecting pond remembering the splendor of that one night there in Adam's arms. He had been so wonderful . . . so warm and tender. She should have realized the danger then, but she'd been too hopelessly naive and foolish. Now, it was too late to worry about the danger. She was his wife, she had his name, and she was bearing his child. None of it really mattered, though, because Adam didn't care.

Suzanne was the woman Adam loved. He'd made that clear from the start. The fact that he spent last night with her only served to emphasize it.

Lianne swallowed with some difficulty, her throat aching as she tried to suppress the emotions that threatened. She remembered the butterfly Alex had caught weeks ago, and she realized that her worst fears had come to pass. She was trapped in a loveless marriage.

A deep sigh shuddered through her, and she turned back toward the house. Soon it would be time for dinner, and she would have to face Adam across the table and pretend, for Alex's sake, that nothing was wrong. Lianne hoped that she was strong enough to do it.

Dinner was a subdued affair, but Alex didn't seem to notice. He was so full of tales to tell Adam about what he'd done all day that there was little room for other conversation.

Lianne was relieved not to have to worry about making chitchat during the meal. She was having enough difficulty coping with the thought of sharing the same bed with Adam again. She wished there was some way for her to avoid it, but remembering what he'd done on their wedding night, she knew better than to try to escape their bedroom

Watching him covertly from beneath lowered lashes, Lianne noted the ease with which he talked with Alex, and she found herself resenting the comfortable camaraderie they shared. Never, in all their time together, had Adam ever spoken with her that way. Their conversations had always been arguments or terse exchanges. It seemed that they had never shared anything except two wild nights of passion, and because of those two encounters, they were now joined for the rest of their lives.

Lianne wondered if there was any point in trying to change his opinion of her. She knew he hated her and would never believe anything she told him right now, but she hoped that in time she would be able to convince him of her true worth. She would be the perfect mother to their child, and then, perhaps, he would come to see that she was not the ogre he thought.

When the meal ended, Lianne excused herself and left the table as quickly as she could, pleading tiredness and the need to go to bed early. Sarah brought her bath for her, and she settled into the steaming, perfumed water with great relish, glad to be away from Adam's somehow threatening presence. She had few enough pleasures left in her life, and she intended to enjoy this one to the fullest.

"Miss Lianne, which nightgown do you want to wear tonight?" Sarah asked as she stood before the wardrobe.

"The same one as last night will do," Lianne replied with little thought.

"You know there are other ones in here that would do just fine," the maid prodded slightly. She knew all about Adam's night away, and she wanted Lianne to do everything in her power to win him and keep him. For all his faults, Sarah thought Adam would make Lianne a good husband once they'd worked through the awkwardness of their forced marriage.

"The one I wore last night will be fine, Sarah," Lianne repeated brusquely. It was the simplest night-dress she owned and not nearly as seductive as the one she'd worn on their wedding night. Adam had made it abundantly clear that he didn't want her, so she saw no reason in flaunting herself before him.

"All right." Sarah sounded slightly annoyed as she answered, but when Lianne glanced at her, she couldn't read anything untoward in her expression.

"You can go now, Sarah. I'll be all right by myself," she dismissed her, needing some time alone more than anything else.

The maid let herself out of the room and closed the door quietly behind her. Sarah was just starting back downstairs to tend to her other duties when she ran into Adam at the top of the staircase. By the time she reached the downstairs hall, Sarah could no longer suppress the smile she'd held back or the twinkle that sparkled in her eyes.

Adam was desperately in need of rest. The long sleepless hours of the night before had caught up with him. Tired as he was though, his nerves were stretched taut at the thought of sharing his bed with Lianne. Remembering the nightgown she had laid out, Adam lingered below with Becky hoping to give his bride time to retire.

Adam delayed going up as long as he could. When he finally did go upstairs, he hoped to find Lianne already under the covers and fast asleep, so he could retire himself and get some much-needed rest. But what Adam found when he opened the door to the bedroom was anything but restful. Standing perfectly still just inside the doorway, he stared in mute shock at the sight of Lianne taking a bath. She hadn't heard him come in, so he took the opportunity to feast his eyes upon her.

Lianne looked gloriously lovely. Her red-gold hair was piled high on her head, baring the graceful arch of her neck. The heat of the water left her skin glowing rosily. Adam felt the all-too-familiar tightening heat in his loins as he imagined himself kissing the dewy droplets of water from her throat and bare shoulders. She lifted her arms to squeeze out the cloth she was using, and the action brought her breasts teasingly to the surface. Adam stared hungrily at the rounded, creamy orbs. The water tantalizingly lapped at their fullness, threatening to but never quite revealing the pale pink crests.

Adam bit back a groan as all trace of weariness left him. Suddenly, sleep was the furthest thing from his mind. Suddenly, he didn't care if she'd trapped him onto marriage. All that mattered was that he make love to her. Damn, but he wanted her as he'd never wanted another! Pushing the door shut, he took a step toward her, intending to follow through on the urgings of his baser instincts.

Lianne heard something and gasped as she turned to find her husband standing there staring at her. His expression was wooden, revealing nothing of his inner thoughts, yet there was something about the way he was looking at her that frightened her. In a shielding move, she grabbed the towel that Sarah had left for her and covered her bosom, not caring if she soaked it in the process.

"Adam! What do you want?" she demanded, conjuring up all the false bravado she could as she faced him. He seemed so overpoweringly male as he stood there, and she felt completely and utterly female, partially exposed as she was to his dark-eyed gaze. She thought him breathtakingly handsome, but, at the same time, knew that he had the power to hurt her and hurt her deeply.

The coldness of her tone jolted him painfully back to reality, and he forced away all thought of taking his pleasure of her. With ruthless resolve, he reminded himself of her treachery. He told himself again that her deceitful ways had almost ruined his plans. He told himself again that no matter how much he desired her, he was not going to make love to her!

"From you, dear wife?" Adam drawled sarcastically. "Not a thing." He spun on his heel and stalked from the room, slamming the door with a finality that jarred her.

Lianne stared at the closed portal, her heart sinking. A great sense of despair filled her at his blunt rejection. There could be no doubt about it, Adam hated her.

The water, which moments before had felt so soothing, suddenly felt chilling. In annoyance, Lianne cast the sodden towel aside and left the tub. She searched

318

the room in dripping splendor for another towel and finally found the one Adam had used earlier. As she began to dry, she moved across the room to where her gown lay, and as she did, her path took her before the full-length mirror.

Lianne was unable to resist the temptation to stare at her own reflection. She had never thought herself a raving beauty, but she did think that she was modestly attractive. Disheartened, she wondered why Adam was in love with Suzanne, and why he found her so much more attractive than herself. Was it because the other woman was more petite than she was, or was it because Suzanne was a golden blond while her own hair was red-gold. The mirror revealed no answers.

Lianne thought about going after him, but she knew it was a useless effort. She slipped into her gown and climbed into her solitary bed. As she drifted off to sleep, she wondered sadly if every night of her married life was going to be as empty as this one had been.

Chapter Twenty-six

Lianne came awake abruptly at the sound of a door slamming below. She sat up sleepily, straining to hear more of what was going on, but all she could make out was the sound of a rider galloping off into the night. Frowning and perplexed, Lianne wondered who would be leaving Belle Arbor at this late hour.

A terrible thought occurred to her, destroying her pleasantly slumberous state. What if it had been Adam who'd just ridden off? What if he'd been unable to stay away from Suzanne and had gone to spend the rest of the night with her, in her bed, giving her his love?

Lianne lay back down and tried to go back to sleep, but she was too filled with despair to rest any more. She had to know the truth. She had to find out if Adam was the one who'd just left the house.

Without bothering to pull on her wrapper, Lianne slipped from the bed and left the room to move silently down the hall. She paused at the top of the staircase. No sounds came from below, but a faint light showed through the partially open study doorway. Thinking that Adam had negligently left the lamp burning when he'd departed, she angrily headed downstairs to extinguish the light before returning to her own desolate bed.

* * *

Adam slumped wearily on the loveseat in the study, wondering if he was ever going to get a good night's sleep again. He had planned to go directly to bed when he'd gone upstairs long hours before, but the sight of Lianne bathing had driven him from the bedroom at almost a dead run. Now, half a bottle of bourbon later, he still couldn't sleep. Every time he closed his eyes, he saw his wife sitting gloriously naked before him in the tub, and his desire would return full force.

Adam just didn't know how to deal with the situation. He could no longer deny that he wanted her. Lianne affected him as no other woman ever had before. It seemed she was a fire in his blood. All he had to do was think about making love to her, and the heat would throb through him anew.

He rubbed his forehead in a weary gesture as he continued his battle against his desire for Lianne. He couldn't want her. He knew what kind of woman she was—or did he? Again, Alex's stories about Lianne haunted him. Could it really be true that this attraction between them was something neither one of them could control? A part of Adam wanted to think so, but the other, more logical side of him denied it. The battle raged on within him.

Frustrated, Adam took another deep drink from the bottle he held loosely in his hand. He had started off using a glass, but had grown tired of continually having to pour himself another drink. After his first two double shots, he'd decided to discard the trappings of civilization and give in at least that much to the way he was feeling—slightly barbarous.

His gaze fell upon the single sheet of paper lying somewhat crumpled on the floor. A sneer curled his lips as he stared at it in disgust. It was a note from Suzanne, who'd sent her messenger over in the middle of the night to deliver it. Her brazenness bothered him, but there was nothing he could do about it. He'd convinced her that she was the woman he wanted, even though he'd married Lianne, and now he had to deal with it.

Suzanne had wanted him to come to her tonight, but he'd refused to go. He'd sent the servant back with the message that he would not be able to get away to see her until the next day. The thought of being with her, of her blond beauty and lush curves, did not appeal to him at all. Instead, he found himself envisioning Lianne in his arms, hungry for his kisses, welcoming his touch.

Adam snorted derisively at the thought. Lianne hated him. She had from the very beginning and probably always would.

It occurred to him rather abruptly that he'd never given Lianne any reason to love him. The thought was sobering. Driven by his own desperate need for revenge, he had taken over her home without a thought as to what she was thinking and feeling. He had taken her innocence in much the same way, and the end result had been that he'd gotten her pregnant even as he announced his engagement to another woman. *Was it any wonder Lianne couldn't stand the sight of him?* he asked himself with detached rationality. Adam scowled blackly and took another drink. It didn't sit well with him to think that he could have been wrong in any of this.

A small sound drew his sodden attention just then, and he glanced up to see Lianne enter the study. He stared in disbelief, for it almost seemed as if his musings had somehow conjured her up. She hadn't noticed him yet, so he didn't speak and instead took the time to feast his eyes upon her.

Lianne was undeniably gorgeous, Adam decided,

and he drunkenly complimented himself on his choice of a wife. Her thick burnished tresses hung unadorned about her shoulders, and he found himself wanting to see her hair fanned out on a pillow beneath her as he kissed her to senselessness. A lopsided smile quirked his lips at the mental image. The white gown she wore was demure in styling. The bodice was cut modestly, revealing little of her cleavage, and a single blue ribbon was tied beneath her breasts in the style of an empire gown. The sleeves were full and flowing as was the body of the nightdress. It was created of a gossamer fabric that enticed even as it concealed, and Adam found himself completely mesmerized by that which he could see and that which he could not.

He watched with intense interest as she seemed to float across the study to the desk where the lamp glowed softly. As she moved in front of the light, its brightness cast her luscious young body into shadowed relief against the filmy material of the gown, and Adam was treated to a innocent sensual display.

The effect upon him was instantaneous and electric as his barely controlled desire for her erupted to full-blooded passion. Adam wanted her. What he felt for her was as old as time, and his body embraced the knowledge openly, even as he consciously denied it.

Adam realized later that he must have made a sound, for Lianne spun about to face him, her expression wary and frightened. He thought she looked much like a doe before a hunter, poised and ready for flight at the first sign of danger.

"You're here . . ." Lianne said breathlessly as she stood before him.

She wanted to look away, but she couldn't. Adam was so handsome, and the physical attraction she felt for him was so potent, that she stood there spellbound staring at him. Her gaze went over him hungrily, taking in everything about him . . . the dark thickness of his hair, the strong column of his throat. He had unbuttoned the neck of the white shirt he wore, and Lianne could see the beginning of the black curling hair that covered the magnificent width of his chest. She found herself remembering what it had felt like to be cradled there against his heart, and a smoldering passion sparked to life deep within her.

"Did you think I'd left you?" Adam's voice was deep and rich, and it went over her in a velvet caress, stoking the already fiery desire she was feeling.

Lianne couldn't tell by his tone if he was mocking her or not, and she certainly didn't want to admit the truth to him.

"Would it matter?" she challenged huskily.

Lianne knew she should flee from his presence, but somehow she just couldn't make herself turn away from him. She discovered that she wanted him. She knew he didn't want her, that Suzanne was the woman he truly loved, but right now, this minute, it didn't seem to make any difference. Lianne wanted to kiss the firm line of his mouth until the sternness of it softened with passion. She wanted to touch him, to caress the leanness of his ribs and tangle her fingers in the fur on his chest. She ached to hold him close and take him deep within her.

The memory of the searing heat of his body melding with hers sent her senses soaring. Vaguely, Lianne wondered if this was what it was like to be in love. If it was, it wouldn't matter, for Adam despised her, she realized poignantly. There could never be anything between them.

Adam's gaze darkened as it met hers, and what she saw revealed there in the molten depths sent a quiver of excitement through her.

"Oh, yes," he said in a voice that was a low, almost

predatory growl. "It matters."

He set the bottle aside as he came to his feet and crossed the room to where she stood. Lianne couldn't move. She stood transfixed before him, watching him come, helpless to do anything but wait for her fate. Adam lifted one hand to caress her cheek with his knuckles. Lianne shivered at his touch, but did not try to evade him.

"We want each other. We always have," Adam told her huskily, thinking that at least they had that much to build a relationship on.

Lianne didn't respond. Her mouth was dry, and her pulses were racing. Every fiber of her being was aware of him.

Adam felt his own desire for her raging to life as he looked down at her. She looked so innocent, so guileless. Was it possible that she had been the one trapped into this marriage and not the other way around? Was it possible that his cruelty to her had all been unfounded?

"You are so beautiful, Lianne," he said softly as he bent to kiss her.

Adam honestly expected her to run away from him, and at that moment he wouldn't have blamed her if she had. To his surprise, she stayed, and as his lips touched hers, he heard her sigh softly.

The gentleness of her sigh touched a chord deep within his heart, stirring something there he'd never experienced before. With the most delicate care, he lifted both hands to frame her face as the kiss went on and on. His mouth touched hers in a sweet, cherishing touch, but Lianne grew anxious for him to deepen the exchange. She opened her mouth beneath his as a flower opens to the sun, and she gloried in the boldness of his questing tongue.

A shudder of ecstasy wracked her at the ardor he

displayed, and, almost without conscious thought, she moved closer to him. Her willingness stirred him to even greater heights of excitement. With an emboldened touch, he cupped one hip and brought her full against him, holding her there so she could feel the proof of his desire for her.

Lianne gave a low rapturous moan as her hips nestled against his. He was so hard against her softness and so very masculine that her knees grew weak. She wanted Adam. She wanted him with a fierce, frenzied need that drove all thoughts of his betrayal from her mind. *Perhaps,* she thought deliriously, *love and hate were only a wit apart . . .*

"I want you, Lianne, more than I've ever wanted any woman," Adam confessed as he broke off the kiss to gaze down at her, his dark eyes mirroring the intensity of his need.

"I want you, too, Adam," Lianne admitted without reluctance. There seemed no point in trying to fight it any longer.

He kissed her again then, a powerful, devouring kiss. This time her knees did buckle, and he swept her up into his arms and carried her to the loveseat as if she weighed no more than a mite. Adam sat down on the sofa and kept Lianne on his lap. With a tenderness born of love, he sought to please her in every way. His every caress was cherishing, his every kiss devoted. He thought only of Lianne and her pleasure.

Lianne was lost in a haze of bliss-filled ecstasy. Their other joinings had been exciting and exhilarating, but this time there was something different about the way Adam was touching her and kissing her. She knew she should try to analyze the difference so she could understand, but her passion won out. She surrendered mindlessly to the joy of his lovemaking.

When Adam slipped the negligee from her, Lianne

did not protest but thrilled instead to his low exclamation telling her how lovely she was. His lips sought her throat and then traced lower to tease her breasts with hot, arousing kisses. She was like a wild thing in his arms as he lay down with her fully against him. Lianne moved restlessly in his embrace, wanting to get closer to him, wanting to know his most intimate possession.

Adam shifted to lie on the bottom and brought Lianne above him, savoring the feel of her wriggling hips against his hard-driving need. He wanted her desperately, but he did not want to hurry. He wanted to make love to her in the deepest sense of the word. Positioning her, he sought the fullness of her breasts as she arched herself to him.

The touch of his mouth at her bosom left Lianne feeling enraptured as she supported herself slightly above him. Her head was thrown back and her eyes were half-closed as she moved her hips against his in a wildly restive motion. She knew she was tantalizing him with her movements, but she was feeling too wonderful to care.

When Adam slipped a hand between her thighs to test her readiness, she gasped at the sensation his touch aroused. He began to massage her then, taking her higher and higher to the brink of love's pinnacle. Complete abandon overtook her as she reached the peak of excitement. She was swept away on the burning fire of her need, spiraling to the heavens in a crescendo of ecstasy and then drifting down to the blissful lull of fulfillment.

Lianne was feeling a bit shy as she rested with her head on his shoulder. Embarrassed by her abandoned response to him, she kept her face turned away from his and her eyes closed as she savored the aftermath of her now-sated passion. Lianne could feel the heat of his desire for her still hard against her, and it filled her with pleasure to know that he wanted her as much as she had wanted him.

Languidly, she opened her eyes, intending to initiate the full completion of their lovemaking. Then, for the first time, she noticed the crumpled sheet of paper on the floor nearby. She hadn't seen it before, as caught up in Adam's embrace as she'd been, but now, staring at the note, she recognized Suzanne's scrawling handwriting.

My darling Adam,
  I miss you so, even though we haven't been apart for very long. Come to me tonight. I need you and I want you. I'll be waiting . . .
                    Love,
                    Suzanne

Reality—Harsh, cruel, and taunting—raised its ugly head, and Lianne went stiff in his arms. *Of course his touch had been different!* she berated herself. *He'd been thinking of his precious Suzanne all the time he was making love to you!* In an almost violent move, she threw herself from his arms.

"Lianne?" Adam had been content for the first time in what seemed like ages. He had given Lianne complete joy and had planned to make slow, magnificent love to her all night. His body was alive with his unsated passion for her. Now suddenly, for no reason, she had left his embrace. "What is it?"

"How could I have been so stupid?" Lianne demanded, more of herself than him. "How could I have let you do this to me?"

"Do what to you? We were making love,

328

Lianne . . ."

She froze him with a look as she snatched up the note from the floor and thrust it in his face. "And then what, Adam? Were you going to leave me and rush off to Suzanne?"

Adam felt his desire fade as he realized the reason for her upset. "No, Lianne. I was—"

"You were what, *dear husband!* Were you going to go from our marriage bed to your lover's bed? Were you going to compare Suzanne and me when you were done and then choose between us?" Lianne threw the note aside in disgust.

In that moment, seeing her anguish, Adam knew that he loved her. He couldn't bear to hurt her any longer with his emotions. He wanted to tell her everything.

"It's not what you think, Lianne," Adam began to explain as he came off the loveseat and tried to take her in his arms.

Lianne gave a cynical laugh as she evaded him. "I should have remembered! Why is it every time you touch me, I forget everything that's important?" she agonized out loud.

"Lianne, I—" He was feeling the full weight of his deception now, and he wanted to clear the air.

Adam reached out to take her by the arm and drag her back to him. But Lianne was not about to allow him to touch her again.

"No, Adam!" Like a savage she-cat she attacked him, slapping him with all her might. "I hate you! I hate you with all my heart and soul! Don't you ever come near me again!" she cried, backing cautiously away from him, her eyes wild. "Go on to Suzanne, Adam! She's the one who's waiting for you! She's the one who wants you! Not me!"

With that, Lianne fled the study, not caring that she

was nude and that she'd left her gown behind, not caring about anything except the need to escape. She reached the bedroom and locked the door behind her. Panting from her mad dash to safety and trembling with fright over the force of the emotions that filled her, Lianne fell upon the bed and clutched her pillow protectively to her.

Lianne was miserable as she contemplated what she had almost allowed to happen. Adam had only to touch her, and her resistance vanished. She tried to fight against acknowledging the truth, but it pounded through her with relentless ferocity. She loved Adam! She loved him desperately! The realization pounded through her, even as she wanted to deny it. Why else would he constantly haunt her thoughts? Why else would it hurt so badly to think of him with Suzanne, making love to her?

Tears fell unheeded as Lianne admitted to herself the hopelessness of her love for Adam. There, alone in her room, she cried, alternately fearing that he would come after her and also that he wouldn't. When she heard the sound of men's voices outside, she left the bed and rushed to the window. She brushed the curtains aside just in time to see Adam ride off into the night in the direction of Willow Bend.

Adam stood helplessly by and watched Lianne run from the study. *She hated him* . . . He'd known it, but for just those few minutes he'd allowed himself to forget all that had happened before and just love her. Like a man in a trance, he picked up the discarded negligee and stared at it blankly. The material was soft and sleek in his hands, and Adam found himself thinking of how satiny Lianne's skin had felt beneath his touch. The ache returned to his loins. With an angry curse, he tangled his hands in the nightgown and tore it to shreds in a single, vicious motion, then cast it aside.

Suddenly becoming aware of what he'd done, Adam knew that he had to get away from Lianne. The torture of living with her and wanting her and never being able to have her was driving him to madness.

He would go back to the *Sea Shadow,* he decided. He and Beau had prearranged a system for relaying messages, and he would send one to him tonight letting him know that he wanted to go back to sea again as soon as he could.

Adam strode from the room and roused a servant to bring a horse from the stables for him. When the horse was brought around, he rode off without leaving word of where he would be or when he would be back.

Chapter Twenty-seven

Suzanne was fairly dancing down the hall with excitement. Adam had finally arrived! She'd been more than a little disappointed the night before when he hadn't come to her as she'd asked. All the doubts Cyrus had created within her had crept back into her thoughts. She'd passed the long hours of darkness imagining Adam making love to his insipid little wife and getting very angry. Now that he was here, she knew all her turmoil had just been the result of her overactive imagination. He'd just been too busy last night to get away. Today, he was here and he was hers.

"Adam, darling." Suzanne went into his arms where he stood waiting for her in the parlor and lifted her lips to his for a passionate kiss.

For the first time since he'd begun his pretended courtship of her, Adam really did not want anything to do with her. Still, he knew his game had not yet been played out, and it was essential that he continue the charade. Grimacing inwardly, he met her in that exchange. No desire flared within him as he kissed her. All Adam felt was disgust. He was relieved when Suzanne broke off the kiss and moved away to sit on the sofa.

"Come join me," she invited, patting the seat next to her, and Adam knew he could do little else. "I've missed you, Adam."

"I've missed being with you, too," he lied.

"I really wanted to see you last night," Suzanne purred, rubbing her breast against his shoulder as she leaned toward him.

"I'm sorry I couldn't get away, but I had some business I had to attend to. I was just leaving when your note arrived, and it was quite late when I got back."

"I understand," she told him. "All that matters is that you're here now. Can you stay and perhaps have dinner with me tonight?"

"I'm afraid my visit will have to be a brief one today," Adam replied, glad that he'd remembered his promise to Alex to spend some time with him. "I have a business appointment this afternoon that I can't postpone."

"Oh," Suzanne pouted, wondering what was more important than their love. "You know, Adam, you don't seem very glad to see me. I wonder why you bothered to come here at all!"

Adam recognized his cue and took her in his arms with what he hoped passed for true ardor.

"You know why I came, Suzanne," he said fiercely. "How could I stay away?"

He kissed her then in a manner he hoped she would believe reflected his undying love, and when he broke it off, he felt decidedly jaded. No longer did his manipulations thrill him. No longer did he feel the tension of the chase.

"Oh, my darling, it's so good to be with you again," Suzanne panted. She gazed up at him adoringly, wanting him desperately, but knowing that they had to wait. "I just wish we could be together always."

"Our time will come," Adam mouthed the words she wanted to hear.

She went into his arms again, her mouth seeking and finding his in a deep kiss. Pressing herself against him, she caressed him as boldly as she dared. Adam suffered her advances, acting the part of the fervent lover, yet all the while he played his role, he was thinking of the night before and Lianne. He remembered the beauty of her nakedness and the creamy fullness of her breasts. He remembered the excitement aroused in him just by being near her. He remembered the sweetness of her kiss and the innocence of her passion. Then he remembered the ending of their momentarily idyllic scene and the reason for it—Suzanne. He wondered suddenly, dazedly, what in the hell he was doing there, kissing another woman. Lianne was his wife.

Abruptly, Adam broke off the kiss and moved away from Suzanne and her cloying embrace. She watched him in confusion as he stood up.

"I really have to be getting back to Belle Arbor," he declared edgily.

Suzanne thought that she'd aroused his passion to the point where he had to leave or make love to her right then and there. The idea pleased her. She had always considered herself something of a femme fatale, and she figured that Adam was the same as any other man. She rose and went to him, planning to tease him just a little more. Brazenly, she linked her arms about his neck and tried to draw him down for another kiss, but he resisted. Suzanne was stunned when Adam actually gripped her arms and loosened their hold on him.

"I have to go, Suzanne."

"Must you really go so soon?" she argued. "It seems that you just got here."

"I'll be back as soon as I can get away," Adam promised. He realized he might be jeopardizing his plan, but at that moment, he didn't care about anything except escaping her aggressiveness.

"I know you will." Though questions and accusations filled her, she tried to sound pleasant. Suzanne knew acting jealous would get her nowhere with Adam. He was a victim of their situation just as much as she was. "I'm just sorry that things have to be this way now."

"It won't be this way forever," Adam said, meeting her eyes forthrightly as he spoke. While he was saying it, he was hoping and praying that Shark would make an appearance soon.

Suzanne, however, read another meaning in his words, and she went to him impulsively, embracing him even when he would have refused.

"It's that thought that makes this all bearable for me, Adam," she confessed.

"Me, too," he vowed seriously as he kissed her one last time and then left.

Adam had traveled to Willow Bend by way of the bayou, and the quiet return trip on the waterway provided him with the time he needed to think things through. He loved Lianne. He had never realized just how much until he had tried to continue on with his act as Suzanne's lover. It had been next to impossible for him to keep up the pretense, and he was glad to be away from her clinging embrace.

Even though Adam was relieved to have gotten away from Suzanne relatively unscathed, the prospect of returning home to spend the rest of the day in Lianne's company left him feeling tense and on edge. She hated him completely. The thought left him feeling deeply troubled, and he wondered how best to handle the situation. He wanted Lianne, and he wanted her badly—there was no doubt about that. But until this thing with Shark was settled, he was trapped in his own deception. Adam knew that there was no way out other than to follow through with his original intent. Once Shark had been brought to justice, he could court Lianne as a true lover would and convince her of the real depth of his love for her. Perhaps when she learned the truth of his motives and came to understand the reason for his actions, she would see him in a different light. He hoped so.

Maneuvering the skiff into the dock at Belle Arbor, Adam tied up and then jumped from the craft. He had just started up the path toward the main house when he heard Alex call out to him, and he spotted the boy running toward him.

"Adam!"

"Hi, Alex," he greeted him.

"You ready to go for our ride?" Alex asked enthusiastically.

Adam glanced up toward the house, thought about the possibility of a confrontation with Lianne, and then quickly agreed. "Let's go."

"I got this great idea where we can go today since it's so hot," the boy told him in a confiding tone.

"Oh? Where's that? The south fields to check on the crops there?"

Alex slanted him a conspiratorial look. "No. This is some place you've never been before." They reached the stable and went in to get their mounts. "It's a secret place where Mark and I used to go whenever we could sneak off. You're gonna like it," he told him with confidence as they rode out.

Adam realized then that this was some place very special, for he knew how much Alex had loved his older brother.

Alex's secret place was a small, secluded swimming hole a goodly distance from the house. As it was shrouded from view by the grove of trees that surrounded it, privacy was guaranteed. Several limbs of the larger trees hung enticingly out over the water, and a strategically placed rope gave testimony to the hours of boyish fun and frolic that had gone on here before.

"What d'ya think, Adam?" Alex asked eagerly.

"I can see why you like to come here, Alex." He grinned at him as they tied up the horses and walked down to the water's edge. "I'll bet you've had a lot of fun here, haven't you?"

"I used to," the boy began slowly, suddenly doubting that it had been a good idea to come back to the place he'd shared so intimately with Mark. It had been their place, and their place alone. He hadn't swum there since his brother's death, and he almost felt as if he was somehow betraying him by bringing Adam here.

"What's the matter, Alex?" he prompted, sensing his sadness.

Alex lifted his troubled gaze to Adam's as he wondered if he should tell him everything he was feeling. Adam saw the pain, hurt, and bewilderment reflected there. He didn't speak, though, for he knew the youth would have to open up to him on his own.

"I haven't been here since . . . since Mark died." He stumbled over the words.

"You came here a lot together?"

"Every summer we'd spend hours here every chance we could! We used to have so much fun!" he answered, remembering all the happy times he and Mark had shared, swimming, swinging from the rope and diving from the low-hanging tree branches. Despite the vast differences in their ages they had been as close as any two brothers could be. Until . . . "But it hurts to be here now, Adam," Alex confessed as tears filled his eyes, forcing him to look away.

"Do you want to go? We can leave if you want to," Adam offered. He waited, watching the tortured expressions flit across Alex's face as he wrestled with his feelings. "Or, if you want, we can stay and have some fun on our own?"

His eyes danced with joy, and he reacted spontaneously, throwing his arms about Adam to give him a big hug. "I'd like that, Adam."

"Good." He hugged him back, thinking of how defenseless Alex was against the power of life's sometimes overwhelming misery, yet thinking how well he had done in coping with all that had happened to him in the past year. Adam found himself wondering if his own child, the child that Lianne now carried, would be as brave and as strong as Alex.

"Last one in . . ." Alex laughed in delight as he started to strip down with wild, youthful enthusiasm.

They raced to shed their clothing, but Alex had a head start and was the first one in the water. Adam followed him only moments later, diving in next to him with the biggest splash he could make. Time was forgotten as they cavorted with carefree, male abandon. Adam tossed a gleeful, shrieking Alex from his shoulders into the cool depths time and again as they wrestled playfully. Their play was a relaxing diversion for the both of them, and they lost track of all except the joy of their revelry.

Lianne was frowning as she sought out Sarah in the kitchen. "I've been trying to find Alex, Sarah. Have you seen him?"

"Not since early this morning. Whatever he's doing, he must be keeping himself pretty busy."

"Why do you say that?" she asked, curiously.

"He didn't even come back for the lunch," Sarah answered, "and it ain't much like that boy to skip a meal."

338

"You're right about that, Sarah." Lianne gave a light laugh.

"Alex was saying at breakfast that he and Mr. Adam were going to be out riding together today. Could he be with him?"

"No," Lianne snapped more harshly than she'd intended. The memory of the night before and Adam's betrayal was still too fresh in her mind to think of him with anything but a flashfire of hate.

"Then you've spoken with Mr. Adam?" Sarah pried. She knew she shouldn't, but she wanted to get to the bottom of what was troubling Lianne. Sarah had never seen her so strained and on edge. Something was terribly wrong, and she thought if Lianne talked about it, it might help her.

"No, I haven't seen him," she bit out tersely.

"Well, why not?" Sarah faced her, hoping that she would open up and talk to her. Lianne was not about to speak of Adam's infidelity. It hurt her too much even to think of it, let alone talk about it.

"Look, I'm getting worried about Alex. I've got to go look for him." Lianne fled the kitchen needing desperately to get away from Sarah's knowing look. Sometimes she regretted that her servant knew her so well.

"Lianne?" Becky was coming down the stairs as Lianne started out the front door. "Where are you going?"

"I'm trying to find Alex."

"Is something wrong?"

"No. It's just that he seems to have disappeared and I was getting a little worried about him. I haven't seen him all day, and it'll be dinner time soon."

"I saw him around midmorning. He said he was going to find Adam so they could go for the ride he'd promised him."

339

"I'll be down at the stables, then. Maybe someone down there can tell me where he's gone. It's not like Alex to just take off and not let me know where he's going."

"Well, I wouldn't worry too much. He's probably with Adam."

Becky's voice trailed after her as she went out the door, but the thought lingered and she grew angry as she headed for the stables. Just because Alex might be with Adam was no reason for him not to let her know where he was and what he was doing. She was his sister! She was the one responsible for him!

The news she received from the stablehands only added to her irritation. Alex and Adam had ridden out several hours before. No one knew for sure exactly where they were going, but they'd over heard Alex telling Adam something about his "secret place."

Lianne knew immediately where Alex had taken Adam, and she grew furious. The swimming hole had been Mark and Alex's place. Adam had no business going there! How dare he try to insinuate himself into her little brother's life! Hadn't Alex suffered enough with Mark's death? How dare Adam befriend him when he knew damn good and well that he would be leaving them just as soon as he could?

Lianne was painfully aware that their marriage was a farce. She knew he didn't love her and that he wanted out as soon as possible so he could marry his sweet little Suzanne! Directing one of the hands to saddle her a mount, she rode out after them.

Adam and Alex were floating easily in the pool, just enjoying the sunshine and the quiet. Alex knew now that he'd made the right decision in staying. He had had a wonderful time with Adam, and he wanted to come back here with him again just as soon as they could manage it.

"It's getting a little late, Alex. I guess it's time to start back," Adam said as he reversed his position and started to swim lazily back toward the bank.

"Do we have to?"

"What do you think?" Adam asked him, his eyes alight as he remembered his own boyhood days and how much he'd always hated to go home after an afternoon of fun.

"You're right. Lianne's gonna be mad enough as it is," Alex grumbled as he paddled after him.

"Why's that?"

"I didn't tell her when I left. I'm supposed to tell her where I'm going so she doesn't worry about me," he explained.

As they talked, they were unaware of Lianne's presence in the grove of trees. She hadn't meant to eavesdrop. She'd meant to make her presence known and to scold Alex immediately for his negligence, but when Adam reached the shallow end and started to stand up, she found herself standing in rigid silence, holding her breath in anticipation of his next step out of the water.

Lianne told herself that she should look away, that there was no point in torturing herself this way. Adam would never be hers, and she had to accept that. Yet, she couldn't tear her gaze away from the sight of him.

She stared at him, mesmerized. The sun was glinting off his dark hair, making it seem almost blue-black in color, and when he smiled down at Alex, his teeth flashed white and perfect in his tanned face. There wasn't an ounce of extra flesh upon him. His chest was broad and his shoulders looked strong and powerful. Lianne found herself longing to run her hands over those firm, corded muscles.

341

As Adam stepped up on the bank out of the pond, she still couldn't bring herself to look away. Lianne had no doubt that Adam was a glorious example of manhood in its prime. His lean waist and long, straight legs only enhanced his very evident maleness.

Lianne thought of the night before and of how intimately they had lain together on the loveseat in the study. Her heartbeat quickened as she remembered his kisses and caresses. A pulse of heavy desire throbbed to life deep in the cradle of her womanhood as she watched him pick up his clothes and begin to dress.

They were still ignorant of Lianne standing nearby as Alex came to join him and began to dress, too.

"Adam, can I ask you something?" After the pleasant afternoon they had shared, he felt close to Adam, and he felt sure he could ask him the question that had been troubling him all day.

"What is it?" Adam asked him.

"How come you went to over to Willow Bend today?"

"I went to see Suzanne," he answered, a bit taken by surprise by his question. Adam had not known that Alex was aware of where he'd gone.

"I know that." Alex gave him an exasperated look. "What I want to know is, now that you're married to Lianne, why do you still go to see her?"

Alex's innocent, but challenging gaze pinned him, demanding an honesty that he wanted to, but couldn't, give.

"It's like I told you before, Alex. Suzanne is a friend. Just because you get married doesn't mean you stop having friends." He tried to make it sound acceptable.

"Then you're going to keep on seeing her?" Alex pressed.

As much as Adam wanted to tell him that he wouldn't, he knew there was no point in lying. He was going to have to continue seeing Suzanne until Shark returned. "Yes, I am," he told him bluntly, and he turned away from the sight of Alex's crestfallen expression.

Lianne had remained motionless, not wanting to draw any attention to herself as she'd listened to the exchange. At Adam's harsh answer she turned and rushed soundlessly away. Her throat ached as she struggled to hold back the cry of sorrow that threatened.

Suzanne was the only woman he loved. Lianne knew that the love she felt for him would always have to remain a secret. She could never bare her soul to him, for the humiliation would be too great. She had only known the bliss of Adam's love twice, and the memories of those nights would have to last her a lifetime.

Chapter Twenty-eight

"I'm sorry," Alex muttered as he stood before his sister an hour later, his head down, his eyes averted.

"I was worried about you. No one knew where you'd gone," Lianne reprimanded him.

"It's just that I was having so much fun with Adam that I—"

Alex's words cut her to the quick. He liked Adam and even trusted him. In his innocence, he had no idea of how much, how greatly, Adam could hurt him. Lianne wanted to warn him not to care for Adam too deeply, but she knew she couldn't without having to explain. Alex thought their marriage was a love match, and she didn't want to ruin that for him. He was too young to know the disillusioning truth.

"Next time think before you go running off, young man. Just let me know where you're going to be."

"Yes, Lianne." He sighed contritely. He knew he'd been wrong and that he deserved the scolding he was getting.

Lianne hugged him impulsively. "Good. I don't like having to worry about you. You're all I've got left."

"That's not true. You've got Adam," Alex said as he hugged her back, then gazed up at her with questioning, brown eyes. "You do love him, don't you, Lianne?"

"Of course," she answered, knowing it was no lie. "I married him, didn't I?"

"I know, but there's something I don't understand."

"What is it, sweetheart?" Lianne kept a supportive arm about his little shoulders as he struggled to find the right way to ask her.

"Well, why does Adam still have to go see Suzanne, Lianne? He says she's his friend and that's why he goes, but I don't like it. *I don't like her!*" The words exploded from him.

"I don't like her either, Alex, but Adam's a grown man and he can do whatever he wants," she explained lamely.

"Can't you make him stop?"

"Sometimes life doesn't go exactly the way you want it to," Lianne counselled.

"But, Lianne . . ." Alex's eyes were huge in his face as he spoke what was in his heart. "I'm so afraid that what happened to Mark is going to happen to Adam."

"It won't."

"But how can you be so sure? Make him stop going to see her, please, Lianne? You love him, and he loves you. He'll listen to you if you tell him not to go." Alex made it sound so simple.

"Honey, just because you love someone doesn't mean they're always going to do what you want them to. Look at you," she said, pointing out the analogy. "You went off today without telling me where you were going."

Alex looked frustrated. "Won't you at least talk to him, Lianne?"

"Yes, Alex. I'll talk to him, and I'm sure everything will be just fine," Lianne promised in her most earnest tone.

The moment Lianne told him that everything would be all right, Alex felt better. Lianne always told him the truth, and he trusted her implicitly. If she said something would be all right, it always was.

"Can I go play now, Lianne?" Alex asked, already on to other things.

"Go on," she laughed. "Get out of here. But remember . . . from now on tell me where you're going. All right?"

"All right." He dashed from the room, lighthearted again.

As Lianne watched him go, she thought of how sweetly young and innocent he still was, and suddenly the stifling melancholy that had gripped her was wrenched away. She grew furiously angry with Adam. It was obvious that Alex had come to love him very deeply, and Lianne realized that the bond could only end in disaster.

Lianne knew she could not stand idly by and watch her little brother be hurt again. She wouldn't allow Adam to do anything that would cause Alex any further pain. He had suffered enough losing Mark, and she didn't want him to suffer any more.

If Adam really wanted Suzanne, she decided vehemently, then he should go to her now and stay with her. Why prolong the torment of leaving them?

Lianne knew that Adam didn't love her. She knew that it was Suzanne he really wanted and that he'd only married her for the sake of their baby, but he wasn't doing them any favors by remaining with them while he continued to see Suzanne on the side. If the break was to be made, then he should do it now. Her mind made up, Lianne felt her long-absent pride return. She was going to confront Adam as soon as possible and demand that he choose.

Even as Lianne convinced herself that she would be doing this for Alex and the baby, her pride taunted her with the knowledge that he'd been making a fool out of her. If Alex was aware of his visits to Suzanne, then so was everyone else. Theirs might be a marriage in name only, but no one else was supposed to know it. Lianne lifted her chin in defiance at the thought. It was time to put a stop to this farce, one way or the other. Tonight, she would demand that he make his decision.

When Adam returned from his outing with Alex, he determinedly immersed himself in plantation business. He did not even leave the study for dinner. Becky encouraged him to join them, but he gave her strict orders that he was not to be interrupted for anything for the rest of the night. Adam continued to work on the ledgers until his eyes grew tired, and when he checked the time, he was pleased to find that it was near midnight.

Only then, when he was too exhausted to continue, did he allow his thoughts to dwell on his real reason for staying locked in the study for so long. *Lianne* . . . Adam's gaze drifted to the loveseat where they'd lain together in a passionate embrace the night before, and he felt the heat rise in his body again in remembrance. In frustration, he wondered what it would take to make him immune to Lianne. Here he was, bone-weary and worn out, and yet just the thought of having her filled him with expectant desire.

Adam shook his head in confusion. He would not force himself on Lianne. She'd made it clear the night before how she felt about him. There was no point in pushing it. He knew the best thing for him to do was to avoid Lianne as much as possible. That way the temptation to take her wouldn't be as strong. *Out of sight, out of mind* — he hoped.

With the last of his willpower, Adam fought down the need to rush from the study to his marriage bed and claim the love that was his by right. Instead, he sought out the barren comfort of the loveseat for his night's rest, grumbling to himself all the while. The too-short, too-hard sofa left him miserable through most of the night, but he did not weaken in his resolve to stay away from Lianne. It seemed an eternity to him before dawn finally pinkened the eastern sky, and he rose from his broken sleep, eager to escape from the house before Lianne awoke.

Adam's tread was silent as he made his way upstairs. He did not want to go into their bedroom, but he had no other way to get the clothing he needed. He entered the bedroom quietly and was glad to find that Lianne was asleep. He wasn't quite sure what he would have said to her had he found her awake, waiting for him.

Adam made a definite effort not to look at Lianne as he sorted through his clothes to find the pants and shirt he needed for the day. It was only when he turned, about to leave the room, that his gaze fell upon her. He froze, unable to look away from the sight of her slumbering so blissfully. He found himself moving to stand beside the bed and stare down at her.

In repose, she was lying on her right side. The covers had fallen away from her shoulder, baring one graceful arm to his gaze. Her hand was splayed out on the sheet, and the sight of his ring, proud, heavy, and dominant, on her finger sent an unexpected feeling of possessiveness surging through him.

Adam's breathing grew ragged as he studied her gentle beauty, taking in the soft swell of her breasts beneath the caressing fabric and the curve of her hips beneath the blanket. Soon she would be rounding with his child. Filled with a deep sense of warm rightness, Adam almost reached out to touch her cheek and smooth back an errant curl. Only the last-minute realization of what he was about to do stopped him. Silently cursing himself, Adam snatched his hand away and backed from the room.

A short while later when he left the house, Adam was hoping that he would soon get word from Beau about a rendezvous time, for he didn't know how much longer he could remain in such close quarters with Lianne and keep from making love to her. Resolved to working out his restlessness through hard, physical labor, Adam rode out to the fields intending to spend the entire day there.

Lianne was dismayed to awaken the following morning and discover that her husband had never come to bed. She had tried to stay awake as long as she could, but had finally fallen asleep some time during the early morning hours. Angry and frustrated, she dressed hurriedly and rushed downstairs wanting to confront Adam right away, only to discover that he'd already left the house and wasn't expected back until sundown.

Becky was up already and asked her if there was a problem, but Lianne denied that anything was wrong. She decided to wait until that evening to try to corner him and speak with him, but again that night her plans went awry. Adam stayed away until well after dusk and then secluded himself in the study once again, refusing any attempts at conversation.

At dinner, Lianne was forced to artfully dodge all of Alex's probing questions about why Adam was so busy that he didn't have time for them. She retired alone, again, staying awake as along as she could and finally drifting off after midnight.

Becky had remained surprisingly reticent through all of Lianne's turmoil with Adam. She honestly believed the change in her brother was directly related to the unexpected turn of events concerning Elise, and she knew there was nothing more she could do to help him through this troubling time.

Her heart ached for Lianne. She understood her confusion over Adam's behavior, but she knew that there was nothing she could tell her. Becky knew she couldn't risk betraying Adam, so she said as little as possible whenever they were together, pretending to be only vaguely aware of his withdrawal.

It was in the afternoon two days later when one of the servants came running into the house to announce that there was a carriage coming up the drive. Becky had gone upstairs to rest and Alex had gone out to play, leaving Lianne alone to greet the unexpected visitor. Curiosity gripped her as she wondered who might be coming to call, and she went outside to meet the new arrival.

The sight of the Labadie carriage making its way down Belle Arbor's drive filled Lianne with fury. She seethed as she thought of the other woman's brazenness in coming here, but she was not about to let Suzanne know that it infuriated her. Instead, she adopted a calm, serene demeanor and stepped from the porch to welcome her as warmly as was fitting for Adam's new bride.

"Why, Suzanne . . . this is a surprise." Lianne was all smiles as she watched her arch rival descend from her carriage.

"Really, darling?" Suzanne drawled, her blue eyes a frigid reflection of her feelings for Lianne. "Is Adam here?"

"No, my husband's working with the overseer today." she answered as coolly as she could. "Would you like me to take a message for you? I expect him back around sundown."

"Pity. I had so wanted to see Adam today, but I suppose it can wait until tonight—when he comes to see me."

"Well, if that's all you wanted, I suppose it will keep. Good-bye, Suzanne." Inwardly, Lianne bristled at Suzanne's open flaunting of her relationship with Adam. Unable to stand the sight of her any longer, she turned on her heel, meaning to walk away.

Suzanne eyed Lianne critically, hating her for the confidence she was displaying and for the way she seemed to be blossoming with good health. She had hoped that Lianne would be growing bloated and ugly, but her figure was still perfect, and she looked as ecstatically happy as any newlywed should. Suddenly, the doubts Cyrus had instilled in her rushed to the forefront, and she found that she wanted to hurt Lianne and hurt her badly.

"You know he's mine, don't you, Lianne?" Suzanne taunted knowingly.

Lianne stiffened at her words and turned back to regard the beautiful blond. "I know no such thing, Suzanne. Adam married me. I'm the one who bears his name."

Suzanne smirked at her statement. "Lianne, honey, you didn't stand a chance with Adam until you conveniently got pregnant. You were just another woman to Adam, someone to use and then cast off. You don't mean a thing to him."

Lianne managed her best smile. "You may think that way, but I don't"

"If he cared about you, Lianne, he certainly wouldn't be coming to me and professing his love, now, would he?"

She shrugged, trying to maintain her cool facade, trying not to let any of her heartbreak show before this vindictive witch.

"I'm Adam's wife, Suzanne. If he'd wanted you so much, why didn't he marry you while he had the chance?" Lianne challenged.

"Honor, little girl, honor. You're carrying his child . . ." She paused for effect, "at least, he thinks it's his child. Tell me, Lianne. Is it really Adam's baby or are you having someone else's brat and placing the blame on Adam just to keep Belle Arbor?"

Lianne's fists clinched at her sides, but she kept them hidden in the folds of her skirt so the other woman wouldn't know how truly upset she was at her accusations.

"Don't judge everyone else's morals by your own standards, Suzanne. We're not all eager to bed any man who'll have us."

At Lianne's comeback, Suzanne knew she had to strike back and strike back painfully. "You're wrong there, darling. I haven't bedded *every* man who wanted me. I'm very discriminating. If your brother had lived, he could have vouched for that. You see, I never thought Mark was quite man enough for me. Adam, however . . . Adam is a different story entirely, don't you think?" Suzanne smiled widely in triumph as she saw Lianne go sickly pale at her vicious remarks.

"Perhaps, Mark was the one who was discriminating in his tastes, Suzanne. Maybe he was the one who chose not to bed you!" Lianne shot back as her enemy climbed back into her carriage.

"Please tell Adam I came by, will you, Lianne?" Suzanne ignored her comment as she directed her driver to head back home.

Overcome with fury and heartwrenching pain, Lianne stood in the middle of the walk staring after the departing carriage with unseeing eyes. It had been terrible enough that she'd had to suffer Adam's visits to Suzanne, but there was no way she could tolerate the other woman coming here to gloat over Adam's love for her. This had to end, and it had to end now, before Alex found out! As soon as Adam returned tonight she was going to have it out with him once and for all.

"Mr. Adam!"

Adam looked up from where he stood discussing the crops with Ray Middleton, Belle Arbor's tall, rangy, dark-haired overseer, to see Fred, one of the men who worked in the stable, riding quickly toward him. Excusing himself from Ray, he went to meet him.

"What is it, Fred? Is something wrong?" Adam asked worriedly as Fred reined in beside him. The speed at which he had ridden in left Adam fearful that something might have happened. The horse was jitterish at having come to such an abrupt stop, so Adam grabbed his mount's bridle to calm him as he regarded Fred.

"This came for you," he said as he held out a sealed envelope. "Miss Becky said I should bring it to you right away."

"Thanks. You can tell Becky that I got the message."

"Yes, sir."

As Fred rode off, Adam glanced down at the missive and recognized Beau's handwriting immediately. A great feeling of relief swept through him. He had not known how long it would take his friend to get his message and arrange a rendezvous for them, but he was glad that it had happened this quickly. The long, sleepless nights he spent thinking of Lianne sleeping nearby were taking their toll. At least once he got away from Belle Arbor, he'd be able to get some rest. Adam opened the letter and read the message.

Adam—

As we'd discussed, Pointe Bayou at midnight. I'll arrange to have men there to meet you and bring you out to the ship.

Beau

He nodded to himself in approval of the plan as he pocketed the letter and moved off to rejoin Ray. There was work to finish before he could leave the plantation.

Lianne was furious as she paced the house. She had seen the messenger arrive with the letter and reluctantly hand it over to Becky. Although Lianne did not recognize the man as being one of Suzanne's servants, she felt sure that the message was from the other woman.

The thought that Adam would go running to Suzanne as soon as he read the message filled her with a tangled mixture of anger and despair. She only hoped that he returned to the house before he went, so she could corner him and face him down.

To Lianne's continued frustration, though, Adam did not return to the house until well after dark. She and Becky had already dined and were relaxing in the parlor when he rode up. Alex had been eagerly anticipating seeing him all day and was waiting at the door for him as he came inside.

"Adam! I'm so glad you're back," Alex greeted him excitedly.

"It's been a long day, Alex. Sorry I was away so long, but I think Ray and I have finally straightened out the problems in the south fields," Adam responded.

"Good. Does that mean you don't have to work so hard tomorrow, and we can go swimming again?" he asked hopefully, wanting to spend some time with him.

"I'm afraid not," Adam told him. He looked up just then and saw Lianne and Becky both watching them from the parlor. "As a matter of fact, I'm going to be gone for a few days."

Alex looked miserably disappointed, and Lianne stiffened. It was starting already. Alex's suspicion and the resulting heartbreak tore at her, and, coupled with her own humiliation, filled her with even greater determination.

"Do you have to go? Can't you stay home, Adam?" Alex pleaded pitifully.

"No, I'm afraid not. This is important." Adam read the emotion in his eyes, but could do nothing right then to dispel his upset. Once he caught Shark and the truth came out, he would clear the air with Alex.

Adam's words were like a knife in Lianne's heart. *This is important* . . . She almost scoffed out loud, but she held her tongue. When she confronted him about Suzanne, they would have to be alone.

"Becky . . . could I see you for a moment?" Adam requested, and then turned back to Alex. "Why don't you go on to bed, and I'll see you when I get back."

Lianne knew her brother well, and she could see that Alex was having a difficult time accepting what Adam had told him. Standing up, she followed Becky to the door.

"Why don't I see Alex on to bed, while you two have your talk?" Lianne offered. Her eyes met Adam's accusingly.

At her look of contempt, Adam cringed inwardly. He wanted to see love shining in her emerald gaze, not hatred. He wanted to see her lovely features

355

flushed with passion, not cold with resentment. He wanted desperately to tell her everything, but he held back. He looked away first, breaking that tenuous contact.

"Fine," Adam answered as he moved off. "Good night, Alex."

"G'night, Adam," Alex said solemnly as he let Lianne lead him upstairs.

Adam directed Becky to close the door behind her as she followed him into the study.

"Where are you going?" she demanded, not waiting for him to offer the information.

"I'm rejoining Beau on the *Sea Shadow*," he replied. "Shark is due back at any time now, so we'll be close-by, watching and waiting."

"And what about Lianne?" Becky demanded.

"What about her?" he returned, feigning innocence at her meaning. "She'll be fine here with you."

"Aren't you going to tell her the truth of where you're going to be? She is your wife, you know."

"I know. Believe me, little sister, I know she's my wife," he answered bitterly, "but I have no intention of telling her or anyone else my business. I expect the same from you."

Becky looked hurt. "Adam, you know you can trust me, and I think you could trust Lianne, too."

He shot her an outraged look. "She's to know nothing of this—not until it's over."

"All right," Becky agreed reluctantly. "I won't say a word. You're on business, if anyone asks. How soon do you have to leave?"

"The rendezvous is set for midnight." He glanced at the clock on the mantel. "I have to leave now."

"Aren't you even going to wait and tell Lianne good-bye?" Becky was incredulous. She could not understand his cold indifference to Lianne. Even if he still loved Elise, even if he had to continue his charade with Suzanne, the least he could do was to treat Lianne civilly.

"No," he said bluntly as he started from the room. "It's better this way."

Chapter Twenty-nine

"Adam's not going to Suzanne's, is he, Lianne?" Alex asked as he climbed into bed. He was trying his best to be brave, but his bottom lip was quivering with the effort.

"Of course not, sweetheart," Lianne soothed as she tucked him in. "He told you, this is important. I'm sure it's business and nothing else." Once he was snugly under the covers, she sat by his side, knowing that he needed to talk for a while.

Alex's eyes were huge in his face as he regarded his sister solemnly. "I'm glad you married Adam. I love him a lot."

Lianne felt a tightness in her chest at his words. "I know you do, Alex, and Adam loves you, too."

"Do you really think so?" He brightened at the thought.

"Of course. Do you think he'd go off and go swimming with just anyone?" she teased playfully.

"No, I guess not. We had fun, Lianne," Alex told her earnestly as he remembered the carefree afternoon they'd spent at the swimming hole.

"And I'm sure you're going to have fun again, Alex, just as soon as Adam takes care of all his business."

The little boy curled on his side as he sighed deeply. "I know. I just wish he'd hurry."

Lianne reached out to smooth back his hair from his forehead and press a kiss there. "He'll be home soon."

Filled with love and tenderness, Lianne stayed with him, holding his small hand in hers. While she sat there waiting for Alex to drift off to sleep, she tried to imagine her upcoming confrontation with Adam and anticipate what he was going to say in response to her demand that he choose between Suzanne and her. Lianne grimly told herself that she knew exactly what he was going to say, but still she knew she had to try.

When Alex finally fell sound asleep, Lianne got up from the bed and wandered about the room, gathering up her courage to face Adam. It was then as she paused by the window to look out that she heard Adam speaking below. Lianne couldn't make out what was being said, but as she watched he left the house alone and headed off across the grounds toward the boat dock.

Lianne's blood ran cold. Adam was going to Suzanne, and he was planning to spend the next several days with her! Propelled to action, she hurried from Alex's room. Lianne darted down the stairway taking care to be completely quiet, for she didn't want to run into Becky right now. All she wanted to do was to catch up with Adam and have it out with him. She was thankful as she made her escape from the house undetected. Racing full speed down the path to the dock, she was frustrated to find that Adam had already gone.

Lianne stood there staring off into the gloom of the bayou, uncertain for a moment, but she quickly put her indecision from her. She had to catch up with Adam! Having traveled the bayou all her life, she knew it like the back of her hand, while Adam had only minimal experience with the intricacies of the waterway. Lianne was certain that she'd have no trouble overtaking him before he reached Suzanne's.

Hurrying to free the rope of the other skiff tied up

359

there, Lianne climbed nimbly into the small craft. Grateful for the pale, guiding light of the moon, Lianne set out determinedly after her husband.

Brody and Michaels, two experienced crewmembers from the *Sea Shadow,* were waiting for Adam when he arrived at Pointe Bayou.

"Captain Trent!" they called out to him in slightly hushed tones as they saw him heading in their direction.

Adam spotted them on the bank and waved his return greeting. He jumped easily from the craft after coasting in near them.

"Good to see you again, men," he told them as they helped him pull the skiff out of the water and hide it behind some bushes.

"Captain Hamilton's waiting for you, sir. We'd better set out right away," the tall, thin Brody said.

"Have you seen anything of Shark?"

"Not yet, sir," Michaels offered.

The news did not surprise Adam, although he was disappointed by it. "We're going to catch him soon, men. It's only a matter of time now," Adam said with confidence as they made ready to head out of the bayou and back to sea in the *Sea Shadow*'s boat.

They were just about to push off when one of the men whispered urgently, "Captain Trent! Someone followed you!"

Adam looked up and suddenly cursed vividly under his breath as he immediately recognized Lianne.

"Damn!" he swore with a vengeance. What the hell was she doing here? But Adam knew he had no time to ponder her totally irrational actions.

"Who is it, sir?" one of the men asked.

"My wife," Adam replied tersely. He glanced

around, trying desperately to come up with a plan to avoid a confrontation. He spoke softly as an idea occurred to him, "She knows nothing of my identity as Spectre, and it's necessary to keep it that way. There's no way we can avoid her, so here's what I want you to do." He was already climbing out of the boat. "Take her captive."

The men looked at him with something akin to outrage. "Captive, sir?"

"Shut up and move before she finds out what's going on! Tie her up and blindfold her. I can't risk her seeing me. Don't use my real name. From this point on I'm Spectre, and don't call Mr. Hamilton by name, either. I'll wait here for you," he snapped, and they hurried to follow his orders.

Lianne had always felt comfortable in the bayou, even at night. She'd always thought it a tranquil, unthreatening place. For some reason, though, as she negotiated the tricky bayou passages this evening, she was filled with a sense of foreboding.

Lianne tried to put the worry from her mind. It was true that she'd heard that bad things did occasionally happen in the backwater areas. Yet, in all of her years, she'd never had any such encounter and had eventually come to dismiss those tales as ridiculous. Lianne told herself firmly that it was nonsense, that she was only nervous about confronting Adam, but still the icy tendrils of fear lingered in her soul as she rushed onward trying to catch up with him.

They were upon her suddenly, seemingly out of nowhere. One moment, she'd been alone in her search, and the next, a boat she'd never seen before was racing toward her. For a moment, Lianne could only stare at the threatening craft. As they drew closer, she could see their menacing expressions. Stark terror filled her. Who were they? What did they want?

Common sense told her to flee, so Lianne quickly tried to turn her skiff trying to escape, all the while cursing herself for not trusting her instincts before this. She knew she should have been more cautious in her reckless pursuit of Adam, but now, it was too late. Lianne had little hope of getting away from this unknown band of cutthroats, and she knew it.

Refusing to give up, she paddled viciously in a desperate effort to make for an area with heavy overgrowth. As a child, she had often played hide-and-seek here with Mark. Lianne hoped that she could lose herself in the concealing brush and elude her would-be captors that way.

However, it was not to be. The men of the *Sea Shadow* were excellent sailors who were more at home in a boat than on land. They anticipated her every evasive move and were upon her quickly.

As Lianne felt the heavy hand grip her boat, stopping her progress in spite of her best efforts, she turned and tried to hit him with her paddle. The big, fierce-looking man snatched it easily away from her, though, killing her last hope for salvation. As the other boat pulled up evenly with hers and the big man reached out to grab her, Lianne reacted on sheer nerve, diving from her skiff into the black, mysterious waters.

"Damn it, Michaels! Why didn't you get her while you had the chance!" Brody complained.

"Where the hell is she?" Michaels stared out across the water trying to see her so he could go after her again, but she hadn't surfaced yet.

"She was wearing a dress," Brody remarked. "You don't suppose . . ."

As the thought occurred to Brody, Michaels had

already realized that she was in trouble. Without further hesitation, he dove in after her.

Lianne had thought to make her escape by swimming away underwater, but in her desperation to get away, she'd forgotten what she was wearing. With the heavy material of her skirts weighing her down, twining about her legs and preventing her from kicking, she sank like a rock. Lianne tried to resurface, propelling herself with her arms, but the heavy, smothering anchor of her clothing held her down.

As water began to fill her lungs, she suddenly realized that she might die. The panic that came with that thought gave her one, final burst of energy. Fighting for her life, she managed to reach the surface. Lianne knew that Adam was the only person within earshot who might be able to save her. With the last of her strength, she called out his name in terrified, choking cry for help.

"Adam! Help!" Almost as soon as she yelled, the weight of her clothing pulled her back under.

Lianne thought it was the end as the dark waters closed over her head. She was about to lose consciousness when strong arms grasped her and hauled her back to the surface.

"Brody! Help me!" Michaels called out as he swam back toward the boat, drawing a limp, unresisting Lianne behind him.

"Is she dead?" Brody asked worriedly as he helped Michaels lift Lianne into their boat.

As if in answer to his question, Lianne began to cough and choke, and Brody and Michaels exchanged relieved glances.

"Get the ropes," Michael told him.

Brody took up the rope and knelt beside her, preparing to bind her as the captain had ordered.

Lianne's chest ached and her throat was raw. She

was exhausted as she lay in the bottom of the boat, waiting in rigid silence for whatever her two captors meant to do with her next.

"What do you want? What are you going to do with me?"

Silence was her only answer.

"Please . . ." she gasped, her voice a mere croak of fear, "can't you just let me go?"

When one man came toward her with a rope in hand, horror seized her. Brody's expression didn't change as he took her by her wrists and started to bind her hands behind her back.

"You don't have to tie me up! I promise I won't fight you anymore." Lianne begged.

"Shut up," he answered brusquely, moved by her pleas, but trying not to look at her. He knew there'd be hell to pay if he didn't follow the captain's instructions. When he moved to tie her ankles, she tried to kick him, but she was so weak, he easily subdued her.

Lianne was completely terrified as she stared at the big, mean-looking man who was hovering over her. She honestly believed that her life was about to end. Her heart ached at the thought of Alex being left all alone in the world, and it hurt her to think that she would never know the joy of holding her child in her arms. Tears burned her eyes, and she wished that Adam would come and save her from whatever awful fate these men had in store for her.

"No! Don't!" she shrieked as the man used a neckerchief to blindfold her. She was sure that at any minute she was going to die, and she didn't want to die in the darkness.

Brody looked at Michaels questioningly and then, reluctantly, gagged her too. It wouldn't do if her shouting gave away their presence in the bayou.

Bound, gagged, blindfolded, and miserable, Lianne

lay motionlessly in the bottom of the boat. As her captors began to paddle again, she wondered where they were taking her and why. Resigned to the fact that she was helpless for the moment, she remained quiet, hoping to listen to whatever was said and figure out a way to escape later . . . if there was a later.

Brody and Michaels headed back to where they'd left Adam, and they could see him standing at the water's edge. Though it was too dark to read his expression, they could tell just from his rigid stance that he'd heard Lianne's call and knew that something had gone wrong.

Adam saw them returning, but did not see Lianne in the boat with them. Horror suddenly struck his heart as he considered for the first time that she might have tried to fight them off and gotten hurt in the process. He had heard her cry out to him for help. At the time, he'd thought that she'd called for him only because he was nearby and might hear her. What if she'd really been in trouble? He went pale at the prospect.

His blood was pounding in his veins as he watched Brody and Michaels draw nearer. *Where was Lianne! Why couldn't he see her in the boat!* Adam wanted to call out to them, to ask where she was and how she was, but he knew he had to remain silent. If Lianne was in the boat, she might recognize his voice, and he couldn't risk being discovered—not yet.

"We got her, just like you ordered," Brody announced as the boat coasted into the bank next to him.

"Good," Adam answered, taking care to disguise his voice.

Lianne heard the hoarse, rasping voice and a chill of fear ran through her. Who was this man that her two captors answered to, and why did he want her?

Suddenly wild with fright, she began to shiver uncontrollably. She felt the boat dip and sway as the other man joined them in the craft. When he was aboard, she felt them push off again. As they sailed away into the darkness of the night, Lianne's thoughts were filled with terrified visions of death at the hands of the mysterious man who'd ordered her taken captive.

Beau had been watching for his men to return with Adam, and when he spotted the small boat heading their way, he went to meet them. Brody came aboard first and immediately sought him out.

"Mr. Hamilton, sir, the captain says to be sure not to say anything to him when he comes aboard."

Beau gave him a curious look. "May I ask why not?"

"The captain's brought his wife with him, sir, but—"

"Lianne? Here?" Beau could not imagine what had possessed Adam to do such a thing. There'd been no mention in his note that he was bringing Lianne along. Puzzled, he awaited Adam's coming, yet still he was not prepared for the sight of Adam climbing aboard with Lianne, bound as she was, thrown over his shoulder. "What the hell?" he muttered under his breath as he stalked toward them.

Adam held up one hand to silence him as he strode on past him and went directly below to his cabin. Beau dogged his footsteps the entire way, wondering why Lianne was tied up this way and why her clothes were all wet. He watched as Adam laid her upon his bunk and then turned to him and gestured for him to go back outside.

"What are you doing?" Beau demanded when Adam had closed the cabin door, insuring that Lianne wouldn't be able to hear them and distinguish their voices.

"She followed me, Beau. What else was I supposed to do? Let her find out about Spectre?"

"She followed you, so you tied her up, blindfolded her and brought her aboard . . ." Beau repeated, stunned. "Why didn't you just hide until she was gone?"

Adam cast him a pained look. "You obviously don't know Lianne very well. She wouldn't have stopped looking until she'd found me."

"So what are you going to do with her now? You know we can't take her on the entire voyage."

"Of course I know that!" Adam snarled, angry at the situation in which he found himself. "If she's missing from Belle Arbor for any length of time, there'll be questions asked."

"So?"

"How soon do we sail?"

"We have to wait for the tide . . . two hours, maybe three," Beau replied.

Adam nodded. "Before we sail, I'll have the men take her back where we found her and release her. Until then, I'll be in my cabin, and I don't want to be disturbed."

"All right. I'll let you know when it's almost time to sail."

When Beau had gone, Adam went back inside. He was annoyed over everything that had happened. He had come to the *Sea Shadow* to get away from Lianne, not to be cooped up in his cramped ship's quarters with her.

He stood near the door, staring across the room to where she lay on his bunk. Even from this distance, he could see that she was shivering, and it occurred to him then that she was probably chilled from the wet clothing. Knowing that it would be hours before he could see her safely back to Belle Arbor, Adam realized he had to do something to help warm her.

Adam moved across the room slowly, soundlessly, coming to stand beside the bed. Lianne's clothing was still wet, clinging damply to her body, and his gaze grew heated as he visually traced her luscious curves. With her arms drawn back behind her, her breasts were thrust forward and he could see the outline of the peaks pressing tautly against the sodden fabric. Desire, thick and heavy, filled him, and he reached out with a gentle hand to begin unbuttoning the buttons at the bodice of her dress.

Lianne had been lying quietly, trying to understand what was happening to her. She had heard the two men leave and then had heard the door open and close once again. She sensed that someone was in the room with her, but she didn't know where he was or what he intended. The feel of his hand at her bodice terrified her, and she gasped as she tried to scoot away from the anonymous touch.

"Easy, my lovely," Adam spoken in the hoarse disguising tone he'd adopted as he stilled her frantic movements with his hands.

Behind her gag, Lianne cried out for salvation from the unknown man who was pinning her to the bed.

"I mean you no harm," he rasped, reaching behind her to untie her hands for a moment.

Lianne could not believe that he was releasing the bonds. She almost had hope until he refused to let go of her wrists once he'd untied the rope.

"But I'll be forced to deal with you severely if you ever attempt to take off the blindfold," he told her menacingly.

His threat sent a shudder of fear through her, and when he stripped her gown and chemise from her shoulders and her arms, effectively baring her to the waist, she began to tremble violently. She tried to struggle free from his grip, but he held her easily. Adam dragged her arms back above her head and tied them to the bunk's frame. Pinioned so, Lianne lay tense and unwilling before him as he stripped away the last of her clothing. She held herself rigidly, preparing for the worst. She longed for Adam to come and rescue her, yet she knew that by now he was with Suzanne, probably making love to her, completely unaware of her own fate.

Adam took great pains not to look at her as he gathered up her sodden clothing and went outside to call for a cabin boy. Adam gave the boy the clothes and instructed him that they were to be taken to the kitchen and dried before the stove, then returned as quickly as possible. He wanted to get Lianne dressed and off the *Sea Shadow* as soon as he could, for the temptation of having her there was nearly overpowering.

Lianne was terror-stricken as she lay on the bed. She had never felt so completely vulnerable before, and she wondered what her captor was going to do to her. When she heard the door open and close again, she knew her kidnapper had returned. She wished the gag was off so she could talk, but she knew it would be useless to try to persuade her abductor to let her go. She'd already tried that once and failed. Lianne waited nervously for his next move.

Adam stood in the middle of the cabin, a man in conflict. The desire that had flamed to life within him moments before had not abated. If anything, the need to possess Lianne had grown even stronger when he'd come back into the room and seen her there in his bed.

Logically, he told himself that he wanted to dress Lianne in whatever clothes he could find and get her off the ship and away from him. He knew he would stand no chance of winning her love later if he took her against her will this way now. But the passion he felt her was so obsessive, he could only think of the joy of having her once more.

Where's the harm? The taunting thought echoed through his mind as his body throbbed with hot awareness. Lianne would never know he was Spectre, he reasoned. Like a man driven, he approached the bunk. His dark gaze was burning with an inner, unquenchable fire as he stared down at his wife. She was lovely, so lovely, and Adam knew in that moment that he was a fool if he didn't take her while he had the chance.

Chapter Thirty

Lianne felt the mattress sink as her unseen captor sat down beside her, and she knew true panic as his hand touched her cheek. She jerked away from his caress, but he only gave a soft, chiding laugh.

"There's no point in fighting me," he told her gruffly. "You're mine, all mine." Adam emphasized the point by making a sweeping caress of her body from breast to thigh.

Lianne clamped her legs firmly together and tried to twist away from him, Adam, however, was not about to be denied. He had waited far too long for this opportunity, and he meant to take advantage of it. His touch was gentle as he stroked the side of her neck and then trailed his hand lower to outline the rounded swell of her breast, teasing but never touching the sensitive peak. He heard her gasp at the sensation his caress created within her, so he repeated it again, this time watching her reaction more carefully.

"So you like that, do you?" Adam murmured.

Lianne shook her head in mute denial, but again her captor only gave a low, throaty chuckle.

"Don't be afraid. I have no intention of hurting you," he promised as he continued to caress her.

Lianne didn't believe him. How could he tell her not to be afraid when he was keeping her bound and helpless? If there was nothing to fear and he wasn't going to hurt her, why didn't he let her go? Why was he holding her captive?

371

When Adam moved to trace the same pattern of fire upon her flesh with his lips, Lianne gave a low moan of terror deep in her throat. She held herself stiffly, trying to concentrate on anything but the feel of his hands and lips upon her. Adam was insistent, though, remembering exactly what had excited her during their pervious times together, and he used that knowledge to his advantage.

Lianne tried to remain rigid in his arms as he continued to press heated kisses to her breasts. Lianne had expected to feel revulsion when he laid his hands upon her, but instead, to her shock and horror, her body was responding to his touch. Forbidded excitement blossomed within her. She was mortified, yet could not deny the need that pulsed through her. How could this be? How could this mysterious stranger's touch wreak such havoc on her senses? Adam was the man she loved! He was the only one who could rouse such feelings in her, yet . . .

Lianne's desperation became a very real thing as she felt her body beginning to betray her. She squirmed away, trying to elude him, but her captor would not to be denied. He clamped a hand firmly at her waist, holding her immobile while he continued his play.

"You can't escape me," he declared in a seductively velvet tone just as his mouth closed hotly over the taut crest of one breast.

The contact was electric, and Lianne arched upward, straining at her bonds as he suckled there. His hands were everywhere upon her then, cupping and molding, caressing and fondling. Lianne felt hot with desire, yet cold with fear at the same time. She didn't understand how she could be responding to him this way, but she was. As his mouth plundered her breasts, he slipped a hand between her thighs with an intimacy

372

that sent shock waves pulsing through her. Lianne was appalled as she found herself being swept away by a stormtide of rapture.

Adam felt her response and suddenly wished he could release her from her bonds. He wanted to feel her arms around him, holding him and touching him, but he knew it was impossible. He didn't like the deception he was carrying out, but the situation made it necessary. Adam realized that the only restraint he could safely remove was the gag, so without further thought, he paused in his lovemaking, untied the offensive cloth, and tossed it aside.

Lianne had a moment of hope as he removed the gag, but before she could speak, his mouth claimed hers in a devouring exchange. She knew she should keep fighting him, but her body was responding to him as wantonly as it had responded to Adam. Lianne didn't understand it, and it frightened her. She didn't want to feel these things. She didn't want to desire this unseen man. She wanted Adam.

Lianne knew she should keep resisting him and the feverish delight that was threatening to overwhelm her. As his lips moved persuasively over hers, not demanding, but gently coercing, her resistance weakened dangerously.

When her unseen captor abruptly broke off the kiss and moved away from her, Lianne lay on the bunk, tormented by what she was feeling. She didn't know what to expect next. Everything was happening too quickly. One moment her captor was beside her torturing her with arousing kisses and caresses, and the next he was gone, leaving her feeling feverish and unsure. A part of her was screaming for release from the sensual bondage he'd created within her with his masterful seduction, and yet, the more sane, more logical side of her was commanding her to fight him to

373

the end, to never surrender to his mastery. All Lianne knew was that she wanted to be free of this nightmare in which she was trapped.

Panting hard, from combined fear and excitement, she whispered, "Who are you? What do you want from me?"

"My name is Spectre," he growled in his hoarse voice, "and you know what I want."

"Please, please, don't do this to me! My name's Lianne Trent. My husband will give you money . . . anything . . . if you'll just let me go!"

Adam had moved away from her to shed his own clothing. At the sound of her plea, he turned back to gaze down at her and felt a renewed rush of desire surge through him. *God, she was beautiful,* he thought as he let his eyes caress her. From the thickness of her lustrous fiery gold hair to her long, shapely legs, she was every inch woman, and he wanted her as he'd never wanted another.

"The only thing I want is you, Lianne," Adam declared, and as he said it, he suddenly realized it was true. Heady with the realization, he walked back to stand beside the bed. "And I'm going to make you mine."

"No! Please no!" Lianne protested, frightened of him and of herself.

He bent down to untie her ankles, running a hand boldly up the slender length of her leg as he did so. Lianne quickly tried to evade him, twisting to her side and drawing her knees up protectively to her chest in an effort to hide herself. Her efforts were useless, though, for he easily released the rope and then joined her on the bed, pulling her into his arms and bringing her full against him. Lianne felt the shock of the contact with his hard male frame all the way to the heart of her, and she trembled. Whether in fear or desire,

374

she wasn't sure, and that made it even worse.

"You want me, too," Adam declared, holding her close.

"No! Never!" she cried fiercely.

"Shall I convince you?" he taunted, beginning to fondle her again.

Lianne tried to keep her legs together, tried to refuse him access to her body, but there was no denying him. With a grip that was painless, yet unyielding, he rolled her to her back and then moved over her. Positioning himself between her thighs, he settled himself deep within her.

"No . . . no . . ." Lianne groaned, turning and bucking beneath him in an effort to dislodge him from her body.

"Oh, yes," Adam murmured, savoring the hot grasp of her tight body around him. He kissed her again and began to caress her breasts.

Lianne didn't want to kiss him back, but when his mouth claimed hers in a demanding, passionate exchange at the same time he cupped her breasts and teased the sensitive peaks, all rationality fled. She was lost in a sea of mindless pleasure. Her legs instinctively entwined with his, and her erratic movements of a moment earlier became seductive and enticing. The strength of his hardness buried in the womanly core of her sent her desires soaring. Lianne began to move beneath him in rhythmic invitation, desperately needing that intimate ecstasy that she knew was only a heartbeat away.

Adam felt her responding and started his rhythm, thrusting deeply within her molten, silken depths. Lianne didn't try to analyze the excitement she was experiencing, she only went along with it — feeling, not thinking. They moved in unison, their bodies perfectly mated, spiraling ever upward in their search for the explosion of joy. When it came, they ignited together, their passions cresting in ecstasy's rapture.

His breathing ragged, Adam lay heavily upon her, savoring the feeling of her naked in his arms. Having her had been heaven, but knowing that he had to let her go soon was hell. He raised up on his elbows to gaze down at her, and when he moved, she quickly averted her face.

Lianne had been lost in a glorious haze of sensual satisfaction until Adam shifted away from her. When he did, she suddenly remembered where she was. A cry of despair escaped her, and she turned her face away from him, tormented by the shocking discovery of her passionate nature.

Her cry pierced him like a saber thrust to his heart, and he lifted one hand to gently smooth back her hair from her face.

"There's no need for tears," Adam told her huskily.

"There's every need," Lianne responded brittlely.

"But why? Didn't you enjoy our lovemaking?"

"That wasn't lovemaking!"

"Oh? What would you call it, then?" he taunted, refusing to feel guilty for having made love to her.

"Torture!"

"Shall I torture you some more?" Adam asked, a bit angered by her denial of her enjoyment.

Lianne started to answer that she never wanted him to touch her again, but his mouth swooped down to capture hers before she could speak. He kissed her with such savage intensity that she whimpered softly at first, but the fever of his kiss slowly melted away her opposition. She realized dazedly, as she began to kiss him back, that if her arms had been freed, she would have looped them willingly around his neck. When he broke off the kiss, it took her a moment to recover.

"Why are you keeping me this way? Why don't you

let me go?" she questioned.

"All in good time," was all Adam could answer as he stared down at her moist, parted lips, mesmerized. His body swelled with desire and it jolted him to realize that he wanted her again so soon.

"If it's money you're after . . ." Lianne began, thinking that he might be after a ransom of some kind.

"I have no need for money. You're all I want," Adam said thickly as he moved suggestively against her to let her know of his renewed passion.

Lianne could not stop the thrill of excitement that coursed through her as he thrust his hips teasingly against hers. When he moved lower to kiss her breasts, she sighed in ecstasy. She knew she was his captive and that he could do with her as he pleased, but at that moment it didn't matter. All that mattered was the raging fire of desire he stoked to life in the heart of her with his kisses and caresses.

"No . . . please . . ."

"Please what?" Adam asked, shifting back up over her to kiss her again.

When the kiss ended, she offered no more opposition, but gave herself over to the breathtaking excitement of his possession.

It was a long time later when Adam left her and tenderly covered her with a blanket. He was pensive as he dressed, and he had just finished buttoning his shirt when the knock came at his door.

"Captain, sir, I have the clothing . . ." the cabin boy called out.

"Leave it," Adam ordered.

"Also, sir, the first officer said I should tell you that it's almost time to sail."

"All right," he answered regretfully. He didn't open the door to retrieve Lianne's things until he heard him walk away.

"You're sailing?" Lianne asked cautiously.

"With the tide," Adam replied.

"You aren't going to take me with you, are you?" Lianne's question voiced all her fears.

"There would be nothing I'd enjoy more," he rasped, "but no, I'm not taking you along this voyage."

A shiver of apprehension shook her. *Dear God*, she agonized, *this is it . . . this is the end of my life . . .* She heard him approach the bed and knew stark, raving terror. When he reached down and drew off the cover, she gave a soft cry of fear.

Adam was puzzled by her reaction. A short time before, she'd craved his touch, and yet now she was acting as if he were going to hurt her in some way. He released her hands from where they were tied above her head and helped her to sit up.

Lianne was certain that he was going to drag her from the bed and kill her now that he'd had his pleasure of her. She visibly shrank away from his touch.

"What are you going to do with me?" she asked, her fear evident in her voice.

"Right now—dress you," Adam answered as he untied the final rope on her hands long enough to help her slip on her chemise and dress. He quickly bound them behind her, knowing he couldn't risk the possibility of her getting her hands free and taking off her blindfold right now.

Lianne had thought to try to escape one last time, but there was no time as he hurried to refasten her bonds. Remaining nervously passive, she sat on the edge of the bed as he helped her finish dressing and then lay back on the bed at his command. She was disheartened when he once again tied her ankles.

"I'll be back," Adam said as he left the cabin. He went straight up on deck and sought out Beau. "I need both Brody and Michaels again."

"All right."

"I want them to take Lianne back to where they captured her, find the skiff they left adrift there, and take them both back to Belle Arbor. Tell them to leave her in her own boat, but to loosen her ropes just enough so that she can work her way free."

"I'll tell them."

"Good. I'll bring her up now."

Lianne lay submissively upon the bunk until she was certain that Adam had gone from the room, and then she forced herself to act. As frightened as she was, believing that her life was about to end, she knew she had to try to flee while there was still time.

It was awkward, but Lianne managed to right herself upon the bunk and then scoot to the edge and get to her feet. Freeing her hands was her first priority, but blind to her surroundings as she was, she knew it wouldn't be easy. Hobbled, Lianne hopped awkwardly away from the bed in hopes of running into a table or desk that might have some kind a sharp object on it. She had not expected to encounter a chair in the middle of the room, and she fell heavily over it, tumbling to the floor.

Adam hurried back to the cabin expecting to find her exactly where he'd left her. When he opened the door, he came to a dead stop as his gaze fell upon the empty bunk. He stood frozen in the doorway, fearful of the possibility that she might have freed herself, removed her blindfold, and could now discover his true identity.

Adam caught sight of her on the floor then, but it took him a moment to recover from the shock of thinking she'd escaped. Finally, when he was in complete control once more, he strode across the room and scooped her up in his arms.

"That was foolish," he scolded as he laid her back on the bunk. "You might have hurt yourself."

Lianne was nearly hysterical by this point, and she wondered wildly why it would matter.

"I hate to have to do this to you," Adam began as he reached for the cloth that had been her gag and prepared to put it on her again, "but . . ."

"Then don't," Lianne whispered. She was petrified, for she didn't know he was talking about the gag. She thought he was going to kill her right then.

"I have to," Adam said, gagging her once again.

Lianne's heart was pounding in a ragged rhythm as she wondered what was going to happen to her next. She was totally shocked when he picked her up in his arms and carried her from the room in an almost gentle, cradling hold. Still, she refused to go peacefully to what she thought was her death, and she began to struggle against him.

"Stop it!" he commanded harshly, tightening his hold on her, and Lianne was forced to remain still or feel the painful bite of his punishing grip.

Adam strode up on deck with his wife in his arms, ignoring the curious looks of his crew. He personally carried her down to the smaller craft where Brody and Michaels waited for him. As he laid her down in the bottom of the boat, he glanced at his two trustworthy men.

"You've been given your orders?"

"Yes, sir, Captain Spectre. We know."

Lianne was paralyzed with fear as she listened to what they were saying.

"Hurry. There's no time to waste. We've got to make sail. Just make sure no one sees you."

Adam returned to the deck of the *Sea Shadow* and watched in solemn silence as they rowed back through the bayou toward Belle Arbor.

"Do you think she recognized you?" Beau asked as he came to join him.

"No. Our secret's safe," Adam told him. Later he wondered why it didn't seem to matter that much to him anymore and why he felt guilty over what he'd done. He wondered, too, what Lianne had been doing following him through the bayou.

Brody and Michaels did not speak as they concentrated on the task given to them. Anxious to return to their ship, they moved swiftly through the bayou back to the rendezvous point. They located Lianne's deserted skiff with little trouble and then drew it along with them as they traveled the waterway back to the Belle Arbor dock. Brody was as gentle as he could be when he lifted Lianne and transferred her to the other boat, but she was holding herself in such rigid protest that it made it difficult for him. When he'd finally manuevered her into the bottom of the skiff, he made short order of loosening the bonds at her feet and hands, leaving her hands just tight enough that she wouldn't be able to free herself before they could get away. They left her then, disappearing silently into the bayou night.

Lianne lay still in complete confusion, not understanding why they had loosened the ropes that bound her. She remained unmoving for some time, waiting for them to return, waiting for the end to come. It only after long minutes that she realized that the men had gone and they were not coming back. *They hadn't meant to kill her! Spectre hadn't been ordering her death!*

Relief, powerful in its intensity, swept through her, and she began to cry as she worked feverishly to free her hands. It took a while, but she finally worked them loose. Stripping away the blindfold, she stared about herself in total bewilderment. *She was at Belle Arbor! She was home!* Lianne took off the gag and quickly untied her ankles.

Snatching up the paddle, Lianne made for the dock. She managed to tie up all right, but she was shaking uncontrollably by the time she climbed from the craft. Stunned by all that had happened to her, she stood on the dock in the darkness, her arms wrapped tightly about her waist.

A violent torrent of emotions flooded through her as she tried to understand what had happened to her. *Spectre, Captain Spectre* . . . Lianne knew with certainty that she would never forget his name. How could it have happened? How could she have fallen prey to him and how could she have actually surrendered to him?

Worse yet, Lianne realized, was how she could have desired Spectre so desperately. She knew there could be no denying that she'd wanted him. The remembrance of her wild response to his passion troubled Lianne for she felt that she'd betrayed Adam. It had been shocking to discover that her body could respond to Spectre that way, even while she'd been consciously trying to resist him, and she wondered how it was that she could feel such sensual joy with two such different men.

Confused, not knowing where to turn, Lianne started back up the path toward the main house, hoping to sneak back into her room unnoticed. When she managed to reach the privacy of her bedroom she breathed a deep sigh of relief. She undressed quickly and climbed in bed, drawing the covers up protectively over her.

Lianne's thoughts were turbulent as the events of the night continued to play themselves out before her in her mind's eye. From the heartbreaking discovery that Adam was going to spend several days with Suzanne to her own shameful betrayal with her mysterious, sensual captor, the night had been a horror. Lianne wished it had never happened, but to her dismay, she knew it had.

Tossing restlessly on the bed, she finally decided that it would be best if she told no one about her encounter with Spectre. She told herself that it was Adam she loved. Yet as the remaining hours of darkness passed and the eastern sky lightened with the promise of a new day, she wondered if she would ever be able to forget the time she spent in the arms of her unseen captor.

Chapter Thirty-one

David Williams kept a supporting arm around Elise's waist as he led her to the wrought iron bench near the center of the garden. The flowers were all in bloom in a riot of beautiful colors, and the fragrance of their perfume delicately scented the air.

"I thought you might like to sit outside again this morning," he was saying as they sat down next to each other on the small bench.

"Yes, David, it's lovely today," Elise answered. "I'm glad we came outside."

David was enormously pleased with the progress she was making. Since the night she'd first spoken, she'd made steady, measurable improvement every day. Though she was still not a fluent conversationalist, she did answer his questions. She'd become much more aware of and familiar with her surroundings, and she was beginning to move about the house freely with some confidence.

Still, David was concerned about her reaction to the pain of her past. He had not yet broached the subject of her trauma, but he knew he would have to do it soon. Elise would not be able to make a healthy recovery unless she faced all her fears and dealt with them.

"How are you feeling today?"

"I'm not sure," she replied, and her response surprised him.

"Oh? Why not?" David probed. During all their previous conversations, she'd always told that she was doing fine. This was definitely a good sign.

"Last night . . ." She hesitated, not quite sure how to tell him what was troubling her.

"Yes? Did something happen to disturb you?"

"I've been having these dreams . . ." Elise told him slowly, "nightmares, I guess. They're so terrible that they wake me up."

"Do you remember what they were about?" David questioned.

"I don't remember much." She shrugged, obviously puzzled by what was happening to her. "Just little things . . ."

"Why don't you tell me whatever you can recall, and we'll see if we can't piece it all together and make some sense out of it for you."

"I'd like that." Elise knew she always felt better after she confided in David. He had a way of explaining things that made everything seem all right.

"What is it that frightens you about these dreams? Is there any one thing in particular?"

Elise frowned, trying to remember details that had faded when she'd come awake. "I'm in some kind of strange room. It's small. There are no windows and very little light. At first, it seems safe enough . . ."

"Does anything in that room seem familiar to you?" David asked, carefully studying her expression as she pondered his question.

"No."

Her answer was firm, so he nodded for her to go on.

"There are loud noises going on. It sounds like thunder, only it makes me afraid." She looked up at him, her face pale, her hands shaking, and David reached out to take her hands in his reassuringly.

"Don't worry, it's only a dream. Nothing can hurt you. I'm here."

"I know." Elise managed a faint smile as she looked deeply into his eyes and saw the unwavering strength and inner peace reflected there.

"Are there any people in the room with you or are you alone?"

"I don't know . . ." Her hold on his hands suddenly tightened as if she'd caught a glimpse of something in her nightmare that she just wasn't ready to face yet. "I don't know, David! I don't know!"

"Easy, love," David murmured as he put an arm about her and drew her head down on his shoulder.

"I want to remember, David!"

"I know. It'll all come to you one day soon, and when it does, I'll be right here with you to help you."

"Thank you," she whispered as she gave a soft sigh.

It was all David could do to keep from taking her in his arms and kissing her at that moment. He wanted to, but she was so sweetly vulnerable that he didn't dare take advantage of the innocent trust she'd put in him. He loved her too much to take a chance on ruining things between them before they even got started.

"Do you want to go back inside now?"

"No, I don't think so. I want to stay here, where it's open and free."

"Then, we'll stay right here until you say it's time to go," he told her with a smile.

"I'd like that," she returned his smile.

The following three days passed in a blur of emotional turmoil for Lianne. She thought of Adam constantly, wishing he would return, yet at the same time dreading having to face him again. The guilt she felt over her response to Spectre's touch haunted her every waking moment, and she grew frightened and insecure.

Lianne feared that Adam would discover her betrayal, and, when he did, he would throw her out. She was even afraid that he might be so vengeful as to take her baby from her. She touched the slight swell of her stomach almost reverently and vowed to herself that she could never let Adam find out about Spectre.

Lianne felt tired as she wandered back to her bed to lie down. Though she'd spent the past few nights restlessly courting sleep, she had managed to get precious little. Now, however, it suddenly seemed that she couldn't keep her eyes open a minute longer. Lianne was glad, for she hoped that at least in slumber, she would be able to escape her fears. Stretching out upon the wide softness of the bed, exhaustion claimed her, and she was soon fast asleep.

Even in repose, Lianne's troubled thoughts would not give her peace. Her subconscious served up dreams of Spectre, faceless yet compelling, to fire the havoc in her soul.

She tossed and turned, trying to escape her mysterious captor in the dream, but there was no escape. As his arms came around her in the vision, though, he suddenly changed. No longer was he faceless and frightening, instead, he became Adam, holding her and loving her. The dream faded then and was gone. Lianne, finally finding a moment's peace, drifted into a deeper, restful slumber.

Adam had thought he would feel better about returning to Belle Arbor after three days at sea. He'd thought that he would have had time to bring his emotions under control and be able to live in the same house with Lianne without desiring her so much, but it hadn't worked out that way.

Having made love to Lianne as Spectre in his cabin aboard the *Sea Shadow*, Adam had found himself reminded of her every time he'd gone into the room. Sleep had been an impossibility for him in the bunk they'd shared. Every time he'd tried to get some rest there, the memory of her sensual surrender to him torched his passions, and he had had to leave the cabin to get himself under control.

Now, as Adam made his way back through the bayou toward the plantation, he was dreading seeing Lianne again. It had been difficult enough before, living in such close quarters with Lianne and never having her, but now that he'd tasted of her love again, he didn't know if he'd be able to keep himself from her.

Guilt stabbed at him over his deception, but Adam tried to dismiss it. She was his wife, and he'd wanted her. No harm had been done . . . he thought.

Becky had been worried the entire time Adam had been gone. She alternately feared that Adam and Beau would find Shark and be hurt trying to capture him or that they wouldn't find him and the limbo they were living in would continue on indefinitely. She was weary of all the secretiveness and was afraid that Adam's plotting ultimately might ruin any chance he and Lianne had for happiness before they could even begin a life together.

It was easy for Becky to see how Adam's behavior was affecting Lianne. Though her friend had said nothing about his lengthy absence, keeping to herself mostly since he'd left, Becky could tell that it was troubling her deeply. Lianne always seemed tired now, and her appetite had lessened. She looked exhausted, and Becky was starting to worry about the baby.

A sound in the hall drew Becky's attention, and because she knew that Alex and Lianne had already retired for the night, she got up to see who was there.

"Adam!" She was delighted to see him, and she went to him quickly and hugged him.

He returned her embrace as he glanced around for some sign of Lianne. When she didn't appear to greet him, he felt greatly disappointed.

"I'm so glad you're back," Becky was saying, "How did it go? Did you have any luck?"

"No," he answered curtly. "Nothing."

"I'm sorry," she sympathized.

"Where is everyone?" Adam finally asked, not wanting to get into a discussion of the fruitless hours he'd just spent with Beau.

"Lianne and Alex both went to bed. I'm sure they would have waited up for you, if we'd known you were coming home tonight."

"That's all right." Adam knew Alex would have waited up, but he doubted cynically that Lianne would have bothered. He led the way into the study and poured himself a bourbon.

"How was Beau?" Becky tried to sound casual as she inquired, but her heart was pounding at the thought that he might have sent a message with Adam.

"Fine," he answered without elaborating. He took a deep drink of his liquor.

Becky frowned, irritated by Beau's neglect. She missed him dreadfully and had been hoping to hear something from him.

Caught up in his own disappointment, Adam was oblivious to his sister's mood as he finished off his drink. He'd been mentally ready to face Lianne again when he'd entered the house, and her absence left him feeling decidedly let down. Suddenly Adam knew a driving need to see her, asleep or not.

"I think I'll go up and look in on Lianne."

His statement pleased Becky. She hoped he was coming to realize how special Lianne really was and that he'd missed her while he was away.

"I'll see you in the morning, then."

"Good night, Becky."

As he went upstairs, Adam was surprised to find that he was nervous. He paused before the closed bedroom door for a moment, then finally opened it and went in. The room was dark except for the faint, pale streams of moonlight that shone through the windows.

Adam approached the bed, his gaze never leaving Lianne's sleeping form. He stared at her hungrily, wanting her, but keeping a tight rein on that raging need. He remained standing in the shadows near the bed, worshipping her beauty from afar and wishing things were different between them.

Lianne didn't know what it was that woke her. She only knew that one second she'd been sound asleep, and the next, she'd been awake. She lay still, wondering what it was that had disturbed her. As she realized someone else was in the room with her, she became terrified. Lianne sat bolt upright in the bed, clutching the covers over her breasts as she stared at the man who stood silently in the shadows. In her sleepy state, she automatically thought the intruder was Spectre.

"You!" Her cry was a strangled whisper, and she was suddenly trembling at the thought that he'd come back for her.

Adam didn't respond immediately, for he was too busy taking in the glorious sight of her, sitting in the middle of their bed with her hair tumbling about her shoulders in sensual disarray.

"What are you doing here? Why did you come back?" she challenged breathlessly, still believing him to be Spectre.

Adam was jarred by her words, for they reaffirmed to him that she still hated him. Despairingly, Adam wondered if he would ever be able to win her love. He took a step forward into the pale light as he spoke, "I came back because this is my home, wife."

Lianne stared at Adam in bewilderment. She had truly believed it was Spectre, and it startled her to discover that it was Adam. She said a silent prayer of thanks that she hadn't called out the other man's name in her fear. But just because she now knew it was Adam didn't lessen her upset.

"What do you want?" Lianne watched him, her eyes wide and wary. She tightened her grip on the blanket she held protectively to her breasts.

Adam knew what he wanted. He wanted her love. He wanted her in his arms, in his bed, in his life, forever. Suddenly nothing else mattered but his love for her. Without speaking, he moved to sit down on the edge of the bed beside her, and he flinched inwardly when Lianne sidled away from him.

"Lianne . . ." He lifted one hand to touch her cheek in a gentle caress. Her skin felt like satin to him, and he found himself longing to caress every inch of her silken flesh.

Lianne didn't trust him one bit. She admitted to herself that his being here like this was a dream come true, that she wanted Adam to love her and share her life with her, but she knew he didn't mean it. Hadn't he just spent three days *and nights* with Suzanne?

Adam's eyes held hers, watching, waiting, as his hand slipped lower. He brushed the obstacle of the blanket away from her nerveless fingers and boldly cupped the curve of her breast.

391

Still, Lianne didn't move away. Her breath caught in her throat as his thumb moved provocatively across the nipple. Excitement radiated throughout her body at that single touch. Lianne was torn. She wanted to give herself over to the wonder of his caress, but the memory of his time with Suzanne loomed before her.

Adam was looking deep into her eyes, trying to gauge her thoughts. He knew a real need tonight to tell her everything and have it all out in the open. He didn't know if it would improve things between them or not, but he was willing to take the chance. He was about to speak, when she erupted in anger and slapped his hand away.

"Get your hands off of me, Adam Trent!" She was shaking in a combination of fury and self-reproach as she pulled away from his touch. Desperately, she wanted to hurt him as badly as he was hurting her. "I hate you! I can't stand to have you touch me!"

Adam's moment of weakness vanished abruptly as her refusal sent his temper soaring. A muscle twitched in his cheek as he struggled for control. Her continued avowals of hatred for him left him grim as well as angry. He stood up and, without a word, left the room.

Much later, when Adam sat alone in the study downing a full tumbler of bourbon, it occurred to him that Lianne had never once vowed any hatred for Spectre during the time she was his captive. She had responded wantonly to his embrace as the pirate, but had continually rejected him as her husband. The thought outraged Adam and left him wondering dismally at her response to Spectre.

Adam was angry and upset as he drained his glass. He felt the need to get away for a while, so he quit the house and headed to the stables to saddle a horse. Mounting, he gave his horse the lead, thundering off into the Lousiana night in hopes that a challenging ride would relieve some of the tension that filled him. As he rode off in the direction of Willow Bend, Adam was unaware of Lianne watching him from the bedroom window, tears streaming unheeded down her face.

Adam urged his horse to top speed as they raced across the moonlit countryside in reckless abandon. When at last his mount slowed, Adam reined in to a walk to allow him to rest. He had hoped his anger would ease with time, but he found himself still furious over Lianne's actions.

As her husband, Lianne had spurned him time and again, but as Spectre, she had loved him. It annoyed Adam that his desire for her had not abated with her rejection. He wanted her just as badly now as he had when he'd been sitting on the bed with her. Adam recalled then how wonderful her breast had felt against his palm, and knew he had to have her again. He sawed viciously on the reins to turn his horse back in the direction of the house. She might not want him, but he'd already proven she wanted Spectre. As he rode toward Belle Arbor, Adam began to plan.

Lianne had tossed and turned for hours after Adam had stalked from the bedroom. She was upset with herself, yet she wasn't quite sure why. She didn't know if she was angry because she'd rebuffed Adam's longed-for advances or if she was angry because he'd dared to make those advances after having spent time with Suzanne.

All Lianne did know was her foolishness in sending Adam away from her had resulted in his rushing right back to Suzanne. Long dormant, her pride surged forth reminding her painfully that nothing of value is easily won. If she really loved Adam, she knew she would have to fight to claim his love. The realization gave her a sense of purpose and eased the feeling of helpless misery that had embraced her.

Lying there alone in the dark, Lianne went over her situation again and again, until fatigue forced her to rest. As upset as she was, she had not expected to fall back asleep.

"Lianne . . ." The hoarse, rasping voice said her name softly.

The room was completely dark, the moon having set long before, when Lianne stirred and opened her eyes. It surprised her to find that she'd been asleep, but she wasn't upset or fearful at coming awake again. She thought that she'd drifted off only moments before, not hours ago as it had really been. Lianne wondered if Adam had returned, and she started to leave the bed to check, when he spoke again.

"Lianne . . ."

Where earlier she'd been deceived by the shadows and thought Adam had been Spectre, this time there could be no mistaking his voice. That deep, gruff tone could only belong to her unseen captor. It was him! Spectre! And he was here in her room! How had he gotten in? What did he want from her?

"Lianne, I came for you."

"No! You have to go!" Her heart was pounding and her pulse was racing. Spectre was here before her, but because of the darkness, she still couldn't see him.

"I can't leave you. You mean too much to me," he confessed the truth into the disguising, inky blackness of the night. "I want you, Lianne. I want you for my own . . ."

"That's impossible!" A thrill of excitement charged through her. "My husband—"

"Your husband is gone, my sweet," Spectre scoffed knowingly.

"No, he's not!" Lianne felt a bit frightened by his boldness in invading the sanctuary of her bedroom. She had thought she would never have to deal with him again, but now he was back, and she didn't know what to do.

"I've been watching . . . waiting. I saw him ride away. He won't be back until dawn. We have the rest of the night together — alone."

"No, Spectre. I don't want this," she declared. "I'm a married woman."

"You didn't fight me before," he pointed out coldly.

"How could I?" she threw back at him.

He was beside her in a heartbeat. "I can prove to you that you want me, Lianne."

Lianne stared at his masked features, shocked.

"You're masked?" Her tone was one of wonder as she reached up intending to strip away the offending disguise so she could see his face.

He gripped her wrists quickly to stop her. "It's necessary, love. There are those who would kill to learn my identity. It's better this way."

"But I want to see you."

"What I look like doesn't matter. All that matters is what's in my heart." He swept her into his arms and kissed her passionately.

His arousing kiss sent her senses soaring. She was alive with desire for him. She wanted him. She wanted him desperately, but she loved Adam. . . .

"Spectre, please, stop. This is madness . . ." Lianne gasped when his mouth left hers to explore the sensitive cords of her neck.

"You're like a fire in my blood. I can't get enough of you. That's why I came back. I need you, Lianne. I

395

need you and I want you as I've never wanted another."

"But I can't . . . I shouldn't . . ." She started to argue, not even noticing that he'd released her arms. She was clinging to his broad shoulders, his mask long forgotten. Her head was thrown back in ecstasy as he pressed heated kisses along the arch of her throat.

"You can," he told her huskily, pushing her nightgown from her shoulders to bare her breasts to his questing caresses. "You can and you will . . ."

There was no more talk then, only passion as they came together in an inferno of molten need. As Spectre, Adam gave her all the love he had pent up inside him, and, instinctively, Lianne returned his loving a hundredfold. It was a tumultuous, elemental joining—man and woman merging as one. They gloried in the union, cresting together and riding the tide of their desire to ecstatic oblivion.

Adam roused first from the blissful exhaustion that had claimed them both. His mood was disquieted as he slowly thought about the moments just passed. Lianne had made love with him as Spectre, openly and freely. He'd had only to press his point, and she'd given herself to him.

Adam suddenly felt as if he were caught on a double-edged sword. She could love him as a roguish mystery-lover, but not as the man who was her husband. The deception had been his from the first, and now he was trapped by it and the guilt that followed.

Adam wanted nothing more than to wake up with her in his arms, but he knew the risks were far too great. Moving easily away from her heavenly embrace, he began to dress.

"You're leaving?"

"It wouldn't do to have your husband find me in your bed," he responded a bit harshly. He heard her sharp intake of breath as his words cruelly struck home. He longed to erase them and comfort her, but he didn't dare. The sky to the east was already beginning to lighten, and Adam knew that if he touched her again, he would not be able to stop until he'd made love to her one last time. He had to go now, while it was still dark out.

"Will you be back?" Lianne asked fearfully, hopefully. She wasn't sure why she was asking, she just knew she had to know.

"I'll be back," he answered with a certainty. Then he was gone, disappearing out through the bedroom window.

Lianne flew from the bed to try to catch a glimpse of him leaving, but it was as if he had vanished into thin air. It surprised her that he could disappear that quickly, but there was no trace of him to be seen. For a moment, Lianne almost wondered if she'd dreamed the whole encounter with him.

As the sun crested the horizon bathing the room in a bright, golden glow, Lianne finally wandered back to her solitary bed. She thought of Adam then and where he'd spent the night, and tears threatened. She fell across the bed and turned her face into her pillow to muffle the sounds of her heartbreak.

Chapter Thirty-two

Several days passed as Adam returned to working the plantation again. No matter how busy he kept himself, though, Lianne was always in his thoughts. Whenever he saw her, it was all he could do to keep from taking her in his arms and loving her. He wanted to convince her of his innocence and see a warm glow of love for him reflected in her eyes, but he knew he had to wait just a little longer.

Since the night he'd made love to Lianne as Spectre, Adam had decided to begin trying to win her over. He knew it would take time, for there was a lot of distrust and misunderstandings between them, but he was determined to start making the effort. The breach in their marriage was great, though, and any small kindness he extended her way was met with a wariness that left him despairing and even more frustrated.

The only time Adam had come close to reaching her was when he'd taken an active interest in the plans she and Becky were making for the nursery. He'd offered several ideas that he thought would work and then had insisted that they decorate the room in blue, stating that he knew his son would not like a bedroom done in any other color. For an instant, he could have sworn that he'd seen a flash of warm emotion in Lianne's usually frosty, emerald gaze, but it had disappeared quickly, and she'd deliberately distanced herself from him after that.

Lianne's unspoken rebuff had hurt, but had not discouraged Adam too greatly. Biding his time, he elected not to appear too eager for fear of appearing unconvincing. He wanted to lay the foundation for a lifetime of love together, not sweep her off to bed for an hour's worth of physical pleasure.

His supposed love for Suzanne hung over him like a threatening cloud. Adam knew he should go see her and keep up the pretense, but somehow he hadn't been able to make himself do it. Lianne was the only woman he wanted, and he seriously doubted that he would be able to carry off the role of Suzanne's devoted lover with any conviction right now.

Still, Adam knew Shark was due back at any time. He didn't want to jeopardize his plan for trapping him, so he'd sent a note to Suzanne the day before explaining that he'd been gone on a short business trip and that he would come to Willow Bend to see her just as soon as he could get away. Adam hoped that would keep her satisfied for the time being.

Adam was sitting at his desk working on the plantation accounts when the knock came at the study door.

"It's me, Adam," Becky identified herself.

"Come on in," he called out, setting the books aside.

Becky entered and closed the door behind her again. Adam could tell that something was bothering her, for her usually pleasant expression was somber.

"Adam, I think we need to talk," she stated firmly.

"All right," he answered a bit cautiously, unable to imagine what could be troubling her. "What is it?"

"I'm worried about Lianne . . . and you," Becky said bluntly and then hurried on before he could say anything. "Now, you know I don't usually interfere in anything you do, but I can't help it this time. Something's terribly wrong between you, and since I love you both, I want to help."

Becky paused almost breathlessly, expecting Adam to explode in anger at her boldness in interfering in his life, and she was completely surprised when he only sat in silence, staring at her for a long moment.

"I don't know that you can, Becky," Adam answered simply as he pushed away from the desk and moved to stand by the window.

"It's Elise, isn't it, Adam? She's the reason you're distancing yourself from Lianne, isn't she?" Becky hit at what she thought was the core of the problem between them.

Adam was a bit shocked by her statement, and the glance he gave her revealed his thoughts.

"I thought so," Becky was saying, believing that she'd correctly identified the problem.

"No, Becky. Elise has nothing to do with it."

"She doesn't?" She was astounded. "You don't love her anymore?"

"I'll always care for Elise, but she's not the woman I love." Distractedly, Adam added, "Sometimes now I wonder if I ever really did . . ."

"Then what is it? What's wrong?"

"I've fallen in love with Lianne, Becky," Adam offered in the way of an explanation.

"Oh, well, that explains it all," Becky responded drolly, glaring at him.

"No. You don't understand," he went on, thinking of all the reasons Lianne had for hating him.

"I guess I don't," she agreed. "I would think that if I loved someone, I would want to be married to them."

"That's true enough, but, Becky, Lianne doesn't love me."

"So make her fall in love with you. There was a time when all the single women in Charleston would have gladly accepted your proposal—if you'd proposed," she teased.

"It's not as simple as you make it sound."

"And why not?" she demanded.

Adam stifled a groan as he thought of the strangling web of intrigue he'd created with his deceit. "Because there's still Suzanne to consider, and—"

"You're married to Lianne," Becky stated with emphasis, "and she's having your baby. You've just confessed to me that you love her. I don't see that Suzanne has anything more to do with your life. Lianne is your life now. Lianne and your baby . . ."

"Becky, there are things you don't know . . . things I can't talk about."

"There's nothing to talk about," she insisted, seeing everything plainly in black and white as she always did. "You love Lianne. That's all that matters. Tell her. Work things out between you."

"You make it sound so easy." Adam rubbed the tense muscles in the back of his neck.

"It can be, if you let it," she urged. "You know you can't go on this way."

"I have to for a while yet . . . until Shark—"

"Can't you give it up?" Becky was suddenly angry. "This need you have for revenge might very well ruin the rest of your life!"

Adam's expression was strained as he turned to look at her. "It's too late to quit now. It'll be over soon."

"I hope for your sake that it's over soon enough . . ."

Suzanne was frustrated and angry as she stormed about the parlor at Willow Bend.

"Why haven't I heard from him?" she ranted out loud to herself. "It's been days, and all he's sent is this one pitiful note!" She stared down at the single-paged letter Adam had written, telling her how he'd been out of town and that he'd come to her as soon as he could.

She felt hurt and rejected, for there was no talk of love in his note at all.

The searing memory of Cyrus's warning taunted Suzanne as she considered the cool missive, and as much as she wanted to put it from her, she couldn't. The possibility that Adam might have fallen in love with Lianne haunted her.

Suzanne thought back and realized how decidedly cool he had been toward her the last time he'd come to call. She remembered how rushed he'd been and how he'd been the one to break off their passionate embrace. At the time, Suzanne had thought that she'd tempted him too fully and that he was trying to restrain his runaway desire for her, but now she was beginning to see things in a different light. Perhaps he'd really fallen for Lianne. Perhaps he was going to end their relationship completely.

Outrage surged through Suzanne at the thought, and she stalked out into the main hallway and called out for a servant.

"Mary," Suzanne commanded the maid, "have a horse saddled and brought around for me."

"But, Miss Suzanne . . ." The servant started to question her request, knowing her mistress always took the carriage. "You know you don't like to ride astride like a man!"

Suzanne silenced her with a chilling glare, then hurried upstairs to change into her riding habit. As soon as she saw the stablehand leading the riding horse up to the house, she went out to meet him.

Suzanne had chosen to ride horseback rather than take the carriage, so she could cut cross-country and reach the other plantation house faster. All she cared about was being with Adam again. She was tired of waiting for him to come to her. She was going to seek him out and find out why he'd stayed away for so long.

As Suzanne rode up the main drive toward the big house, she was surprised to find that the place looked a little deserted. There were numerous workers out in the fields, but there seemed to be no one around the main house. She dismounted without help and tied her horse to the hitching post herself.

Suzanne waited there for a moment, expecting someone to have seen her coming and to emerge from the house to greet her. When no one did, she grew bold. It was not unusual for guests to enter a house unbidden, so she mounted the front steps with confidence. The main door was wide open, and Suzanne took advantage of its unspoken invitation by walking right on inside.

She could hear the sound of Adam's voice coming from behind the closed study door, and so she moved down the hall to listen, curious to hear what he was talking about. Suzanne didn't know what she'd expected to learn, standing there eavesdropping outside the door, but what she did hear made her go deathly pale.

"It's not as simple as you make it sound." Adam was saying.

"And why not?" Suzanne recognized the woman he was talking to as his sister Becky.

"Because there's still Suzanne to consider, and—" Suzanne knew a moment of victorious delight.

"You're married to Lianne," Becky stated with emphasis, "and she's having your baby. You've just confessed to me that you love her. I don't see that Suzanne has anything more to do with your life. Lianne is your life now. Lianne and your baby . . ." Suzanne went rigid.

"You make it sound so easy."

"It can be, if you let it. You know you can't go on this way."

"I have to for a while yet . . . until Shark—" *Shark!*

"Can't you give it up? This need you have for revenge might very well ruin the rest of your life!" Adam was after Shark? Suzanne wondered why.

"It's too late to quit now. It'll be over soon."

"I hope for your sake that it's over soon enough . . ."

Suzanne backed away from her door, her hands shaking and her temper flaring as Becky's damning words echoed through her very soul. *You've just confessed to me that you love her . . . You've just confessed to me that you love her . . . You've just confessed to me that you love her . . .* Damn Lianne Ducharme! Damn her! It had happened just like Cyrus had said it would!

A terrible, swift need for vengeance against the woman who'd stolen Adam from her and caused her so much humiliation filled Suzanne. She was going to take care of Lianne once and for all. Then when his precious little wife was out of the way, Suzanne knew she could use her knowledge of Shark's activities to her benefit with Adam. She would have him for her own yet!

She was furious as she hurried back outside. She wanted to leave before someone saw her, but when she caught sight of Lianne working in the garden at the far side of the house, she was unable to resist the opportunity to torment her.

"Why, Lianne, still working like a fieldhand, I see," Suzanne remarked cattily as she watched her digging in the soil.

Lianne had cringed at the sound of her voice, but she straightened from her work to give her a grimace of a smile.

"I happen to *like* working in the garden. It's quite peaceful—most of the time."

"Oh," Suzanne put a lot of disdain into that one word as she stared at Lianne's soiled clothing.

"What do you want, Suzanne?" Lianne asked impatiently. She knew the other woman had sought her out for a reason. She wanted to find out what it was and get this over with as quickly as she could.

"Why, Lianne." She faked amazement. "Do I have to have a reason for coming to Belle Arbor?"

Lianne turned back to her task in disgust. "If you want Adam, I think he's inside," she said, hoping Suzanne would leave.

"Oh, I've already had my visit with Adam . . ." Suzanne let the sentence hang to give Lianne something to think about. "Tell me something, Lianne," she began in a confiding tone after a long, silent moment.

"What?" Lianne looked up at her again, struggling to control the hatred she felt for her.

"How does it feel to be married to a man who doesn't love you?" Suzanne watched with something akin to glee as Lianne blanched.

"I don't know what you mean."

"I mean, darling, why in the world would you want to stay married to someone who doesn't want you? Everyone knows how you tricked him into this marriage of yours. Adam loves me. He always has and he always will," Suzanne told her smugly.

Each word was like a slap in the face to Lianne. She wanted to attack the smirking Suzanne and slap that knowing smile from her face, but she knew it would do no good. Suzanne was right. Adam did love her. If she attacked her, she would only be making herself look like a fool. It was better to let her think that she didn't care.

"I think you'd better go, Suzanne."

"Of course." The other woman gave her a condescending smile as she started back to her mount. "I'm sure I'll be seeing you again."

After Suzanne had ridden away, Lianne went to sit

on the small, secluded bench near the center of the garden. Her heart was heavy as she tried to sort out the turbulent emotions that were beseiging her. The near-violent jealousy that had revealed itself to her as she'd spoken with Suzanne only served to emphasize to Lianne how deeply she really did love Adam.

Lately, Lianne had thought that she had noticed a subtle change in Adam, a new gentleness in his manner toward her, and she had hoped . . . But Suzanne's little visit effectively shattered that illusion and left her realizing just how futile her love for him really was.

Even as she acknowledged her feelings for her husband, though, memories of Spectre plagued her. Could she fault Adam, when she herself had made love to another? She didn't understand what it was she felt for Spectre. He was a mystery. She'd never even seen his face, and yet there had been something so compelling about him that she'd been unable to resist him. She'd wanted him. A blush stained her cheeks as she thought of just how much.

Remembering her betraying, unbridled response to Spectre, Lianne vowed to herself that she would never give herself to him again. She would control her wayward desires at all costs! Adam was the man she loved. Adam was the man she wanted to spend her life with. If Spectre returned as he'd said he would, she was going to deny him completely and send him away from her forever. Only then could she concentrate on winning Adam's love.

That decided, Lianne felt a little better, but as evening neared, she wondered nervously if this would be the night Spectre returned.

After stopping at Willow Bend to get her carriage and driver, Suzanne made the trip to New Orleans in something close to record time. She entered Cyrus's bank knowing exactly what had to be done.

"I'd like to see Mr. Shackelford, please," she told the clerk out front.

"He's with someone right now, ma'am. If you'd care to wait . . ." the clerk offered, motioning to a chair nearby.

"I'm Suzanne Labadie. Mr. Shackelford will see me now. Announce me immediately."

"But, ma'am . . ."

"Now!" she snapped, not about to be put off by some lowly clerk. She watched with satisfaction as the timid little man rushed to do as she'd ordered. She was even more pleased when he came quickly back out of the office with Cyrus's other visitor.

"He'll see you now, Miss Labadie," he announced, a little resentful at being so abused.

"Thank you." Suzanne swept past him into the office, closing the door firmly behind her.

"Suzanne, how good to see you." Cyrus came to his feet behind his desk to welcome her, his expression carefully guarded as he watched her cross the room to stand before him.

"I want Lianne out of Adam's life permanently. What's your plan, Cyrus?" she stated bluntly.

A cunning smile lit up the banker's features. "So, you've come around to my way of thinking have you?"

"Yes, now what do we have to do?" Suzanne's voice was flat and revealed no emotion as she spoke.

"Very little," he said as he sat back down. "Why don't you take a seat while we discuss the finer details?"

Suzanne did as he'd bid, and she listened with avid interest as he described his devious plan to have Lianne kidnapped and sold into white slavery.

"We'll need the help of your business partner to do

this, of course," Cyrus ended his explanation.

"Of course," she agreed, thrilled with his plan. She could think of no more fitting end for Lianne than at the hands of the brutal slave traders.

"How soon do you think you could get in touch with him?"

Suzanne knew that Shark was due back within the next week to ten days, and she told him so.

"That will work out just fine. Can you arrange a meeting between Shark and myself?"

"I'll contact you as soon as I hear from him."

"Good."

"Cyrus?" Suzanne was suddenly curious about the other man's motives. "When this is over, I'm going to end up with Adam, but what are you going to get out of it?"

"One night, my dear, just one night."

"I don't understand."

"All I want is one night with Lianne, alone, in some isolated place. I'm sure your partner will be able to arrange it for me if I promise him that I won't do any lasting damage to his 'merchandise.'"

The thought of Lianne at the banker's mercy pleased Suzanne inordinately, and she smiled widely as she stood to leave. "I'm sure we can work something out. I'll be in touch."

When Suzanne had gone, Cyrus leaned back in his chair feeling quite confident that everything was going to work out perfectly. All that was left for him to do was to make his private deal on the side with Shark arranging for Adam's death. It wasn't enough to just make Lianne suffer, he wanted Trent to know the taste of his vengeance, too.

Chapter Thirty-three

"Have you heard from David?"

The anxious tone of Elise's question caught Nurse Halliday by surprise as she sat alone in the parlor, and she looked up to find her patient standing in the doorway. It took her a moment to answer, for it was a shock to see Elise up, dressed, and already downstairs at this early hour. Her pattern had always been to sleep late and require help with her toilette.

"Elise . . . good morning," Nurse Halliday greeted.

Impatiently, Elise asked again, "David . . . have you heard from him yet today?"

"No. It's much too early," she finally replied. "Dr. Williams won't be here until around eleven."

Elise's expression grew strained at the news. "I see. Is there anyway you can contact him now? I need to see him."

Nurse Halliday noticed that there was a tenseness about her, and she knew immediately that she should try to locate the doctor.

"I'll send a message right away," she offered. "Would you like to have some breakfast while we wait for him?"

"No . . . no, I can't eat anything right now," Elise answered anxiously. "I'll just wait for him outside in the garden."

The nurse was astounded as she watched her patient go outside alone. In all the time she'd been there, this was the first occasion that Elise had dared to move so freely and determinedly about the house. Before there had always been a timidity, an uncertainty about her actions. Today, though she was obviously a bit nervous, she seemed to be more assertive and almost in control. Halliday rushed to send off the missive to Dr. Williams, knowing that he would come as soon as he got word of the change.

David was still at home when he received Halliday's note and he left the house at once. *Come at once. There's been a change in Miss Elise. She wants to see you right away,* the note had said. He was fearful and elated at the same time—fearful, because he was afraid she was going to remember her love for Trent, want him, and then, as a result, be hurt again; elated, because it meant that at last they might be able to progress in their relationship.

David loved Elise with all his heart, but he'd taken great care not to reveal anything more than carefully offered, unthreatening devotion. He'd always known that he had to help her fully reclaim her own identity before he could try to win her love.

It took all his willpower not to race through the streets of New Orleans at breakneck speed. When he reached the house, Nurse Halliday was waiting expectantly for him.

"What is it?" he demanded. "How is she?"

"I'm not sure."

"What do you mean, you're not sure?" David asked with uncharacteristic sharpness. "Is she worse?"

"No, not at all. She came downstairs earlier fully dressed, and told me that she needed to see you. When I told her that you'd be here later this morning, she was very disappointed. That's why I sent the note."

David was unware that until today, Elise had always required help with her morning toilette. It was quite a change, and one for the better, that she had performed her morning ablutions independently today. He was anxious, even as he was cautious.

"Where is she now?"

"She told me that she would wait for you in the garden." Nurse Halliday met the physician's look of surprise and nodded in affirmation.

"We're not to be disturbed," David directed as he headed from the house in search of Elise.

Elise was standing near a flowering bush, toying absently with one of the fragrant, fragile blossoms. She knew the truth now—all of it—and she was nervous about facing David again.

The thought of David brought a soft smile to her lovely features. He was such a good, kind man. He had been strong and supportive during all these long weeks of her recovery, and Elise knew that she loved him deeply. She thought it would be the easiest thing in the world to spend the rest of her life loving him, but she knew from experience now that nothing in life was easy.

Adam . . . Elise's expression turned sorrowful. Last night she had remembered everything. Sometime after midnight, the dreams had come again, but this time her subconscious had revealed it all. She had remembered Adam, their whirlwind courtship, and the fateful voyage to Charleston that had ended in disaster.

Elise had been awakened by the force of the emotions that had swept through her. She'd spent long hours crying out her misery as she realized that her aunt was dead and her own innocence stripped from

411

her violently, lost to her forever. It had been near dawn when she'd finally come to grips with it all, understand at last the reasons for her months of withdrawal.

With that understanding, though, also came the realization of what she now had to face. She had fallen in love with David. He was the man she wanted. The time she'd had with Adam was like a distant, fading dream, and she knew she didn't want to return to that part of her life. She wanted to go on from here and start over, anew.

A sudden fear shook her. What if David didn't return her love? What if he was only being kind to her because it was his job? What if he was repelled by her? Certainly, her violation had not been her fault, but there were those who would look down upon her because of it. Elise worried desperately that David might condemn her for it.

Tensely, she picked a flower from the bush. She closed her eyes and lifted the blossom to her nose to inhale the sweet scent, all the while saying a heartfelt prayer that everything would work out.

David was hurrying through the winding paths of the garden trying to locate Elise, and it was then that he found her. She had her back to him, but, even so, he could tell right away that there had been a change in her. Just the way she was carrying herself revealed an awareness of self that hadn't been there before.

For one of the few times in his life, David felt insecure. He swallowed nervously several times before he finally spoke.

"Elise?" His tone was a bit huskier than usual, and he wondered at it.

Elise's eyes flew open at the sound of David's voice. He looked so dear and so wonderful to her that she had to restrain herself from throwing herself into his arms.

"Hello, David."

He heard the new cautious edge in her voice, and his heart sank. *She'd remembered*—he knew it without her saying another word.

"Nurse Halliday said that you wanted to see me. I came right over." He tried to sound professional, as if this was strictly a medical matter.

"Yes . . . I . . . " Elise found herself awkwardly searching for the right way to phrase what she had to tell him. "The dream . . . I think I understand now."

He heard the torment in her words and wanted to hold her. Instead, he kept an iron hand on the rein of his emotions and remained standing where he was.

"Do you want to tell me about it?" David encouraged.

"How much do you know?"

"Just what Adam Trent's told me . . ."

"Adam . . ." she said his name in a gasp.

"Do you want to see him? I can send for him. He could be here soon."

"No!"

Her response completely confused David. "No?"

Elise turned to face David fully as she hastened to explain. "I don't think I'm really ready to see Adam yet. I—I wanted to talk with you first."

He knew a moment of hope, but told himself sternly that she probably only wanted to talk to him about her fear of facing Adam again, that it had nothing to do with him personally. He was her doctor. She was his patient.

"Why don't we sit on the bench like we always do?" David wanted to take her arm as he always did during their walks, but today he held back.

Elise wanted him to escort her as he always did, and she was crestfallen when he didn't offer to take her arm. Holding herself stiffly, she led the way up the path to the secluded bench where they'd previously passed many afternoons in quiet companionship. When she'd settled on the seat, she kept her gaze averted, for she was afraid she wouldn't be able to conceal the love she was feeling for him.

David could feel the tension mounting between them, but he knew he had to encourage her to talk to him. He didn't understand her reluctance to see Trent.

"Why don't you want to see Adam, Elise? He's very concerned about you."

"He is?" The thought distressed her, and she knew a pang of guilt.

"He's the one who brought you here to New Orleans to me. He's taken care of everything for you. He's a very good man, Elise." David knew he couldn't be the one to break the news to her that Adam had married another woman, but he did want her to realize how much he had really cared for her.

"I know," Elise agreed miserably. "It's just that . . ."

"Are you afraid of the memories that will come with seeing him again?" David asked, incisively, thinking that was the reason for her hesitation.

"No. I've remembered everything now."

He noted how pale she became as she made the statement. "Then, what is it you're afraid of? Why don't you want to see him again?"

"I don't want to hurt him any more."

He was confused. "I'm sure seeing that you've made a full recovery won't hurt him, Elise. If anything, he'll be overjoyed. I've kept in regular contact with him and apprised him of your continuing improvement."

"Oh. Still . . ."

"I don't understand," David told her, puzzled by her obvious distress over facing Trent again. He had thought she'd be thrilled to reclaim her lost love. "If you're afraid that he's going to react differently to you because of all that's happened, I'm sure you're wrong. You're not to blame for what was inflicted upon you. You were, and still are, an innocent."

At his statement, Elise finally felt brave enough to lift her gaze to meet his.

"David, I'm afraid to see Adam because I don't love him any more," she stated firmly.

"What?"

"It's not that I don't care about him. I do. He's a wonderful man. It's just that . . ."

"Just that *what?*"

"Adam's not the man I love, David, you are." *There,* she thought with relief, *it was out in the open between them.* Elise felt pleased for a moment, but when David didn't immediately respond, her heart sank.

David was stunned. He'd known that they were close, but he'd had no idea that she felt the same way he did. He had thought she was just responding to him as a patient.

"Are you sure about this?" he finally managed to croak.

Elise let her gaze slide away from David's, thinking that he was going to try to convince her that she was wrong. "Yes. I'm sure."

David's tenuous control over his runaway emotions broke at that moment, and he took her into his arms. "I love you, too, Elise," he vowed devotedly. "I have for so long, but I was afraid . . ."

"You do?"

"Oh, yes," David groaned as he bent his head to kiss her for the very first time.

The kiss was gentle, tender, a tentative exploring of the fragile emotion they were both just beginning to accept, and when David ended it, their eyes met and held.

"I've loved you from the first," he told her, "but I was afraid it could never be."

"I love you, David. In the beginning, when I was first starting to remember, I'd wake up at night thinking of you. You're everything I want and need, David, everything." she confessed breathlessly, but then the thought of Adam intruded on her bliss.

David saw her expression darken. "You're worried about Trent?"

She nodded.

"Don't be," he told her with a smile.

Elise looked up at him questioningly. "Why? What's happened?"

"I spoke with him not too long ago . . ."

"Yes?"

"It seems things have changed drastically in his life, too." He paused for an instant before telling her the truth. "He's married now, Elise."

Elise blinked in surprise at the news and then smiled. There was no hurt or rejection, only a wonderful sense of freedom. She felt as if a great burden had been lifted from her. Her spirit felt light. Without hesitation, she threw her arms around David and hugged him.

David held her close to his heart. "Will you marry me, darling?"

"Yes . . . yes, oh yes!"

They held each other for a moment before David drew away to speak again. "You'll have to see him again, you know."

"I know." She gave him a bright smile.

"He was very worried about hurting you, too."

"Adam's a wonderful man," Elise said, her eyes filling with tears.

"You're crying?" David touched her cheek reverently, wondering what was wrong.

"Only because I'm so happy," Elise said. "As long as I have you by my side, I know I can handle anything."

"I'll never leave you, darling," David vowed. "I'll stay with you always."

"Send the messages to Adam," she told him with conviction. "I'm ready to see him now."

Adam received David's note late that day and could not arrange to get away until that evening. He confided only in Becky and then made the trip into New Orleans alone, glad for the chance to be away from Lianne's intoxicating, tempting nearness. His mood was dark as he lay awake in his room at the St. Louis that night, contemplating the confrontation to come the next morning.

The note from the doctor had been short but informative, letting Adam know that Elise had almost completely recovered now and that she wanted to see him as soon as he could manage to make the trip to town. Williams had given Adam no hint as to her current state of mind or the state of her affections. He was anticipating a very painful scene when they met. The last thing he wanted to do was to hurt her further, but he knew he wouldn't be able to rest unless things were fully resolved between them. Elise had meant a lot to him, and he owed her the complete truth.

Adam was on edge as he was admitted to the house by Nurse Halliday the next day. "Dr. Williams said that Elise was ready to see me," he said as she ushered him inside.

"Yes, sir. If you'll wait in the parlor . . . ?"

As Adam went into the parlor, Nurse Halliday went to find Elise. Adam was too tense to sit down and try to relax, so instead, he wandered to the window to gaze out at the serenity of the lush gardens beyond.

Then he saw her standing in the garden, and, with a shock, he realized that, indeed, her recovery was complete. No longer did she appear the distant, unaffected woman he'd dealt with during these long months. She was the Elise he'd once known . . . lovely, vibrant, happy . . .

The last thought jolted Adam. She looked so wonderful, so unexpectedly content, that he almost turned and left. He didn't want to be the one to cause her any more pain.

Still, Adam stood his ground, watching in silence as he saw Nurse Halliday go to her. He tried to read Elise's expression as the nurse gave her the news that he'd arrived, but the distance was too great to judge her reaction. Turning away from the window, he waited, and it was only a few moments before he heard her coming down the hall.

"I'll be in the parlor with Adam, Nurse Halliday, and we're not to be disturbed," she was saying.

"Yes, ma'am."

Having dismissed her, Elise turned then and faced Adam with full recognition for the first time since they'd last spoken on the ship.

"Adam . . ." She said his name with deep, heartfelt emotion as she went to him. She could tell that he was nervous, and without hesitation, she put her arms around him and hugged him. Since David had explained everything, she wanted to put him at ease. She wanted him to know that she still loved him in her own way.

Adam returned the embrace with a tenderness that came from deep affection. When Elise moved back to look up at him, he finally found his voice.

"It's good to see you, Elise. You look beautiful," Adam told her, thrilling at the sanity he found in her eyes. He touched her cheek gently, tenderly, thinking her a stunning woman, understanding how he'd believed himself in love with her all those months ago. Yet even as he admired Elise, Lianne was there in his thoughts, her hold on his heart unchallenged.

"Thank you, Adam. It's good to see you, too," she responded as she drew him down on the sofa beside her. "I'm so glad you're all right. There was a lot I couldn't remember in the beginning, and David helped me through it. He told me all the rest of what had happened. I'm so sorry, Adam."

"You're sorry?" Adam asked in amazement, wondering what she had to be sorry about. "You have nothing to be sorry about." This last he said bitterly, his own self-recrimination not yet fully put to rest.

The moment grew awkward. Adam didn't know what she was expecting from him or what he should say next. He did not want to discuss all the ugliness of the past, and yet, he didn't know what to say to her about the future.

Elise, too, didn't know how to begin. She wanted to tell him that she knew of his marriage and that it was all right. She wanted to tell him that she too had fallen in love with someone else, and they should both go on with the rest of their lives happily and without guilt. What was over, was over. It was time for each of them to begin anew.

At the exact same time, they both decided to bring the truth out in the open.

"Adam . . ."

"Elise . . ."

They both began to talk, and then they both fell silent as their eyes met and held.

"I want to thank you for everything you've done for me, Adam," Elise started again. "I know this couldn't have been easy for you, and—"

"For me?" Adam scoffed in self-derision, thinking she was the one who'd suffered the most.

"Yes, you," she boldly interrupted before he could say anything more. "Yes, you. If it hadn't been for you, God knows what would have happened to me."

"I care about you, Elise," Adam said seriously. "In the beginning, when they told me that you'd never recover, I nearly lost my mind. I was lucky to find Dr. Williams."

"We both were."

She sat it with such impact that Adam suddenly knew a bust of hope.

"Adam, David told me about your marriage." Else was relieved when she finally blurted it out.

"He did?" Adam stiffened in surprise.

Elise smiled at him sweetly as she lay a hand on his arm. "I'm happy for you, Adam, and I hope you'll be happy for me . . ."

"You've come to care for Williams?" Adam ventured.

"Yes. I love David very much, and I've agreed to become his wife." There was a very real glow of joy about her as she told him the news.

"Elise, that's wonderful!" For the first time since Shark's terrible raid Adam felt almost lighthearted. He took her in his arms and embraced her. "I wish you only the best of everything."

"Thank you, Adam. I feel the same way about you."

When he left her some time later, Adam's mood was better than it had been in months. He would never have believed it before, but it seemed that things did have a way of turning out for the best.

As his thoughts turned to Lianne, however, Adam grew a bit more somber. It was not going to be easy. This problem he'd created by making love to her as Spectre had made things far more difficult than he'd ever dreamed they could be, but he knew that somehow he was going to find the way to win her heart.

Suzanne intruded on his thoughts then, too, and he found himself wishing that he'd already finished with Shark, so he'd never have to see her again. It was getting harder and harder to pretend to be her lover. The thought that he had to stop on the way back to Belle Arbor to see her in order to keep up the charade left him feeling jaded.

Still, Adam knew he had to complete his revenge against the smuggler. Then, when it was over, he would put the past from him and get on with his future — a future that included Lianne and their child.

Chapter Thirty-four

"Miss Suzanne has gone into New Orleans, Mr. Adam. She's been gone since yesterday, and I'm not sure when to expect her back," the servant informed him.

Relief swept through Adam, for he was glad to have avoided the awkwardness of courting her. "Would you please tell her that I came to call?"

"Yes, sir. I'll tell her just as soon as she gets back."

As Adam left Willow Bend, though, he wondered what had drawn Suzanne into town. Since Beau's close call in capturing Shark weeks ago, had the smuggler changed his method of operating and somehow managed to elude Beau's diligent patrol? Adam knew it bore looking into, and he resolved to relay the possibility to Beau as soon as he made it back to Belle Arbor.

Night laid its shadowy claim to the land as Adam journeyed on the final leg of his return trip home. Elise's newfound happiness had released him from the torment of long-held feelings of personal guilt. His thoughts turned to Lianne as he rode through the darkness. The prospect of returning home to find her suspicious and doubting him again troubled him. He longed for a warm, loving welcome, but knew he had to be patient. He was weary of the deception, but could see no way out of it just yet.

The memory of her response to Spectre still bothered Adam, too, but he knew it was ridiculous to feel jealous of his own alter ego. As he anticipated seeing Lianne again, his body came alive with desire for her. It always amazed Adam that he reacted so strongly to her, but he realized now that this was love—this all-consuming, overpowering need to possess and be possessed. He'd never felt it with another, and he knew he never would again.

Suddenly, Adam needed to know the absolute truth of Lianne's feelings. He needed to know if there was any hope left for their marriage. It didn't seem possible to him that Lianne could respond to him physically the way she did if she hated him as thoroughly as she professed. Adam wondered, too, why she had followed him into the bayou that fateful night. She obviously had come after him in hopes of forcing a confrontation, but why? If she despised him, why would she have cared what he did? She had her home back and a rich husband. Wouldn't his absence from her bed greatly please her if, as she vowed, she couldn't bear his touch? Adam longed to find out, but he knew she would never reveal anything to him, personally.

At that point, he decided to assume Spectre's identity with her one last time. Adam knew he shouldn't. Logic told him that he should wait and take things slowly with Lianne. Logic, however, didn't rule his heart.

Lianne had found herself watching for Adam all day. After he'd left so abruptly the night before, Becky had assured her that his trip into town definitely was business. That has eased her anxiety somewhat, but the memory of Suzanne's tauntingly vicious conversation left her despairing. Lianne knew that the other woman's hold on Adam was considerable and that her own efforts to win Adam's love might well prove futile. Still, Lianne knew she had to try.

Lianne retired early again, her disappointment over Adam's continuing absence evident as she made her way slowly upstairs. Though she hadn't expected to be able to rest, sleep claimed her quickly, and she dreamed of Adam and the night they'd made love beside the reflecting pond.

The caressing touch at Lianne's breast was warm and gentle even as it aroused, and she smiled in her sleep.

"Adam . . ." she murmured, caught up in dreams of his loving possession, feeling desire's sweet heat flooding through her. "Adam . . ."

The touch stopped abruptly, and Lianne came awake. She stirred sleepily, her body still glowing with the fiery tension her sensual reverie had evoked. Lianne realized slowly that it had all been imagined, and the disappointment was heartbreaking. Even in her sleep, her body betrayed her.

Lianne opened her eyes, hoping to dispel the desire that throbbed deep within her, and she saw Spectre looming above her. She started to cry out in surprise, but he clamped a hand firmly across her mouth to prevent it.

"Be quiet," he commanded in his hoarse, rasping tone.

Lianne nodded. She was relieved when he immediately took his hand away, but her heart was still pounding wildly in her breast.

"Why did you come back?" she demanded in a whisper.

Spectre looked at her for a long time before he

answered. His dark eyes, gleaming behind the disguise he wore, seemed to bore into hers as if searching for something.

"I couldn't stay away from you," he confessed earnestly, and he reached out boldly to touch her breast again. Adam had been shocked to hear her call out his name and not Spectre's as he'd caressed her. Certainly, she had sounded pleased as she said it, but then, she had been asleep.

Lianne was mesmerized by his caress for a moment and didn't immediately move away from the seductive touch of his hand as he toyed with the already aching crest of her breast.

"I want you, Lianne," he told her gruffly. "I want you more than I've ever wanted another woman. You're everything I've ever desired . . ."

He was just about to kiss her, when Lianne finally came to her senses. She scrambled across the bed, taking care to keep out of his reach.

"No, Spectre! I won't let you do this to me again!" she blurted out desperately.

"Do what to you? Make love to you?" he asked, puzzled by her withdrawal when he'd knew her body was responding to him.

"Yes," Lianne declared firmly, remembering her vow to herself. "I don't want you to touch me anymore. You have to go!"

"But why? You're alone, and you know you want me," Spectre said simply. "Do I have to show you again how much you really desire me, Lianne?" he taunted her with her past surrender.

"I know you can make me respond to you physically," she returned, trying not to let her fear that she might succumb to him again show in her voice. "But that doesn't mean anything!"

"It doesn't?" There was a mocking tone to his voice.

"No." She shook her head to emphasize her determination.

"Tell me, Lianne. Why this sudden reluctance?" Spectre chided. "You know the joy I can give you. You know the passion we've shared."

"I don't want that any more. It means nothing."

He gave a soft laugh. "I know you so well, Lianne. Why is it I'm finding it so difficult to believe you?"

"You don't know me at all, and I don't know you! Why, I've never even seen you!"

"That never mattered to you before," he told her in a seductive tone.

"I know, but . . ."

"But what?" His words were a sneer.

She caught herself before she blurted out everything to him. "Why should I tell you what I'm thinking and feeling? You've never trusted me! You've always hidden behind that mask!"

"For good reason," he remarked fiercely, snaring her by her arms and bringing her fully against him even as she knelt on the bed. "You love me, Lianne. I can tell by the way your body responds to mine."

"No! I don't love you!"

"Oh? Then just who do you love, Lianne? Have you suddenly found that you love your absent husband more than you do me?"

"You may be able to make me desire you, Spectre, but you can never touch my heart. Adam's the only one who can do that. My husband is the only man I love!"

Adam was elated by her unexpected confession. He kissed her devouringly, forgetting for a moment that he was Spectre and not himself. When Lianne began to struggle against him, he realized his mistake and broke off the kiss.

"Don't, Spectre!" Lianne gasped, trying to deny the

426

stirrings of passion he'd aroused when his mouth had moved over hers in that demanding exchange. Crushed to the hard width of his chest now, she could feel his own desire for her pressing hotly against her thigh. Her need was great, but her love for Adam was stronger. Tears filled her eyes as she tried to free herself from his arms. "You must let me go. I can never betray my husband this way again! I love him too much! Please, Spectre, if you care for me at all, you'll release me."

Her words stung Adam. He wanted to make love to her. He wanted to take her right then and there, but he knew any chance of that had disappeared when she'd confessed to loving him.

As ecstatic as Adam was over discovering that she really loved him, he now found himself in an even more complicated situation. There was no way he could reveal to her, as her husband, that he knew her deepest feelings without giving himself away, and Adam was certain that she would be outraged if she found out about his deception. He wouldn't blame her for really hating him then, for he certainly wasn't proud of what he'd done. The unshed tears glistening in her eyes sent a pang of regret through him.

"If that's what you really want, Lianne," he managed, hating the thought of releasing her when she felt so wonderful held tightly against him.

"It's what I want," she reaffirmed, her eyes never leaving his. Lianne was amazed when he pushed her slightly away from him and stepped back.

"You're husband is a very lucky man to have your love, Lianne."

Lianne had to fight to keep from laughing bitterly. She watched in silence as Spectre turned his back on her and left the room through the balcony window. She was frozen in place for a moment, but then raced to the window to look out. Lianne felt oddly disappointed when there was no sign of Spectre anywhere. It was almost as if he'd vanished.

Returning to her bed, Lianne felt very proud of herself. It had been difficult to send Spectre away, but she had to do it. She loved Adam, whether he loved her or not, and she wanted to be a good wife to him. He was due to return home tomorrow, and when he did, she was going to tell him of her love for him and how she wanted to try to make a life together. Lianne knew there was a good chance that he would reject her outright; still, she knew she had to try. Her whole future depended on it.

Suzanne entered her room at the hotel late that night after spending the evening with friends. She had left a low lamp burning on the night table when she'd left, and she was surprised to find that it had gone out while she was away. Leaving the door open slightly to provide some illumination, she made her way to the dresser to light the other lamp. That accomplished, she returned to close and lock the door.

Suzanne had only started to turn around when the man's arms went around her and she was hauled against a rock-hard, unyielding chest. His hands moved brazenly over her lush curves with insulting familiarity.

"Shark!" Suzanne gasped in immediate recognition.

"It's about time you got back," Shark remarked as he trailed hot, wet kisses down the side of her neck.

"What are you doing in New Orleans?" she asked, twisting free of his grasp to turn and face him. Shark usually avoided the city. It was strange for him to show up here like this.

"We had a close call when we sailed last time," he

informed her.

"What kind of close call?"

Shark was not about to let her know the depth of his concern about this "Captain Spectre" who was supposedly after him.

"I'm not sure. It might have been the authorities. I didn't stay around long enough to find out, and we took a different return route this time, just in case."

"What about our cargo?"

"You don't have to worry about your profits, Suzanne. The cargo has already been dropped off. It's safe."

"I always knew you were resourceful when the situation called for it."

"That's not all I am," he said, leering at her lustfully.

With deliberate seductiveness, Suzanne lifted her hands to begin to unbutton her bodice. "What else are you, Shark?" she asked huskily. Adam's meager kisses had left her longing for more, and she was hungry to know a man again. Certainly, she would have preferred Adam, but she knew Shark could satisfy her the way she needed to be satisfied.

Shark brushed her hands away and hurriedly finished the job she'd started. When she stood nude before him, he swept her up in his arms and fell upon the bed with her. His caresses were bold and demanding, and Suzanne responded wantonly. She had been without a man for far too long. She wanted him as desperately as he wanted her. Shark's need was so great that he didn't even bother to strip off his clothes. He only freed himself from his pants and mounted her, taking his pleasure quickly and forcefully.

It was as they lay together, momentarily sated, that Suzanne smiled. If nothing else, Shark did always manage to satisfy her.

"I'm glad you're back. I've missed you."

"I could tell," he replied, thinking of her wildness during their lovemaking.

"I need your help with something . . ."

"Oh?" Shark raised up on his forearms to stare down at her, wondering what it was she wanted.

"It could prove very profitable to you."

The thought of profits always interested Shark. "What is it?"

"I have a friend, Cyrus Shackelford. He and I are mutually interested in having a certain woman disappear and never come back."

Now he was really intrigued. "What did she do to you, Suzanne? Is she the one who married your 'fiancé'?"

Suzanne glared at him. "So, you've heard?"

"Oh, yes. I was surprised to hear of your 'engagement,' no matter how short it was. Is that what this is all about?"

"Yes. She's a bitch and I want her gone! Cyrus does, too!"

"Why? What did she do to him?"

"She rejected him."

"And just what do I get out of this?"

"Money," she told him with a cunning smile, knowing that greed was his one weakness. "I'm sure Cyrus will pay whatever you ask."

Shark considered her proposition for a minute and then nodded, feeling certain that it would be easy money. "Set up the meeting."

"I'll send the message now," Suzanne said, and she started from the bed only to be pulled back down.

"Not yet. There's plenty of time to meet with Shackelford. First, let's have a meeting of our own . . ." His mouth covered hers as he moved over her once more.

* * *

It was the next afternoon when Cyrus faced Shark across the table in the secluded corner of the waterfront saloon.

"There is one other thing . . ." Cyrus said as he met the other man's eyes. He could read nothing in the black, obsidian depths, but rather than feel intimidated by his lack of revealed emotion, Cyrus felt more secure. He could tell that Shark was a predator by nature—he would do whatever was expedient at the time to achieve his goals—and that was exactly the kind of person Cyrus wanted to deal with.

"Such as?" Shark's gaze narrowed. He sensed in Cyrus a man who was as ruthless as himself, but who disguised that ruthlessness beneath a veneer of sophistication. Shark knew that Cyrus Shackelford was a man who should be carefully watching.

"I have one other matter that needs to be taken care of, and I'm certain you're the one who can handle it." Having already discussed with him the details of how he wanted Lianne's kidnapping handled, he was now ready to broach the subject of arranging Adam's murder.

Shark didn't bother to reply, waiting for him to go on.

"I want the girl's husband killed?"

"Trent?"

Cyrus nodded. "I don't care how it's done. I just want him dead."

Shark knew that Suzanne was hoping to have Trent to herself once the woman was out of the way, and he understood now the reason why Shackelford had wanted to meet with him privately without her.

"How much is it worth to you?" Shark asked, not in the least concerned about what Suzanne wanted. She meant nothing more to him than an exciting bed companion. Money was Shark's only trusted friend.

431

"Name your price," Cyrus told him. When Shark quoted an outrageous sum, he agreed without flinching.

"This Trent must have caused you *some* trouble, Shackelford," he said, eagerly anticipating collecting the pay for murdering this Trent.

For a moment Cyrus's civilized expression slipped, and Shark could see the hatred and contempt he felt for the other man. "That he has, that he has. I deal viciously with those who cross me, Shark. See that Trent gets the message just before you kill him."

Shark returned to Suzanne's hotel room to find her waiting expectantly for him.

"How did it go?" she questioned anxiously as she let him in.

"Everything's settled."

"You've agreed to do it?"

"Shackelford's price was right."

"How soon?"

"As soon as I can make the arrangements. It shouldn't take more than a day or two to set up everything."

Suzanne's eyes glowed at the prospect of Lianne's getting what she deserved. With Lianne out of the way, Suzanne expected it would be a simple matter to win Adam's love again, especially since she now knew that Adam was hunting for Shark. She didn't know the reason for his search, and she didn't care. Suzanne firmly believed that all she'd have to do to win his confidence and love would be to betray Shark to him. Still, however, she wouldn't do it until after Lianne had been completely disposed of. Adam had loved her once, and she was sure that she could make him love her again.

432

"How soon do you have to leave?" She suddenly wished Shark was gone, so she could fantasize about her future with Adam.

"Not for some time yet," Shark leered at her, wondering what she would think if she knew that he'd already begun to plot her other lover's death. The thought amused him as he reached out to take her in his arms.

Suzanne did not resist his embrace, and as Shark overwhelmed her with his sensual power, she gave up clinging to her thoughts of Adam and surrendered willingly to his mastery of her senses.

Chapter Thirty-five

Adam stayed away from Belle Arbor until the following morning. It was still early when he returned, and only Becky had already come downstairs.

"Adam!" Becky had been waiting nervously to hear from him, and she rushed to greet him. Her dark eyes searched his for some clue as to the outcome of his visit with Elise. "How did it go?" she asked.

"Come into the study and I'll tell you everything," Adam directed, leading the way into the room and then closing the door behind them for privacy.

"Well? What did the doctor say?"

"I never had a chance to talk with him."

"You didn't?" Becky was puzzled. "Then what . . . ?"

"I was with Elise, Becky," he told her as his gaze met hers across the room.

"You were?" She couldn't read any telltale emotion in his expression and wasn't quite sure how to react to the news.

"Elise has made a full recovery," he told her with a smile.

"That's wonderful . . ." Becky ventured a bit hesitantly, suddenly worrying how her recovery had affected Adam. Had he found he still loved her?

"Yes, it is wonderful, Becky," Adam reassured her, seeing the worry in her eyes. "Elise had also fallen in love with Dr. Williams and has agreed to marry him."

"She has?" Becky's face lit up with the happiness she felt for him. "That's perfect. Now—" she began eagerly, about to blurt out that there was nothing to keep him and Lianne apart any more, but she knew he still had not given up his thirst for revenge against Shark.

"Now, there's only one thing I have left to do," he interrupted her, "and then I can put this entire nightmare behind me." Adam's expression darkened as he thought of Shark and Suzanne. He knew he had to get the message regarding her trip to New Orleans off to Beau right away.

"You still won't give it up?"

"I can't Becky, not yet, not until Shark's paid the price," he vowed, not wavering in his purpose.

Knowing it was useless to press the point, Becky started from the room. "Lianne's missed you while you were away, Adam," she remarked easily.

"Did she tell you that?" he asked quickly.

"No, but I could tell. Adam . . ."

He looked up at her expectantly, questioningly.

"Adam," Becky continued, "if you love her, tell her now, before it's too late." She didn't wait for his response, but left him alone with his thoughts.

Adam scowled at his sister as she left, closing the door behind her again on her way out. He knew she was right. He knew he should tell Lianne that he loved her, but he wondered if she would believe him after all of his declarations of devotion to Suzanne. Adam flinched as he thought of how cruelly he'd treated Lianne since their marriage and of all the humiliation she'd suffered because of him. It was a wonder that she harbored any tender feelings toward him at all, he realized with brutal clarity.

The memory of Lianne's profession of love the night before filled Adam with vibrant emotion then. Suddenly he wanted to rush upstairs, sweep her up into

435

his arms, declare his love, and make passionate love to her for the rest of the day. Adam knew his behavior might be suspect if he followed through on that particular impulse, though.

Instead, Adam hesitated, remaining where he was, struggling to find a way out of the deceitful situation in which he found himself. It came to him in a blinding flash of common sense — there was no real reason to keep the truth from Lianne any longer. She loved him and he knew he loved her. She hated Suzanne, and so, when he told her the whole story, he knew he could count on her to help him, rather than cross him . . . except . . .

Adam knew if he told her everything that he would have to tell her about Spectre, and that was where the danger was. He glanced longingly at the bottle of bourbon sitting out on the liquor cabinet, but he dismissed the idea as quickly as it came. Liquor would not ease the problem he now faced, only honesty would.

Girding himself, Adam decided that he would tell Lianne everything. He would tell her that he loved her. He would explain about the raid and Elise and his "involvement" with Suzanne. He wanted no more lies between them. He would even confess the truth about Spectre and hope that she understood, for nothing else really mattered except that they loved each other . . . he hoped.

Feeling confident that he was doing the right thing, Adam left the study and went upstairs to talk with his wife.

Lianne had not fallen back asleep after Spectre's visit. She had spent the balance of the night hours thinking solely of Adam. Her thoughts were still centered on him as she sat at her dressing table brushing out her hair the next morning. Lianne was so deeply lost in her musings as she ran the brush through the silken thickness of her hair that she didn't hear the door open behind her or notice when Adam moved soundlessly into the room.

Adam started into the room, but stopped suddenly at the sight of Lianne sitting at the dressing table clad only in her gown. A shock of awareness coursed through him at the delectable sight she made, and memories of last night, when he'd held her and caressed her, returned full force.

Realizing that she was unaware of his presence, Adam took advantage of the moment and remained standing quietly just inside the doorway, watching her with hungry intent. His gaze darkened with desire as it raked over her. The gown was a demure one, yet its very absence of daring held Adam enthralled. He *knew* what delights lay beneath the soft fabric—that they were hidden from him now only served to entice him that much more.

Lianne didn't know why she looked up into the mirror just then, but she did. The sight of Adam standing there watching her so intently, caused her to stop in midmotion.

"Hello, Lianne . . . " Adam said huskily as he pushed the door shut behind him. Like a man possessed, he moved across the room toward her, his eyes meeting and locking with hers in the mirror. He wanted her with a driving desperation, and he wondered how he was going to be able to keep from touching her until they had finished talking.

"Adam . . . you're back," Lianne murmured in soft surprise. She had known that he was due to return, but she hadn't expected him to make an effort to seek her out. She wasn't sure whether to be pleased or

437

cautious. She decided on the latter.

Adam came up behind her and took the brush from her hand, placing it upon the tabletop. When she said nothing, he grew emboldened and rested his hands on her slender shoulders. Lianne felt so delicately feminine beneath his hands that he suddenly knew an overwhelming need to protect her, to keep her from harm. He never wanted to cause her any pain again as long as he lived. He wanted only to spend the rest of his life making her happy.

Lianne was mesmerized by the gentleness of his touch. This was what she'd wanted for so long! This was what she'd longed for! Yet even as she allowed herself a moment of hope, reality returned. He loved Suzanne.

Lianne's heart ached as she fought not to give in to the desire to let him have his way with her. It would have been easy to pretend that he really loved her for a few minutes, to fall into his arms and make love with him. The trouble came afterward, when she would be forced to face the truth of his feelings again. Knowing the pain it would bring, Lianne knew there was no way she could allow Adam to make love to her. She didn't just want sex with him. She wanted his love. She wanted all of him—not just Suzanne's leftovers.

"Adam, we need to talk . . ." Lianne finally managed, and she was startled by the unexpected huskiness in her voice.

"I know," he agreed reluctantly, his eyes still clinging to hers in the mirror, his hands beginning a mesmerizing massage of her shoulders.

"Adam," Lianne began again, trying to ignore the warmth that was flooding through her from his caress. "Adam, I can't go on with this farce of a marriage any longer," she declared forcefully, shrugging away from his touch. Lianne left the dressing table and moved

438

across the room before facing him again. Somehow, she felt safer and more in control when she was out of reach of his intoxicating touch. It was a proven fact that she couldn't think straight whenever he touched her.

"What?" Her statement shocked him completely, for it was the last thing he'd expected her to say. Last night, she had declared herself in love with him. Now today, she was telling him that their marriage was over. Adam was confused, and with that confusion came reactive anger. His expression grew thunderous.

At Adam's suddenly fierce look, Lianne wrapped her arms about herself protectively. She didn't understand why he looked so angry. She had thought he would be thrilled that she was going to set him free. Why would he care that she wanted the marriage to end? He loved Suzanne, didn't he? Suzanne was the one he wanted, wasn't she?

"Look, Adam, I know you're in love with Suzanne. You made it perfectly clear from the beginning how you felt about me . . . about our marriage."

"Lianne—"

"No, let me finish!" She silenced him, not wanting to be interrupted now that she was finally telling him everything. "I knew how you felt about her, but for some misguided reason I kept hoping that, eventually, you would come to love me. I was wrong, and I've come to accept the fact that you're always going to love Suzanne." Lianne paused to draw a deep breath, and Adam took the opportunity to get a word in edgewise.

"Lianne, you're wrong. Suzanne really has nothing to do with us." He started to explain, but Lianne took his statement wrong.

"Oh, you're wrong there, Adam. Suzanne has everything to do with us! You see, Adam Trent, I love you. I love you very much. It would be the easiest thing in the world for me to go to bed with you right now and make love to you, but I'm not going to do it. I won't make love with you just because you're stuck in this marriage with me, and I certainly won't make love with you while you're in love with someone else. I want all of you, or nothing, Adam. I can't go on living this way any longer."

"Lianne." Her name was a loving caress on his lips as he met her gaze across the room. In her emerald eyes, Adam could read all the doubts and fears she was trying so hard to conceal, and he knew that he was the only one who could erase them. His movements were slow but determined as he crossed the distance between them.

Lianne watched him as he came toward her, her eyes widening in alarm. She didn't want him near her. She didn't want him to touch her again. She just wanted him to go! His dark eyes never left hers as he approached, and she felt trapped by the blaze of emotion she saw reflected there.

"I don't love Suzanne, Lianne," Adam said with a growl as he took her in his arms.

His mouth took hers in a dominating exchange, and she resisted with all her might. She would have kept fighting him, too, but after an instant of holding her in his arms, Adam's anger disappeared. He wanted to please her, not punish her. He wanted to prove his love to her, not convince her that she was right about his affections.

Adam's kiss went from overpowering to seductive, from force to gentle persuasion, and Lianne felt her determination to refuse him waning. When he broke off the kiss, she gazed up at him in confusion, her conflicting emotions plainly revealed on her face.

"Adam . . . I—"

"Lianne." He cut sharply across her words before

she had a chance to tell him to leave. "Lianne"—
Adam's tone softened to a thick whisper—"I love you."

Lianne was truly stunned by his revelation. Adam
loved *her?* How could he declare his love for her, when
all along he'd sworn he cared only for Suzanne? She
stared up into the dark, fathomless depths of Adam's
gaze, trying to decipher the secrets he had hidden
there.

Adam saw the sudden wariness of her expression.
He knew he deserved that look of suspicion, and much
more, but it only made him more determined to convince her of his love. There would be no note from
Suzanne to tear them apart this time. Lianne was
going to learn the true depth of his caring for her, and
she was going to learn it now.

"There are so many things I need to tell you . . ."
Adam said as he lifted one hand to cup her cheek,
fearing that she might reject him again, but knowing
that he had to try. "Just know this, Lianne." He bent to
her, his lips almost, but not quite touching hers.
"When we make love, there'll be no room for anyone
else in the bed with us."

Although he hadn't meant them to, his words
brought back her memories of Spectre and sent a shaft
of guilt lancing through her. She tried to drop her
gaze from his, but he framed her face with his hands
and kissed her.

A part of her told Lianne to keep fighting him, that
this was some sort of trick, but her heart demanded
she accept the joy Adam was offering her. Could
Adam be telling her the truth? Did he really love her?
It made no sense, but at this very moment, she didn't
care . . .

Lianne gave herself over to the glory of his embrace. His lips moved over hers, evoking a wildfire of
desire in her. In response, she instinctively arched

against him, pressing her soft womanly curves against the hardness of him.

Again and again Adam sought her lips, tasting of her honeyed sweetness there. His hands never stopped caressing her through the soft gown. When he could bear it no longer, he swept Lianne up into his arms and strode to the bed with her. Adam placed her upon the welcoming softness and then moved to lay down beside her.

Lianne welcomed Adam to her with open arms, holding him close as they kissed once more, heatedly, passionately. Their bodies strained together hungrily. Adam pushed the gown from her shoulders, trailing a searing path of kisses over the creamy flesh he exposed. Lianne groaned in ecstasy as his lips sought and found her breasts, bared now beneath his questing caresses. She moved restlessly in his arms as he traced patterns of fire upon her pliant flesh. When his hands moved lower, seeking the softness of her, she moved to accommodate him. Lianne thrilled at his practiced touch, and she found herself writhing against Adam, desperately needing to be one with him again.

Adam could no longer restrain himself from taking her. He drew away from her embrace just long enough to shed his own clothing, and then returned to take her in his arms once more. Moving over Lianne, he fit his body intimately to hers. Lianne arched up to him and took the strength of him deep within her.

Theirs was a joining of hearts as well as bodies. It was the first time they'd made love as husband and wife, and Adam wanted it to be perfect for her. He lay embedded in her sweetness, the urge to take her quickly almost overwhelming, but he fought it down. With the utmost of patience and care, he began to kiss and caress her again, taking the time to arouse her desires to the same fever pitch as his before beginning his rhythm.

When Adam started to move within her, Lianne was ready. She matched his hard, driving hips stroke for stroke, arching and twisting beneath him in love's most sensuous dance. The memory of his declaration of love played over and over in her mind as she moved beneath him and with him. Lianne told herself that he loved her, that he wanted only her, that they were going to be this happy forever.

Adam was caught up in the heat of his need for Lianne. Making love to her was his heaven and his hell. He remembered with burning desire the way she'd denied him the night before as Spectre, declaring her love for him as her husband. Adam also remembered, all to starkly, the look of doubt and suspicion that had haunted her before he'd overwhelmed her with his kisses. In the back of his mind, he worried that she would still be distrustful of his motives even after they'd made love.

Adam's uncertainties were swept away, though, as Lianne drew him down to her for a flaming kiss. Her openly willing move sent his senses spiraling out of control. Thrusting avidly into her, Adam took them both to the heights of ecstasy's splendor. They gloried in the breathless release their mating brought them.

In the aftermath of the storm of their loving, Adam and Lianne clung tightly to one another. Neither spoke right away for fear of losing the closeness that each of them had waited so long to experience. They rested that way, locked in their cherishing embrace.

Much later Adam levered himself up on his elbow to stare down at his wife.

"I love you, Lianne," Adam told her huskily as he

brushed one errant curl from her cheek.

"Adam," Lianne sighed in heavenly contentment as she opened her eyes to gaze up at him. The doubts she had put from her returned, and she grew afraid now that he might have lied to her about his love just to get her into bed.

Adam could see the shadow of doubt that still troubled her. He wanted to have it all out, to tell her the entire story, but suddenly he felt a chilling fear. What if she hated him after he told her about his deception as Spectre? What if she came to despise him for his callous trick?

What had seemed like the right thing to do before, now seemed suicidal. What had happened between them had been so perfect, so magical, Adam didn't want to risk ruining it. He swallowed nervously as he struggled to make the decision. *What Lianne didn't know couldn't hurt her,* he reasoned, his decision made.

"I do love you," he told her sincerely. "I'm sorry about Suzanne. I . . ."

Lianne saw the earnestness in his gaze and surrendered fully to her heart's desire, blocking out any need to hear his explanations. All that mattered was that he loved her. "Adam . . . please, don't explain. Don't say a word. I don't ever want to hear that woman's name again."

He looked down at her a bit confused. "But . . ."

Lianne lifted one hand to press her fingers to his lips. "I don't want to hear about the past, Adam. All that matters now is our future. I love you, too . . . I have for so long."

Adam breathed an inner sigh of relief at her words. He groaned as he bent to kiss her with ardent devotion. "And I love you, Lianne, with all my heart."

Lianne was in his arms then, wrapped in his powerful embrace. His mouth slanted across hers in a fiery claim that stole her breath away. Lianne clutched at his shoulders as ecstasy claimed her again. *This was Adam! He loved her . . . he wanted her! They were going to be together forever . . .*

the boat, he had often his sleep depend on dependable
crewmen to aid him with thousands of dollars worth of
merchandise aboard their ship, his crew was top notch
he could count on them.

Chapter Thirty-six

Cyrus was beside himself with excitement. It should
be happening at any time now! It had been three days
since his meeting with Shark. He knew the smuggler
was as eager for his money as he himself was to have
Lianne all to himself for one, uninterrupted night.
The arrangements had all been made. All that was left
was for Shark to notify him when the deed had been
done. Then they would meet at the rendezvous point,
Shark would be paid, and he would get Lianne.

Cyrus paced his office, rubbing his hands together
in eager anticipation of that night. A cruel smile
curved the hard line of his mouth as he imagined her
pleading with him for mercy. He would take great
pleasure in giving her none. By the time Shark came
to take her away the following morning, she would
know a true taste of humiliation. He'd see to it.

Anxiously, Cyrus glanced down at his watch. It was
growing late in the day, and still there had been no
word. Cyrus hated waiting for anything, but he supposed this time it was worth it. Sitting back down at
his desk, he picked up some papers and tried to work.
All he could think about though was Lianne, naked
and humble before him. It was pleasant daydream.

Shark glanced at the three men who sat with him at
the table in the saloon. Having left Will in charge of

the boat, he had chosen his three most dependable crewmen to aid him with the murder-kidnapping. The men had readily agreed to help him when he'd told them of the extra money they could make. The promise of financial rewards carried great weight with Shark's greedy, murderous crew.

"You understand what you're supposed to do?" Shark glared at each one of them pointedly, wanting to make sure that there would be no mistakes made the following morning when they coordinated their attack. "Morley? O'Malley?"

"O'Malley and me, we're going after Trent, and we're supposed to tell him right before we kill him that Cyrus Shackelford sent us," the big, burly man answered for himself and his tall, skinny, mean-looking friend.

"How about you, Drago?"

"I go with you. We grab the woman, tie her up, and keep her quiet until we get back to the ship."

"I don't want any mistakes made, do you understand me?" Shark glowered at them threateningly. "If this goes off the way I got it planned, we'll all be a lot richer by nightfall tomorrow."

The other pirates exchanged smug, confident looks among themselves.

"Anybody who doesn't get their part of this done might as well count themselves as a dead man. Understand?" he threatened, knowing that overconfidence on their part could ruin everything.

"Yes, sir, Captain Shark. We're ready. We're just waiting for the word from you."

"We leave here tonight before midnight. We'll stay at Willow Bend until daylight and then move out." He looked around him once more and felt reasonably certain nothing would go wrong.

* * *

The days since she and Adam had reconciled had been idyllic for Lianne. Since the morning when they'd first talked and declared their true feelings for one another, Adam had become the most considerate of husbands. Before this, Lianne had never known his more gentle side, and she found herself falling even more deeply in love with him. He was everything she had thought he was and more.

All the doubts and suspicions Lianne had harbored during the early days of their marriage were slowly beginning to fade. She didn't question her good fortune in winning Adam's love, she just tried to relax and appreciate it. There was still a lot about him she didn't know, but she didn't dwell on that. The past was over. Today and the rest of their lives together were all that mattered.

Adam was being so attentive and kind that she almost felt as if he were paying her court. It was a delightful experience for her. Being courted by the man she loved was something she'd always fantasized about, but had never actually experienced before. Lianne was discovering that she enjoyed it very much.

Now, as she rode across Belle Arbor at his side, Lianne was caught up in the joy of just being with him. Adam had sought her out at the house a short while before and convinced her that she had to take a ride with him. Alex had tried to talk Adam into taking him along too, but Adam had resisted his efforts, promising to ride with him some time the following day.

"Where are we going?" Lianne had an idea where he was taking her, but she wasn't quite sure yet.

"It's a surprise," Adam teased good-naturedly. He flashed her a sensually wicked smile, and Lianne felt her pulse quicken in response. "It's a little place Alex showed me earlier. I think you might like it . . ."

Lianne knew then where they were headed, and her breath caught in her throat at the thought of swimming with Adam . . . alone. She said nothing, but her anticipation grew until she was tingling with excitement.

"Do you know where we're going yet?" Adam questioned as they turned down the narrow trail that led to the secluded swimming hole.

"Yes, I know," she told him, her eyes alive and sparkling at the prospect. When she was here the last time, her heart had been broken. This time, she knew she would make new memories to replace the old painful ones.

Adam said no more, but reined in ahead of her and dismounted. He would have helped her down, but Lianne was too fast for him. By the time he finished and turned to help her, she had already tied up her own mount and raced to the water's edge.

"Lianne!" Adam shouted eagerly following after her.

"What?" She turned to him, her expression radiantly happy.

"I didn't want you to start without me," he told her as he joined her on the bank.

"Start what without you?" Lianne asked archly, leaning lightly against him when he took her in his arms.

"Swimming . . . among other things," Adam told her gruffly just before he kissed her.

Lianne felt the desire spark between them, but she wasn't ready to surrender to him just yet. He had brought her here to swim, hadn't he?

"Oh, no, Adam Trent," Lianne laughed as she pushed herself free of his embrace. "Since we're here, I want to go swimming!"

As Adam watched with feigned dismay at her rejection, Lianne began to undress. Seduction was not on her mind as she started, but by the time she'd stripped down to her chemise, she could tell that it was on Adam's. His dark eyes were glowing with an inner fire as he watched her, and it gave Lianne great female pleasure to know that she could arouse him that way. She stood posed before him for just an instant before diving into the cool water.

"If you want me, Adam, come and get me!" she teased with a lighthearted laugh, then started swimming across the pool away from him.

Her challenge spurred him to action, and within moments, he was in the water racing toward her with hard, powerful strokes. Adam was upon her in no time, and he slipped beneath the surface to snare her by the ankle and drag her under into his arms.

Lianne didn't resist, and when they surfaced, she wrapped her arms securely around his neck, allowing him to do all the work of keeping them afloat.

"I think I could come to like this," she murmured, kissing his neck.

Keeping one arm around Lianne's waist, Adam managed to keep both of their heads above the surface as he swam back toward shore. The water was a silken caress against their bodies that added to the sensuousness of the moment. By the time they reached shallower water to where Adam could stand, Lianne could feel him hot and hard against her. She gave a soft, enticing laugh as she reached down to caress him in a bold ploy.

Adam groaned at her brazenness and, switching his hold on her, brought her fully around in front of him. Positioning her legs around his waist, he buried himself in her sweetness. The heat of her body was a direct contrast to the coolness of the water, and Adam's passion flared hotly.

Lianne was enthralled by the novelty of their position, and she began to move excitedly against him using the buoyancy of the water to help her. Adam sought her breasts as they moved together in a tidal wave of desire. Arching her back, she continued to move in an abandoned, primitive rhythm, ecstasy building within her. They crested together, rapturous in their loving. Wave after wave of excitement throbbed through them as they stood locked together in that most intimate embrace.

When the storm of their passion had passed, Adam lifted Lianne into his arms and carried her to the moss-covered bank. He held her near as they lay quietly together, savoring the newness of their relationship.

"I love you, Lianne," Adam told her in a love-husky voice.

"I know," Lianne sighed as she lay nestled at his side, her head resting on his shoulder, one hand splayed out across his chest. "But sometimes, these last few days seem more like a dream . . ."

"What do you mean?" He frowned.

She pushed herself up on one elbow to gaze down at him. "Things were so difficult between us for so long . . . you were always gone, and then when you were here, you avoided me . . ."

"With good reason." Adam gave her a lopsided, pained smile as he raised up long enough to give her a quick, hard kiss.

"What good reason?" Lianne demanded, wanting to know what his reason had been for being so cruel to her.

"If I hadn't stayed away from you, we would have ended up spending all our time like this." He chuckled at her amazed look. "Yes, my dear, lovely wife, I had to fight to keep my hands off you. I wanted you desperately, but being manipulated into marriage . . ."

"Adam, you know—" She started to interrupt, to tell him that none of it was planned, but he silenced her with another kiss.

"I know the truth, love . . . now. I was too blind then to see it. It was a matter of pride. Not only that, but there you were, declaring your hatred for me at every opportunity."

Lianne gave him a soft, seductive smile as she pressed a tender kiss to his cheek. "I did hate you," she said softly. At his surprised, questioning look, she went on, "I hated you for what you made me feel. I wanted you to love me desperately, but it all seemed hopeless. Suzanne's little visits didn't help, either."

"Suzanne was here?" He hadn't been aware that the other woman had come to Belle Arbor.

"Of course Suzanne was here. It was only last week when she was here last."

"Last week? I didn't see her here last week."

Lianne gave him a puzzled, doubting look, wondering why he would try to hide Suzanne's visit from her. "Look, Adam, I saw her. It was one of the afternoons when you were working in the study. She came to talk with me in the garden right after she'd finished seeing you. She told me—"

"I didn't meet with her, Lianne," he vowed seriously, troubled by the news of this mysterious visit. Why would Suzanne make the trip all the way there to see him and then not announce herself? Unless . . . "What did she say to you?"

"The usual things . . ." Even now, safe in Adam's embrace, the memory of her taunts had the power to hurt her, and she dropped her eyes from him.

"Like what?" Adam put a finger under her chin and tilted her face up so she was looking at him again.

Drawing a ragged breath, she told him everything

Suzanne had said. After hearing it, Adam pulled her close and kissed her in soft devotion.

"I didn't speak with her at Belle Arbor last week. She didn't come to see me in the study. The only thing I can think of is that, as brazen as she is, she might have eavesdropped on a conversation I had with Becky."

"What conversation?" Lianne asked, wondering what could have been said to evoke such a vicious response from Suzanne.

"The conversation where I admitted to Becky that I loved you, not Suzanne."

"You admitted that you loved me to Becky that long ago, but you didn't tell me until now? Why did you wait? I would have given anything to know that you loved me."

"I didn't know that you'd believe me for one thing. You have to remember that I still thought you hated me." Adam knew that was a lie, but things were too wonderful between them to worry about it.

"And I thought you hated me . . ." she murmured. "It's a shame we wasted so much time."

"Indeed it is, my love. Indeed, it is," Adam agreed, and then proceeded to make up for all the lost time.

Suzanne came awake abruptly as Shark boldly entered her bedroom. "Shark? What are you doing here? Has something gone wrong?"

"No, nothing's wrong. I'm just paying a social call while I wait for sunup." Shark grinned at her leeringly as she started to undress. He had left the others outside in the stables with orders to wait for him there while he'd gone up to the house. He didn't want to take the chance that one of them might say something that would reveal their plot to kill Trent. Suzanne

453

didn't need to know about his and Cyrus's private deal. All she needed to know about was the girl's kidnapping.

"Then, you're going to do it in the morning?"

"Yes, first thing."

"What's your plan?" she asked eagerly. She wanted to know everything.

"I've got some men with me. We'll watch the house, and as soon as we can snatch her without causing a scene we'll make our move."

"Then?" Suzanne was listening avidly.

Shark shrugged as he joined her in bed. "We're meeting the ship at our usual rendezvous point. I notify Shackelford that everything's been taken care of, he gets his night with her aboard the *Banshee*, and I get my money."

"What are you going to do with her then?"

"I know some buyers who'd be interested in a white woman. She'll bring a good price if she's pretty. If not, there's still a profit to be made." He was tired of talking, and he reached out and pulled her roughly to him.

Suzanne had grown excited at hearing all his plans, and she chose to thank him in a very elemental way. She didn't resist his manhandling, but melted against him, eager to please him.

Knowing that this was probably the last time he would share her bed, Shark took full advantage of her willingness. They passed the remaining hours of darkness in a heated, animalistic mating that left them both spent yet satisfied.

The sky had only begun to lighten when he left her bed to get dressed.

"Will you be back?" Suzanne questioned as she watched him prepare to leave her.

"No," he answered. Shark knew she wouldn't be

454

wanting anything to do with him once she found out he was responsible for Trent's death.

"Are you going to leave again after you take care of Lianne?"

"Yes. I'll ship out as soon as I can. Things'll probably get pretty hot around here, so I'll lay low for a while."

"Let me know where you'll be in case I need to contact you." She needed to know what he was going to be doing and where he would be going, so she could arrange to betray him to Adam when the time was right.

"I will," he lied, anxious now to be away from her so he could begin work on his devious scheme.

Shark went to her for one last kiss and then left. He sought out Micah, the young stableboy Suzanne used for a messenger, and handed him a sealed envelope.

"Your mistress wants this delivered to Adam Trent right away. No one else is to see it, understand?" Shark ordered in a fierce tone.

"Yes, suh," the youngster replied hurriedly as he took the note.

"This is for you." He handed the boy a coin.

"Thank you, suh." He looked up at the big man, his eyes wide in appreciation.

"Just make sure you give it directly to Trent."

"I will, suh, right away!"

As the first rays of the morning sun shone through the bedroom window, Adam awoke. It was a wonderful sensation to wake up with Lianne in his arms, and he wanted to linger there in bed with her, savoring the intimacy of the moment. This particular morning, though, he knew he couldn't. He'd arranged to ride out with the overseer, and he was due to meet him at

455

the stable in less than an hour.

Adam's regret was great as he gently eased Lianne from his embrace, trying not to disturb her peaceful slumber, but she awoke up the instant he tried to shift away from her.

"Adam? Where are you going?" Lianne asked in a sleepy murmur as she reached out to draw him back to her.

"I've got to see the fields this morning, love, but I'll try to be back by midafternoon."

"Ummm . . . the fields." She nodded in understanding, keeping her eyes half-closed in pretended sleepiness.

Adam started to move away again, but Lianne reacted too quickly for him, looping her arms around her neck and pulling him down for a good-morning kiss.

"Lianne." Adam was laughing as he returned her embrace. "I really do have to meet him."

"I know," she said throatily, kissing him again.

"Lianne, I arranged to meet him . . ." He protested, sounding less and less convincing.

Lianne pressed herself fully against him. "I know," she sighed in mock sorrow, her eyes alight with loving mischief. "You have to go."

Lianne gave Adam a teasingly seductive smile and shifted away from him. Since they'd been together, she'd taken to sleeping in the nude, and she deliberately let the covers fall from her so that she lay enticingly before him, every lovely inch of her bare to his gaze. She could read the riot of emotions that played across his face as he wrestled with his desire to stay and his need to go, and her heart filled with tender love for him.

"I guess if you have to go . . . you have to go . . ." Lianne stretched in sensuous splendor. Playing the vixen, she arched her back and lifted her arms over her head. She never looked away from him, and she knew the moment Adam's tenuous hold on his desire was lost.

"The hell with him. Let him wait!" Adam growled in desperation, going into her arms.

Lianne gave a throaty chuckle in celebration of her victory as she lifted her lips to his. It was nearly an hour later when Adam finally left her. Having spent so much time lost in the rapture of her loving, he gave up any thoughts of breakfast and rushed to the stables to begin his workday.

Chapter Thirty-seven

By the time Micah reached Belle Arbor, Adam had already ridden out with the overseer. It was midmorning before the boy finally managed to locate him on the vast plantation. He was intimidated by the scowling look Adam gave him when he delivered the letter to him, and he hurried to leave, wanting to get away as quickly as possible.

Adam watched him ride away and then glanced down at the note he held in his hand. Though the handwriting didn't look particularly familiar, he was certain that it was from Suzanne, for he recognized Micah as one of her servants. Adam was sure that the missive was an entreaty to come see her, and he dreaded the prospect even though he knew he had to go. Moving away from the overseer, he opened the note.

> *My dearest Adam —*
>   *It's important that I see you right away. Please meet me at the grove of willows near our boundary line.*
>   *Suzanne*

Adam thought it unusual that she didn't want to meet at her home, but since the grove was closer, he gave it little thought. Excusing himself from the overseer, he mounted up and rode off toward the arranged meeting place.

"What the hell is takin' him so long?" O'Malley complained as he waited with Morley near the willow grove.

"How the hell am I supposed to know!" his partner snarled.

They had been crouched in their secluded hiding place since early that morning waiting for their intended victim to show up, but so far there had been no sign of him.

"You think he's gonna turn up soon?"

"I hope so. I want to get this over with and get back to the ship," Morley grumbled.

Only Shark's promise of a big payoff held them there as the hours dragged on.

Lianne had wanted to linger in bed after Adam left her, but she'd found herself unable to fall back asleep. Giving up the effort, she'd dressed and gone downstairs to breakfast with Becky and Alex. The morning was a quiet one as they enjoyed each other's company. Alex ran off to the stables to play, and Becky decided to join Lianne in her garden work. They labored there contentedly weeding and pruning back her plants until late morning when the warmth of sun encouraged them to rest for a while. Lianne pocketed the small knife she used for the pruning as they wandered down to the cool, shady banks of the reflecting pond beckoned to sit and relax.

"I'm really glad that you and Adam have worked things out, Lianne," Becky confided as they sat together in easy camaraderie beneath the shade of the massive trees.

"So am I, Becky," Lianne told her.

"I always thought you were perfect for him," she said with a laugh.

"You did?" Lianne was amazed.

Becky nodded. "I'm sure he's loved you from the first time he saw you, even though he didn't show it until now."

Lianne couldn't believe what her friend was telling her. "From the first time he saw me?" she asked, stunned. She remembered their first encounter quite well, and she knew that she looked little better than a fieldhand that day. "You've got to be teasing."

"Oh, no, I'm serious. You're the only woman I've ever known who's run Adam off with a shotgun!" Becky chortled with delight as she recalled Adam's outrage at being faced down.

"But Adam was so arrogant and so mean to me all this time."

"I know he was, Adam had a really good reason for everything he did. You may not always understand him, but trust him, Lianne. I know he loves you deeply, and now you know that too." Becky said, wanting somehow to prepare her friend for when the whole truth was one day revealed.

Lianne sensed an unspoken urgency in her words, and she wanted to know what she meant. "I know he loves me, Becky. But what do you—"

As she was about to ask, she was interrupted by a big, ugly brute of a man who emerged from the words near them, rifle in hand.

"Don't neither one of you move or say a word!" he ordered, leveling the gun straight at them.

Becky and Lianne froze as they stared at the threatening stranger, wondering what he wanted. Only when she heard someone come up behind them did Lianne know a true moment of terror.

"Don't move or we'll kill you right where you sit!" the menacing voice said.

Shark had been watching the two women from a distance, trying to decide which one was Lianne Ducharme. In frustration, he'd finally decided to take them both. They were both comely wenches, and he knew they would each bring a good price on the slave market.

460

Eager to be gone before they could be found out, Shark grabbed Becky and quickly bound and gagged her.

Lianne remembered when she had last been bound and gagged and knew a moment of panic.

"If you're from Spectre, there's no need for this!" she told him earnestly. "You don't have to tie us up! I'll go with you willingly."

At her mention of Spectre, Shark reacted violently, shoving Becky brutally aside and spinning Lianne around to face him.

"You know Spectre?" he demanded, his hands biting into her upper arms where he held her.

"Yes, and I'll go with you without a fight. You don't have to—"

"What do you know about Spectre?" Shark asked, his black obsidian eyes boring into hers.

"You aren't from Spectre, are you?" Lianne gasped and went pale at the realization.

Becky lay on the ground, her eyes wide and questioning as she listened to what was being said. How did Lianne know about Spectre when Adam had never told her the truth about their situation? What had Adam done? And who was this thug that he should know about Spectre and be so interested in him? She didn't have long to wait to find out.

"Get that one, Drago, while I take care of her," Shark directed.

"Aye, Captain Shark," he answered.

Becky felt a chill of doom descend upon her. She knew about Shark—the man was a killer. She also knew it was hopeless to try to escape; she didn't doubt for a moment that they would kill them right there if they tried.

As Shark reached out to begin tying Lianne's hands, she finally reacted. Throwing herself sideways, she tried to elude him in hopes that she could get to her knife and fight back. She managed to evade him for an instant, but Shark was not about to let her get away. Lianne got out only one short scream for help before he was on her, one hamlike hand closing over her mouth with suffocating effectiveness. In minutes, she was bound and gagged like Becky.

"Let's get out of here. Stay down low. I don't want to be seen. With any luck, these two won't even be missed for several hours."

Sick at heart, Lianne listened dazedly and knew that he was right. Since Alex was busy playing, no one would come looking for them until it was time for the midday meal. She groaned in misery as Shark heaved her over his shoulder and moved off through the brushes with Drago carrying Becky following behind.

"Morley! Look! Here he comes now!" O'Malley jabbed him in the ribs and pointed toward the lone rider heading their way.

"Think that's him?"

"Who else would it be? You ready?" he asked, lifting his own rifle and talking careful aim.

"Yeah, I'm ready. Let's get this over with," Morley growled, sighting down his own weapon.

O'Malley fired first and they were both jubilant to see the rider fall from his horse and lay still.

"Come on," Morley urged, afraid the shot might have alerted someone to their presence. "Let's get outta here!"

"You know we can't leave until we're sure he's dead," he told him. "We gotta be sure. If we want to get paid, there's no room for mistakes on this one."

Grumbling in annoyance and nervousness, he followed O'Malley to where the rider lay motionlessly on the ground. His shirt was bloodstained, and they could see that it was just a flesh wound and that the bullet had passed completely through.

"He ain't dead," O'Malley said in disgust. "You want to finish him off or shall I?"

"I'll do it," Morley said eagerly as he aimed his rifle at Adam's head. "This is from Cyrus Shackelford." He repeated what Shark had told him to say as he prepared to pull the trigger. He was not ready for what happened next as Adam quickly scissored his legs, tripping him. The rifle flew from his grasp as he fell heavily.

O'Malley was momentarily stunned by what had happened. Adam took advantage of his element of surprise, launching himself at him and knocking the rifle from his grasp. Operating strictly on bloodlust, Adam threw him down and then grabbed up the fallen weapon. Without thought, he turned and fired, laying low both of his would-be assassins.

In shock, Adam stood staring down at the scene before him, the attacker's words still echoing vengefully inside his mind. *This is from Cyrus Shackelford. . . .*

As rationality returned, Adam wondered if either of them were still alive, and he went to check. To his dismay, Adam found that his marksmanship had been all too good.

A searing, burning anger filled him then as he thought of Shackelford. He had always known that the banker hated him, but he'd had no idea that his hatred ran this deep. Snatching up a rifle, Adam vaulted onto his horse's back, paying no attention to the hot stickiness of his own blood on his chest. He put his heels to his mount's flanks and raced across the countryside heading straight for New Orleans and a showdown with the cowardly Cyrus.

It was the noon hour, and the bank was empty except

463

for Abner, the clerk, and Cyrus. Cyrus was trying to immerse himself in his work, but his anticipation was so great that he was again having trouble concentrating. All he could think of was Lianne and the night he would have her in his power. The thought filled him with overwhelming desire. In irritation, the banker stood up from his desk and strode to the window to stare out, hoping to distract himself from his heated imaginings. Soon, he told himself, soon it would be a reality. Lianne would be his.

Cyrus was even considering the prospect of buying her from Shark himself, if the night was enjoyable enough. He knew there were ways to handle such delicate situations, and if Lianne pleased him as much he thought she was going to, he would make her his permanently.

In his mind, Cyrus pictured a windowless room in the cellar of his house where he would keep her locked up in perfect seclusion until he tired of her. The idea had merit, he decided with a wicked, lustful smile.

The door to his office crashed open at that moment, and Cyrus looked up to find himself staring down the barrel of a rifle.

"How does it feel to be on the receiving end, Shackelford?" Adam demanded.

Cyrus went deathly white as he saw the blood and realized that Shark had failed. "What do you want? What are you doing here?!" he demanded trying to retain some dignity and bluff his way out of the situation. "Abner! Get the law!"

"I've already sent him for them, Cyrus. I want them to hear your confession."

"Confession?" He gave a short laugh as his eyes shifted nervously to his desk. If only he could find a way to get the gun he had hidden there and kill Trent before the law arrived! Then he could claim that Trent barged into his

464

office with a gun, ready to shoot, and he'd killed him in self-defense. "I really have no idea what you're talking about." Cyrus was cool as he turned slowly and moved back toward his chair.

"I'll tell you what I'm talking about." Adam was seething as he spoke. "I'm talking about 'This is from Cyrus Shackelford.' That's what I'm talking about! Lucky for me the men you hired were terrible shots or you'd have gotten away with it."

Cyrus realized then how stupidly arrogant he'd been in telling Shark to let Adam know that he was the one who wanted him dead. He silently cursed himself as he edged closer to his concealed gun.

"I didn't hire any gunmen to kill you, Trent. Why would I? The whole idea is absurd," he said smoothly, dismissingly.

Adam was not taken in by his outward display of calmness. He had seen his expression when he'd first burst through the door, and he knew the truth.

"I don't know, Shackelford. You tell me," Adam taunted. "Tell me why it was so important for me to end up dead? Do you want Lianne that badly that you'd kill me to get her? I've got news for you. She wouldn't want you if you were the last man on earth. You had your chance with her, and she turned you down flat . . . or don't you remember?" He said the last with a sneer, wanting to push him to the brink and reveal him for the snake he really was.

Adam's words had just the effect he'd wanted. Cyrus was livid. He wanted Trent dead! *Dead!* Time was running out! Cyrus dove for the desk, grabbed the gun from the secret compartment where he kept it hidden, and fired.

Adam knew Cyrus for the swine he was, and he fired as soon as the other man made his move. Cyrus's shot went wide as Adam's bullet caught the banker full in the chest and sent him sprawling to the floor.

Adam heard Abner's and the constable's shouts behind him, but he paid no attention as he threw his rifle down and ran to Cyrus's side. Blood trickled from the corner of Cyrus's mouth as he smiled grimly up at his most hated enemy.

"You may think you've won, Trent, but you haven't!" He began to cough violently as death tightened its hold on him.

"Won?" Adam stared down at him in confusion. *What kind of game was this man playing?* "Won that, Shackelford? What are you talking about?"

"Lianne . . ." Cyrus groaned.

At his uttering of her name, Adam grabbed him by the shirt front and hauled him upward.

"What about Lianne!" he demanded viciously, knowing that the man's life was draining from him and that he had to know what was happening.

"You've lost her . . ." he told him with a defiant gleam flaring in his eyes for an instant before fading to a pain-filled daze. "Suzanne arranged it all . . ."

"Suzanne?" Adam thought of the note and realized that they had worked together to exact their revenge.

"She hates Lianne as much as I hate you," Cyrus spat viciously.

"Lianne!" Adam suddenly recognized the danger she was in. He lowered Cyrus back to the floor intending to rush to her rescue. But Cyrus's next words stopped him before he could stand to go.

"That's right . . . Suzanne has plans for her." He gave a hoarse, coughing laugh. "But you're too late already, Trent! Even though she'll never be mine now, at least I know she won't belong to you any more . . . She'll pay for what she did to me . . . She'll pay with her body, and she'll pay with her soul!"

Adam knew true fear. If Suzanne's and Cyrus's hatred

was savage enough to cause them to arrange his murder, God only knew what they could have planned for Lianne.

"What have you done to her?" he demanded fiercely, nearly out of his mind with worry. Adam was torn between the need to race to Belle Arbor and the need to stay and get the whole truth out of Cyrus.

But fate took the decision from him as Cyrus went tense, groaning Lianne's name in a despairing lover's whisper. He slumped visibly then, his life over.

Adam got to his feet, intending to leave immediately for home.

"We saw and heard everything, Mr. Trent. There'll be no charges filed," Horace Watkins, the constable, told him.

"Right," Adam answered distractedly, anxious to be on his way.

"What he was saying about this Lianne . . ."

"Lianne is my wife," Adam told him tersely, "and she's in some kind of terrible danger. I have to get back home . . ."

"Of course. I'll send help with you."

"I can't wait for your men. It might be too late already! Send them to Willow Bend plantation. Suzanne Labadie is the one you want."

"They'll be on their way within the hour," Watkins promised. "What about your shoulder? Don't you think you should have a doctor take a look at that?"

"There's no time for that," Adam answered, hurrying from the room, and he never looked back.

The ride to Belle Arbor had never seemed so long as Adam again took off cross-country in an effort to get back home and save Lianne. The miles were endless to him as he and his tiring mount struggled to reach the plantation. When he finally charged up the drive to the main house, his horse was foam-flecked and near exhaustion. He dismounted before completely coming to a stop and raced up the steps, shouting out her name.

Sarah heard Adam's call and came to meet him. Her eyes widened in horror at the sight of his bloodstained shirt. "Mr. Adam . . . what is it? What happened to you?"

"It doesn't matter, Sarah. Where's Lianne? Where's Becky?" he asked impatiently.

"They're not in the house. They were working in the garden earlier, but I haven't seen them for a while."

Adam rushed to the garden. He found their discarded tools, but no further sign of them. Sarah had followed him, and he turned on her furiously.

"Where else could they be? Where else could they have gone?"

"Mr. Adam, I don't know. Why don't you tell me what's wrong? What's happened?"

"Cyrus Shackelford tried to have me killed this morning, and there are plans to hurt Lianne, too . . ."

"Dear God!"

Adam's exhausted mount had drawn the attention of the stablehands, and, hearing the talk that something must be wrong up at the big house, Alex went to see what was going on. He found Adam in the garden with Sarah. At the sight of Adam's wound, he thought of Mark, and tears of fear filled his eyes. Without hesitation he ran to Adam and wrapped his arms possessively around him.

"Adam! You can't die like Mark! I won't let you!"

"I'm not going to die, Alex," he promised, giving him a reassuring hug.

"But somebody shot you!"

"Some very mean men, but they've all been taken care of already."

"They have?" He brightened a bit.

Adam nodded, keeping his arms around the boy to comfort him and ease his worries. "Have you seen Lianne or Becky?" He tried to sound casual, not wanting to upset him.

"Not for a long time," he said, "but we'd better find her. She's going to be worried about you."

"You're right, Alex, she will be. You didn't see her with Becky down at the stable, did you?"

"No, she wasn't there."

"Sarah, I want Lianne found now!" Adam snapped with firm authority, and Sarah ran to do as he'd instructed.

The search proved fruitless, as he'd feared it would. Adam finally allowed Sarah to nurse his shoulder, and then he donned a clean shirt. Leaving a frightened Alex in her care, he got a fresh mount and headed for Willow Bend and Suzanne . . . the true link to Lianne's and Becky's disappearance.

Though his shoulder and arm were beginning to ache, Adam dismissed the pain. Nothing mattered but saving Lianne and Becky from whatever horrible fate Suzanne had plotted.

Chapter Thirty-eight

Since Shark had left Willow Bend at dawn, Suzanne had been beside herself with excitement. As the hours passed, she became convinced that everything had gone just as Shark had planned. Certainly, she reasoned, she would have heard something if it hadn't.

Suzanne was thrilled to think that Lianne had disappeared from Belle Arbor without a trace, and she could hardly wait for the time to come when Adam would once again be hers. Judging from what little she'd been able to learn from Shark, it would be a matter of another six weeks or so before he returned to her. By the time he got back, she intended to have Adam's full attention again. She would betray Shark to him then, winning even more of his confidence and, hopefully, all of his love.

Suzanne sighed in dramatic fashion as she pictured herself wrapped in Adam's strong embrace. The memory of his avowal of love for Lianne intruded on her happiness, but she shoved it away. She knew Lianne really meant nothing to him. The stupid chit had trapped him into marriage by getting herself with child. Suzanne was positive it would be easy to win him back now that she was gone.

The sound of a horse dashing madly up to the house brought her out of bed. Suzanne ran to the window and was absolutely delighted when she caught a glimpse of Adam below. Her heart filled with joy at the thought that he'd come to her so soon, and she raced to her dressing table to make sure that she looked her best before she went out to see him.

"Where is she?" Adam challenged as he pushed aggressively past the maid and into the house without waiting for an invitation.

The servant recognized Adam, but was puzzled by his obvious anger. She answered promptly, hoping to placate him, "Miss Suzanne is in her room, sir. Shall I get her for you?"

"Never mind. I'll go get her myself." He brushed past her and started up the steps.

"But Mr. Adam, sir . . ." she protested, trailing after him, but there was no diverting him.

Adam stalked down the hall with the maid at his heels. "Mr. Adam, I don't think this is a good idea—"

Even as the servant tried to stop him, Suzanne's bedroom door opened, and she stepped unawares out into the hall.

"Adam!" Suzanne had no trouble sounding surprised as she came face to face with him right outside her bedroom door, for she was indeed. The fact that he'd come upstairs looking for her filled her with confidence. Her eyes were aglow with a fervent fire as she stared at him hungrily. "It's all right," she told the girl. "You can go."

"Yes, ma'am."

"Adam, it's so good to see you . . ." She cooed, stepping nearer to stand close in front of him. She was hoping he would take her in his arms and kiss her, for it had been a long time since they'd been together.

"Yes," he bit out, barely controlling his fury, "it's good to see you, too." For what it was worth, Adam really meant his words. During his ride to Willow Bend, he'd been afraid that Suzanne might be gone when he got there, and he was pleased to find her still in residence.

"I've missed you terribly," Suzanne said with emphasis as she rested a hand on his forearm.

Adam flinched as she touched his injured arm, the pain reminding him all too vividly of her viciousness. When the maid had at last gone out of sight, he stopped all pretense of being the courting suitor. Grabbing her wrists in a viselike grip, Adam glared murderously down at her.

"I want the truth and I want it now!" he snarled, pushing her back against the wall and holding her pinned there.

"Adam . . . stop! You're hurting me!" Suzanne's look of wide-eyed confusion at being so manhandled was not fake. She was used to roughness from Shark, but she had never expected it from Adam. His actions alarmed her, and she realized with a terrible, sinking feeling that something must have gone wrong.

"I'll do more than hurt you, Suzanne. It's going to be a while before the law shows up. I want to know where Lianne is long before they get here. Do you understand me?" Adam questioned savagely, tightening his already brutal hold.

"Lianne's gone? Why do you think I'd know where she is? Maybe she's left you because she knows how much we truly love each other. Maybe—"

Adam gave her a hard, teeth-rattling shake. "Lianne didn't leave me, Suzanne. I know you're in on this with Cyrus. He told me everything."

"Cyrus . . ." She blanched at this.

"Yes, my dear, Cyrus. His little plot to have me killed didn't work, though."

"What? Cyrus tried to have you killed?" Suzanne stared at him aghast. "That can't be true! He only wanted to get Lianne. He said so. We agreed—"

"So, you agreed on everything, did you?"

"*No! No!* I never wanted you dead! Adam, I love you!" Suzanne was suddenly crying as she kept trying to free herself from his restraining hold. She wanted to throw her arms around him and kiss him, to tell him she loved him over and over until he believed her. The thought that Cyrus and Shark had double-crossed her left her furious.

"Love?" Adam stared down at her with loathing. "What you feel for me is the furthest thing from love I've ever known," he sneered.

"No, Adam, really . . . I do! I love you! I only wanted to get Lianne out of the way so we could be together. I know she forced you into marriage. I know you don't love her. You proposed to me! I'm the one you want. I'm the one you love."

"That's where you're wrong, Suzanne. I don't love you."

His words were like a knife to her heart, and she rushed to use her most powerful weapon to win him.

"Adam, you will! You will when I tell you . . ." She hurried to tell him about Shark just so he would see her in a different, more favorable light.

"Tell me what?" he interrupted, glaring at her with a deep, abiding hatred.

Suzanne saw the emotion reflected there, but she went on anyway, desperate to convince him of how wild she was about him. "About Shark . . ."

He stiffened. "Shark?"

"Yes. I know you're looking for him, and I can help you find him. I can! I was going to tell you later, but I'll tell you now," she went on quickly, all the while praying inside that Lianne would be nowhere around when Adam caught up with the smuggler. Suzanne was totally dumbfounded when Adam did not react enthusiastically to the news.

"Save it, Suzanne. If you think I care more about

473

finding him than locating Lianne and Becky, you're wrong. What's happened to them? Where are they? What did you and Shackelford have planned?"

"Shark's got Lianne, Adam, and probably Becky, too," she answered immediately. "Don't you see? My plan was perfect!" Suzanne went on a little crazily. "You're rid of the wife you didn't want now, so we can be together. You and me. Just like it was before . . ."

Tears were streaming down her cheeks, but Adam didn't even notice. He had gone completely still at her announcement that Shark was involved in this—that Shark had Lianne and Becky. Without conscious thought, he released her arms and closed his hands about her neck.

"You let Shark have them? You turned two good women over to that animal!" Adam went wild at the thought, his hands tightening menacingly on her throat. He had seen what Shark did to women! He had lived through it once . . . "Where are they, Suzanne? Where has he taken them? Tell me now, or so help me, I'll strangle you right here!"

"Cyrus is supposed to meeting them tonight at Pelican Passage," she croaked beneath his brutal hands. Weakly, she grabbed at his arms in an attempt to break his murderous hold. She was gasping for air.

"Cyrus won't be meeting anyone tonight, Suzanne," Adam ground out coldly. "Cyrus is dead."

"You killed him?" Suzanne swayed weakly as she felt her consciousness fading.

It was the bite of the chain against his palms that brought Adam back to reality. He released Suzanne abruptly, staring with blazing eyes at the fine golden chain and crescent medallion she was wearing.

Suzanne was choking and struggling to regain her breath, when she noticed the strange stillness about Adam. "What is it?" she whispered, fearful of what he would do next.

Adam grabbed the chain in a tight fist and tore it from her neck. "Shark gave you this months ago, didn't he?"

"Yes," she replied weakly, trembling violently as she cowered against the wall before him.

"Did he tell you where he got it? Did he tell you where it came from?" he thundered.

"No . . ."

"Shark stole it from a woman who was very dear to me — after he'd raped and brutalized her during a raid on my ship." Adam lifted his medallion from beneath his shirt to show her that they were identical. "You see, Suzanne, it matches the one I'm wearing."

Suzanne gasped as she stared at the jewelry. Suddenly, she knew the cold hard truth of Adam's feelings for her. He had never loved her! He had hated her this entire time. Using her had only been a means to catch Shark and now she had given him what he'd wanted freely!

"You were only using me! All this time you were using me!" She erupted into viciousness at the realization. "I hope you never find your precious Lianne! I hope Shark's long gone by the time you reach the rendezvous! I hope you never see your wife or your sister alive again! They deserved what he's got planned for them!"

Adam grabbed her again and shook her hard. "What's his plan, Suzanne?"

"He's going to sell her into slavery!" she spat out, and she knew a moment of wicked glee at telling him the news. "After he's used her himself, of course. Who knows if your brat will even live long enough to be born!" Suzanne taunted, hating him as she'd never hated another.

At her words, Adam threw her violently from him,

afraid that he might really kill her if he kept his hands on her for a moment longer. Knowing that he had to get to Pelican Passage as quickly as possible, he turned his back on her and started to walk away.

"You'll never find her, Adam! You're a fool to even try! Why would you want her now anyway, when you know Shark and his men have already had her?" she called after him.

Adam was beyond listening to her. His thoughts were focused solely on Lianne and Becky and the terror they must be feeling at being held at Shark's mercy. As he reached the top of the stairs, the maid was just admitting the constable from town.

Watkins looked up to see Adam. "Trent! You're already here!"

"Suzanne Labadie's up here, Watkins, and she's all yours. She's part of an illegal slave-smuggling ring. She's got a partner named Shark."

Watkins sent his men upstairs to take Suzanne into custody as Adam descended and started out the door.

"What about your wife, Trent?" he asked as Adam hurried passed him.

"Don't worry about it. I'll take care of my own," he answered tersely as he strode from the house.

Watkins stared after him for a moment, puzzled by his strange reply. He would have gone after him to ask him more, but his men were already returning with the Labadie woman in tow.

Adam raced back to Belle Arbor, praying all the while that there would be some word from Beau. It had been days since he'd sent the message to him, and he hoped that Beau had received it by now. Adam knew his only hope to catch Shark would be as Spectre aboard the *Sea Shadow*.

476

Beau stood in the main hall, his expression growing more and more outraged as he listened to what Sarah was telling him about what had happened.

"Both Lianne and Becky are missing?" Beau repeated sharply in disbelief.

"Yes, sir," she answered nervously.

"And Adam's gone to Suzanne's alone looking for them?" he asked worriedly.

"Yes, sir, Mr. Beau. He left a long time ago, and we haven't heard anything . . ."

"I'll go right now. He may be in trouble . . . big trouble . . ."

"What kind of trouble, Beau?" Alex asked, emerging from the parlor where he'd been hiding to listen to the adults' conversation.

Beau turned to the boy, wishing he'd known of his presence before he'd made his statement. "Nothing good ol' Adam can't handle, Alex, but I'll go see if I can help him. What do you say?"

"Don't let him get hurt again, Beau . . ." Alex's dark eyes were huge, and his fears were easily discernible.

"I won't," he promised, and he gave him a quick hug before turning to leave. Beau and Sarah had just stepped outside when he spotted Adam coming up the drive at breakneck speed.

"It's him!" Beau quickly ran down the steps and along the drive to meet him.

"Thank God!" Sarah cried as she hurried after Beau.

Adam had never been so glad to see anyone in his entire life. He threw himself from the horse and embraced Beau heartily.

"Where's the ship?" Adam asked immediately when they'd broken apart.

"At the rendezvous point. Why? What happened?" Beau returned.

"We've got to leave *now.*" Adam was already starting to head down to the dock.

"Wait a minute. What's going on? Where are we going?"

"After Shark."

"Shark?! What's he got to do with this?"

"He's got Lianne and Becky! Come on, I'll explain everything on the way!"

Sarah caught up to him and grabbed him by the arm to stop him from leaving without some kind of explanation. "Where are you going, Mr. Adam? Where are Miss Lianne and Miss Becky?"

"They've been kidnapped by some friends of Suzanne's and Shackelford's," he explained. "We're leaving right now to get them back."

"What should I tell Alex?"

"Tell him to try not to worry. We'll be back just as soon as we can, and we'll be bringing Lianne and Becky with us," Adam vowed.

Sarah nodded and watched in tense silence as the two men headed off to rescue the women.

Becky had a lot to think about as she sat alone, still tied and gagged, in the small, dark cabin aboard Shark's ship. She'd been separated from Lianne as soon as they'd been brought aboard. She had heard Shark tell the other man that he was taking Lianne to his cabin, and she had been worried about her friend's fate ever since. Becky shuddered now as she imagined what the pirate might do to Lianne.

Becky prayed for rescue, but she knew it would be hours before they were discovered missing, and then God knows how long after that before Adam could figure out what had happened to them. She realized that their only hope for rescue was Adam, Beau, and the *Sea Shadow*, and she said a prayer that they would come for them soon.

Thoughts of Adam and the *Sea Shadow* caused her to remember Lianne's confessed knowledge of Spectre. Becky knew her brother had never confided in Lianne, so it was a mystery how she could know anything about him. One thing was certain judging from the way Lianne had talked, she had no idea Spectre was her husband.

Letting her mind wander for a moment, Becky wondered what was going to happen when Lianne found out. The prospect was an amusing one, and she knew she certainly wanted to be there to watch the explosion. A moment later, when the true danger of their situation intruded on her musings, Becky also wondered if Lianne would ever have the chance to make that discovery.

Lianne was tied in a chair in Shark's cabin. Her gag had been removed, but it made little difference now. She knew there was no one to hear her screams. The knife in her pocket was her only consolation. Though it wasn't much, it was better than being completely defenseless, and she hoped that she'd be able to get to it and use it if the chance for escape presented itself.

Shark had been sitting at his desk across the room from her studying her unblinkingly for some time now. His expression was so devoid of emotion, his eyes so black and cold, that Lianne thought his name most appropriate. He looked like the amoral killer from the sea . . . big and dangerous and extremely deadly.

"How is it that you know all about my old enemy, Spectre?" Shark asked in a smooth, cool voice.

Lianne lifted her eyes to his unflinchingly. "I don't know him . . . not really . . ."

"If you don't know him, why were you so eager to go to him?" Shark scoffed.

Lianne's color heightened, but she didn't answer.

The pirate's gaze hardened, for he thought that she was playing games with him. "Why, woman?" he demanded angrily.

"I wasn't eager to go to him! I just didn't want us to be hurt, that's all."

"When did you see him last?"

"It's been a week or so . . . He found me in the bayou and forced me to go aboard his boat. I tried to fight him, but it was useless. This time, I thought if I went agreeably . . ."

"So you've been with Spectre, have you?" he asked rhetorically, a thin smile curving the hardness of his mouth. "And you thought he might want you again . . . ?"

"I—"

"Perhaps Spectre would be interested in knowing that you are mine now." Shark was already plotting how to use her to draw his enemy into a trap. Once Shackelford had had his fill of her, he would be free to do with her as he pleased. "And I can use you to draw him out."

"No . . . no. He's gone. I sent him away."

"So, that's the way of it. Well, at least I've made myself a small fortune by taking you for Shackelford."

"Shackelford!" Lianne gasped.

The smuggler chuckled mirthlessly. "Ah yes, that's right, you didn't know about Shackelford's involvement."

"What's Cyrus got to do with this?"

"Everything, my dear. Kidnapping you was his idea to begin with, and it's a good one. He can tell you all about it himself, later tonight, when he joins you."

"Cyrus is coming here?"

"Of course, that was part of the deal—one night, uninterrupted, with you. I've already sent a messenger to him with the news that you're waiting anxiously for him to come to you." He gave a cold laugh at the stark terror that showed in her face. "Shackelford's paying handsomely for the privilege, too, but I wonder if you're really worth it . . ." Shark rose from where he was sitting and came to stand before her.

Lianne trembled uncontrollably as he touched her cheek.

"I suppose he'll tell me tomorrow morning if he thinks you were worth the price. Maybe, if you're that good, I'll permit you to share my bed for a few nights of pleasure before I sell you and your friend to the slave traders," Shark told her, his eyes burning with a black fire.

"Slave traders?" Lianne whispered faintly.

"Ah yes, my dear. You'll both fetch me a good price. White women are a rather rare commodity, and I should do quite well with the two of you." Shark turned and left the cabin, locking the door behind him.

Lianne was pale and shaking as she thought of the terrible ordeal that was to befall them. She wondered if they'd been missed yet at Belle Arbor, and she wondered if there was even the remotest hope of rescue.

Thoughts of Cyrus and his cold-blooded plan unnerved Lianne. She'd known the man was angry with her, but she'd had no idea he would exact such a terrible revenge. It occurred to her that if Cyrus really wanted her that badly, she might be able to use his desire to her advantage and somehow convince him to save her and Becky from the auction block. The fact that she'd been able to figure out a plan that might

481

work, no matter how remote the chance, left Lianne feeling a little better, and she girded herself for the upcoming confrontation.

Chapter Thirty-nine

As they boarded the *Sea Shadow* at the rendezvous point, Beau listened incredulously to Adam's explanation for Lianne's and Becky's disappearance.

"I can't believe this . . ." he muttered, stunned.

"Believe it," Adam answered tersely.

"Suzanne teamed up with Shackelford and together they got Shark to kidnap the women . . . What did she hope to gain?"

"Me," Adam told him with a grimace as he gently massaged his sore shoulder, "but Cyrus had plans for me that Suzanne didn't know about."

"So Cyrus's revenge would have been complete . . . You'd be dead and he'd have Lianne," Beau repeated. "If that was what he wanted, why did they complicate things even more by taking Becky, too?"

"That's not all they wanted Beau," he added solemnly. "Their ultimate goal was for Shark to sell Lianne into white slavery after Cyrus had had his fill of her. When Shark went after Lianne, Becky was probably with her, so he took her too. I'm sure he thought she'd bring him a good price. Becky's a very pretty woman."

"Becky's beautiful!" He declared vehemently, stricken by the thought of the woman he loved being sold into slavery.

Adam looked at Beau questioningly and for the first time he saw revealed in his expression the true depth

483

of his feelings for Becky. "So you're in love with her, are you?" Adam asked perceptively.

"Yes, and I intend to marry her, Adam, just as soon as we find them," Beau declared himself. He was half expecting Adam to argue with him.

"Good. Becky's been in love with you for years. It's about time you came to your senses." He smiled slightly at Beau's obvious surprise. Their gazes met and held in solemn understanding as they thought of the women they loved.

"We've got to find them," Beau vowed passionately.

"I know. Shark will be waiting at Pelican Passage until he finds out Cyrus is dead. We've got to hurry. If we miss him there, we'll be combing the gulf for him again . . ."

"Let's sail!"

Shark was growing impatient as he paced the deck of the *Banshee*. Shackelford was supposed to have met them long before sundown to claim his prize and pay up. As per their plan, Shark had sent two of his men to meet the banker in the arranged place and row him out to the ship, yet it was already dark, and there was still no sign of them returning.

The absence of O'Mally and Morley troubled Shark, too. If everything had gone according to the way it was set up, they should have been back to the ship by midafternoon at the very latest. But there was no word from them, either.

"Keep a sharp watch, Will," Shark instructed, becoming more and more uneasy as time passed. He sensed that something was not quite right, but he didn't know what.

Another two hours passed before the call went up that the skiff had been sighted. Shark went to the rail to meet Cyrus, eager to get his full payment for taking Lianne. He was puzzled when his own two men climbed back aboard without him.

"Where the hell is Shackelford!" Shark demanded angrily, irritated over the banker's absence.

The two crewmen exchanged worried looks before the braver of the two answered. "He's dead, Captain."

"Dead?" Shark eyed them both suspiciously.

"Yes, sir. When he didn't show up, we went into town looking for him. That's when we found out."

"How did it happen? What did you hear?" The fact that O'Malley and Morley were still missing was beginning to take on an ominous meaning.

"Word was out that someone named Trent shot him in self-defense."

Shark exploded in fury, cursing O'Malley and Morley vilely at the news. "Damn them! They didn't kill the bastard!"

"Who, sir?"

"Never mind. If Trent has found out about Shackelford, the odds are he knows about Suzanne and her connection to us, too. We'd better make sail now. Tell Will to head for the Gulf."

Shark quickly began issuing orders to get the ship under way. When the sails had been raised, the clipper caught the night breeze and started to move.

Once they were under way, the tension Shark had been feeling eased a little. He was furious that Shackelford's demise had cost him a lot of money, but he took consolation in the fact that he still had the two women. They were worth a good deal on the market, and he was looking forward to having some private showings aboard the ship for his more preferred customers.

Satisfied that everything was under control on deck, Shark headed below to relax for a while and to start making new plans. He wasn't sure yet how he was going to use Lianne to lure Spectre out into the open, and he wanted to come up with a scheme that would guarantee him victory over his enemy.

Can't we get this thing going any faster?" Adam snapped as he stared out across the night-shrouded water.

"Sorry, sir, but this passage is tricky in the best of times, and at night, it's downright dangerous," the helmsman, Carson, told his captain.

Adam stifled a groan of frustration, but did not argue, for he trusted his helmsman's judgment. Striding across the deck, he joined Beau who was scanning the darkened horizon for some sign of the other ship.

"Nothing?"

"Nothing."

"Damn! We've got to be close!" Adam slammed his fist against the rail.

"The moon should be up soon. Maybe then we can catch sight of him. If he was scheduled to meet Shackelford here tonight, he wouldn't have left without him or at least word of him."

Adam grunted his agreement as he strained to watch for a glimpse of white sails against the black sky.

"There!" The word erupted from Adam excitedly as he pointed to the pale, distant vision of the *Banshee*, sails unfurled, heading out away from them toward the freedom of the Gulf. The image of that boat had been seared into his consciousness long ago, and this time Adam knew there was no mistake. It was Shark. There was no doubt in his mind.

"That's him! Damn him, he's heading straight for open water!" Beau swore.

"Carson, follow them at top speed! Beau, see that the guns are manned and tell everyone to be ready! We're going to catch that bastard this time. He's not going to get away from us again!" Adam vowed as he started belowdecks to don his Spectre garb.

Shark was sitting in his cabin at his desk contemplating Lianne where she sat still tied to the chair before him. She was certainly a lovely wench, and he was going to enjoy tasting of her charms. Once they'd safely made it to the Gulf, he was going to sample what Shackelford had missed.

"Shark!"

Will's shout was so alarmed that Shark was on his feet even as he called out for this man to enter the cabin.

"What is it?" he asked. "What's wrong?"

"It's another clipper, Shark, and she's comin' up on us mighty fast."

"Why the hell didn't you see it sooner?"

"It just seemed to come out of nowhere!" Will said as he led the way up on deck. "That ship is flying . . ." he told him a bit in awe.

"Tell the men to get ready," Shark remarked with considerable calm as he turned to glance back at Lianne who was watching them anxiously. He gave her a feral smile. "I've got a feeling I know exactly who this is. It looks like we won't be needing a plan to catch Spectre after all. He's coming to us!" With that he turned and was gone.

Lianne felt the color drain from her face as she watched him leave the room. *Shark thought it was Spectre who had come after them! But how had Spectre known of their predicament? How had he known where to find them?*

Her heart raced at the thought of being rescued.

Then, with some excitement, Lianne realized that Shark had forgotten to lock the cabin door when he'd gone. Now was the time to use the pruning knife, if she could just get it out of her pocket! Awkwardly, she began to struggle.

Adam stood at the helm of the *Sea Shadow* issuing orders hard and fast to his crew. He knew his ship as well as he knew himself, and he intended to get every ounce of speed out of her he could. This was the moment he'd been waiting for—his final confrontation with Shark. There was no way he was going to act cautiously and give the pirate the opportunity to slip away. Shark was his!

Adam's expression was fierce and deadly as he kept an eye on the other boat. Every move Shark made, he countered with a better one. He was going to catch him, and he was going to see that Shark paid the price for all his murderous ways. Adam smiled grimly as the distance between them narrowed.

"We're almost on him, Beau! It's only a matter of time now . . ."

Shark watched the closing clipper with growing apprehension. He'd always believed the *Banshee* to be the fastest ship around, but Spectre's boat was definitely giving him a run for it. Shark remembered one night in a bar when a sailor had told him of how swift Spectre's craft was. He'd scoffed then, but now he realized how wrong he'd been to underestimate his enemy.

The pale light of the newly risen moon glinted off the massive guns that protruded threateningly from the sides of the *Sea Shadow,* and at first sight of them, a cold, gnawing fear clutched at Shark's chest. Panic threatened. He had never known a real challenge. All the ships he'd raided had been slow, lumbering merchants, not well-armed clippers like the one swooping down upon him now. Barking orders to Will to get to top speed from the *Banshee* at all costs, he watched nervously as the other ship drew ever closer.

"All right! Bring her about!" Adam shouted, his blood pounding fiercely in his veins as he prepared to do battle. "Aim to disable, not to sink!" he commanded his men. With Lianne and Becky aboard, he knew they had to be careful.

Beau and the others hurried to do as he ordered. This was what they'd waited for during all these months of searching, and they were more than ready to wreak their own vengeance. Most of the *Sea Shadow*'s crew had been on the *Windwood*, and they remembered Shark's lack of mercy in dealing with them. They were going to take great pleasure in boarding his vessel.

Aboard the *Banshee*, Shark was preparing to take the initiative. It was obvious that he would not be able to outrun Spectre, so he planned to maneuver shrewdly and fire first. His guns were easily the equal of the other ship's, so he had no fear that his firepower would be any less deadly.

Shark's determination came just a little too late, though, for Spectre's cannon were already targeted. Though they were still just a little out of range and the first volley fell a bit short of its intended mark, the speed with which Spectre was closing left Shark's men frightened for the first time in their lives.

"Hold your positions and prepare to fire," Shark snarled, trying to gauge the *Sea Shadow*'s distance so they would be accurate in their aim. *"Now!"* he roared.

The *Banshee* and the *Sea Shadow* fired their weapons simultaneously, with the *Banshee* getting the worst of the exchange. Adam cheered along with his crew as their second barrage strafed the *Banshee*'s rigging and sent much of it crashing to the deck, taking most of Shark's weapons out of commission at the same time. The *Sea Shadow* suffered damage to only one mast, leaving her completely maneuverable and ready to sail in for the kill.

"Fire another broadside and then take her in!" Adam commanded, wanting to make sure there was no way the other ship could flee. Pistol and sword in hand, he stood ready to board. If he had to fight his way from one end of the ship to the other to save Lianne and Becky, he was going to do it.

Adam's dark gaze was riveted on the other vessel, watching . . . waiting. It appeared that chaos reigned there, but he didn't allow himself the luxury of believing it. No matter what condition their ship was in, Shark's men were killers. No one knew that better than Adam did.

"Prepare to board!" Adam ordered, and then turned to Beau. "Stay here and take command."

"No, Adam, I'm going with you. Becky's on that ship and I'm going to find her. If she's been harmed in any way, I'm going to find whoever did it and kill them!"

Adam could tell by his friend's determined expression that there would be no convincing him to stay behind with the *Sea Shadow*. "All right, but be careful, damn it!"

"I will. Don't worry about me, just take care of yourself."

As they remembered the last time they'd faced Shark, they exchanged one last, solemn look, then turned their attention back to the pirate ship.

Shark was livid. He had never been bested before, and he wasn't about to allow it to happen now. He was going to fight to the death — *Spectre's death,* he swore savagely. Exhorting his men to defensive action, he armed himself to repel the invaders.

As the other ship drew near, Shark searched its deck for some sign of his arch enemy. He had heard much about the infamous Spectre, and he found that he was eager to face him at long last. He spied the masked, black-clad figure leading his men as they prepared to board, but he didn't recognize him and that puzzled Shark. He'd thought he would know him when they finally met. Still, he smiled wolfishly in anticipation of stripping the disguise from his face after he'd run him through. Spectre wanted a fight, and he was going to get one.

Heavily armed, the men of the *Sea Shadow* swarmed onto the hated vessel with Adam and Beau leading the way. With pistols and swords, they battled the very men who had locked them in the hold of the *Windwood* and left them to burn to death so many months ago.

Adam and Beau remained side by side in the thick of the fighting. Adam's mask and black clothing added a dangerous mystique to his presence, and many of Shark's crew ran rather than fight him. Adam fought head-on all who would challenged him as he tried to scan the deck for Shark. Shark was the one he wanted.

Screams of agony from the dying and wounded echoed across the deck, but nothing stopped the carnage. The struggle continued unabated. Shark's crew would never surrender. They would fight to the last man rather than face the wrath of their vicious captain.

Shark attacked savagely, cutting down several of Adam's men in his frenzy to defend his ship. He knew things were not going well, though, for his own men were being forced to fall back and give ground, and the damned Spectre was leading the fight.

The sight of his avowed enemy fighting on the *Banshee*'s deck sent a shiver of trepidation through the normally fearless Shark. Quickly, he judged the ferocity of the other man's assault and knew there was only one way to guarantee the safety of his ship. Dodging through the wreckage, he headed for the companionway and Lianne.

Adam finished off one opponent and looked up, trying to find Shark amidst the fighting. He wanted desperately to face the pirate one on one. This was what he'd waited and planned for. He did not intend to let the savage brute get away. Adam spied Shark just as he disappeared into the passage leading belowdecks.

"Beau! He's headed below! I'm going after him!" Adam called out as he gave chase, mowing down one of Shark's men who tried to stop him.

Though it had been a long, difficult struggle for her, Lianne had finally managed to get hold of the small pruning knife in her skirt pocket. It seemed to take forever to saw awkwardly through the restraints that held her hands, but when the sturdy rope finally began to fray, she knew a surge of triumph.

Before she could break completely free, though, the *Banshee* and *Sea Shadow* exchanged volleys. The jolt aboard ship from taking the hit sent Lianne sprawling, chair and all, to the floor, and it was a painful ordeal to retrieve the knife and continue her effort to escape.

When at long last Lianne managed to free her hands, she was able to loosen the rest of her bonds much more quickly. The sounds of the battle being waged up on deck frightened her, but she bravely decided to leave the cabin anyway. She had to find Becky so they could be ready to escape should the chance arise. Though Lianne knew it would be of little real protection, she clutched the small knife tightly as she started from the cabin.

Lianne had only opened the door when Shark grabbed her by the left arm. His laugh was demonic as he twisted her arm up behind her and held his pistol pointed at her. Despite his surprise assault, Lianne kept a grip on the knife and hid her right hand in her skirts.

"So, you thought you could get away, did you?" he breathed hatefully in her ear. His grip on her was brutally tight as he started back up the companionway, dragging her along with him. "We'll see how Spectre reacts when he sees that I've got a gun pointed at your head . . ."

"Now you know, Shark." Spectre's booming voice filled the narrow passageway, and Lianne felt her knees sag in relief. He was here! He had come!

Shark looked up to find his enemy standing on the stairs pointing a pistol directly at him.

"Let her go, Shark. Now! This is between you and me. Lianne has nothing to do with it."

"Ha!" Shark gave a sharp bark of defying laughter as he tried to ignore the feeling of doom that overcame him. "I want you and your men off my ship now or I'll kill her right here."

Spectre saw the madness in the pirate's eyes and knew he would do it. Did he risk trying to rescue Lianne or did he back down and leave her helplessly in his hands? Spectre's dilemma was a real one, for he knew Lianne might be lost to him either way.

Lianne was not about to let these two men decide her fate. Taking matters into her own hands, she moved with lightning speed to stab Shark in the thigh with the small knife. She knew it wouldn't do much damage, but it might afford her the chance she needed to get away from him and give Spectre a clear shot.

Her action took Shark by surprise, and as the searing pain jarred him he momentarily loosened his grip on her. Taking advantage of it, Lianne used all the strength she had to tear herself free and fling herself out of the way.

Shark recovered almost immediately, and, realizing he'd lost his advantage, he fired his gun in Lianne's general direction just as Adam's pistol roared to life. Spectre's shot took him full in the chest and sent him crashing to the floor.

Spectre came charging down the steps and ran to Shark's side.

"Who are you?" Shark croaked, but that final truth eluded him as he drew his last breath.

Relief swept through Spectre as he realized the pirate was dead. He turned away from him and went immediately to Lianne, who was crouching fearfully against the wall. He pulled her into his arms and held her crushed against his chest.

"Thank God, he missed! Thank God, you're safe!" he groaned in real agony, tangling his hands in her hair and tilting her head back so he could look at her and be completely sure. Their gazes locked, and they stared at each other in silence for a timeless moment before his mouth descended to take hers in a deep, sensual possession.

Lianne was shaking as he kissed her. She wasn't sure if it was from the terror she'd just experienced or from the force of emotion that was surging through her as she was being held in his arms. For an instant she allowed herself to glory in his protective embrace, but then thoughts of Adam intruded, and she started to pull away.

"Captain!" the man's voice rang out behind them as some of his men came thundering down the stairs to assist him. "The fighting's all over on deck, sir!"

"It's over down here, too," he told them, keeping one arm around Lianne's waist as he indicated Shark's lifeless body.

"Wait! Have you found Becky? Where's Becky?" Lianne asked in sudden remembrance of her friend. "Shark had her taken captive, too."

"Where was he keeping her?" Spectre demanded quickly, fear for his sister's safety returning.

"I don't know . . ."

"Here, Robbins! Take Lianne back to my cabin while I search the ship," Spectre ordered his man.

"Yes, sir."

"But, Spectre, I want to help! Becky may need me!" she argued, but he wouldn't listen.

"Go, Robbins!" Spectre repeated, remembering the condition Elise had been in when he'd found her. He didn't want Lianne to be witness to anything that might have happened to Becky.

Spectre wanted to talk to Lianne, to tell her everything, but he couldn't until he was certain that Becky was safe. Once he'd found Becky, he would go to Lianne in his cabin and tell her the truth . . . all of it.

Chapter Forty

It took Beau some time to see that the survivors from Shark's crew were all placed in irons, but as soon as he'd finished, he raced below to join Adam.

"Where are they? Did you find them?" Beau asked as he found Adam searching the cabins.

"I just sent Lianne back to the *Sea Shadow* with Robbins. You didn't see her?"

"No."

"Good." He breathed a sigh of relief as he took off his mask. "I was afraid that she'd see you and figure out everything herself before I had the chance to explain things to her."

"If you found Lianne, then where's Becky?" Beau worried impatiently.

"I haven't found her yet," Adam told him as they hurried on to the next cabin and went inside.

"She's here on the ship, isn't she?" Beau paused in their search, suddenly worried that Shark might have killed her earlier.

"Yes, she's here somewhere. Lianne said they were both brought aboard together."

Beau began to search in earnest then, throwing the cabin doors wide in his haste to find his love. He called her name, loudly, desperately, but there was no answering response. He had to find her! She had to be safe! He remembered what had happened to the women aboard the *Windwood*, and he felt sick with concern for her. Room after room turned up empty, and Beau's fears became near to overpowering.

"Damn it, Adam! Becky's got to be here somewhere! She's got to!"

Becky was terrified. When she'd first heard the sounds of the battle, she'd been excited to think that Beau and Adam had come for them. But the excitement turned to terror when she realized that the ship she was on might be sunk and that she'd be trapped helplessly upon it.

When the cannon fell silent, Becky wasn't sure whether to celebrate or fear for her life. She prayed continually for salvation as she waited breathlessly — fearfully — for someone to rescue her. She hoped it would be Beau or Adam, but as the minutes passed and no one appeared, she grew more and more nervous.

The door to her cabin was locked. Becky could hear the muffled sound of men's voices outside, and she saw the knob turn as whoever it was beyond the closed portal tried to open it. Suddenly the door was forcefully kicked open, and Becky would have screamed in horror had she not still been gagged. Her blood ran cold as she waited for the men to enter.

Though Becky had prayed for Adam and Beau to save her, she really hadn't believed it would be them coming for her now. She had expected only the worst. When she saw Adam storm into the room, she knew a moment of pure ecstasy. They had come for her! She was safe!

"Beau! Becky's in here! She's all right!" Adam bellowed as he hurried to untie her gag.

Beau nearly knocked Adam down in his haste to get to Becky. He'd been so afraid that she would suffer the same fate as Elise that his relief at finding her safe and

497

sound was tremendous. He began to untie her as Adam finished removing her gag.

"Are you all right, Becky?" Beau asked, tearing at her bonds in a desperate attempt to free her.

"Yes . . . yes . . . oh, yes!" Becky was sobbing almost hysterically with joy. The moment she was finally free, she launched herself into Beau's arms, pressing delirious kisses all over his face and neck. "Thank God, you came!"

Beau hugged her close, crushing her to his chest, and then kissed her with an almost violent need.

"I love you, Becky. I love you . . . I love you . . ." he repeated in a litany of heartfelt devotion.

Becky suddenly drew away. She left his arms and went to Adam, hugging him, too, as she asked urgently. "Lianne . . . have you found her yet? They separated us as soon as we were brought aboard."

"Yes, she's safe. She's already back on the *Sea Shadow.*"

Becky sighed in relief and returned to Beau's embrace, kissing him with a hunger born of frantic need.

"Don't ever leave me again, Beau!" she pleaded.

"Don't worry, love. I won't. As soon as we get back to New Orleans, we're getting married, and I'm never going to let you out of my sight again!"

"Oh, Beau!" Becky sighed and gave him a long and lingering kiss.

Adam started to back out of the room, but Becky broke off their kiss to speak with him.

"Adam?"

He looked at her questioningly. "What?"

"I was wondering . . . how did Lianne know about Spectre?"

"What do you mean?"

"When Shark took us captive, Lianne told him that if he was from Spectre there was no need to tie us up, that she would go with him without argument. I thought she didn't know about you."

"She doesn't," he answered flatly.

"Well, if she doesn't, how can she be familiar with Spectre?" Becky was confused and she grew even more so when she saw a dull flush stain her brother's cheeks. It had been years since she'd seen him embarrassed, and she wondered at the cause. "Adam?"

"Someday I'll tell you about it. Right now, I've got to get back to the *Sea Shadow* . . . and Lianne."

"Has she seen you yet? Does she know the truth now?"

"No, not yet," he answered curtly.

Becky could tell that he was apprehensive about telling Lianne the truth. "Adam, go to her and tell her everything. She'll understand. She loves you."

"She may love me now, but once she finds out what I've done . . ."

Becky understood, but she urged him on. "Go to her, Adam. She may be angry for a while, but she'll get over it."

Adam wanted to believe this, but he was more worried about going to Lianne now than he had been about attacking Shark a few hours before.

"Beau, will you take charge here?" he asked.

"For as long as it takes," Beau promised, and he and Becky followed Adam from the cabin. "I'll get a skeleton crew of our men to repair the riggings enough so we can get this ship back into port."

"Good. As soon as you're ready to sail, let's head home."

Becky was smiling as she watched her brother return to the *Sea Shadow*.

"What are you smiling about?" Beau asked, curious.

"I'd love to know the details of how Lianne found out about Spectre. It's going to be something when she finds out he's Adam."

"Do you think she'll forgive him?"

"Of course, but not before she gives him some trouble."

"Poor Adam," Beau groaned sympathetically.

"You're right." Becky nodded.

Lianne was apprehensive as she paced Spectre's cabin. Becky . . . where was Becky? She had to be safe, but what if she wasn't? What if Shark had done something terrible to her after he'd separated them? The possibility filled her with anxiety, and Lianne cursed her helplessness as she waited here alone for Spectre to return with news of her friend. Lianne wished he'd let her stay with him and help him search so she could have been there when they found Becky, but he had been firm in his determination to send her away. She wondered agonizingly if Spectre had done it to protect her because he suspected that something might have happened to Becky. The thought only served to deepen her anxiety. In agitation, Lianne wandered to the cabin window to stare out into the darkness.

As eager as Adam was to go to Lianne, he still hesitated nervously when he reached the *Sea Shadow*. He thought of their last few days together at Belle Arbor, of the love they'd shared so completely, and he knew he wanted that to go on. *No matter what it took,* Adam told himself, *he was not going to lose Lianne now.* Determination filled him with a firm resolve, and he went below to his cabin to share his past with her.

Adam reached the door to his quarters and paused. He had meant to just walk in and declare himself, but on second thought, he realized that might leave her so furious that she wouldn't even listen to his explanation. Reluctantly, Adam donned his mask again.

Lianne heard the door open behind her, and she whirled about to face him, dying to know the fate of her friend.

"Lianne . . ." His voice was hoarse as he stared at her. Her beauty never failed to overwhelm him, and he had to fight the instinct to go straight to her and sweep her up into his arms.

Lianne tried to ignore the effect his rough-edged, velvet voice had on her. Becky was her main concern . . . only Becky.

"Did you find Becky?" Her troubled gaze met his across the width of the cabin, searching for some clue as to what had happened.

Adam gave her a reassuring smile as he strode farther into the cabin. "Yes, we found her. She's fine."

Lianne's relief was so complete and total that she swayed on her feet and had to reach out quickly to brace herself. Adam saw her distress and immediately rushed to her, thinking she was about to faint, but Lianne held up a hand to ward him off. As vulnerable as she was right now, she didn't trust herself in his arms. The kiss he'd given her aboard Shark's ship had been near to overwhelming, and she didn't want to risk his touching her right now when her defenses were so low.

"Spectre, we need to talk," Lianne told him, moving a little away from him.

"Yes, I know. That's why I was so long coming back. I wanted to make sure that everything was taken care of before I came to you, because I didn't want us to be interrupted," Adam tried to explain, but somehow his words didn't come out the way he meant them.

"Oh . . ." Lianne stiffened at his declaration. *He didn't want them to be interrupted . . .* She was thrilled that he'd rescued them from Shark, but she had the terrible feeling that he wasn't going to be satisfied with a monetary reward or a heartfelt thank you. What was she going to do? She knew he wanted her—his kiss had left no doubt about that, but she loved Adam. She couldn't, wouldn't betray him ever again! What would she do if Spectre pressed her? He knew how to break down any resistance she might offer. How could she manage to convince him that she loved only her husband and desired no other? She was not afraid of Spectre in the same way she had been of Shark, but she was worried about what he wanted from her.

"Lianne, I . . ." Adam took another step toward her, wanting only to take her in his arms, kiss her and tell her everything. But when he saw the flash of fear in her green eyes, he forced himself to wait.

"Spectre, I want you to know how very grateful I am for your help. God only knows what would have happened to Becky and me if you hadn't shown up when you did," Lianne interrupted him, wanting to blurt out the truth of her feelings before he had a chance to try to sway her.

"Lianne, I don't want your gratitude . . ." he replied.

His words almost sent Lianne into a panic, for she believed she knew what he really wanted. She tried not to think about being in his arms or kissing him or the last time they were in this cabin together.

"I'm afraid gratitude is all I can give you, Spectre." Lianne bravely lifted her eyes to his. She wanted him to know that she was being completely honest with him. "You see I love my husband. He's the only man I want."

Adam felt like a damn fool, standing there listening

502

to her profess her love for him.

"Lianne," he cut her off, ready to put an end to the charade, "do you remember the last time we were together when I told you that there were those who would kill to know my identity?"

"Yes."

"That's over now." Adam was resolved to go through with this even though he knew she would be angry.

"It is?"

"There's no more need for the disguise, Lianne. I'm free of the past now . . ."

The tension was thick in the room as Adam reached up to take off his disguise. Lianne watched breathlessly as Spectre untied the mask.

"Adam!" For just a second, she didn't react as she stared in total disbelief at her husband. Then her temper erupted. "Adam! It was you all the time? You were Spectre!"

Lianne glanced from the discarded mask to Adam and back again. Rage filled her. *Adam was Spectre . . . Spectre was Adam . . .* He had taken her captive! He had made love to her on this very boat, knowing she was frightened, knowing she believed he was going to kill her! That night in their room . . . of course, he had known her husband was gone! She gave a bitter, slightly hysterical laugh as she turned flashing, anger-filled eyes on him.

"Lianne, I can explain everything . . ." he offered a bit lamely.

"Oh, I'll just bet you can," she snarled, "but that doesn't mean I have to listen to you! All this time, you led me on! You tied me to that bed and—"

"And I'll do it again, if you don't shut up and listen to what I've got to say," Adam finished for her with some satisfaction.

She gasped and started to rush from the room, but

503

he moved more quickly, blocking her path and catching her in his arms.

"Let me go, Adam Trent! You're a no-good, low-down, swine! You're a—"

"Enough!" he thundered, and he was relieved when she fell silent. True, she was sulking, but at least she was quiet. "Now, I want you to sit down in that chair and not say another word until you've heard me out. When I'm finished telling you everything, if you still want to leave me, I won't try to stop you. Just keep in mind that I love you more than anything in this world, Lianne—anything."

Their gazes met and locked. When Lianne tried to move away from him, this time Adam let her go. She sat down where he'd directed, giving him a frigid glare.

Adam was nervous as he began to talk, but he knew it was too late to worry about anything except explaining himself and his motives.

"You know Becky and I own a plantation home in Charleston," he said and at her answering nod, he continued. "I also own a successful shipping firm with Beau—Crescent Shipping." Adam saw the flicker of surprise in her eyes. "It was almost a year ago . . . I was in Houston on business when I met and became engaged to a young woman named Elise Clayton."

This news sent a shaft of pain through Lianne, but she betrayed no emotion as he went on with his story. Her anger was still vibrant within her, and all she wanted to do was get as far away from Adam as possible.

"We were returning to Charleston with her aunt so she could meet Becky, when we were attacked by Shark. The *Windwood* was a merchant vessel, easy prey for someone like him. We had little chance to defend ourselves." Adam's expression turned bleak as

504

he remembered.

Lianne found she was holding her breath as he talked. She could hear the anguish in his tone as he described the carnage Shark wreaked aboard his vessel.

"Many of my men were killed. Beau was seriously injured. Elise's aunt was attacked and killed. Elise was . . ." Adam paused, trying to find the right way to phrase it. "Elise was raped, but they didn't bother to kill her when they were through. They just left her lying there . . . I vowed then and there that if we were rescued, I was going to get even with Shark—someway, somehow."

Lianne couldn't believe what he was telling her. "What happened to Elise?"

"We were rescued. When we made it back to Charleston, Becky and I sought out every doctor available, but none of them gave her any chance for recovery. She had withdrawn completely from reality and showed no sign of ever returning to normal."

Lianne found herself imagining Adam's torment to see the woman he loved in such condition.

"I had my fastest ship—the *Sea Shadow*—outfitted with guns, and I became Spectre. Once Beau had recovered, we went out and began searching the Gulf for Shark. From what we'd overheard during the attack, we knew that Shark was really a slave smuggler and that he had a woman partner in New Orleans. When our search of the Gulf didn't work, I decided to come to New Orleans and try to find him through his partner. That's what led me to Suzanne."

"Suzanne? And Shark?" Lianne was taken completely by surprise at this.

Adam nodded, sensing that her outrage with him was fading a bit. "Evidently, they'd been bringing slaves in illegally for some time. I got engaged to her

505

just to be able to keep an eye on her activities. I knew Shark was due to show up at any time, and I had to be there to catch him . . . but then there was you." Adam gave her a long, searching look.

"Me? You hated me then," she charged.

"I never hated you. I just didn't want to fall in love with you, Lianne. I didn't want to feel the things you were making me feel. I fought it desperately. Trapping Shark was my only priority. That was all that mattered to me—that and Elise . . ."

"Elise . . . Where is she now?" Lianne was startled when her question brought a smile to his face.

"I brought Elise here to New Orleans with Becky and me, because I wanted to be sure she was getting the right medical care. I rented a house for her in town and set up round-the-clock nursing care. I even hired the best doctor I could find here to treat her, although in the beginning he wasn't any more encouraging than the others had been."

"No one could ask for more," Lianne said supportively, finding herself sympathizing with his plight.

"Then, right after we were married, I got a note from Dr. Williams telling me that Elise had begun to make progress. The odds were good that she would recover."

"Oh, Adam . . ." Lianne's heart went out to him. "I'm sorry."

"No, don't be, Lianne," he replied quickly. "I was in love with you, but I still wouldn't admit to it, especially since you kept telling me that you hated me."

"I hated what you made me feel," she confessed, suddenly wanting him to understand. "Every time you came near me, I wanted you, yet you were 'in love' with Suzanne."

"I had to keep up the pretext. I had to get Shark," he said simply.

"What about Elise? Did she get better?"

"Yes. As a matter of fact, it turned out that Dr. Williams had fallen in love with Elise during all their time together and she with him. She's fully recovered now and happy. I've seen her and we've talked. She's ready to start her life over again with him."

"I'm glad for her."

"She's a lovely lady, and she deserves all the happiness she can find. But Elise's recovery didn't help my situation. I still couldn't break completely with Suzanne until I had what I wanted from her . . . contact with Shark."

"And I believed that you loved her and were with her every time you left me alone!" Lianne mourned all the misunderstandings that had kept them apart.

"Hardly," Adam replied. "I tried to avoid her, if you want to know the truth. Suzanne held no attraction for me, but I had to act the part. You were the only woman I wanted. Most of the time when I was away from you, I was either here with Beau, or I was in town with Elise and the doctor."

Lianne almost got to her feet so she could go to him, but the memory of his little game as Spectre held her back. A flare of fury remained, but it was much abated compared to what she'd felt at first.

"But why the charade with me as Spectre? Why did you have to kidnap me that night in the bayou?"

"First," Adam countered, "you tell me what you were doing there."

"I followed you to force you to choose between Suzanne and me. I couldn't bear the humiliation any longer, and I was so afraid that Alex would be hurt if you left me and went to her after the baby was born."

"Would Alex have been the only one hurt?" he asked.

"You know better than that now, Adam. But that

night I was going to face you down and demand that you make your choice."

"I'm glad you got sidetracked," Adam told her with a wicked grin.

"Adam Trent!" Lianne said with justified outrage. "You kidnapped me. You tied me up. You—"

"I didn't know what else to do with you! I didn't know what you were doing there or why you'd followed me. All I knew was that I couldn't let you discover my other identity. As for the rest . . ." Adam looked contrite. "I never have been able to control my desire for you with any great success. I was desperate to make love to you, and since you'd vowed that you hated me, I decided to take you as Spectre." Before she could say anything more, he went on, "I know it was wrong. I know I took advantage of you. But, Lianne, I was crazy in love with you, and you rejected me at every turn."

"I turned you away because I thought you loved Suzanne."

"I know. That's what I wanted you to think in the beginning," he answered. "I only hope that you can forgive me, Lianne. I love you as Adam, and I love you as Spectre. You hold my heart, love. You're my world, my future . . . you and our child."

Adam fell silent as he waited for her to make her decision.

Chapter Forty-one

Lianne stared up at her husband, seeing with joy the total openness and trust in his expression. She got to her feet slowly, her eyes dark with emotion. Until this moment, she'd had no idea of the torment Adam had been through. Now she understood what Becky had been trying to tell her in the garden, and her heart filled with love for him. He was her world, too, and her future. It was as she'd told Spectre. She loved her husband and wanted only him.

Adam was uneasy as he watched her stand. Her expression was inscrutable, and he worried that she was going to leave him. Preparing himself for the worst, he remained perfectly still and waited.

Lianne saw the momentary flash of fear in his eyes, and without another moment's hesitation, she flew into his arms. "I love you, too, Adam. It seems I have forever . . ."

Adam clasped her to him in a joyous embrace as his mouth sought hers. Enraptured they stood wrapped in one another's arms, savoring the newness of their commitment. Without ending the kiss, he lifted her into his arms and moved to the bunk. He laid her gently upon its softness, then helped her strip away her clothing. He shed his own and joined her there.

"No ropes this time?" Lianne asked teasingly as she eagerly reached for him.

"No ropes and no more deception," Adam told her,

his voice hoarse with emotion as he moved over her and fitted himself to her intimately. His gaze was loving as he looked down at her. "There'll never be any secrets between us again, Lianne."

Lianne shivered pleasantly as she recognized Spectre's husky tone for the first time.

"The past is over, Adam. Let's put it from us and think only of our future," she murmured as she drew him down for a flaming kiss that ignited into a wildfire of desire.

They came together in a blaze of passion that took them both to the searing splendor of breathless ecstasy. The heights of rapture attained, they clung to each other knowing that the rest of their lives would be as perfect.